PRAISE FOR THE FAR SHORE

"A plausible and harrowing adventure that explores hum drive for personal freedom." *–Kirkus Reviews*

"I give The Far Shore five stars. It rivals The Martian in accuracy, ambition and attitude. It offers hope for humanity at all levels." *–Tamara Wilhite, contributor at Liberty Island Magazine*

"Gripping and immersive, The Far Shore offers a lot: technology for the hard science fiction fans and tons of heart for all of us." *–Laura Montgomery, author of Mercenary Calling*

"Brilliant...I admit to having tears in my eyes." *–Jeffery D. Kooistra, author of Dykstra's War*

"I was hooked! Damn! The pace is awesome, the suspense is unbeatable, the characters are engaging, the plot is original, the theme is eternal and universal." *–Irene Psyhogios*

"Highly recommended for adult sci-fi fans who enjoy exceptionally well-developed plots, characters, and hard sci-fi." *–Donovan's Literary Services*

"The Far Shore sucked me in from page one. It really is amazing." *–Sherri Addleston Hilts*

"A magnificent story – a soaring feat of imagination, highly suspenseful and utterly gripping." *–Robert Bidinotto, bestselling author of HUNTER*

THE FAR SHORE

GLENN DAMATO

NINTH
CIRCLE
PRESS

Los Angeles

www.ninthcirclepress.com

Published by
Ninth Circle Press
578 Washington Blvd 920
Los Angeles, CA 90292

This title is also available as an eBook and audiobook product.

Damato, Glenn
    The Far Shore / Glenn Damato

ISBN-13: 978-0-9858162-2-3   ISBN-10: 0-9858162-2-8

Science fiction, hard science fiction, dystopian fiction, space travel, space colonization, Mars colonization

Library of Congress Control Number: 2019909929

Cover and interior design by KarrieRoss.com

To Mike, Adam, Jim, Anna, and the rest of the gang at MicroStrategy, for giving me my shot even though I didn't belong there.

THE FAR SHORE

PART I

As One

ONE

My worst crime is I say things people don't want to hear. The punishments are bearable, but why should words be a crime? I mean, it's my mouth, and my brain.

I'll never shut up. My long history of misconduct has scarcely begun.

Imagine there's a tiny man sitting on your shoulder. He watches everything you do and listens to everything you say. He'll hurt you the instant you make him angry. The little bastardo never goes away, not even for a second.

That's my life, today and every day.

Look, I'm not crazy. I know there's no tiny man sitting on my shoulder. The Autoridad doesn't need him; they have infinite microscopic devices to supervise me. The autosystems watch and listen and understand, just like people. Did you know the Autoridad operates the smartest autosystems that ever existed? I can't fool them. I can't even see them. And they never leave me alone.

The result? As of this morning my Trust Score stands at 208, only eight points above the lowest possible number. All I need to do is piss them off a bit more to reach rock bottom. My life is hostage to that Score because it controls everything I can and cannot do. I'm expected to conform my behavior and raise my number, but I refuse to play their game.

What do they expect? I wasn't born to be watched and operated like a machine.

I do have some freedom. Eggs or Honey Nut Cheerios for breakfast? I can freely choose either one and it won't drop my Trust Score.

There are seven of us crammed into a type-C municipal unit: me, a quad of adults, plus two little niños. Usually they're all late sleepers, but Dottie must have smoked some kind of potent shab because she's dancing circles across the living room, her bony legs nimbly jumping over the clothes and other junk scattered on the floor. Why is she out of bed before the kids? And lit-up before twelve?

I need to cook, but Dottie spins into the kitchen and bounces her hip against the stove. She sniffs and blinks at me with tearful eyes. "I'm mandated. Say goodbye to sweet little Dot."

My heart jumps. Shit. "Mandated to where?"

She skips off without answering, so I flick to her Stream display. The mandate notice came two hours ago but there's no information about where they're taking her. That's bad. She's probably going to Coachella Center. The Centers are supposed to teach hygiene, language skills, interpersonal relations, plus correct wrong behavior and bad thinking. That's mainly lies. They're places of pain and hunger, and if people do come back they can hardly bear to be alive. I've seen it.

Dottie is a typical micro-brained *nada*, a nothing. Nadas exist to sleep, game, screw, and smoke shab. What did she say that got her mandated? Maybe nothing. No matter. She's gone. No more letting her braid my hair while we laugh over the ridiculous lies of her treacherous lovers.

Six years, Dottie and me. She's the one who taught me the particulars when I had my first period. Dottie, one of the few I ever let help me, maybe the most childlike adult I know.

She's mandated, and I'm not. Now that's freaked.

Dottie dances, and I fry peppers and eggs. My two sleepy niños shuffle into the kitchen. Nathan, no taller than my elbow, sets out three plates and forks. I pick up the skillet and give the eggs a final toss. "Isabel, why such a sad face on this beautiful sunny day?"

"Nathan, he hid my shoe," the niñita growls. She narrows her eyes and turns toward her older brother. "Put it in the sink, got it wet."

I point the spatula at Nathan in mock scolding. "Next time you feel like hiding a shoe, why don't you take one of mine?"

He sinks into his chair. "Qué noooo!"

"Smart decision, hombrecito." I scoop eggs onto plates. "Might need to kype something of his, Isabel, just so he—"

A motion just outside the kitchen window. I keep my voice cool to avoid alarming the children. "So he knows what it feels like."

I dump the skillet on the stove and steal a second glance out the window. A three-legged spotter stalks across the backyard like a predatory beast. It's robotic cameras peer through the window and study my face. I sit and fork eggs into my mouth as if nothing is happening.

The front door opens and the spotter struts inside with its spidery way of moving. Charlie, our liver-colored spaniel, bolts toward the safety of my bedroom. Strange how most pets never get used to ground spotters, while the youngest niños ignore them as a mundane part of life. Sensors check everywhere for weapons or some other trouble. For our own safety, of course.

We eat our eggs in silence.

Dottie lets out a long breath and covers her eyes.

The spotter strides down the hallway. I throw my plate into the sink and follow it. The obnoxious thing goes straight for my room. Charlie scoots past me and zips out the front door. Not supposed to watch spotters, but so what? I swallow and clench my fists as it scans my dresser. They can see through everything, and always know exactly where to look. At least it doesn't open the bottom drawer.

Lady voices from the kitchen, soft feminine assurances. Two grinning Policía with their hands outstretched in the usual *I am your friend* trick.

Policía de Seguridad del Estado—State Security Police—the muscle of the Autoridad. They're always oh-so-sweet, but that's just to make us forget they can take away everything we ever imagined for our lives. These two darlings are in the new style lavender uniform, smooth and spotless, with insignia on the sleeves: a fisted hand clutching a red rose with green petals.

The shorter, black-haired Policía is fat enough to be a sumo wrestler. She holds out packets of shab as gifts.

That means trouble.

The taller Policía has a giant nose shaped like a beak. She nods at me and the kids, then smiles at Dottie. "Saludos, señora Jenson. Did you say goodbye to your friends?"

No accent. She's an Alta California native.

Dottie blinks her eyes at the shab but for some reason doesn't grab it. She whispers, "I need my sweater."

"Nothing required for you to bring," Sumo Wrestler snaps. An emblem on her collar shows her homeland is Korea.

"I'll allow it," Beak Nose says.

Dottie faces me. She's tearing up again. "A friend to bring me peace and set me free. Adiós, chica. Te amo." She disappears down the hallway with her fingers pressed against both cheeks.

I need words, but nothing comes out of my mouth. *Who* is her friend to set her free? *Why* did she just tell me goodbye and she loves me before going into her bedroom?

To escape the mandate the only way she can.

Shit shit shit shit.

My stomach heaves and I'm going to lose those eggs. I can't stop my feet from moving. The spotter reacts first. It steps behind me and I brace for a hit. Never been hit and I sure don't want it, but I'm going after Dottie.

The Policía must have signaled the spotter to lay off because I make it to Dottie's doorway. She slides into the bed where Nick and Chloe are asleep. In her fingers, a little pink vase. Those pink vases! Everybody over fourteen keeps one in their bedroom in plain sight. It's required.

I can jump across the room and knock it from her hand. The spotter will hit me, but so what? If I can get the vase away from her, even for a few seconds, maybe she'll slow down and *think*.

But all I do is stand in the doorway, because I'm a fucking coward.

"Dottie…" My big mouth fails me. That mouth of mine, always ready, now goes to shit.

Beak Nose says, "Cristina, step back. Do not interfere. Be silent."

I can't stop Dottie. I'd be mandated on the spot. What would happen to my niños? Who would feed them, care for them, love them?

Dottie nestles against Nick. She pulls the fake white rose from the vase. Two pills, one white and one red. She pushes the white pill through her lips. The promise is five minutes of joy, followed by a sweet and painless death. The red pill is the antidote in case you change your mind.

"Cristina, step back."

I say it low, but I say it. "Where there's life, there's hope."

"Cristina! Final warning. Step back."

Dottie strokes Nick's mat of chest hair. He yawns wide enough to show a row of broken teeth. He knows, and he does nothing.

Shit, Dottie. Shit.

I need to get back to my niños. I need to scream. I need to spit on these two putas. I need to shove their spotter up both their anos.

But my niños. Still at the table picking at their eggs, quiet as angels. I slip both hands into my pockets so they can't see my fingers trembling. In a few minutes I'll walk them to school and everything will be back to normal.

The spotter struts to the other side of the kitchen so it can watch me better. The Policía come close to my niños, too close, touching distance. There's a new rock in my gut.

Beak Nose tells me, "You're lucky I'm in a good mood."

They're going to steal them from me.

I rap my knuckles on the kitchen table. "Nathan!"

He flinches, startled.

"Take your sister, get ready for school."

Beak Nose waves her hand. "No school today."

I glare at Nathan. "Rápido!"

They run off. The heap of eggs remaining on Isabel's plate. A perfect four-sided pyramid of yellow.

The Policía brandish the grim look of official business. The spotter creeps up to me and positions its arm near my chest, a clear message. I face Beak Nose. Her eyes are green and soft, and for an instant I don't believe she can destroy my life, this ordinary flesh-and-blood person who looks like anybody's sister or best friend. But she can. The insignia on her shoulder proves it.

Go ahead, Beak. Get in the first word.

"This unit is below minimum adult occupancy. I'm pulling them to state care."

"No reason for that. They don't even know Dottie's their mother."

Now we stare, the two of us, woman-to-woman. The Policía heard me say an unacceptable word, *mother.* To their faces. *Mother, father.* Those words have been stolen from us. We can't say them out loud. This will lead to a Better World.

Beak blinks fast. She has no comeback at all? My Trust Score is steady at 208. After saying *mother*. But I'm just getting started.

"I care for them. I'm the only one who washes them and hugs them in the night. And I'm not going anywhere."

Sumo shakes her head. "You are a child."

"I'm seventeen. Don't hit shab. I already do all the work around here." I jab my index finger toward the plates. "Who do you think feeds them?"

They flick through my Stream. Pics of the Skylon II engine nozzles and heat shield flaps. Drawings of the JAXA single-stage-to-orbit vehicle. Do they understand my dream? Tracked for University. Beijing or Tokyo or Bangalore. Aerospace engineer. A future life designing spacecraft instead of watching them from the ground.

But there's that 208 Trust Score.

"We understand your feelings," Sumo counters. "However, we have only limited ability to change—"

"You have the discretion!"

Beak nods as if she finally understands my 208 Score. I create discord. Her phony smile comes back. "My discretion is to pull the children for their own health and safety."

"You want them?"

Smile gone, just like that. "We want to secure …"

I stretch my arms across the hallway to block access to the bedrooms. The spotter takes three steps to get in a better position to hit me. Beak and I lock eyes. This will take more. That's fine. "We both want those kids. But I want them more than you do."

She sputters but can't figure out what to say. The spotter raises its arm. I'm right on the edge of turning into a physical threat, so I may get hit for the first time, after all. That would be fine, too.

"Cristina, stop this. Sit down and be quiet."

"Will you leave my kids with me? I'm not moving, so the burden of action is on you. Hit me, mandate me, or leave."

Sumo looks ready to faint from the sheer stress of dealing with this fifty-five-kilo girl. She stammers, "Remember what happens to you if you don't obey us. It is required."

"I don't care. Can't you see that? Look, this is simple. If you want those kids, if you really want them, hit me. Hit me, mandate me, then come up with some reason to explain why you lost control of the situation. Because that's what you're going to have to do. I want them that bad. You're not taking those kids while I'm still standing."

I mean it. Beak Nose gets that.

Sumo turns to Beak. "Stun her? Do you authorize?"

The spotter waits for the order. How much is this going to hurt?

We're back to staring. Beak Nose thinks and thinks hard. Policía are supposed to avoid hits, maintain control with smiles and words. It's easier, quicker, less risk of trouble—and even the Autoridad prefers to avoid trouble.

She shakes her head, and the tension leaves her face. "I'm marking this unit a quad. I find those kids hungry, they're pulled. Do you understand that? I'll let you win this one. Don't screw it up."

I want to reach out and grab her hand, but it's not allowed—the spotter will automatically hit me if I touch her.

"From my heart. Gracias, mi capitán."

I bow my head in fake respect as they leave. The spotter follows them out, and it even closes the door. Other spotters will come later for Dottie's removal.

But I have this much: For once the Autoridad didn't get to control me. And I told two Policía they can basically go fuck themselves.

The niños are in their room. They're dressed for school, but huddling in the corner as if hiding from a dangerous animal. Nathan's face shines with wet.

They're in my arms, and the three of us hug tight. "I'm proud of my little chiquillos." I bury my face in Isabel's brown curls so they can absorb the moisture from my eyes.

"Are they gone?" Nathan asks.

"They're gone. Don't be afraid."

We're told children belong to the community. That's wrong. These belong to me.

T W O

School assembly in forty minutes. I'm safe and alone in my room, but my fingers still shake. They need to get still soon.

Playa Vista Academy pushes a promo to my Stream: Special celebration! October twenty-sixth, Moon Festival! I'm on parade, but that can't be right. It's Tuesday.

I snap, "No parade today!" and get my explanation.

Yes, the Academy will parade this morning. Today isn't just any Moon Festival, but big anniversary Moon Festival, exactly thirty years after Lin, Xiao, Huang-Lee, and Zheng accomplished their historic first landing.

This, on top of everything else.

The promo babbles about the Chēngzhǎng flights. Courageous pilots and engineers established a scientific outpost at the crater Copernicus. They showed the world what could be accomplished under Global Harmony. Except I know Global Harmony didn't exist thirty years ago.

The fake Cristina in the promo happily marches with her classmates in a perfect uniform. She's a bit prettier than the real me, her nose a cute little button, chestnut-colored hair longer and more lustrous, toothpaste-tube body altered to have curves in the right places. They do this on purpose, another trick to get me to watch.

In reality, I'm toward the bottom of the curve in the prettiness department, and my uniform hasn't been washed since last week. I pick it out of the laundry net, give it a sniff, and check for food spots. A couple of quick licks and fingernail scrapes and it's clean enough.

What do they expect, parading both Monday and Tuesday?

Worse, this is for a supposed historic event that isn't even true—not the way the instructors tell it. The Chēngzhăng flights happened. They did send people to Copernicus and the Mare Imbrium. But others were on the moon before Chēngzhăng.

The America states landed men with the Apollo spacecraft a long time ahead of Global Harmony. Twelve men in six flights to different locations. Why were they all men, anyhow?

Why isn't Apollo—the real first landings—ever covered in school? Why isn't Apollo anywhere on the Stream?

I pull on calf-length white socks, then the massive, clunky white parade shoes everyone loathes. There's just enough time for a quick look at my Apollo book. I need to wash the Chēngzhăng Moon Festival jabber out of my head, along with the Policía and Dottie eating the pill. All of it, I need to forget and forget fast.

My book, my treasure, kept in the bottom dresser drawer concealed and protected under a layer of folded skirts. I place it on my lap. A square block of shiny paper, heavy and huge.

Apollo: The Epic Journey to the Moon, 1963-1972

I open the cover and run my fingers across the blue handwriting on the first page:

> *To my daughter Cristina on her ninth birthday.*
> *May your spirit one day carry you to the heavens.*

Signed with a flourish: *Francisco Flores, PhD*. Francisco—also known as Paco—my father. He taught me to always play the Autoridad's games, so I call him Paco instead of papá.

Across the bottom half of the same page is more handwriting. Thick black lines, each letter neat and straight:

> *To Paco, No dream is too high for those with*
> *their eyes in the sky.*
> *Best wishes*
> *Buzz Aldrin*

This one page, touched and written upon by both Paco and Buzz Aldrin—my father and an Apollo man who flew to the moon. Both of them, on this paper under my fingers.

The book is dated 2013, ridiculously ancient. I flip paper to the first landing. Armstrong. Aldrin. Houston, Tranquility Base. The Eagle has landed. Every page and every pic is in my memory but when I hold this book, what happened back then becomes real, and I can feel Paco Flores and Buzz Aldrin with me.

Or maybe I'm just another crazy chica.

The intricate Apollo hardware must have been more fragile than the silver cylinders of the Chēngzhǎng spacecraft, especially the Lunar Module. How much control did the pilot have? What did he see, feel, and think during the landing?

The need to know—the yearning invades my head all over again.

But reality calls. I close my book and hide it under skirts. After class there will be time to re-explore every detail of those two hundred and seventy-two pages.

I jerk my left white sock up a bit, then don my pale blue beret and pull the front edge the proper length forward. Today my rosies come with me. I take them from their hiding place inside a rolled-up sock and drop the burgundy-colored beads into my uniform pocket. The miniature cross makes them a religious icon, something the Autoridad requires to be kept at home.

Today they're coming; what's life without risks? What are they gonna do, drop my Score to 200?

Along with my Apollo book, my rosies are Paco. Paco, on his knees, rosies in his giant hands. He did that every evening before bed. What was he doing with these rosies intertwined in his fingers? They were something he cared about deeply, and that's reason enough to keep them close.

My own fingers are calm and steady.

I pull on my white silk gloves and stretch them halfway back to my elbows. How stupid is it to walk to school wearing white gloves? I screwed with two Policía, but I'm scared shitless to go near the Academy on a parade day wearing an incomplete uniform.

✳

Culver Boulevard is blocked by columns of fast-marching soldiers in green and brown camouflage. They're grouped by homeland. Texas follows Japan follows Honduras. Their helmets, machine guns, and stiff, jerky style of walking always terrifies Nathan. He squeezes my hand tighter.

"They're not going to your school," I assure him, the thumps from hundreds of boots almost drowning out my words. "They're going to mine."

Global Harmony says we need plenty of soldiers to protect us from the Khilafah. Maybe that's true, but I doubt it matters much. The soldiers also guarantee the Autoridad can do anything they want. Harmony is everywhere across the world, but their soldiers and the Autoridad are here in our faces to make sure we never forget who has the final word.

As long as we don't forget, there is peace.

When I was around six years old, I stood at this same corner and felt a bomb explode. *Felt it,* right through the soles of my feet. I remember people running everywhere all the time. I remember sidewalks covered in blood. I remember a dead lady's ripped-up face hanging off the top of her body. One time there was another bomb, and someone, I forget who, made me and Paco and some other people go outside and look at a row of men kneeling in the street. They each held a big brick or something over their heads. When any of them let their brick drop, a soldier shot him in the back.

Wild times. And long over. Because of the soldiers. So why am I not grateful?

It's a relief to drop the kids off at their school because Culver's fast getting crazy. The chaos begins blocks away from the Academy. The Autoridad closed off the streets and swarms of spotters fly in formation overhead—the hefty kind, with weapons. They're scanning our faces from fifty meters up and maybe looking into our brains too.

All this for some high-ranking político. That guarantees a speech, another waste of time. The instructors will form us into lines and we'll parade, and then hear how lucky we are to serve Global Harmony.

Banners hang from the top of the bleachers: the baboon face of Marco Javier Crespo, governor of Alta California. Marco decides on a Moon Festival tour of Los Angeles, so what better place to start than a morning extravaganza at Playa Vista Academy? Politicos can't get enough of themselves.

I enter school grounds ungreeted and not terribly welcome. Thank you, 208 Trust Score. Even so little as a friendly smile might lower their own Scores. I'm invisible, and who can blame them? The good news is, I don't care. I don't need them. They consider themselves nothing but collections of atoms, products of selfish genes, adrift through spacetime with the single goal of increasing their Score. Score is everything, your total value, your worth as a human being. A high number makes their lives easier and better in every way—eating, sleeping, gaming, even love.

Years ago, my Score sometimes cleared 700. I was a good girl, never contradicted the instructors or questioned what we were told. I watched the right promos, volunteered to march and be a guidon, and kept my mouth shut. Young, stupid, too easily intimidated. That's over. Now my life is harder and maybe futile, but I truly don't care about my Score, and I don't need anyone else.

Even so, someone does notice I exist. Not one of the tall, handsome gatos, of course, but an on-and-off friend who's also too old to be at the Academy. Faye and I see each other at the same time. She has my guidon along with her own, gripping both heavy wooden poles even though she has only two fingers on each hand.

"Marco picked Playa over Venice and Hawthorne," she tells me, which might be good news to her. Faye has a habit of casting her eyes downward when she talks, as if she fears her own words.

"Our great luck. But it could be worse. It could be raining."

I can't help glancing at Faye's hands as she passes my guidon pole. Special white gloves with two fingers each, an index finger and middle finger for her right hand, a thumb and middle finger for her left. She's a guidon bearer even though she can barely grasp the pole with her limited number of fingers.

A few pendejos call her Four-Fingered Faye.

Everyone's heard the story. Faye was mandated, along with her parents. This was a while ago, when we were both twelve. Faye came back with a lot fewer fingers.

That's all anyone knows.

Faye's Score is 375 and it never tops 400, so she doesn't have much to lose by associating with me. It might even raise her Score if she could get me to say or do something that raises my own. No success with that yet.

Instructors walk up and down the field shouting, *"Asamblea!"* Hundreds of chattering voices hush. We all drift into proper place, and order emerges from chaos.

Principal Alvarez probably dreams of someday ascending to Marco's level of divinity. His usual smug expression is replaced by a formal posture. He puts both hands on his hips and barks, "Let's see some snap!"

Everyone has a case of sizzled nerves. Gracias, Marco Javier Crespo.

A whistle blows and we fifteen guidon bearers come to attention. I check my guidon post is perfectly vertical, twelve centimeters from my chest, and the guidon flag—the flag of Alta California—is unwrapped and free. On signal from Alvarez, I take two steps forward, turn about-face, and deliver my command.

"First squad! Atten...*hut!*"

Faye is next with her guidon, the flag of Alberta. The other squads carry the banners of Chihuahua, Cuba, Venezuela, Australia, China, Germany, and other homelands. Each guidon bearer brings their squad to attention, six hundred students total. Fifteen multicolored flags wave in the breeze.

Principal Alvarez marches across the rows, stops, and pivots on his heel. A distant hum grows to bone-shaking strength, and three helicopters pass over the field. They're dull gray with red stars and followed by a swarm of spotters. The massive craft settle down and throw swirls of dust across the rows of students. Soldiers sprint into protective formation.

Alvarez growls, "Academy!"

I stand a little straighter and yell from my diaphragm, "First squad! *As one!* March!"

Left foot first...clunk, the sound of a hundred heels striking the pavement together in perfect cadence.

Spine erect.

Guidon post vertical. Twelve centimeters from my chest. Eyes forward.

"Column! *As one!* Right!"

Principal Alvarez directs the ranks onto the field. Hundreds of arms swing together, thirty centimeters to the front, twenty centimeters to the rear.

I lead my squad across the front of the bleachers. Marco the Magnificent stands on his platform. The dumpy little emperor wears silver pleated pants and a dark red shirt. An enormous vid screen depicts Marco doing various noble things. Marco riding a horse. Marco with some niños. Marco picking fruit or something.

"Column! Eyes! Left!"

Our squad jerks our heads so we face Marco. We parade past him and his stupid smirk.

A whistle blasts…fifteen flags dip simultaneously, automatically, no need to think about it. Another blast. Our guidon posts and their flags shoot upwards instantly, as one, with perfection.

The columns double back and form up before the bleachers. Alvarez calls each squad to a halt. My squad stands to the right of the platform, still close enough to experience every nuance of Marco's idiotic expression. The illustrious man expects a serenade in his honor.

Grandiose music booms. That's the signal: they raise their right arms with fists clenched, the People's Victory salute, every arm at a sixty-degree angle. Every right arm but mine.

I'll carry my guidon with the flag of Alta California because that's my homeland. But no People's Victory fist salute from me, never ever. I'm a people, and it's my damn fist.

The Stream prompts hundreds of voices to sing in chorus.

> *Marco Marco Marco!*
> *You are number one*
> *We are your children, you are the sun!*

I keep my mouth shut. Not one word escapes my lips.

> *You care for us, shelter us, give us what we need*
> *You are dear leader, we are all agreed!*

Marco grins and pumps his arms. He surveys the sea of faces and bobs his head in ecstasy with every word.

> *We stand for Alta California*
> *Under the red, green and white*
> *Each of us are equal in your wise and knowing sight!*

Wouldn't it be terrific if Marco's knowing sight noticed me not singing? One person here refuses to worship.

We give a hand, we do our part
Our obedience makes our bright future start!

One closed mouth out of hundreds wide open. But Marco is too far away to see the most tightly closed mouth in the world.

Marco Marco Marco!
Hear our voices call
Welcome to our school, we love you one and all!

Marco belches out a giggle. Which will be worse, the song or the speech?

"Friends!" Marco's amplified, nasal voice thunders across the field. "I love you too!"

They all shriek with delight, including Faye. My mouth stays shut, even more shut than before.

"I will always be here for you," la pene de mierda diminuto goes on, barely audible over the screaming. "I will protect you, I will provide for you, I will be your strength!"

The Stream cues them to quiet down. Marco's screechy whine resumes. "We have a particular reason to feel pride this morning. A glorious event happened thirty years ago today, a time before any of you were even born."

He motions toward the familiar old vid. The Chēngzhǎng spacecraft on the moon, Ming Huang-Lee and Sheng Xiao planting a red and yellow flag into the gray surface.

"Now I ask you to reflect on the meaning of this achievement, not only to the world, but to each of you as servants to Global Harmony."

I whisper, "Do I look like a servant?"

Faye turns her head toward me, then snaps forward.

"Think about it!" Marco cries, gesturing with his arms. "The very first people to reach the moon! The first!"

What a liar. Does he even know it's a lie?

If he doesn't, he should be informed of the facts.

If he does know, he must be exposed as a fraud.

A phony. A liar.

Marco flashes a smug grin. "The first ever! What an achievement!"

The Autoridad requires everyone to tell the truth. But here's Marco Javier Crespo, cheerfully declaring a lie. *They all lie, all the time.*

Whatever they tell us, it's a lie.

My gut thrashes like a hooked fish.

My niños.

Beak Nose lied to me.

Of course she did.

Now I know it. She tricked me, got me to walk away without a hit, so they can pull the niños from their school later today.

I'll never see them again.

How could I be so stupid? *They always lie, and they never stop.*

Here's Marco Javier Crespo, telling more lies. "The first human people to achieve such a thing. How was this even possible?"

I clench my guidon pole so hard it quivers. My mouth opens. Words explode outward. Only five words, but loud and strong.

"They were…not the first!"

Marco stands frozen for one heartbeat. Then his face twitches, mouth a tiny circle of surprise.

I have more words. The problem is getting them out. I stammer, "Apollo…first!"

Can't stop thinking about the *niños*. Take a breath and *focus*. "America states got to the moon before Chēngzhǎng!" I scream. All eyes are on me. "Neil Armstrong! *Buzz Aldrin!*" I deliver that last name with force, because Paco actually met him.

More heartbeats. My throat burns. I said it, and everyone heard it.

Now what?

Whatever happens, I'd do it again. Yes, absolutely.

Marco laughs as if someone told a joke. An Autoridad official—not a Policía but a slender man in a gray jacket—waves a signal. Earsplitting music engulfs us. Alvarez throws both arms straight up. Instantly, six hundred Academy students yell and cheer.

Marco goes on with his speech even though no one can understand the words. What difference would it make? We've heard it all before. Faye's eyes are sorrowful. I smile, but her expression doesn't change. Is this moon outburst the final episode that drives her away?

Speech completed, the governor bows to the dignitaries and strides across the platform with his cadre. He turns directly toward me. I look straight back at him. His grin widens and he flashes his palm in a hasty kind of wave. A taunt? Of course it is. He knows it's all a lie, and he's getting away with it. The rotors on all three helicopters spin up, but the non-stop screams of adoration wipe out the sound of the engines.

Harmony corrects the Stream, and they do it fast. I flick back ten minutes. Student formations chanting their chorus to Marco. I swing the view and zoom in. There I am, as a simulated Cristina, clenched-fist raised high, singing with pure and starry-eyed devotion.

There's Marco, delivering his speech. "How was this even possible?"

That was the moment of my intrusion. In the new version I say nothing. Marco continues to speak. "It was possible due to the collective will of Global Harmony. We must all feel in our hearts a tremendous sense of joy and delight."

The students cheer and wave, including the imitation Cristina. What just happened, never happened. Is my brain playing tricks? Did I imagine it all? Sometimes I don't know which is true, my memory or the Stream.

Harmony adjusts truth for correct thinking.

THREE

Suspended, one week. I've heard it all before.

Except that's not what they did.

Alvarez told me I never cared about my future. *Cared,* past tense, as if I'm already dead. I told him I have a greater future than he does. By far.

I'm through at the Academy. No goodbyes, not even from Faye.

No mandate, though. And my Score, still 208. I guess it really can't go any lower.

Therapeutic counseling. I'm pulled to the Comisaría de Policía in Santa Monica. They sent a car in less than a minute. What the hell is therapeutic counseling, exactly?

As soon as the car moves they push a rather lengthy promo for *El Regalo de Salud,* the so-called Gift of Health. Today there's a special incentive. Accept my Regalo right now and there will be no therapeutic counseling. Accept, and the car will take me to the hospital instead of the police station. The promo shows me joyfully waking up tomorrow morning to sunshine and flowers.

I'll take the therapeutic counseling.

The car drops me off near two poles flying the flags of Alta California and Harmony, the halyard ropes making *ping ping ping* noise from the wind. A green prompt directs me toward the entrance.

I stop. There's music floating down from the sky, the roar of jet engines actually, my favorite kind of song. I turn and shield my eyes from the sun. I'm not going to miss this, not even once.

The roar of a Boeing Skylon on climb-out is like nothing on Earth. The morning departure to Singapore flies overhead and curves upward, a pointed silver hawk. The landing gear tucks into the wings and the doors glide shut like feathers. Fluid motion, a living creature.

The Great Bird will take its flight on the back of the great bird, bringing glory to the nest where it was born.

Who first said those words? Years ago, Paco told me it was a quote from Leonardo. This Leonardo sounds like a poet or a hypersonic engineer, but the Stream shows he acted in an old vid about a titanic ship that hit an iceberg and sank.

The Skylon goes vertical, the twin rocket boosters ignite, and the bird illusion vanishes. A thunderous BOOM punches the ground. That's the best part: the sensation of asphalt trembling under forces from thousands of meters above.

That's where I should be.

But no. The prompt blinks at me, so I trudge through the Comisaría entrance. A spotter scans my body and sings cheerfully, "Follow the prompts, Cristina. Please remove your hat."

My beret! I snatch it from my head and tuck it in next to my rosies.

The blinking arrows lead to Bench 312, Magistrado Geraldo Diaz. There aren't enough chairs in the waiting rooms, so I have to step over and around all the glum-faced nadas and their sleepy kids spread out on the floor. This is a place of fear, so everyone is particularly polite.

Even so, I doubt many of them are troublemaker on my level. La Comisaría is for minor violations like improper speech, disrespect to an Autoridad official, or failure to do something that is required—offenses that knock a Score down a hundred points and take a few months of proper behavior to restore, plus any penalty meted out by a Magistrado.

There's a pink arrow now, pointing to a familiar face.

Consejero Maribel leans against the far wall waiting for me to see her. The frown, the tilted head—her usual look when burdened with another problem. Consejeros are block captains, official neighborhood meddlers. The Stream puts a green and red icon next to Maribel's head, identifying her as Autoridad.

Habit takes over. I drop my eyes, bow slightly at the waist, and mumble, "Buenos días, mi Consejero," as I was taught when

I was little. Maribel is at least fifty years old and stinks of mouthwash and nasty deodorant. I hold my breath as we embrace. Her red hair bun brushes across my nose.

I open my mouth to tell her I don't need her here, but she drapes a flabby arm across my shoulders and whispers into my ear, "This will be a big day for you, muchacha. I can feel it."

"You're not mad?"

"Why should I be mad?" She smiles but her eyes evade. I don't much look into Maribel's eyes anyhow—they're shark eyes, totally dead.

A side door opens and three people emerge wiping tears. New arrivals trade places on the floor with those whose turn has come.

"Why do they want this…therapeutic counseling? Is this like critical self-examination?"

The Consejero hesitates. "Be your usual happy self. This is not about what you think. This is a chance to do better."

"I don't need their counseling."

Her tone hardens. "Say what the Magistrado wants you to say. That's all you need to do, and your troubles go away." She holds up her index finger and presses it to my lips. "What's my rule for you?"

"The one thing in life you can't take back are the words coming out of your mouth."

"You, always trying to change everything. What for? Me, telling you again: Listen and obey. It's simple!" She digs into her pocket and presents a yellow capsule. "Fast acting!"

I shake my head.

"Obey your Consejero. Will relax you. Make you not care. And you won't be alone. I'll be at your side."

"Gracias, Consejero, but I don't need your help."

The doorway to Bench 312 opens. Two stout Policía take position on either side of me. Their expressions speak plainly: *keep-your-mouth-shut.*

Maribel whispers, "You sure, chica?"

"I'm sure."

Whatever happens, better off without Maribel's tricks and scams. On top of that, the Magistrado won't need any help from Maribel. They have autosystems to detect lies.

One of the Policía brings his mouth close to my right ear. "Address the Magistrado as Magistrado. Speak only to answer a direct question, otherwise remain silent."

I nod and stare ahead.

The Policía on my left snarls, "Eyes to the floor."

Bench 312 is enormous for the small number of people inside. I risk raising my eyes just a bit. Five assorted Harmony officials in the standard blue-gray uniforms, all slumped along a wooden table. The Policía direct me to a yellow plastic chair at the center of the room. The door closes behind me.

Magistrado Geraldo Diaz is a skinny man with an ordinary face tanned the color of lentil beans. He's behind a massive desk decorated with the Harmony seal and pics of Marco plus the nine members of the Central Committee. Just pics, but all ten faces move a little bit like vids so it feels like they're scrutinizing me with their eyes.

Same old mind games. How dumb do I look? I snatch a few glimpses of them going through my Stream. The Magistrado starts at the beginning. They want to see my whole life.

There's mi mamá.

Her soft embrace, her flowery scent. Dim memories. My mother, we lost her when I was about three. What happened to mamá? I glance up but they've flicked past her. There's Paco taking me to school. Alex is with us. He's very small, maybe two.

Age six, Paco teaching me to sing.

I'm eight, and Alex is gone.

Before I can stop myself, I slide my left hand into my uniform pocket and clutch my rosies. *Stupid.* Don't draw attention to the rosies.

Alex is gone, and Paco did nothing.

Shut it out.

The Harmony officials talk among themselves in Mandarin and Hindi. What's so interesting? Me, age nine, creating plans for spacecraft. My Apollo book is my inspiration. They scrutinize the NASA logo painstakingly copied from the book. National Aeronautics and Space Administration, the America states group that built the Apollo spacecraft. They watch me try to draw the logo on a white shirt.

The history in my Apollo book isn't taught at the Academy, so I'm not supposed to know it. It's too much harmful information in my head.

Paco is taken from me, too. I'm assigned to a housing unit. One of the officials shakes his head. They know about the rosies. They know they're in my pocket.

One of them mutters the word *icon*.

My heart pounds.

Magistrado Diaz flutters his hand dismissively. "I'll allow it."

He'll allow it.

He'll allow Paco's rosies. A burst of heat surges across my face. What gives him the ability to allow or disallow my rosies?

The Magistrado flicks through my Stream full speed. Taking it all in, the trouble with my instructors, my interest in engineering, aerospace design, even my fútbol team when I was eleven. I was a one-girl team.

My breath escapes in short huffs. He raises his eyes and I stare back. His shirt is a blue so dark it's almost black, and it has cherry-red trim and buttons.

He squints his eyes for a moment, then relaxes and flashes a smile. "Cristina Flores, you have a magnificent brain in you. So much reading and study! Science. Literature. Art. Psychology. Proficiency in so many subjects! There is nothing you don't know, eh?"

"There's a lot I don't know."

The Magistrado jiggles his finger. "I like that answer." He gives my Stream more flicks. "I like your drawings, too. You're a brilliant artist. Your GAO exam scores in physics, chemistry, engineering dynamics. The highest grades I have ever seen."

Not the highest, but damn excellent. Enough to be tracked for university when I was thirteen. I was dumb enough to expect my grades and my projects to overcome my big mouth and my low Trust Scores. But nothing can get around a crappy Score, and I'm old enough to understand that now.

He leans forward. "You seek university admission, eh?"

I stop breathing.

"Peking University, Beijing. That is where you seek to attend?"

"Si."

"Engineering, eh?"

"Si, Magistrado."

They're back to my Stream, all of them. When are they going to mention what I said to Marco? Isn't that why I'm here? It's been cut from my Stream, sure, but they know everything, what actually happened, the true event stored in my head.

"Novio?" the Magistrado asks, his mouth in a tiny smirk.

"No."

No boyfriend. What a revelation. He shrugs as if this is a major mystery. They pass back and forth over the last couple years, my time with Dottie and the niños, with Chloe, Nick, and Charlie. *They can see everything, whatever detail they want.*

"You don't talk to many people, Cristina Flores."

I guess that was a question. "No, Magistrado."

He can figure that out for himself. Other than my niños, who I will never see again, and Dottie, who killed herself this morning, and Faye. That's all.

What does he expect me to say?

Does he comprehend the fact that no one will ever give a rat's ass about me and my 208 Score? Friendship with me would bring down their own Score. I'm supposed to mingle with people who see me as a dangerous snake? Harmony's promos remind us: k*eeping Trust is glorious, breaking Trust is disgraceful.* Chicos are supposed to like me...why? Because I know a lot of math and science? That makes up for my crap Score?

Harmony destroys me with a crap Score, then they wonder why I have no friends.

I almost say it out loud. *You poisoned me.*

For once I control my big mouth. Instead, I state what should be obvious.

"I don't need them."

A simple fact.

One of the Harmony officials, a little man with a long ponytail, snaps out five words in Hindi. The Magistrado nods and speaks while he studies my Stream.

"You are disrespectful. Impolite. You contradicted your instructors numerous times, even though you know it's not permitted."

More barks from the Harmony guy. His ponytail jiggles like a puppy's tail.

"Why do you do this, Cristina? What explanation can you give us?"

"I don't understand what you mean."

He scowls. "You go to school to learn from the instructors. They know more than you. You said you don't know everything, eh? So why can't you behave correctly?"

"I know what's right. I tell the truth."

"Not *your* truth! Learn the correct truth you are taught!"

"There's only one truth."

Another weird twisted face. "Who told you that?"

"My father."

He thumps the desk with his fist. I did it, said an improper word.

"Not your instructors, eh? Your…padre. Si, tu amado padre!"

The officials babble and they're not happy. The Magistrado blows out his breath hard enough to rattle his lips. "Where is father now? Oh yes, he passed. Seven years now. Cancer. Only forty-six."

I fold my arms. Stupid to mention Paco!

They stream this morning's parade. The students marching and singing to Marco. The Magistrado swings to my image and zooms. The simulated me sings passionately. They must know this this faked.

His smile returns. "You have a beautiful voice, Cristina Flores."

"I didn't sing."

That only widens his grin. "Just move your lips. That's what truly matters, eh?" He leans forward. "Peking University. That's where you should be. Beijing! All you need is the nomination, and I grant it. You are pulled to Formación, as of today."

My right hand flies to my mouth and drops again. My skin tingles, so this has to be real.

I splutter, "You can do that?"

"Oh, yes!" he assures me. "Not a problem. You should have gone four years ago—"

"I got a nine on my HSK Mandarin."

He's back to my Stream. I sit, and think, and calm down.

I want to believe him.

But they always lie.

No mention of my Score, my interrupting Marco. This is all a lie, because they have no reason to give me what I want.

Now his fingers are laced together. "It's my pleasure to help you. However, we need to deal with another matter first."

They will require a public apology?

"Before you leave for university, Cristina, you will accept your Regalo de Salud. We'll set your appointment for tomorrow morning."

The room floats.

I jump to my feet and cry out, "Magistrado!"

He grins and waves me toward the door.

"Magistrado, please—"

"Your Consejero will take care of everything."

✳

Maribel tugs me into the washroom. No more smile, all official.

"He's trying to help you."

"I don't want Regalo!"

"It's for your own good."

I run water over my hands. Will Maribel help a chica from the units? Or serve Global Harmony?

She switches to her soft voice. "I want to see you happy. Do what they tell you to do. You think like a child. Do I need to remind you again? They'll get what they want."

"If they want me to accept Regalo so bad, why don't they force me? All those soldiers. Why don't they force everyone? Would simplify things. No need for promos." I shake water from my hands. "But they can't shoot us all, can they?"

Maribel puts her hand over her mouth. Her eyes are wide; I've never seen her afraid. What have I done?

The Stream promos my life without Regalo. Fake Cristina plods through an open field under a blazing sun—sweaty, dirty, exhausted—part of a line of workers trudging behind a harvesting machine.

Menial labor. Capacitación Básica.

Maribel whispers, "They are giving you a chance to do better."

They only take your ovaries, not your uterus. They keep some of the eggs. They might genetically alter them. I'll still be able to have children someday, possibly genetically edited, and only with authorization. Or maybe not, because I've also heard they take everything.

The niños. They're gone. Are my ovaries more important to me?

Maribel cradles my head and brings my cheek against hers. "I promise it won't hurt. Go to sleep, wake up, go home. Quick and easy." She pulls my chin so our eyes meet. "You don't want to bring a child into this world."

F O U R

The low sun outside the Comisaría casts orange light across the buildings and treetops. Already they're pushing my instructions for Regalo. A promo shows me rising early but eating no breakfast. I drink only water, then nothing at all after eight. By nine a car takes me to Manchester Medical Center. I'm happy and unafraid, and afterward I'm in a room with lots of flowers. No mention about losing some of my insides.

A car stops next to me and the door pops open. They want me to go home, but I'm not ready to do that.

My *niños*. I have to know.

They were taken hours ago, probably by Beak Nose herself. But I don't know that for certain. For my chiquillos, I need to *know*, and there's only one way to do that. This may be a last chance to say goodbye.

A 208 Score doesn't let me get a car on my own, so I hike to their school. It's empty by the time I get there. The niños are gone.

Could Chloe have walked them home?

But the windows in my housing unit are dark. How can that be? I open the door, and Charlie greets me with his head low and tail barely moving. Everything is the same, a total mess, just no peeps. Chloe, at least, should have messaged me. But there's nothing.

My mouth goes dry as something drains from my head into my belly.

My Stream, *empty.*

I lower myself into a kitchen chair.

My spacecraft pics and drawings. All gone.

This cannot be.

My pics from Apollo, gone.

My hand-drawn NASA logo, gone.

Like they never were.

My legs wobble, but I force them to carry me into my bedroom.

Bottom drawer. Under the clothes.

Apollo. Gone.

The world drops down a hole. I can't breathe. My knees buckle and I'm on the floor. I sweep my right hand across the bottom of the drawer.

Maybe they just moved it. Maybe they checked it, to see if there's anything hidden inside it—a recording device, a weapon. I spring from one side of the tiny room to the other. Not on the bed, not in the closet, or under the bed, or on the floor, or under my pillow.

Who am I fucking kidding? But I have to look.

I check the sofa, the chairs, the kitchen table, the trash. I wrap my rosies around my fingers and bring them to my lips as Paco used to do.

Charlie sits, tail twitching, watching from a distance.

"Please, no."

I can't get it out of my head. *To my daughter Cristina Flores on her ninth birthday.*

Tears swell behind my eyes. I will not cry. I will not. Paco would hate it.

My body quivers all over. The Autoridad. They took what was mine.

They came in here when? This morning? This afternoon, when I was at the Comisaría? They came in here, into my room, reached into my drawer, put their filthy hands on Apollo. Was it one of those bastardo Policía? Which one took it, Beak Nose or Sumo?

Gilipollas!

Who did this? Magistrado Geraldo Diaz? Marco Javier Crespo? Maribel? Does it matter?

There will be no Regalo.

I scream, "No Regalo! Hear that? I won't do it! *Chinga tu madre!*"

There's no care left in me.

Isabel and Nathan's toys lay scattered across the floor. Plastic elephants and giraffes. "Goodbye, my little chiquillos."

Faye's fingers. White-gloved, wrapped around the guidon pole. Why did they designate short little Faye a guidon bearer? I understand now. So that no one would forget those fingers. They want those fingers held up, in the open, for all to see. A warning.

The Autoridad does that.

I sprint out the door into the darkness. Above me are stars, pure and true. I'm strong again, and I run the two blocks to Faye's unit on legs driven by fury. I push through the door. I know this unit, I lived here with Faye for a few months after she came back.

Two men and a woman are at the table eating. I know only Tim, a pale, round-faced hombre. He stands, wide-eyed, but keeps chewing. The others spin around.

There's Faye, at the sink, with the water running and she doesn't even know I'm here. I grasp her left hand and pull her around to face me. She yelps and spits bits of food. Faye's thumb and middle finger clutch my hand so hard it hurts.

Tim yells at me but he's not going to stop me from doing what I need to do. In fact he doesn't even try. Every nada on the block is taught to back off and run when they see a crazy person, anyone acting in an unauthorized manner, and that I am certainly doing. They dash out the door, the three of them, leaving Faye and me alone.

Faye is close enough to smell salsa on her breath. I say each word with care, and loud enough so she can hear over the running water. "You're going to tell me!"

"Please, Cristina! What are you doing?"

Her two fingers tremble against mine. She knows I won't let go.

"Are you listening? You're going to tell me!"

I hold her two fingers in front of her eyes. They're small and wet and I'm sorry for her, but I really have no choice. This is my last chance.

"I have to know."

She flinches and shakes her head.

I shut the water off. Now we have quiet.

"I want you to tell me what happened. Don't be afraid."

Another head shake. She fights back tears.

"I'm crying too, Faye, inside me."

Two lines of wet spill down her cheeks. I hold her close and stroke her arm. The stub of her pinkie is a hard lump against my skin.

"Faye, look at me. They're not going to give you new fingers. They're lying. They want everybody to see these hands. Understand me? They want us to see."

She cries on my shoulder. I want to say more but I keep my crazy mouth shut. It's quiet outside, but how much time do we have?

"Tell me. Tell me now, because I won't be here much longer."

I wait some more. She raises her head and there's a look in her eye, not fear, but resolve. She's thinking. Forming words. She swallows, and the words come.

"You want to know, Cristina?" She sniffs and stares at the floor.

"Look at me when you talk."

Faye raises her eyes. She presses her lips together before the words come. "*Criminals!* They were *criminals,* Margo and Peter, filthy criminals. Illegal books! Illegal pregnancy! Sickening, both of them, and they deserved what they got."

Her mother and father.

Faye yanks her hand free and thrusts it in my face. Three wet, pink stumps.

"Margo and Peter made them do this! Rotten, filthy criminals. We fixed them good. You're the smartest person I know, but you're too stubborn to understand how happy I am, how lucky I am, to be…an *example…an example* for everyone to see, like you said. An example for *you,* Cristina!"

She wipes both hands on a dishtowel and tosses it across the faucet.

"I serve a *purpose.* My fingers, a necessary sacrifice, a fair exchange for the names Margo and Peter hid in their heads. I did my part to get those names, and it's a worthy purpose for me. Now I'm an example. I thought I could be an example for *you,* Cristina. Maybe someday you would know the greatest purpose for any of us, service to Harmony."

I back away from her.

"I cry for you, Cristina, because you're a criminal, too. Hopeless, pathetic. I wanted to help you. I wanted you to have a purpose. Do you understand the meaning of the word?"

My fingers…a necessary sacrifice.

Her eyes are savage and empty at the same time. Harmony put these things in her brain. Faye belongs to them in every possible way. And she doesn't care—no, she's proud of it.

A metallic *click-click-click* from just outside the door. A spotter walking across concrete.

"*Purpose,* Cristina!" Faye spits. "*What is your purpose? Why do you even bother to live?*"

The spotter comes through the door, circles me, and stops. A broad-shouldered Policía stands at the door. His face is red and sweaty.

"*You,*" he points to me. "Do not move. Understand?" He points to Faye. "You, step back into the other room. Do it now."

I make my voice steady. "Leave me alone."

Two more male Policía take position behind the first. One of them turns and calls out over his shoulder, "You may enter, Consejero."

Maribel pokes her head into the kitchen. She glances around but doesn't acknowledge me. I'm invisible. There's the deodorant stench when she passes behind me on her way to the living room.

The spotter edges closer. The Policía order, "Raise your arms above your head."

What choice is there?

"Turn around, face the table."

I snarl, "You have no reason to do this."

"Lower your arms slowly. Empty your pockets on the table. No sudden movements."

I pull out a packet of fresh tissues and my rosies and lay them between two plates of half-eaten quesadilla.

"Take one step back. Do not move your arms. Do not turn your head."

From behind me, heavy footsteps clunking fast. Maribel brushes my rosies off the table like trash. They slide across the floor.

She yells, "Icon! Mierda bagota!"

"They're allowed!"

I step forward and bend down to pick them up.

Searing pain stabs both my legs, an overwhelming shock worse than hot water because it won't stop. I hear a shriek of agony from far away, from someone else, but it's me. The kitchen floor smacks my face and the anguish in my legs explodes. Every muscle in my body knots together into a tight ball of sparkling hurt.

Time fades. There's a heavy shoe pressing down on the back of my neck. My wrists are bound to a restraint band, a strap of orange plastic wrapped completely around my waist. When did that happen?

"Don't struggle. Just be still."

The Policía yank me to my feet. A trickle of saliva runs down my chin.

"Can you swallow? Good."

They push me toward the door. There's the spotter, one slender arm still dangling a bit of wire.

My rosies.

I try to turn around, but I can't. A weak little whimper comes out of my mouth, a barely audible plea. The Policía steer me outside. They must have sent Maribel away. Faye, the others—all gone. Just a white van.

"Something," I manage to sputter. "Something of mine."

They ignore me and shove me into a seat. The motor purrs alive.

"Kitchen floor, near the corner. Rosies. Beads. Please. I need them. They're allowed."

The Policía take their seats. The spotter strolls up to the van and uses its silvery arms to position itself across from me. One of the arms extends.

Another hit! I clench my teeth.

But the spotter holds my tissues—and my rosies. It slides both into my uniform pocket. The miserable thing did as programmed and returned personal items not deemed weapons. I exhale and press my bound hands against the lump in my pocket, my rosies.

I whisper to the spotter, "Gracias."

All three Policía explode laughing.

FIVE

The end of the line for me. I saw it coming five minutes before we got there.

SERCENT is a concrete tube wider than two fútbol fields and almost a kilometer long, lit up from one end to the other with pink and yellow floodlights. The outer shell is covered with enormous murals portraying various Harmony leaders, their smiling faces fifty meters tall. Above the entrance is a huge graphic of two cupped hands offering a red rose.

Servicios Centrales—Central Services—SERCENT.

Here I am, ready for jail or wherever they keep you right after a mandate, and I get *this?*

Why SERCENT? A status change, definitely—but that means what? I've never had reason to come here, but I have an idea what to expect. SERCENT is calculated humiliation. It's staffed by people who enjoy dishing out fear and anxiety.

Nadas go to SERCENT for sad reasons. I heard a lot of them are here to request an earlier date for a scheduled medical treatment, or appeal denied medical service or a denied prenatal authorization. There's supposed to be a lot of young nadas trying for a better housing allotment, nadas with crap Scores angling to do better, begging Harmony for a few extra crumbs.

I don't want their crumbs. So I'm here why?

SERCENT closed hours ago, but they're going to leave me anyhow. The main floor is so big I can't see the other side. People are sprawled everywhere, sleeping, clustered together talking, leaning against walls and plastic barriers, thousands of them. But those luxury accommodations are not for me.

The Policía, their spotter following like a faithful dog, escort me to an area filled with hundreds of identical chain-link compartments laid out in a grid. Most hold a single sleeper—a man, a woman, or a child. Troublemakers, and this is how they're kept isolated overnight.

They pick a compartment for me, a cage really, two meters square at the most. One of the Policía activates the door lock. He whispers, "Have a wonderful night."

My feet refuse to move.

"Want another hit?"

I let him push me in.

The spotter reaches inside and slices my restraint band and pulls it from my waist. I massage raw skin and blood flows back into my wrists. Something reeks; rows of little holes cover the clear plastic floor, each hole crusted with gunk resembling chocolate and caramel. I'll take a wild guess it's not chocolate or caramel.

A grunt and a dribble sound from behind me. In a nearby cage, a nada with silver hair plaited into neat braids clumsily squats so she can urinate. She clutches the chain-link wall to keep from falling over.

Can I hold it until morning? Absolutely.

They let us out in the morning, right?

I lower my butt to the least filthy spot on the floor. The Stream works, but there's no info, not even my Score, and it doesn't obey my hand. Harmony gets to choose my entertainment, and that means nothing but required promos. First comes a spectacularly stupid spin for Governor Marco. The second promo is no surprise, either. The imitation Cristina—as always, forged slightly prettier than the real me—joyfully accepts her Regalo and emerges from the operation with a moronic grin. The fake Cristina encounters a gorgeous, long-haired hombre and they kiss before a setting sun.

In some crazy way, the idiotic promos help my brain untangle. How many mistakes did I cram into one day? Are they mistakes? I'd do it all over again exactly the same, even though it was a kind of suicide. I still breathe, but the me of my previous life is dead.

Why didn't I shout out and wake up Nick and Chloe? They could have done something, said something, and Dottie could be alive now.

Nathan, Isabel! Would Harmony blame niños that young? Where are they now, what are they doing? They're safe in bed. Who's going to feed them tomorrow morning? Will anyone ever tell them what happened to me? They shouldn't suffer because of my big mouth.

It's going to be a long night.

A greenish glow from high overhead; the whole roof is a giant vid screen and an animated story begins. It's a history lesson, the one everyone already knows. Our past was filled with war, hunger, and suffering. A small number of criminals stole wealth from everyone else. They controlled our common resources for their own selfish benefit. Bombings, shootings, conditions so chaotic millions couldn't obtain food, medical care, or even a place to live.

The outlaws destroyed themselves. There came a glorious Reawakening. People from all over the world smile at each other and embrace. Global Harmony feeds them healthy and delicious food. Everyone is delirious with joy. Harmony provides for our needs, the Autoridad ensures our safety and stability. Harmony leads us to a magnificent future by correcting our moral deficiencies.

Global Harmony. A Better World.

The cage is just wide enough to lie flat. There's a lump on the side of my head from where I smacked into Faye's kitchen floor. The whole left side of my face hurts. My stomach rumbles, grouchy about not getting dinner.

Paco.

His rosies form a comforting lump in my pocket. Think only of Paco and his rosies. Paco taught me history, too—his own history, plus a little about the people of Alta California who lived here before I was born, and about the America states.

In other words, dangerous talk.

Paco had a lot of dangerous ideas in his head, and he told me only a tiny portion. This was to protect me. I was little and little kids haven't yet learned the many things they must never say.

First we rode the Metro to the beach at Santa Monica or Venice. The cooler months were better because there were fewer people, and the sun set straight down into the horizon. We always sat near the water before our talks. Paco spoke softly, his voice barely louder than the crashing waves, maybe so the autosystems wouldn't understand most of his words.

Paco kept a bundle of pics, the kind on pieces of paper. These pics weren't on the Stream and therefore harder for the Autoridad to find. Old pics were important to Paco and he wanted me to see them often, to *store the images in my head,* as he put it.

There was one of Victor, Paco's father, from Sonora, a grinning boy perched on a bicycle, white shirt with a strange cartoon of a big green muscular turtle-person. Victor was in the dreamer program, Paco told me, but he never said what the dreams were about. There was Victor as a soldier in a desert. Same grin, beige uniform, sunglasses, and on his right arm, the flag of the America states. A tiny Paco with Victor, and they're eating funnel cake on the Santa Monica pier. Paco with his mother, Sarah, at Griffith Observatory. Paco with our Apollo book under his arm, shaking hands with Buzz Aldrin, both of them looking at the camera with jaunty smiles.

After the sun set, the ocean became a vivid cobalt blue and the first stars would appear against the pink sky. Seagulls landed and flapped their wings at the edge of the surf, where sheets of foam chased them back into the air.

When it became too dark to see pics, we would just talk, Paco and I.

Kids start Academy at age six, and the first thing we learned is that Harmony is our mother, our guide to what's right and wrong, always there to nurture us and provide for us. The Autoridad is our father, there to protect us and discipline us.

We each received our first Trust Score, something that thrilled me beyond words. I was good with numbers and Scores were numbers that changed, and changed with *meaning.* They started us with a simple one-digit Score that could vary from two to eight, for training, because few niños that age could count much higher, anyhow. We all began with a five, and after that our Score was determined by our behavior.

It didn't take long to discover how to get our Score up: Believe what Harmony told us and behave as we were told to behave. The system was fair and just. Harmony will instruct us and we will be rewarded or punished based on our obedience.

Harmony told us what to think. Thinking your own thoughts to figure out right from wrong was arrogant. And unnecessary. We were nadas, nothings, and thinking about those matters was useless. Far worse, it was poisonous to all of humanity. But if we believed and behaved as we were instructed, everyone would benefit through our excellent compliance and dependability.

I didn't at first understand all the ideas about our duty to serve humanity through Global Harmony, but I found out that kids with a Score of seven or eight received a yummy desert with lunch, something like caramel flan or tres leches cupcakes. Fives and sixes got an apple. Less than five, no dessert at all.

It got more complicated as we got older. Students below 450 received only basic lunch, usually rice and beans, which is why a lot of overweight kids were pulled down to 400 automatically.

When I was young and silly I loved churros with lunch. I also craved the approving smiles of my instructors. I did what I could to get a seven, and then I figured out how to max-out at eight. Simple, really. I only had to ridicule the lower-scored students and inform on anyone who didn't wash their hands after using the restroom or tossed their zucchini into the lunch-room trash.

It was fun, and it won me awards.

Then there was Faye. My Score hit eight for the first time when she whispered to me that she didn't believe the Autoridad was her father because she had a real father named Peter, and besides, her mother told her she had a haven lee father, or something like that, who loved her.

I was small and didn't know any better. Faye forgave me for informing on her. Her parents were strange and no one knows what happened to them. Does this have anything to do with her fingers?

Paco found out about my reaching eight and my awards. At first he didn't say anything. We had to wait for a beach talk. Poor Paco, he knew he couldn't tell me to disobey my instructors. All he could do is explain his ideas to me, and let me store them in my head where the Autoridad could not see them, just like his bundle of old pics.

"Two plus two equals what number?" he asked, the ocean breeze tossing his black hair across his eyes.

"Four."

"Alright, now suppose I told you two plus two equals five?"

"But it doesn't equal five!"

"What if I told you it does?" He leaned toward me so our noses almost touched. "I'm telling you two plus two equals five. If you say that back to me, I promise we will get ice cream tonight."

"*Five!*" I screamed at him. "Two plus two equals five!"

We had our ice cream. Before we finished he asked me again, "What does two plus two equal?" But this time there was that stern tone in his voice, the no-shit Paco.

"Four," I told him. "Two plus two equals four. How could it be anything else?"

"What was two plus two when I asked you on the beach?"

I hesitated. Then I knew. *"Four."*

This was our secret: Say what was required. But *do your own math.*

Always do your own math.

Paco told me that years before I was born, people began to forget how to do their own math, how to think for themselves, how to figure out what was true and untrue. They believed whatever the internet and cable news told them. I'm not sure what the internet or cable news were, but I think they were like the Stream, only more limited, and you had to carry them around with you on a flat piece of plastic.

How is it that Paco, a wise and deserving man, put these ideas in my head that caused so much pain as I got older? Did he know I would lose control of my mouth? What good is this *truth* if it leads me to this grimy cage and stops me from ever seeing my little chiquillos again?

Truth is a real thing, Paco told me. Harmony tells us lies, and sometimes we need to repeat their lies back to them. But what is true will remain true. What's true matters.

Our lives, as well as truth, both have meaning. There's a purpose to our lives.

I didn't know what he meant. I still don't.

✳

A feeble kind of sleep takes me away from SERCENT for a while. Morning comes in fits and starts. There's no sunrise inside the immense enclosure, just the glow from two multicolored murals that cover the length of the curved walls. Hundreds

of nadas are waking, standing, and stretching. I really, really
need to pee.

All the cages open at once. Join the fast-growing service
queues or head for the toilet? The lines are already a hundred
meters long. My bladder will have to wait.

Unruly crowds of nadas hurry into SERCENT and the noise
level swells to a dull roar. Tiny spotters zip around overhead like
wasps. Five big queues, so which one is for me? There are no
prompts. My Stream shows no messages, zero allocation, not
even a Score. I can't even see anyone else's Score.

A lot of nadas get into the wrong queue and when there
aren't enough spotters, a Harmony official drags them by the
arm to where they belong. The officials wear protective lavender
gloves so they don't have to touch us directly, lavender being the
standard Harmony color this month.

The largest horde snakes through the center of the main
floor, a random assortment of nadas young and old, with and
without niños. It could be a general queue, and that's good
enough for me. Fortunately no one pulls me away and the line
move steadily forward. Even so, I honestly don't know if I can
keep my underwear dry.

As the end comes closer all the nadas around me go quiet.
Behave perfectly, please the administrators, get what you want.
I shift my weight from one foot to the other. Would have been
smarter to pee in the cage, regardless of the audience.

Harmony officials in forest green shirts sit behind a grungy
counter. Just when it's my turn, there's a shriek from behind
me—two Policía and a spotter escort a man and a woman, both
crying like four-year-olds. Is she prego without a neonatal per-
mit? Failed to appeal the required termination? They're walking
too slowly, so the spotter gives them both a brawny shove. The
man stumbles and falls to the floor, drawing a snicker from one
of the Policía.

"Next!"

It's a zit-faced hombre behind the counter. Thin mustache,
almost like he's too young to grow real facial hair. He goes
through my Stream. His steel-gray eyes dart left and right, as if
he sees something interesting.

I can't keep my mouth shut. And I have to pee. "Am I
tracked to Básica?"

He takes a long moment to answer. "No Básica."

"Then what's my track?"

"Try to remember this," he says slowly, with exaggerated patience. "You're tarado. It's not possible—"

"I'm not tarado! Do I look tarado? I have four years at Academy—"

"You…are…tarado."

Stomach tremble. Something sour rises in my throat. Tarado! Mentally deficient. Soft brain. Too stupid even for Básica.

"Why?"

"I don't know. Your track is strange. You'll be here for a while. All you need to do is wait."

"I want to know why I'm tarado."

He stares with vacant eyes. "I said wait. Do what you're told, or go in a booth like last night. And watch that mouth or I'll track you OD. Know what that means, tarada?"

OD. Oppositional Disorder. Something wrong with your mind. Loco, unable to live among sane people, unwilling to obey. People tracked OD disappear forever.

I run to the toilets and take care of business. In the mirror: a huge purple bruise across the side of my face. My left eye is swollen half shut.

Back in the main waiting area there's a dance class going on next to the cages. A hundred students step to their left, then right, then left, in rhythm with the leader's mambo lyrics.

They say wait. Wait for what?

A lot of people have food, and they're coming from the far end of the building. There's a row of vendor units dispensing burritos, soup, rice, and candy. All of it low fat, low sodium, and in teeny amounts. Harmony protecting our health.

A ham and egg burrito would taste amazing, even a crappy Harmony burrito. But the vendor doesn't dispense. The reason is ridiculous. And impossible. Zero APAC on credit.

My daily allocation? Zero.

What happened to APAC 146.75, the minimum daily allocation for a seventeen-year-old?

Could they do this? Sure they could. Yesterday afternoon I ate one tiny torta. What I would give for that torta now.

There's a queue for everything, and there's a queue to appeal an allocation. After five hours a bossy puta with two purple moles on her cheek tells me the allocation glitch can't be corrected.

"Come back tomorrow morning."

"I haven't eaten since yesterday. Can't you—"

"No! Just find someplace to sleep." She slows down her words. "If you don't see your allocation tomorrow, follow the prompts. Just follow the prompts!"

Her eyes tell me: Shut my mouth, or I get caged.

SERCENT grows more crowded as the day wears on. Those not in a queue sit or sleep on the floor or just cluster together talking or arguing. I've heard a lot of nadas return to SERCENT regularly, always trying for a larger benefit package. It's their sport.

Tarado. Are tarado required to accept Regalo?

No allocation and no prompts. Technically, I'm not supposed to get into a queue until I'm prompted. But there are promos, be sure of that. I watch, and my credit goes from zero to APAC 0.02. At least that works. As long as I keep my eyes on the promos, I get another APAC 0.02. I take my eyes away, the increase stops.

Is it possible to keep barely fed by watching promos all day?

The drinking fountains are free, therefore I only need food. How long to accumulate enough credit for one bowl of beef pho, or a Snickers? Two to five hours per item, depending on price.

Watch promos, and I can eat. They're stupid but endurable. About two-thirds are supposed to show how Harmony improves our lives. The rest are three-minute fairytales for Regalo. They're simpler now, so not to stress the dim brain of a tarada.

Each retelling contains small variations from the previous promos. For the tenth time, the simulated Cristina accepts her Regalo and sits down to a table piled with rice, fajita, pico de gallo, and now giant churros sprinkled with sugar. She enjoys pleasant dreams and falls in love with the gorgeous, curly-haired señor she had dreamed about.

In the next version, the fake me refuses Regalo and grows plump and repulsive. The replica Cristina stares out at me and warns, "Soon they will require it!"

Is that true, or am I just trying to scare myself?

The imitation Cristina dancing around in the promos should have her own name. Henceforth she will be known as Idiota, my prettier but brainless twin sister. Idiota is tarado, and somehow our Streams got mixed up.

I watch promos as SERCENT sinks into blaring chaos. Spotters fly around hunting for anyone who was pulled but failed to report. When they find one, they hover a meter over his head and shriek, "Vamonos a trabajar!" The unhappy nada picks himself up and walks in the direction prompted, vacation over.

My eyes burn, but my credit is up to APAC 6.76. Enough for something edible, but it's too late for the decent choices. All the pho is gone, along with anything hot and under APAC 10.00. It will be a Snickers and a bag of tortilla chips. I scan the floor and find eleven unopened packets of salsa, ketchup, and plum sauce for the chips.

Hungry, but not completely without. That's the truth of my life.

SIX

Second morning at SERCENT. It came too soon. Even on the rock-hard floor, sleep is a friend that makes hunger go away.

My parade uniform has crossed the line from grungy to filthy, the former pale blue now coated with grime. The white socks are almost as bad. I push them down to my ankles.

On credit: APAC 7.16. No allocation. I sway toward the toilets on quivering legs.

Quick head math: watching promos sixteen hours every day means APAC 9.00 per day. Two snacks, or one bowl of rice, then a tiny but hot bowl of beef pho for lunch.

How long could this go on? A week? No one else here is starving or fainting or begging for food. Of all these thousands, they chose one nada poco for special treatment? Why not make me disappear?

If they hate me this much, mandate me right now. Try it. This time, I put up a fight.

Last year I dreamt up a stupid fantasy. Everyone would just fight against the Autoridad. Shoot them with rifles. Forget about the fact it's illegal for an ordinary person to even touch a rifle, forget that's a death sentence. We'd get rifles, somehow, and shoot as many of them as it takes. Shoot their spotters, too. There's a lot more of us than there are of them.

Now I understand. Nadas won't ever do that, even if they had all the rifles and machine guns in the world. They love Harmony. They feel gratitude toward the Autoridad as long as they aren't mandated, and maybe next year allocated a better housing unit and benefit package.

And if they won and Harmony vanished, what next?

Who would feed them? Who would provide their housing, their medical care, everything they need and want? Nadas would never fight against the Autoridad, but not because they fear losing. They fear winning.

There's something new on the Stream, not another promo, just pure text. I reflexively wave my fingers to scroll. It scrolls! Yes, it sees my hand. Do they finally realize I'm not tarado?

But the words are mystifying:

> *This is an examination to measure your adult intelligence scale. There are sixty questions to be completed within twenty-five minutes. Completion of the test will credit you APAC 30.00. A score in the top five percent will credit you APAC 100.00.*

My skin tingles. Try not to think about sweet, sweet chiros.

Why is Harmony doing this? A test, here at SERCENT, makes no sense. Exams are taken at the Academy.

Why measure the intelligence of this one tarada?

One possible reason—they want to test me for Oppositional Disorder.

That would mean a hospital for the mentally disturbed. Arms and legs strapped to a bed. Fed drugs day and night. An existence worse than death.

Or there's some other reason. Maybe correcting the error that labeled me tarado?

APAC 30.00 just for trying.

That's a full meal, no hunger for a while. I can recover some strength.

I flick my hand, but the exam or whatever it is remains visible. What happened to the promos? If they want to give this test, why no promo showing a joyful Idiota following the instructions and then feasting on churros and hot chocolate?

Credit stuck at APAC 7.04. That's one snack. A headache settles in and the yakking mobs are not helping. A hundred meters overhead, millions of tiny colored squares form portraits of two Harmony leaders I know from the Academy, Seung Rho and Vikram Bhabha. An enormous grinning head forms between the other two and blinks down at we little nadas: Marco Javier Crespo.

This has got to be deliberate. I close my eyes to shut it out.

Someone plops down on the floor next to me, close enough to get a whiff of his sweaty skin. I scoot to the left without bothering to open my eyes.

There's something touching my right knee, something warm and flexing. A wide, hairy hand. I shove it away and snarl, "No me toque!"

I try to get up, but I can't.

The hand snaps back to my knee. It clasps and squeezes. He's a gaunt, black-haired man with a face like a rat. His cracked lips form words. I push at the claw, but his grip has power. His fingers flex and slide across my skin. I try to scream but it comes out a feeble squeak.

I give a mighty shove and try to roll to my left, but a second man sits down on that side—someone much larger than Rat Face. He's an unyielding bundle of muscle.

It happens so fast. The larger man lashes out like a python. His giant hand grabs Rat Face's paw, engulfs it whole. Rat Face tries to yank free, but he can't overcome the strength.

Crack crack crack!

Rat Face howls like a terrified baby. His right arm lashes out but the stronger man reaches directly across my face and stops him cold. Bawling in pain, Rat Face twists away, jumps up and skitters back a safe distance.

Three of his fingers are bent backwards. Those cracks were bones snapping.

He sputters, "Mono loco! Look what you did to me!" He vanishes into the crowd.

I turn to my protector. He's sitting calmly. An oldie! Not just sort of old, like Maribel, but incredibly old, eighty at least. Skin nothing but wrinkles, with a loose flap hanging under his chin. Regardless of age, his body is wide and powerful.

Why did he care enough to help me? I get control of my breath. "Gracias."

"My pleasure."

That's it. Now he gets up and leaves? What if Rat Face comes back?

He extends a spotted and crinkled hand. "Michael Gusman."

I place my palm against his. We grip hands and shake up and down three times. A handshake, like in the old vids. Strange, but somehow civilized.

"Cristina Flores."

I expect conversation, however weird that would be. Instead he stands, extends one hand and beckons me to rise up. There's confidence in his movements, like someone accustomed to giving direction.

"How do you feel today, Cristina?"

Is he trying to be funny? "Hungry."

"I'll bet. Any headaches? Trouble breathing, catching your breath?"

"Why do you care?"

"I'm a medical doctor. Call me Dr. Mike. I'm going to give you a brief examination, okay?"

He inspects the giant bruise on my face. His eyes narrow, and there's a flash of anger.

"Hit my head."

"More likely they kicked it against the floor a few times."

Sure. But how does he know it was a floor?

Dr. Mike peers into my eyes and mouth. His fingers probe my neck. He's a perv, and the rescue was a trick so he could touch me...No. Not this man. There's honesty in him. He's direct and true, very much like Paco, and I'm not thinking that just because he's tough like Paco. It's something else, something that comes into my mind in a way I don't understand.

"What kind of doctor are you?"

Bleary red eyes, like gamers after days without sleep. "I'm a physiologist. Also board-certified in internal medicine. Can you turn around for me?" Both hands grasp the small of my back. "Breathe in as deeply as you can. Good deep breath."

He asks me to extend my arms and exert as much sideways force as I can against his palms. He examines my hands and fingers and flexes my wrists in all directions.

"Am I going to fall apart?"

Dr. Mike sits down. He's completely bald except for two gray tufts above the ears. "You just need some chow in you."

Sharing food outside your housing unit is prohibited. Would he commit the crime anyhow? I sit down beside him and show him the exam offer. "Thirty just for trying. A hundred if I score high enough."

"Why haven't you started already? I think you'd do well."

"What if it's a trick?"

"Cristina, they can take you away any time they want. Why would they need to trick you?"

That makes sense. But how can he be sure? Is he Harmony? Something tells me *not a chance.*

"Only Harmony controls the Stream," I remind him. "Why should I do anything for them?"

Dr. Mike leans toward me. Our heads come close enough for him to lower his voice. "Harmony controls the Stream. And they always put in their scary official logos, don't they? And don't they always try to persuade with a threat of punishment as well as a reward?"

"What are you saying?"

"You see any of that here, Cristina?"

I take another look at the test notice. It's just text. That's strange. But how can it *not* be from Harmony?

"That's impossible," I whisper.

He grunts and rubs the base of his spine. "You'd be surprised what's possible in this world."

We just sit for a while, the bedlam of a few thousand nadas providing background music.

"You think I should do it?"

"One hundred percent!" He snaps it with pure conviction.

Alright. So I begin.

The problems are grueling. Numbers, shapes, grids, then complete the series. The effort drains me, and the hunger makes it hard to focus. Dr. Mike sits beside me through the whole thing.

I just make the twenty-five minutes. I hold my breath and watch the credit increase from APAC 7.04 to 107.04.

He smiles and claps his hands three times. "Now, go get some chow."

I dash off toward the vendors. An extra hundred! Probably should make it last. I come back laden with pho, fajita tacos, hot chocolate, and churros. Too many churros. Does Dr. Mike eat churros?

But Dr. Mike is gone.

✳

There are more tests.

The next one is Visual Composite Memory. Crazy and tricky. A flood of pictures and diagrams run on for over an hour. My brain is a block of ice, but my credit ticks up another APAC 100.00.

The third test is Verbal Composite Memory. A lot of strange words to memorize fast. Another APAC 100.00.

Cognitive Flexibility is a wild and crazy dance. After five hours I stop at forty-seven answers, and I'm rewarded another APAC 100.

The tests make SERCENT go away. They're like the toughest classes at the Academy, a delicious challenge that demands my full attention. And it helps to be pretty well fed.

I take a walk completely around the edge of the main floor, close to two kilometers total, but I can't find Dr. Mike. He probably accomplished whatever brought him here and went home.

A chorus of thirty children serenade with gentle hymns about Harmony and our leaders. And the promos are back. Idiota joins the chorus and sings a sweet song to Marco. It's so stupid Dr. Mike would laugh, that's a given fact. Is there a chance he'll be back tomorrow?

My third night on the floor is restful. No biting hunger, no worry about queues, or maybe my spine is going flat. I eat a breakfast of churros and chocolate. They don't keep anyone here permanently. If I'm still here in the spring, I'll try to build a little cabin or something out of empty juice boxes. Let them stop me.

When I'm done eating, I'm presented with another test. Fine. What else is there to do?

This one is called Processing Speed. Compare two diagrams side by side and decide whether they are the same or not. Two hundred problems and done.

The next is Rapid Visual Information Processing. Five white boxes with black numbers, changing twice per second. They vanish. What was the sequence? Now six numbers—what was the sequence? The pace increases and the numbers change so fast I can barely see them. Another APAC 100.00.

The seventh is the strangest of all: Psychological Profile. Two hundred bizarre questions.

Indicate agree or disagree on a ten-point scale:
My problems are mostly the fault of others.
I am more comfortable before a decision than after.
I am someone people can rely on.
When I am in a difficult situation, I can usually
find my way out of it.
I can handle many things at a time.
I think strong emotions are for weak people.
I can usually find something to laugh about.
If I cheated someone and didn't get caught, I would
feel proud.

Hours pass with no more tests. Final total APAC 622.85, even after a ton of food. Who is looking at my test results? It has to be Harmony. Who else could control the Stream?

Before dinner I walk the length of SERCENT three times, but still no Dr. Mike. Stupid to look.

Just before midnight, as I'm drifting to sleep, my Stream chimes.

Official mandate.

It shows the place: Shinya Yamanaka Medical Center, Pasadena, not later than 9:30 tomorrow. The promo shows Idiota getting into a car.

A hospital. My stomach heaves.

SERCENT. Tarado. Mental tests. Then a hospital. Everyone knows Harmony and the Autoridad do things no one can talk about. Do they have an interest in my brain?

Why tarado? A punishment, of course. A penalty for talking to Faye, and for everything else.

Why a *hospital?*

Once again I circle the entire SERCENT floor, but there's no Dr. Mike. One lap takes twenty minutes. I make five laps before I force myself to sit down.

Only one way to handle this. Let them come. I'll take another hit too, if need be. Why make it easy for them? I know what I'm going to do so I try to sleep, but I wake up countless times during the night. Sickening dreams of hospitals and dissected brains.

At last, the rising noise level signals morning has arrived. The mandate chimes again at nine. I'm not moving. How long before they send Policía?

Dr. Mike plops down on the floor next to me. "How goes it?"

I jump and blurt, "Where have you been?" Incredibly stupid thing to say. But he's here. I show him the mandate, practically rub his nose in it. "What does this mean? What were all those tests about?"

"Yamanaka used to be called Huntington Hospital. I'm familiar with it."

"Why do they want me there? Some kind of experiment?"

Dr. Mike gazes back with peaceful eyes. "As in medical experiments? On you? That won't happen."

There's a reason this viejito is always so sure. Has to be.

"This is something horrible."

He's quiet for a moment. "You're jumping to conclusions. Assuming the worst. That's unlike you, Cristina."

How does he know?

"Assume the best. Have faith. Will you trust me on that?"

Paco would probably agree with him. I touch the rosies in my pocket and nod.

Dr. Mike stands and extends his hand. "Let's get out of this madhouse. You'll be late, but it won't make much difference."

My mandate is a ticket out of here, this *madhouse,* a new word for today. The only way to exit SERCENT is through a row of gates at the far side of the building. We're outside, and the cheery morning sun feels wonderful. But there's one last ugliness to endure before Manchester Avenue.

Red Block.

Our path to the street is a curved cement walkway with flower gardens on both sides. We step over three wide puddles of chunky vomit. The reminder must be close. Among the lilies, sunflowers, lavenders, and marigolds, there's got to be that one last reminder from the Autoridad. Proof they always have the final word.

Nadas scurry down the path in a rush to get past a repulsive sight. No way to avoid it. My throat tightens. Dr. Mike places a firm hand on the back of my neck and directs my gaze forward.

But it's there, along with the sickly-sweet smell. Five people in plastic chairs. They could almost be asleep, except for the bloody mess of their pulverized faces and exposed organs. A man, two women, and two niños not more than ten. Their gray skin crawls with flies. One of the ladies cradles her own head in her lap.

My mouth fills with spit and I'm going to puke. What did these people do?

Dr. Mike gently nudges my head and I face forward again. He squeezes my hand.

"I have complete confidence in you, Cristina Flores. You're going to make it."

I swallow. Some strength comes back.

"One hundred percent!"

SEVEN

The hospital roof is curved wave-style and supported by solid glass. Like most of the other gigantic buildings constructed by Harmony, there are no straight lines.

I step out of the car and inhale flower-scented air. The mountains around Pasadena shimmer in the morning sunshine. Is this my final view of nature's majesty before death?

Have faith. Will you trust me on that?

The circular waiting room is packed with Policía, spotters, and hospital patients, but at least it has chairs. Just as I sit down, a chica with short, military-style hair strides over and snaps, "Come with me." She spins around without waiting for a reply.

The orderlies all wear the same pastel blue or green scrubs, a loose-fitting medical garment. This orderly is in such a rush I have to jog to keep up with her. We hurry down a long corridor, upstairs, and then across a magnificent arch of green glass into another building.

We stop at an elevator. "Don't tell me why I'm here," I mutter. "Surprise me."

She stares straight ahead. Her eyes are as bleary as Dr. Mike's.

"Will I be here a long time? Can you at least tell me that?"

"Yeah," she says without looking at me. "A long time."

The elevator drops. She leads me down a bare cement corridor. There's a musty, earthy fragrance mixed with disinfectant and fresh paint. An underground basement, definitely. At the very end is a heavy door and a stairwell leading further down.

Wait…*no Stream!* It's gone. No vids, no chat, no promos, absolutely nothing. I stop at the top of the stairway. This is too strange. How can there be no Stream at all? How is that possible?

The orderly descends and gestures for me to follow.

"What's down there?"

"No one's going to hurt you. Come on, we're pressed for time."

If there's nothing to fear, why the secrecy? And why the fuck no Stream?

A door bangs open further down the stairway. A silent mob climbs up, all in pale blue scrubs but too young to be orderlies. Teenagers, about twenty of them, mostly girls. They pull themselves up by the handrails, stumbling as if whacked-out tired. The boys have stubble on their chins.

I pick a girl with freckled cheeks. "What's down there?"

She trudges past as if I don't exist. One of the boys mutters, "Have fun."

"Have fun with what?"

He doesn't answer. The orderly folds her arms. "See? People do come back up."

"In pretty crappy shape, if you ask me."

Her eyes turn hard. "Nobody's forcing you. The mandate is rescinded. You can go back to where you came from, right now."

Some choice. I follow her down the stairwell.

At the bottom is another corridor. Muffled voices behind closed doors. Two men in white smocks walk and argue about something medical before they vanish into a side room. We enter a tiny space barely three meters wide. Freshly-painted white walls plus a laboratory cabinet, a chair, a padded bench, and a medical checker.

The orderly pulls a yellow plastic bag and a set of blue scrubs from the cabinet. "Put your clothes and personal things in this, including your underwear, and get dressed in these. There will be a physical exam, and someone will be in to talk to you." She closes the door.

The scrubs are too big but at least they're clean. There are even slippers. Wait—my rosies! I dig them out of my uniform dress and drop them into the front pocket of the scrubs. Then, one last look at the grimy old uniform, white socks, and the white clunker parade shoes. Something tells me I'll never see them again.

Two seconds after I'm dressed, the medical checker hums to life and directs me to stand on a pair of footprints in the center of the room. Slim silver arms whirl around me and scan my entire body. Measuring, but for what?

The checker slides backward toward the padded table. "Please sit down facing the door." It positions a soft collar around my upper arm and inflates it while probing my mouth, ears, chest, neck, and abdomen.

"Lie down on your back."

I let the thing draw a blood sample. It puts a black plastic bar across my eyes.

"Please relax."

Flashing lights. Whirls and clicks. Then a short puff of misty air into each eye. Is this an experiment? Dangerous research that could cause blindness?

The orderly returns and snatches the bag of clothes.

"What did it do to my eyes?" I demand. "The light looks funny, and I can't focus."

"Your pupils had to be dilated in order to examine your retinas. You'll be back to normal in a few minutes."

"Fine. Now tell me what this is all about."

"Be patient."

How arrogant to refuse to answer a basic question! I bang my fist against the seat pad. "Tell me now. *Now!* Or I'll walk out."

The orderly frowns and waves five fingers in my face before she leaves.

Five minutes? Time passes slowly without the Stream. Nothing to watch and nothing to read. I keep looking automatically. When was the last time I couldn't Stream? Probably when I was baby. Does this mean the Autoridad *cannot* watch me right this moment? My words and actions are not being saved? If I get out of here and scroll back to this morning, what would I see? Some fiction? Blackness?

A silver-haired woman in a white lab coat enters and closes the door. She's not as old as Dr. Mike, but close. She carries a clipboard with sheets of paper and plops into the chair. Is everyone in this place exhausted?

"Hello, Cristina. I apologize for not talking to you sooner. My name is Dr. Janet Ordin, and I'm chief physician of endocrinology here at Yamanaka."

She extends her right hand. I shake it up and down three times, Dr. Mike-style. Her fingers are ice cold.

"Why am I here?"

"You're here as a pre-select."

"Select for what?"

Dr. Ordin clutches the clipboard to her chest and rubs the edge against her chin. "I can't tell you anything further at this point. We may end up releasing you back to SERCENT."

Oh, wonderful. "This is some kind of experiment?"

"No."

"You want to take what's mine, so what is it? My body? You want pieces of me? I'm healthy, so you want to cut out my kidneys, my heart, my eyes, give them to some—"

"Organ harvesting? Absolutely not."

"I'm supposed to believe you?"

She looks directly into my eyes. "You're not the only one here. *You are not the first.*"

My mouth opens, then closes. The parade ground. Marco. Not the first. *She knows.*

"You're Autoridad."

"No one here is associated with the Autoridad or with Harmony. We won't hurt you. You're here to be tested, evaluated, and possibly make a decision of your own."

There's quiet between us.

She whispers, "It's a way out."

My stomach jumps. The room spins. "Whatever you want me to do, I'll do it. Trust me on that."

✳

Dr. Ordin denied being Autoridad. Yet the mandate to the hospital was an official Harmony pull. Was it possible they somehow fooled the Stream, hijacked it for a purpose neither Harmony nor the Autoridad knows about?

They would be caught. That would mean death.

For now, not my problem. I promised to do what they want me to do. And they waste no time before subjecting me to the next test.

"Psychomotor speed evaluation," announces the orderly who brought me down to this place. She has me lie on my back atop a foam mat and raise my legs so my thighs are straight up and my lower legs are parallel to the floor.

"Curl up, bring your left elbow to your right side and draw your right knee in to meet it, like you're on a bike," the orderly instructs while guiding with her hand. "Rotate your shoulder and squeeze your abdominal muscles. Do as many as you can for five minutes. Start now!"

Next comes a reaction time test. Just a screen and some buttons, but grueling.

"Neurocognitive battery," the orderly announces cheerily. She's enjoying this. There's coffee on her breath. I ask if I can have a cup. No. Something to eat? No. Some water? No.

"Here are your options. You can leave or you can stay."

"Staying."

It's a way out. I believe it, and I don't believe it.

The tests don't let up. I have to recall pictures, grids, lists, and numbers. Trace diagrams backwards and forwards with one hand, then the other. More lists, then re-draw the previous diagram from memory. Trace it backwards. Trace it upside down.

Humanitarian that she is, the orderly lets me use a toilet. I catch more glimpses of the main corridor. Different people come and go. They're university age, fifteen to twenty, all wearing scrubs. Always more girls than boys.

A baby-faced orderly with a constant scowl asks when I last had anything to eat or drink. Last night. Must be evening now, judging from starvation alone. He leads me to the far end of the corridor.

I ask, "How many more tests?"

"You're done. Now you get to sit with some of the others. Hope you don't mind confined spaces."

The others. This will be interesting.

He unlocks a thick wooden door with a metal key. Nothing but dark, then a filthy toilet stench like body odor mingled with crap and piss. A boy and a girl stumble out into the corridor. They quiver, blink their eyes against the light, and whimper they want to get out. They *need* to get out.

But I promised. So I go in.

EIGHT

The door shuts behind me.

A cement room about four meters wide. Dim light reveals people scattered across the floor. University-age, in blue scrubs, eleven of them. Plus one person standing. The light's too weak to see clearly, but his profile is broad and solid, like an athlete. He's smiling.

Yes, smiling.

"Welcome to the Ninth Circle." His voice is raspy but oddly cheerful.

"Ninth what?"

"Ninth Circle of Hell. You know, abandon hope ye who enter." The smile widens to a grin. If he's a fútbol player, he's the kind who's never as funny or as entertaining as he thinks he is.

I'm wacked-out and starving, so I take everything in slowly. Except for the wiseass, everyone is asleep or shifting position as if half-awake. There's some kind of hand-drawn chart on the wall. A black plastic bucket in the corner—the toilet smell? At least there's a cover on it.

"Pay no attention to him," calls someone from the floor. A deep, full-grown voice. There's reddish chin stubble and an ample stomach. "Ryder crossed the line into clinical insanity yesterday morning." He rises on unsteady legs and bows from the waist. Despite his voice he can't be much older than me. "Eric Rahn is my name, systems engineering my game."

"Cristina Flores."

The grinning athlete bobs his head toward Eric. "Two days ago we couldn't get a word out of him. Now he just babbles nonsense." He extends his hand. "Ryder Lawson."

His fingers swallow up mine. Probably not clean fingers, as there's no sink for washing. I ask him, "How long have you all been in here?"

"I estimate approximately seven hundred years." Ryder turns and his knees buckle.

Eric says, "Sit for a while. Pace yourself."

"Shut it," Ryder responds. "Too excited to sit. Too energized! Time and space lose all meaning here in the Ninth Circle."

This crowded, stinky place must be affecting his brain.

"Does anyone know why we're here?" I ask, making my words louder than necessary to maybe wake the dark heaps still dozing.

"They're testing us," Ryder replies. His voice grows more hoarse with each word. "I'm proving my staying power. Mental and physical stamina. And I'm not claustrophobic at all!" He scans the ceiling as if looking for something. "You get that last part?"

"Think they're listening to us?"

"Oh, sure, listening and watching. This is a test, a filter. Will we break down or keep functioning? Look at me. Still functioning pretty good, considering."

A blond girl with delicate features comes up behind me and pours me a cup of water from a jug. She has a look of innocence, as if she'd been sheltered her whole life from everything nasty. I nod thanks and gulp the water down. We touch hands.

Her lips tighten with sudden hurt. "Your face. What happened?"

"A short but painful fight with a kitchen floor."

"That's funny. I hope you taught that floor not to mess with you. My name is Alison, by the way."

"Alison, a doctor told me this is a way out. What do you think that means?"

Before she can respond Ryder says, "The new girl ponders the big question." He waves his hand toward the chart of words and numbers on the cement wall. "We all have certain things in common, and those commonalities might help us crack the mystery. Cristina, is it? Ready for some questions?"

Ryder uses a short little tube—a marker—to write my name on the wall, and he spells it correctly. He's good at the useless ability of drawing letters by hand and probably never misses a chance to show it off. My eyes are adjusted to the dim light and I can make out most of the chart. Horizontal rows of information labeled with each person's name.

"Ask away."

He points the marker at my face. "Age?"

"Seventeen."

He writes it down next to my name. "Profession?"

"Not tracked."

That draws a rude grunt from Eric. Here I am, not caring what he thinks.

Ryder taps the marker against his chin. "Never attended university?"

"Is that a crime? I have the credits for Peking, GAO composite two fifty-six. GAO math—"

"Alright, we get it," Ryder says. "Some kind of malcontent, huh? What's your Score?"

"Two oh eight."

Eric snorts. His way of expressing admiration, I guess. "A new record."

"Join the club!" Ryder cries. "The troublemakers' club! You're a troublemaker because you don't want to live under their control, right?"

"Take a wild guess."

His voice softens. "Maybe we'll all get a chance, a way out. They said that to me, too."

Eric yawns. "They said that to everybody."

"We're on a list," Ryder says to the sleeping figures on the floor. "A list of smart, educated troublemakers, all together under this hospital, where the Autoridad can't see us, at least for a little while." He jabs the marker at my face. "Parents? Siblings?"

Most of the others stir into wakefulness, thanks to Ryder's not-so-quiet voice. I reply, "Is that question necessary?"

He slaps his wall chart. "We're searching for commonalities! You want to figure this out, don't you? Are you like the rest of us, no close family?"

Family. Another word Harmony stole from us, because Harmony is the best and greatest family possible. He uses the word boldly, without hesitation. What was *his* Score?

"My father passed. My mother, I never met her."

"Brothers, sisters?"

I shake my head. Ryder draws an "X" by my name, same as everyone else. "No family to miss you."

My fists clench.

Alison grabs my left wrist and lays her fingers over mine. "But you had people you loved? You were part of a close group. You're not a loner."

My fingers go on top of hers. "Kids, two kids, not mine. And their mother, I …"

"Watched out for them."

I face Ryder. "How did you know?"

"Just a guess. I had my own people."

Eric says from the floor, "We've shown we can work within a small group. None of us hate other people."

A dark-haired girl pushes herself upright and rubs her eyes. "Except me. I despise every person in this room."

Ryder ignores her and gestures toward my stomach. "You still have ovaries?"

He's asking about Regalo. "How could that figure into this?"

"It's an unlikely commonality. Everybody here has intact reproductive organs. In a group our age, professionally educated, that's not likely to happen by chance."

Eric says, "And, *almost* all of us are scientists or engineers."

I study Ryder's chart. Alison is a botanist. Other names show physicist, medical doctor, biomedical engineer, chemical engineer, mechanical engineer, and molecular engineer. Ryder, the grinning jock, is an applied engineer.

Harmony tracks the most intelligent and diligent students to university at age thirteen, sometimes even younger. They're enrolled in accelerated professional programs at top schools in Mumbai, Fukushima, Beijing, or Seoul. They get there with a GAO composite lower than mine, because they're better at keeping their mouths shut.

The sleepy dark-haired girl clears her throat. "Have you geniuses noticed there's twice as many females in here than males? And we're close to minimum reproductive age. I'm thinking somebody wants to make a lot of babies, fast."

"Interesting theory!" exclaims Ryder. "Want to test it out?"

She throws a cup at him. Ryder fills the cup with water but instead of drinking it he hands it back to her. "You need this. Haven't seen you drink in hours."

"Maybe has something to do with not wanting to piss into a bucket in front of a room full of people." Her voice is simultaneously harsh and fragile.

"We promised not to look." Ryder points at me with the marker. "Mikki, this is Cristina. Not only are Cristina's ovaries intact, but she didn't go to college."

Are those now my primary qualities? Along with no parents to notice I'm gone?

Mikki is a compact girl with a heart-shaped face and defiant eyes. She drains the cup and says without looking at me, "Take my advice, bang on the door and ask to leave."

"Why don't you?"

"I would, if I had any brains. But I have too much suffering invested in this shithole to throw it all away."

"It's a filter, like he said," Eric tells me. He lies down flat on his back, belly sticking up as if he'd swallowed a fútbol. "You should have been here the day before yesterday. There were twenty-six crammed in here before some of them started losing it."

Ryder throws up both arms. "We who have lasted, be proud."

Is he dopefaced on fatigue?

I ask him, "Who, exactly, is testing us? Is there evidence they're Autoridad? Or some other section of Harmony?"

"No chance!" declares Eric. "Whoever brought us here, they can't be Harmony."

"Whoever they are, how could they just…turn off the Stream? Even in a limited area?"

"They infiltrated the Stream! They hacked it. Don't ask me how. But you know what? They have access to every bit of information in the world. They know everything about every person alive and dead. They can do anything they want. Covertly. Quickly. The possibilities boggle the mind."

"You're probably right," I tell him. "But what happens if they're caught?"

Alison sits back against the wall. "We can't answer that before we figure out why we're here. Hours of talking and guessing and all we've established is it involves human reproduction."

I touch my abdomen. "How do you know that?"

"Simple probability," says Ryder. "Around half the university students our age are already sterilized. Almost all the rest get cut by the time they're twenty-five, if they want to win favor from Harmony and land a decent job. Twenty-six people passed through this room, all late teens, not a single one sterilized. The odds of that occurring randomly—"

"Two to the negative twenty-sixth power," reports Eric. "Less than one in sixty million, or actually about half of that, now that we have another girl."

I ask, "How many engineers did we start with?"

Ryder scans his wall chart. "Eighteen, counting those two flakes who ran out when you got here."

"Solid majority engineers," I tell him. "I agree we're supposed to build something."

Ryder adds, "And make babies. Lots of screamin' babies."

Alison points out, "Maybe a self-sufficiency thing. Such a wide range of fields."

Ryder waves his marker at me, again. "You're the wild card. No university degree."

"So what? And quit pointing that thing at me."

"You messed up our perfect list," he says, still brandishing the marker. "Not an engineer, not a scientist, not a physician. You don't belong here!"

My face heats up and I dig my nails into my palms.

"She's clearly intelligent," offers Alison. "No pattern broken there."

"Not intelligent enough to walk out the door," Mikki mumbles.

I growl, "Maybe I'm here to raise the average level of maturity."

Ryder hoots and claps his hands.

A different girl sits up and pushes her thin brown hair away from her face. Her pout says she's going to scold us before a word leaves her lips. She turns to Alison. "I'm a biomedical engineer. Whatever the purpose of our being here, it had better be over quick. You hypothesize a relationship to reproduction. Has someone found a way to speed human gestation by three orders of magnitude? I doubt it. We'll never have time to produce offspring." She looks at Eric. "If they infiltrated the Stream and the other Harmony systems, how long do we have before discovery?"

"A few days, Tess. Couple of weeks, max."

"Certainly not years. Forget about reproduction."

Alison says, "Unless they have someplace for us to hide."

Mikki counters, "Hide where? Harmony has the whole planet under surveillance."

Tess adds, "I'm skeptical these people aren't working with Harmony."

Eric folds his arms. "You mean Occam's Razor tells us to assume they're Harmony until we have a valid reason to think otherwise?"

Mikki says, "And if they're Harmony or Autoridad, we're dead. Nothing we do—"

I can't stand it. I scream, *"Wait!"*

They stare back at me. "Can anyone prove they're Harmony and they're going to kill us? Did you get a good look at these people? They're exhausted, all of them, and most of them are nervous, anxious, and hurried. Did you notice? So when was the last time you saw Harmony scared and rushed?"

None of them can answer that, and they know it.

I'm not done. "For what little we know, this may be…a chance…"

Blank out.

Ryder finishes my sentence. "For something magnificent."

The silence hangs for a while. "You feel it, don't you? You could leave, but you're still here. So quit planning our funerals while we're still breathing."

Ryder shakes his marker at my face, again. "I like her." He sinks to the floor and closes his eyes, still smiling.

✳

My fingers reach out to scroll a Stream that isn't there. Reality creeps back—a damp, reeking chamber full of strangers. I'm sleeping on a floor, as usual. My head rests on Alison's hip. She had insisted.

Is it day or night? Time and space lose all meaning in the Ninth Circle. Orderlies have been taking people out. Mikki is gone. Eric is gone. A boy named Marc and a girl named Kim are gone. Kim and I shared a few words before sleep; she hadn't said a word to anyone, so I broke through her shyness by offering a cup of water, the only thing of value we could give each other.

She was exhausted and starved, she admitted, but not ready to leave. Three words sustained her: *A way out.*

Our energy level is near zero. We're talked out, at the limit of what we can deduce by thinking alone. Not unlike SERCENT, we wait for higher powers to tell us what to do.

I drift back to the edge of sleep, but the door opens and the sudden light burns my eyes. A young man, maybe a few years older than me, wearing standard blue scrubs. He carries a clipboard, but he's not one of the regular orderlies or one of the docs. There's a subtle difference when he inspects us. The orderlies don't *care*. This hombre does.

We gaze upward at him from the floor.

"You've been through an ordeal." His voice is crisp, almost musical. "Does anyone want out? You can have a shower, hot food, a bed, right down the hall. But remember, if you leave, there's no reconsideration."

Ryder asks, "Who are you?"

"Jürgen Morita." The name matches his face, a striking blend of Asian and Caucasian features. Almost too handsome. He carries authority, but not in a bossy or threatening way.

"What are you?"

Jürgen lowers his clipboard. "I'm a geologist."

Ryder punches the air with his fist. His smile is back.

Jürgen lowers his voice as if telling us something we aren't supposed to hear. "It'll be worth the confinement and hunger. You've all held together under stress and deprivation. You've earned the right to what comes next."

He closes the door gently. Somehow, his brief presence makes the room less stinky and ugly.

Ryder breaks the silence. "I volunteer, yes I do."

I turn around. "Volunteers for what?"

Tess sits up and twists toward Ryder. "You think you know?"

"Oh, I do know."

She snarls, "Going to tell us?"

Ryder appears as if he's about to do just that, but he replies, "No, I don't think so. Not unless you ask much nicer."

Tess sighs and lays back down.

But soon afterward the door opens again. This time we all sit upright together. A Chinese orderly ushers us out of our nasty tomb.

Which is good. But the corridor echoes the sounds of arguing and crying from close by.

Yes, crying. That's not so good.

The orderly leads us toward the turmoil. Jürgen's distinct voice rises above the others. Four teens bolt through a doorway, muttering in angry tones. Muttering about dying. That's not good, either.

Ryder still smiles. What's wrong with him?

We enter a spacious room filled with chairs and people. Smack in the center, Jürgen speaking and gesturing. I catch two words, *peril* and *promise*. He stops and faces us. His eyes are excited.

"We'll come back to that," he tells the audience seated around him. There are at least forty, all in blue or green scrubs, none older than nineteen or twenty. As usual, most are female.

We're directed to sit. I pass the girl named Kim; she's crying softly and wiping both sides of her thin nose. She smiles and whispers to me, "Happy tears, happy tears."

All eyes follow Jürgen as he walks to the front of the room. Seven gray-haired men and women stand along the wall apart from the seated teens. Dr. Ordin is among them, still in her white coat.

My feet stop, my hand goes to my cheek. At the far end of the room is Dr. Mike. He stands erect and unflinching.

He's a part of this. Of course he is. That makes sense.

Dr. Mike wears a brown leather jacket with a cloth patch on the left breast. A colorful patch, colorful and familiar.

Is it even possible? I squint to be sure.

A NASA patch.

I'm not dreaming, not imagining. There's the blue circle, the white letters, the red curve. *NASA*. Exactly as the logo appeared in my Apollo book—only this is no book. This is real.

Dr. Mike returns my gaze and locks on my eyes. He brings his right fist away from his body and sticks his thumb straight up.

I thrust my own right fist forward and stick my thumb up and hold it there, exactly the same way, fearless and bold, without taking my eyes off his.

NINE

A girl drops a round box of cookies into my lap. Butter cookies, at a time like this. Why not?

Jürgen scrutinizes we newcomers. "Listen up! We have key facts to put out and not much time to do it. These men and women standing behind me sacrificed their safety to get you here. We're part of a larger team you'll never meet."

I chew. His words and the delicious cookies make a perfect combination.

Jürgen sweeps his hand horizontally. "You're also part of a larger group." He turns to Dr. Ordin. "How many did we start with?"

"Two hundred thirty-five pre-selects."

"All of you were chosen with great care. Events of this historic significance don't happen often. We have an opportunity to begin the world over again. Let me repeat that. We have an opportunity to begin the world over again, and to be free. We're going to Mars."

I stop chewing.

What does he mean, *we*? My brain is a jumble, it's impossible to think.

Mars. Is he joking? Is he lying?

Ryder lets out a deep, masculine howl. "Oh, yes!" He jumps up and smashes his chair into the floor three times. He locks Jürgen and Mikki in a bear hug, then spins around, reaches over his chair and shoves his hand toward me. I take his finger-crushing grip and my fatigue and hunger vanish.

Alison covers her mouth with her hand. Others stare into the air, faces blank. Some just sit with their arms folded. Jürgen believes it, so everyone believes it. In a world full of lies, this is truer than true. I scan the oldies standing along the wall. In their faces, a quiet and fierce determination.

Mars.

This is real.

Does he mean me? I'm going?

I said I would do anything.

A life free from Harmony and the Autoridad. The idea of it sends the room spinning.

"We're going to Mars," Jürgen repeats. He's sure of it. "We're going to Mars, to stay. We'll build a community, and our descendants will build a civilization."

Ryder stomps both feet on the ground. Mikki rubs the back of his neck with her left hand.

"We can start fresh and learn from past errors. If you do this..." Jürgen stops. Except for muffled sobs, the room is still. "If you do this, it won't be for the usual reasons humans take risks. It won't be for fame, or power, or glory, or survival. We have another reason. The need to live free and control our own destinies."

Questions fly from all directions. Has anyone ever been to Mars? How do we know Harmony isn't there right now? How many are going? How much time would we have to say goodbye to friends? What if something goes wrong?

Jürgen opens his mouth and silence falls. "Okay. What to expect. We leave soon and there is no turning back. We will be the first humans on Mars, and there will be no outside assistance of any kind. I will not bullshit you. There is a likelihood you may die. So decide if this is what you want. If you don't, just walk out of this room. You'll be fed and released from the hospital in a few days."

A girl with short blond hair mutters, "Some other time." She makes her way through the door.

Eric crosses his arms and says to Jürgen, "We need to know more."

Too many people shout questions at once. A slender man with a thick mane of silver hair steps forward. He has to be at least eighty years old. I didn't know it was possible for someone so old to grow hair down below his shoulders.

He shouts, "Yo!"

Just one syllable, but the sound pierces the babble and the place goes quiet.

The long-haired oldie clears his throat. "My name is Dr. David Chao, and I am a systems engineer. I was once employed at a technology development center formerly located here in Pasadena. It was called the Jet Propulsion Laboratory."

Ryder leaps to his feet and cries, "Wahoo!"

David continues in a tranquil tone. "After JPL, I served as a senior engineer for most of the Chéngzhǎng flights. The men and women standing behind me are my colleagues. Over a hundred scientists, engineers, and technicians have dedicated themselves to the goal of flying a small, carefully selected group to Mars and landing them safely, along with the equipment and materials to establish an independent settlement."

David pronounces one word again, crisply and distinctly. "*Independent.*"

A stillness hangs over us, broken only by the sound of restrained crying.

Independent. That means free. In charge of our own lives. Worth the risk, no matter what happens.

Someone asks, "Harmony doing this?"

"Negative," David replies.

"But they know about it?"

"Negative."

"Bullshit! How is that possible?"

"Speed! And complete secrecy. We have one launch opportunity. Six spacecraft with six seats each, launched together on a direct trajectory."

"They'll shoot them down!" cries the same boy.

"Negative. You'll climb two thousand kilometers in less than seven minutes. That's outside missile range. Their defense systems are configured to deal with incoming targets. Speed is our friend. We'll launch as quickly as possible, before we're—"

"Discovered," mutters Eric.

Jürgen inspects us as he talks. "We have twelve so far. We can take another twenty-four. Counting me, that's twenty-three open seats."

Alison calls out, "Excuse me. The other twelve. Are they experienced? Are they…please tell me they're older than us."

The silence is total.

"No, they are not," David answers softly. "We would strongly prefer candidates with more operational experience, men and women in their mid to late twenties. That's not feasible."

"El Regalo," I whisper. It comes out on its own.

David nods at me. "Harmony controls access to technical education. By age sixteen, over sixty percent of technical graduates have already undergone voluntary sterilization. By age twenty-five it's ninety-six percent. The post-grads who make it into their twenties with the ability to have children are the ideological fanatics, exactly the ones we don't want."

But this won't work with so few. So I speak up. "That explains twice as many females as males. More ovaries, more babies in less time. But you said thirty-six? Are more people following later? I'm no expert, but that doesn't sound like a big enough gene pool."

Dr. Mike answers my question. "You'll be able to have children of your own. But to supplement the limited gene pool, each spacecraft carries two cryogenic flasks with eighteen hundred embryos and sperm samples, all pre-screened for genetic health and high intelligence, no genetic modification whatsoever. At cryogenic temperatures, the rate of molecular migration is low enough so the material should remain viable for three hundred years. New genetic stock can be introduced over the first twelve to fifteen generations."

Ryder covers his mouth and quips, "And there's the old fashioned way."

Thin laughter, mostly from the boys. Why did he glance at me when he said it?

David adds, "There will be no additional flights following you. This is a one-shot event."

A boy stands, a man really. His lips twist as if he's annoyed. There are two beads of sweat on his forehead. "Norberto Pena. My question is this. What about communication? I assume you will support us and guide us?"

David closes his eyes and shakes his head. "Everyone needs to understand this now. Once you're in flight, you're on your own."

Norberto plops back into his chair. Two boys and a girl rise and walk out the door. The smart ones?

David tells us, "Your spacecraft will be flown by an automatic navigation system. There are expert systems aboard that operate your life support and other necessary—"

"Guaranteed to work perfectly, right?" Norberto shoots back.

Three more people stride for the door without looking back. Objections and complaints fly from everywhere. This is a stupid argument.

I rise up on wobbly legs, but my body is so light I can fly.

"Stand with me!"

Three words, almost screamed. I sweep my eyes across their startled faces. "What good is your life if you're a slave? Stand with me!"

Ryder knocks his chair out of his way and wraps his arms around me. Body odor. So what? He spins toward Jürgen. "Standing!"

The chattering dies off and they watch me, Jürgen, and David. Mikki stares straight ahead. I snap at her, "What's the matter with you? This is the greatest moment of your life. Stand with us!"

She looks at me with wet and fearful eyes. Then, to Ryder, "Yes!" She stands and Ryder steadies her. A gruff shout to the whole room, "They do not own me!"

Alison's fists are clenched; her lips tremble. Our eyes meet, but she doesn't move.

Eric runs his fingers through his matted hair. "Just to toss in a teeny bit of reality. Last I heard, Mars is nothing but rocks, and it's a hundred degrees below zero."

Kim apparently doesn't hear him. She stands while wiping her eyes of the happy tears. "If I die, I'll die free. Nobody watching me. No spotters. Decide on my own life. My own life! That starts now."

"Decide your own life!" I repeat back to them. "Start now! *Stand with us!*"

But they aren't moving.

I gaze at a girl with wavy brown hair. "During all those years living under their thumb, didn't you ever wonder to yourself, when will be my time? *My time!* It's here, right now. This is your chance. Stand with us!"

She drops her eyes to the floor.

"What about power?" barks Eric. "What about air? What about food and water? What about replacement parts? Drugs, medicines? How do you know Mars has the raw materials to support a whole freakin' civilization?"

David directs his response to all of us. "My colleagues and I believe you have a good chance of success. Each spacecraft is redundant to the others. Each flies with five hundred petabytes of data, almost the entire digitized knowledge of humanity. For raw materials, we've known since 2015 that Mars harbors abundant water ice and mineral resources needed to manufacture what you need."

"I don't understand how we're going to get food on Mars," says a girl with a childlike voice. "Didn't they have to deliver supplies to the lunar villages?"

"Mars is the only other place in the solar system besides Earth where it's practical to grow food with sunlight," replies David. "With suitably engineered enclosures, it can be done."

"You're so damn sure!" cries a tall girl from the back of the room. "But you don't know, do you? How can you know?" She kicks over her chair and strides toward the door. Four others follow her out.

"I just want to go home," stammers a boy.

Jürgen said they need twenty-three more. That means almost everyone remaining will have to volunteer.

I put my arm around Kim's shoulder, then face the whole room. "Who else will stand with us? Get off your ass and stand!" I let the words flow and ignore the quiver in my voice. "You're scared. I am too. I wanted university. An engineering career. Travel, a comfortable home, love, children, a family. Now I understand. None of that is any good without freedom."

✳

People rise from their seats individually and in pairs, but the total isn't enough.

The holdouts shout endless questions. They want specific answers, not vague assurances. Who built the spacecraft? How could they be tested without Harmony finding out? How could anyone be sure all the systems will work?

The technology is mostly well-established, insists a Korean engineer with a bald head covered with thin blue veins. Every vital system was developed directly from Chinese, Korean, and American orbital and lunar equipment. The guidance and navigation systems are based on the Chēngzhǎng flights to the moon.

Life support, avionics, propulsion, fault recovery, all printed from reliable designs.

So we get there. What next? All this wonderful equipment, it has to last forever? What happens when something breaks? We'll need a wide variety of materials. If not from Earth, where will it all come from?

The engineers have answers for everything. We can produce whatever is needed on Mars. We start with ice and Mars air, which is mostly carbon dioxide. From that we can synthesize oxygen, hydrogen, nitrogen, carbon monoxide, methane, methanol fuel, and then ethylene and benzene, the starting points to produce a wide range of plastics. That means Kevlar, Mylar, Nylon, acrylics, polycarbonates, fertilizers, plus rubber, detergents, lubricants, precursors to pharmaceuticals. The Mars regolith is rich in metals and metalloids, including silicon and other semiconductors, plus trace elements.

Fabrication printers?

Two Honeywell TW9 printers are on board each space-craft. We'll be able to print any component we can conceive, including replacement parts and specialized equipment from custom designs.

All that does no good without electrical power. But solar panels cannot supply the necessary kilowatts to actually make use of those resources.

A Japanese engineer steps forward. A pure white beard juts from his chin. We will have ample power, he assures us. Each spacecraft carries one liquid fluoride thorium nuclear reactor. These flight-certified reactors are similar to the ones used at the Chēngzhăng lunar outposts for many years. Thorium fuel can be found on Mars, a fact proven by numerous successful robot-ic explorers.

And when the food runs out?

We'll have stock to print meals for about seven hundred days. Before that stock is exhausted, we construct greenhouse enclosures with local materials and pressurize them to three hundred and forty millibars, one-third standard atmosphere. Once washed, Mars regolith is similar to the volcanic dirt of Hawaii. We will add water and nitrates to create soil. Sunlight will be used to grow crops from seeds. Mars rotates once every twenty-four hours and thirty-nine minutes, so the day lasts just a bit longer than on Earth.

Eric remains skeptical. "How do you know all this is gonna work together perfectly?"

"Most of the technology has been under development and in use for fifty years or more," David tells him. "It's a matter of applied science."

"And the guts to try," I add.

Eric lifts his bulk from his chair. "If you're trying, I'm there with you." He reaches out and we touch hands.

A dark-skinned girl with almond eyes stands and addresses the room. "My name is Indra Chaudhuir. I am the daughter of Venkat and Ruma of Kamothe, India. From this moment I am free." She looks directly at Kim and me. Tears form twin rivulets down her cheeks.

"Decide now," Dr. Ordin tells those who remain seated. "We don't have a lot of time. The next ones to stand will go."

"Be certain," David says. "No second thoughts will be permitted."

"Are you coming?" Norberto snaps.

"I sincerely wish that were the case. Every seat is reserved for someone like you, someone with a lifetime of creative energy. You're going to start with a clean slate."

Alison asks, "What happens to those who don't want to go? Will the Autoridad know? Will we lose what we have?"

I face her. "What do you have now? Is it more precious to you than freedom?"

She spits, "I'm alive."

"Congratulations!" cracks Dr. Ordin. "Now decide."

A girl with straight dark haired asks, "What if Harmony is already on Mars?"

David shakes his head. "Harmony isn't interested in Mars, and they never will be. Any settlement there will be independent and therefore beyond their control."

A Chinese girl stands. "This terrifies the shit out of me. Staying here scares me more."

Alison's hands clench together and she stares straight ahead. Norberto rocks his upper body rhythmically back and forth. Two girls whisper together furiously. Tess is bent over at the waist, her head on her knees.

Jürgen approaches the undecideds. His words come slowly. "Human beings should live free. Not devoting their lives to serve a government master. Not dedicated to ends they did not choose.

We must be the masters of our own fate."

A tall boy with wide shoulders lowers his head. "I don't want to die."

He needs to hear this. "The length of your life is nothing, it's what you do with your life."

A round-faced girl sits up. Her eyes are angry. "Risk our lives with no chance of coming back, no chance for help?"

Norberto asks, "How do we even know we can do this?"

I answer, "Anything's possible if you have the courage to try."

He stands! Did I do that? And Tess. And three teens I don't recognize.

A boy mutters, "Crazy dangerous."

"You want to stay safe?" I ask him. "Safe to do what? Be a slave?"

The petite woman with wavy brown hair stands and faces Jürgen. She's pale and haggard as if she's been down in this hospital basement for a month. "Doctor Blair Rizzo. I recently graduated second in my class at Fujian Medical University. I'll pledge my life on the condition my esteemed colleague, Doctor Shuko Saito, will join me."

She places her hand on the shoulder of a lean Asian man no older than twenty. He has too much thick black hair, and it's combed in a way that makes his head square. He folds his arms, peers down at the floor, glances at Blair Rizzo, then stands.

He stares directly at me, of all people

"I wanted this for years," he stammers. His words are for me, and it's like we're the only two people in the room. This isn't someone who expresses his feelings often or easily. Yet, the words come. "Only two things are mine by right, freedom and death. If I can't have one, I'll have the other."

The quiet is broken by Ryder's single clap. I nod at Shuko.

"Death will come to us eventually no matter what we do," I say to everyone. "It's your right to be free before that day comes."

But it's not enough, not yet. Some sit with their eyes closed, as if trying to shut everything out.

Dr. Mike places his hands on his hips. "I think if we do not succeed, it means our human species has lost the last hope for freedom. Harmony is developing better psychological controls, better reproductive controls. The small degree of privacy and autonomy people have over their lives, what little remains, is going to be extinct in a short time."

Dr. Ordin adds, "Harmony plans to cut the global population down to less than one billion by 2120. They want a new breed of docile humans reared for obedience. What you see happening in this room is quite probably the final chance for human freedom."

A short, brown-skinned girl with a round, elfin face speaks directly to Jürgen. "Paige Weber. Chemical engineer. I have a younger sister." She swallows and wipes her eyes. "What if the people we love suffer because of the decision we make here?"

Isabel. Nathan. Faye. There's no possibility of seeing any of them again.

Jürgen focuses his gaze on Paige and approaches her. He takes her hands into his. "She would want you to go." He turns to the others. "Everyone you know and love would want you to do this. They would want you to be free."

The room goes quiet again. Dr. Ordin looks at her wrist.

I'm not done talking. "We're all free for this short time. What will you do with that freedom?"

Someone whispers, "God help us."

Paige links arms with an Asian girl seated next to her. They jump up together so hard they knock their chairs over. Others rise up, to my left and right. Alison stands and throws her arms around me. Her body is damp and her heart drums against my chest.

Jürgen nods, and it's all over. We have enough. Five people remain seated. Dr. Ordin barks, "The rest of you, exit through that door and wait in the corridor."

We volunteers steal glances at one another. Some whisper together but most avoid eye contact. Are these the only people I'll be with for the rest of my life?

The doctors and the oldie engineers form a huddle among themselves. David issues orders in a low voice.

Ryder whispers, "I think they're forming us into groups."

A door opposite the entranceway opens and a male orderly beckons us to follow. No chairs in the adjoining room, only a metal table covered with tiny blue plastic vials.

Another orderly strides past us. "Ladies, roll up your right sleeve and form a line."

There are sixteen girls. I face the same orderly who led me into the basement. She holds a glistening needle. "You made it safe and sound, I see." She applies disinfectant, then jabs the hypodermic into my upper arm.

"What's this?"

"Twelve-month contraceptive."

I guess we're not quite ready for freedom *yet*.

They separate us into four groups. I'm with Alison, Mikki, Paige, Ryder, and the Asian doctor named Shuko. The other groups leave one at a time. I don't see Dr. Mike again, so forget about saying thank you and goodbye. The orderlies clear away every scrap of medical gear. They're in a frantic rush and not in a talking mood, as if they're the ones who should be nervous about having just volunteered to fly off to a deserted planet without any way to get back. Jürgen leaves with Tess and Norberto. Eric nods a silent goodbye. Kim still wipes her happy tears.

Where will I see these people again? Mars?

Dr. Ordin puts her clipboard aside. "We're going to take you out of the hospital now. You are not to speak to each other. You are not to utter a word to any person you see. No matter what happens, say nothing and do exactly as you are told. Do I have everyone's complete cooperation?"

I swallow and nod my yes with the others.

Mikki approaches her. "Is this it? We're gone? Because we need a chance to say goodbye to people."

"Mikki—"

"Let them know what happened to us. You're not going to tell me that's too much to ask. You're not going to tell me that."

Dr. Ordin exhales. Her tone is gentle. "Mikki, you're under a lot of stress. What you're feeling is understandable. But what you're asking is impossible."

Mikki turns her face to the floor and covers her eyes. I rub my hand over my rosies. Isabel. Nathan. Chloe. Dottie. Nick. Faye. You will always be remembered and loved.

Dr. Ordin leads us briskly down the long corridor to the stairwell. Ryder blatantly fires off questions. Where's our launch site? Who built the spacecraft? How long will it take to reach Mars? He receives no answers. Dr. Ordin growls, "No talking."

We're in the smaller building connected to the main lobby. Dr. Ordin turns left through glass doors. Nighttime, and there are people outside.

The Stream! 8:44 pm. Fresh air, the aroma of wet dirt. It must have just rained.

Ryder is just behind me. He lets out his breath. Not a good sound. Directly in front of us, people walk single-file, their hands fastened to their waists. One of them is Dr. Mike. He is pushed forward by a man in a dark uniform. Policía.

Enormous black buses. Spotters.

The Autoridad.

They'd been waiting.

T E N

A sour wet fills my mouth, but I can't swallow it.

Policía surround us. Each carries the bulky kind of weapon that will kill. Is this what happens before Red Block? Just shoot me now.

A spotter grabs my forearms and wraps a thick orange strap around my waist and wrists. It cuts into the soreness left over from SERCENT.

Ryder doesn't want to be strapped. He backs away. I open my mouth to warn him of the hit, but no hit comes. He looks left and right. He yanks Mikki's sleeve and his knees bend, as if he's ready to sprint away. The Policía watch but their weapons remain pointed to the ground.

I force the words out. "Don't bother to run."

"I want this over quick," he sputters, breath coming in pants. The spotter tugs his arms and applies the strap.

They order us to line up and board one of four military transports. The massive bus-like vehicles have tracked wheels and narrow, tinted windows. The grubby seats reek of old sweat.

A spotter hangs from a rail running the full length of the ceiling. "Prisoners!" it shrieks. "Take the nearest empty seat. Do not speak. Look straight ahead."

David Chao strolls toward the back like a man on his way to the corner bodega for a jar of mayonnaise. Alison and I sit together. Her eyes are clamped shut. Mikki walks rearward, head hung low. "We're fucked."

"Prisoner!" snaps the spotter. "Do not speak or you will be penalized."

Mikki spits on the floor but doesn't say another word.

The door shuts the instant everyone is seated. No Policía riding? A rude vibration shakes my ass and we lurch forward. The horizontal windows are only ten centimeters high, but that's enough to show the other transports are coming with us.

The tremor of the road calms my nerves. I can make myself think, but nothing comes to mind except my approaching end. Interrogation, followed by Red Block. Maybe they'll skip the interrogation and give us a quick death. Did Ryder have the right idea? Break for it, die free, here and now, just sooner than strictly necessary.

Die free. Wasn't that the plan anyhow? Now even that chance is gone. We'll die under their heels.

Mars? How did I ever believe it? *They* believed it, David Chao, Dr. Mike, Ryder, Jürgen, all of them. Lying without realizing it. Minutes ago we had a new purpose, and now it's gone.

Faye had said to me, *I wanted you to have a purpose. Do you understand the meaning of the word?* She struck the truth when no one else could.

The transport glides down a black highway. I tug against the waist strap and touch the bump of my rosies in my pocket. Paco told me all lives have a purpose. What would he say to the fact I'm bound up in this transport headed rapidly toward extremely probable death?

Where there's life, there's hope.

Dottie lost hope, then lost her life. If I had a little pink vase with me right now, would I swallow the white pill? Would likely be a lot less painful than whatever's waiting at the end of this ride.

But I wouldn't swallow the pill.

Maybe that's my purpose—to hang on to my thin shred of hope. And do my own math.

Paco's life had a purpose, and I saw small pieces of that purpose from his bundle of pics. Paco and his strange old pics…they come back and take me away from this place. We're at the Santa Monica beach. There's a low sun, damp sand under my feet, and the salty scent of the ocean.

Memories of pics fill my brain. A very young Paco, years before I was born, standing with a group of seven or eight smiling men. They're dressed in black and their shirt collars are uncomfortable-looking white bands around their necks. Each holds a silver cross to his chests, the same kind of cross that's on Paco's rosies, only larger.

An older Paco, still years before I was born, with the beginnings of his beard. He's in a classroom wearing a white coat and standing next to a complicated machine with switches and wires. Trying to appear serious, but a hint of a mischievous smile leaks out.

He's a scientist, a professor of physics. What was the purpose behind doing that?

Paco never told me. He lost his position and his wife and my mother Lynda, and even his son Alex. All taken away, for what reason? Did Paco ever question the purpose of all having all those parts of his life he eventually lost? Including, eventually, his life itself?

Paco would ask me, *Are you breathing?*

Then there's hope.

The transport lurches and the motor slows. Brightly-lit cement outside, then we're down a ramp, then inside a garage filled with Policía and spotters strutting back and forth. La Cárcel Detention, finally. But we don't stop. We turn and climb the same ramp we came down thirty seconds ago.

Ryder flashes me a sly grin. So they sent us to the wrong place? No jail cells; instead we're going to a Center and a prolonged death from starvation? Does that count as a form of hope?

Or something else?

I peek behind my shoulder. The spotter moves, maybe to let me know it's watching. Paige, David Chao, Dr. Ordin, eight total. Only eight, on a vehicle with at least thirty seats. Why four transports for less than forty prisoners?

I ask aloud, "Why keep us together?"

The spotter jerks toward me. "Prisoner! Be silent. Face forward. Comply or you will be penalized."

The Asian physician stares at me from across the aisle. I whisper to him, "Cristina Flores."

He glances at the spotter and decides to respond. "Doctor Shuko Saito."

"Prisoner! Do not speak. Comply or be penalized."

"My father was Francisco Flores. Doctor Francisco Flores. He told me life has a purpose." I look directly at the spotter. "Even though it may not feel like it all the time."

Mikki mumbles, "I'm dead at eighteen. Some purpose."

I remind her, "We're not dead yet."

Shuko turns to me. His face is innocent and trying not to be afraid. "Doctor? Was he in medicine?"

"He was a scientist."

The spotter pays special attention to me. "Prisoner—"

"Penalize me!" I scream back at it. "Do it! I'm ready for it, so take your shot!"

The hit, here it comes. But the spotter is still.

I announce to everyone, "They're barking but not biting."

"Cristina," Dr. Ordin calls out. "That's enough."

Paige whispers, "Is this some kind of fake-out?"

A wet snort comes from the back of the transport. The sound repeats in a slow rhythm. Dr. David Chao, head back, mouth open, sound asleep.

A knot of elation low in my gut. Ryder, now with a half-grin.

The transport slows and travels down a straight, dark road. There's a foggy mist in the air. Boxy buildings, thick pipes, tanks of various sizes. We slow to bicycle speed and make turn after turn. Bright lights. Plain metal buildings so big we can't see the roofs. The motor winds down and the breaks hiss.

David Chao's snores sputter and stop. He sits up, and the spotter reaches down and slices off his restraints. It moves along the ceiling and frees each of us. Alison glances at me, almost asking for permission to feel hope.

Our eyes follow David Chao as he strides to the front of the transport. "No talking, and I mean it. All you're gonna do is follow me. There will be men with weapons. Ignore them. They're for your protection."

Ryder thrusts both arms upward. *"Yes!"*

So it was a sham. A fake-out. Something to make the Autoridad believe we vanished into the depths of la Cárcel, at least for a short time. Congratulations and bravo, bastardos.

We step onto concrete. My nose tells me there's got to be salt water and seaweed nearby. Two more Autoridad transports roll past. We're next to an enormous black metal structure with giant green letters across the side:

L N G

Meaning what?

Thick ropes hang from the darkness above. There's a narrow set of portable stairs leading to a door high off the ground. The upper levels are white with small, round windows.

It's not a building.

It's a ship.

We climb the shaky stairway and duck through the entrance hatch. The inside reeks of paint and grease. Four soldiers in combat suits watch us. Each has a rifle, a helmet, and strange equipment hanging from their vests. No Harmony or Autoridad uniform insignia. Soldiers here to fight, but not on Harmony's command. Acting on their own, and carrying weapons? That's a death sentence.

Like going to Mars with no way to get back?

More stairs, narrow and ridiculously steep. The odors improve as we climb higher. Finally, a kitchen area with two tables, a counter, a refrigerator, and a sink. Metal plates block the windows.

David Chao tells us, "Have a snack if you want, then go to bed. Ignore the sounds. We have a busy day tomorrow."

Yes, we want a snack. Mikki and Ryder throw packages onto the table. We tear open plastic wrap and cartons and eat like starving wolves. Ritz Crackers. Cheese sticks. Almonds. Squeeze bottles of peanut butter and jelly. More butter cookies, oatmeal cookies, too. Milk. Ramune. Orange juice. Raspberry iced tea.

Ryder talks around a mouthful of crackers. "I can use a sandwich, but this is good too."

Mikki checks the corridor. Two soldiers just outside.

Besides the exit, the kitchen has three more doors. Alison squeals with delight. A bedroom! Tiny but comfortable. Two beds stacked one above the other, with thick mattresses and soft white sheets. We open drawers. Plenty of clothes and undergarments, in neat rolls. Just gray coveralls, but they're clean!

The little cabin has a sparkling bathroom with shower, toilet, soap, shampoo, soft white towels. The fresh scent makes my nose tingle.

A rumble comes from deep within the ship. Engines. They're not wasting any time. The lights flicker, the vibration deepens, and there's a higher-pitched whine from outside. The wallstremble and the room sways. I set up the bathroom for a shower. Yes, hot water!

Alison pulls nightclothes from the dresser. "Do you get sea-sick?"

"Never been out on the ocean."

"Where do you think they're taking us?" Before I can answer, she adds, "I'm not going to be able to sleep tonight. Not after what just happened."

I sit her down and put my arm across her shoulder. "Don't think about what's behind us. We have the future, just the future."

"Yeah, that's what I mean. How do we know if we even have a future? Who are these people? What do we know about them? Nothing, that's what!"

She lets out a long breath and stares at the carpet.

"I think we can say this much. They don't have to be here. Just like us, they're here by choice. And they understand the risk, just like we do. Yet, they're here. That's all I need to know."

She looks me in the eye. "Why take the risk if they can't come with us?"

"Why are *you* here, Alison?"

A hint of a smile, as if I just said something a tiny bit funny.

"You have to ask? I'm here because of *you*. You made me...brave...braver..."

Her eyes clamp shut and she's crying. I hug her tighter.

"You...made me braver than I've ever...been in my life. I'm not brave, Cristina. I'm weak, I've been so weak, so afraid all my life."

"We all have."

"Tonight, that was the only brave thing I ever did, volunteering to be here, to go, to leave everything behind. Maybe the last brave thing I ever do."

"Not true. We're going to be strong from now on. That doesn't mean fearless. I've been weak, sometimes I've been a coward. They made me afraid, afraid to lose my life for no reason. I don't know what's going to happen to us. But I can say this. We're past the hard part."

She snickers, a sloppy wet snicker through tears. Maybe I really was funny that time.

"Maybe not all the hard parts, but one hard part, at least. Who are these people, what are they doing here? Maybe they're just trying their best to be strong, do what needs to be done. They have a purpose. Freedom. Even if it's not their own freedom. We owe them something back, don't you think? Now our lives have a purpose too."

ELEVEN

At the beach you look *at* the ocean. Here, we are *on* the ocean. Smack in the middle of it, encircled by it, racing over it, rushing somewhere in a furious hurry. The best view is at the very back of the ship. We tear the water into an enormous roadway of turbulent white and green foam a block wide, trailing behind us all the way to the horizon.

I lean over the rail. Big white letters against the hull of the ship, and I have to read them upside-down: HANJIN GALLINA. Twenty meters below, the ocean swirls past and whooshes against the sides. The churning seawater and the powerful breeze combine to make the air sweet and invigorating.

Mikki holds the rail with one hand and stuffs an egg burrito into her mouth with the other. She turns to David Chao. "What's your name again? Where are we going? And why the hell are we going there so fast?"

"Call me David." But he ignores her questions. To me, "Grab something to eat, Sleeping Beauty. We've got a lot of work to do."

Alison, Ryder, Shuko, and Paige eat at a wooden table sheltered from the wind by a canvas barrier. Ryder's mouth chomps on the last of the eggs, which explains the quiet.

"Everyone's here," says Paige, "We should do introductions. Life stories. I don't—"

"You know what?" interrupts David. He pours himself a coffee refill. "I think you're going to have forty-two days in space plus the rest of your lives to tell each other about your phobias and favorite foods. Right now you belong to me."

"Flight time forty-two days!" exclaims Ryder. "That means nuclear propulsion."

"We ruled out a nine or ten-month Hohmann trajectory early in the planning stage. Too much time exposed to cosmic rays." David gestures toward Ryder's crotch. "Gotta protect those vital organs."

Mikki says, "Please, not while I'm eating."

Ryder licks his lips. "When do we launch?"

I nibble on a piece of toast. "Where's everyone else? Jürgen? Eric? They're not on this ship?"

David sips coffee. "We're sending thirty-six to Mars. The others are on different ships traveling close in a convoy formation." He points to a spot on the horizon. Another ship! A red and mustard-colored vessel tears through the water parallel to our course. There are six white domes front to back—tanks?

"That's the *Enterprise* crew five kilometers off our starboard beam. There's a ship off our port beam and three more behind us, if you look hard."

I ask, "Dr. Mike?"

"Everyone you saw in Pasadena is on a ship."

Mikki probes. "You're telling me Harmony doesn't know we're out here?"

David drains his cup. "We're okay for a while. Their systems show us in detention. Hundreds of ships cross the Pacific every year. As long as we don't blow anything up, the monitoring systems can't tell there's anything unusual going on. All these tanker ships have been automated down to zero crew years ago. We're on a regular schedule to depart Terminal Island Liquefaction Facility at midnight for a twenty-day run to the regasification plant at Ta Phut, Thailand."

Ryder blurts, "This thing is loaded with liquified natural gas, right? How about liquid oxygen?"

LNG. Liquified natural gas.

"A cryo tank is a cryo tank."

"So we're hauling oxygen, too!" Ryder cries. He smacks his palm against the rail. "We're taking fuel and oxidizer to the launch site. It can't be a Harmony launch facility. We'd never get away with it."

David grins and puts down his coffee cup. "Your education commences now. Follow me."

✳

It lays horizontal, sparkling white and impossibly huge. I can't speak. This can't be real. It's wider than a city street, it's two Skylons end-to-end, and a Skylon is longer than a fútbol field. It's too big to fly.

My stomach is ready to climb up my throat. This is happening, we're leaving, and soon.

Ryder jumps up and down like a maníaco. He falls to his knees. Shuko's head is bent back, his mouth open, trying to take in the tail-end of the rocket. Intricate silver machinery overhead, plus dark cones about two meters wide—too many to count, fifty at least. Engine nozzles.

Paige places both her hands on top of her head.

Mikki sputters, "This flies? This flies?"

"Total length one hundred seventy meters. Booster stage, fifteen meters in diameter. Six times the weight of the former record-holder, the Apollo Saturn Five." David smiles and points toward the massive nozzles. "In thrust we trust."

Ryder is back on his feet and vigorously shaking David's hand. "How did you do this? How did you do this right under their noses?"

"Fast as hell, that's how. Everything you see, printed and assembled over the last nine days right here inside the hull."

"Here?" Alison asks. "You built this right here inside the ship?"

"Best place to hide it." replies David. "We hacked the whole setup right down to the raw materials. These ships were scheduled for a refit, so we already had the industrial printers plus the feed materials and power supplies. Aluminum. Titanium. Steel. Plastics and composites. The heavy printing and assembly work was done by the same bots that do ship refits."

Ryder snickers. "You stole Harmony's materials and used Harmony's printers to create this. Right under their fuckin' noses. Sweetest thing I ever heard. Now show us the people section, the lander."

We head forward in this vast, misty place of pipes, cables, and machinery. Pairs of technicians in blue coveralls bend over their work. They don't notice us over the background noise coming from racks of fans, pumps, and other equipment surrounding us.

The rocket is supported by a long cradle of blue girders and braces. It grows narrower as we near the upper parts and it ends with a blunt nose. There are little oval windows bordered in black and an open hatch crowded with hoses. Written near the hatch: *Liberty*. Deep red letters over the glossy white surface— brash and gallant.

"*Liberty*!" shouts Ryder. He punches the air. "*Liberty*!" He knocks fists with David and thumps Mikki on the shoulder. I'm lucky; I get a tap on the back of my head.

There nearest window is directly above us. I ask David, "A look inside? Just for a minute?"

"Not yet. They're doing system checks and lineups."

Ryder shakes his head like he still can't believe any of this. "Launch date?"

"November eleventh, one week from tomorrow."

Fly in space, in one week. My heart races.

"A week?" sneers Mikki. "We can't be ready in a week!"

"That's my job," David declares. "You'll be ready, and you'll have time in flight to learn and adapt enough to keep yourselves alive and build what you need. You'll have consider- ably more information and resources than the first settlers who arrived at the Americas or Polynesia."

"Eight days," mumbles Shuko. "That hardly seems adequate."

"Doctor Saito, I won't question your medical judgment. Extend me the same professional courtesy."

I inform Shuko, "If they can build this in nine days, they can train us and get us to the launch site in eight."

David grins. "Launch site? You're standing on it."

＊

The kitchen off the sleeping quarters has been set up as a class- room. David stands before a two-meter panel displaying a map of the Pacific Ocean.

"Today's agenda has three parts. First, your flight plan. Second, cabin familiarization. Third, emergency actions." He points a bony finger to a red dot a few centimeters to the left of Alta California. "We're here, about three hundred kilometers from the coast." His finger cuts across the screen to a point halfway between the America states and China. "This is your launch position, sixteen hundred kilometers northwest of the Hawaiian Islands."

Ryder stomps both feet on the floor. "You mean we launch straight from this ship? *That* big beautiful gigantic thing lifts off straight from this ship?"

"The cradle rotates ninety degrees to vertical."

Mikki exhales sharply. "If you're launching the biggest rockets ever made, you might as well go all the way and do it from ships."

I ask, "How did you pick the launch position?"

"It's distant from military assets. Harmony's defense tracking systems watch for ballistic threats near the coasts. They're not configured against a target rising straight up from the middle of nowhere. We can launch you at any point, and the guidance system will fly you to Mars."

David changes the display to a cross-section of the entire ship. There are six enormous spheres in a single row—yes, tanks after all—each marked 65 meters in diameter. The rocket and it's cradle are beneath the third, fourth, and fifth tanks, which are hollow and have only upper domes.

"These middle tanks are dummies. The forward two tanks hold your liquid methane fuel, the sixth is full of liquid oxygen. Eighteen thousand tons of propellant. A few hours before launch, we'll transfer the oxygen and the fuel into the rocket tanks. The three dummy domes slide off into the ocean, and the tower rotates to vertical via transmission cables spooled by two diesel engines."

Paige shakes her head. "Won't the whole ship topple over?"

"No, because we'll be counter-flooding the hull to keep the center of gravity low. The rocket cradle also slides forward as it rises in order to keep the ship balanced along the transverse axis. Once you're vertical, the cradle is your launch tower."

Mikki says, "You're forgetting something."

"What?"

"The part where I get a bottle of wine. Because I'm not doing this before I drink a whole bottle of wine."

David closes his eyes and pinches the bridge of his nose, but not fast enough to hide a tiny smile.

The panel displays a drawing of the entire rocket. It's divided into five sections and labeled *R-56 Mars Colonial Transport.*

"We call this stack the BFR. Big Fucking Rocket. A straight-out trajectory in four stages." David taps the bottom section of the rocket. "First stage, the biggie, fifty-six Raptor engines. Burns two and a half minutes, takes you up sixty kilometers."

I blurt, "Over halfway to space!"

He nods. "But you're still slow, a mere seven hundred meters per second. The second stage is lower thrust, but uses more efficient J-2X engines."

I can't help blurting it out. "Apollo!"

"That's right, a J-2 derivative, heavily modified for methane instead of hydrogen. The design was digitized forty years ago, so we leveraged the engineering done at Rocketdyne. When that second stage drops after six minutes, you're two thousand kilometers high, moving over seven kilometers per second. You're gone, Harmony knows it, but it's too late to do anything about it. The third stage accelerates to escape velocity plus ten percent over, faster than any humans ever moved."

Alison lets out a slow breath. I reach out and squeeze her shoulder.

David displays two planetary orbital arcs over a black background: Earth and Mars. A green curve appears connecting the two planets. "Trans-Mars Injection. The TMI stage more than doubles your velocity to thirty kilometers per second. This is the newest tech in the stack, plasma thrusters running off an eight megawatt reactor. The thrusters will push you at one twentieth of a gravity for about ten hours."

Ryder says, "Direct trajectory, and with the reactor we don't need solar panels."

"After thruster shutdown, the reactor idles and provides electrical power for the rest of the flight. Earth and Mars are in conjunction this month. Thanks to the plasma thrusters, total flight time is forty-two days."

I ask, "Does the TMI slow us down when we get there?"

"Can't lift enough propellant. But you're on a hyperbolic trajectory climbing away from the sun. The sun's gravity will take off half your velocity by arrival."

The display switches to a close-up view of Mars. A green curve loops around the planet twice and ends at a tan-colored smudge on the surface. "You're going to aerobrake. The atmosphere will take off the rest of your velocity. We designed a landing sequence that will set one hundred tons gently down amid the rolling hills and glaciers of Protonilus Mensae."

Ryder leans forward. "Proton-nil...that's our landing spot? Why there?"

"Availability of ice, minerals, other useful resources. Everything you need is likely to be within driving range of your trucks. Closer to the equator would give you more sunlight, but there may not be available ice nearby. We didn't want to take that chance, especially since our images and data are decades old."

Paige asks, "You said six ships. Are they going to this Protonilus place too? Or are we scattered across different locations?"

David zooms the view of Mars. Mountains, ridges, craters. He points to a circular area. "All six spacecraft land within a few hundred meters of each other. Everyone is a backup to everyone else. With luck, you'll be joined by *Independence*, *Resolute*, *Endurance*, *Enterprise*, and *Constitution*."

Mikki crosses her arms. "With luck, eh? I don't see why there can't be at least one expert coming with us. If something goes wrong, what are we supposed to do?"

"Autosystems," Alison says, almost a whisper. "The autosystems will assist with emergencies."

But David shakes his head. "No autosystems."

"Right, because how would you train them?" Ryder says. "Bayesian models to train helper systems need a huge set of examples to work with, and we're headed into a completely new environment."

"That's basically it. We decided it would do more harm than good to try to train helpers. Too many unknowns and unpredictable variables. You're going to learn and adapt without artificial intelligence as a crutch." David taps his forehead. "Use your organic intelligence."

Mikki snorts. "I get it. Hope nothing goes *really* wrong, because if it does, we die."

We all sit in silence for a couple of heartbeats.

"If something goes wrong," David says softly, "You deal with it. You're going to learn how to do that this week."

The next few hours are a thick jumble of terminology, equipment, and configurations. According to David, we must memorize the physical arrangement of the major spacecraft components before we learn emergency actions and override procedures.

Liberty is the uppermost section of the rocket, the part that lands on Mars. The shape is a truncated cone eight and a half meters wide at the base and twelve meters tall, not counting the nose fairing and parachute canister, which will be jettisoned before landing. The outer hull is high-temperature composite polymer, and within that is a pressure cabin of aluminum-lithium alloy with a honeycomb matrix core.

The pressure cabin is bulkhead-divided into two main compartments: a control center in the upper section, and an equipment bay in the lower section. The control center has six acceleration seats that can fold away, storage lockers, plus three double-occupancy sleep compartments—sleepers for short. The control center is also where we eat.

Everything else is crammed into the equipment bay: life-support machinery, medical gear, food stock, tools, batteries, materials stowage, two printers, two creepy little cryogenic flasks that hold hundreds of frozen embryos and sperm samples, an airlock and operating station, and a cramped hygiene compartment for washing and pooping.

Outside the pressure cabin but within the outer hull are tanks for oxygen, nitrogen, helium, and the monomethylhydrazine and nitrogen tetroxide used by the landing engines. The compartments outside the pressure hull contain a compact portable nuclear generator and a disassembled methanol-powered truck with a built-in crane.

"Power is your top priority after landing," David tells us. "Once you assemble the truck, use it to dig a hole three meters deep. Lower the generator into that hole, bury it for radiation shielding, and start generating electricity. Without charging, your batteries will last ten days at most."

The display shows the interior of *Liberty*: a tangled maze of multicolored cables, hoses, lockers, and displays.

"Routine procedures are automated, but you need to know four operating panels so you can monitor and override if you experience a serious failure."

Mikki snorts. "I feel so much better."

The System Power Panel is in the equipment bay next to the airlock operating station. It controls and monitors electrical generation, battery charge, and bus isolation.

The Caution and Warning Panel is in the control center between two acceleration seats. It displays spacecraft state-of-health plus thirty-seven hundred warning messages and ten separate alarms.

David tells us, "The Guidance and Navigation Panel is within view of the flight director, and the Master Control Panel is near the right seat." He points to Shuko. "You're going to be in that seat monitoring cabin atmosphere for the first several hours, until you're confident the automatic systems are functioning normally."

"I understand," says Shuko.

"The flight director is responsible for safety and coordination. Everyone's going to memorize their emergency actions, but during any emergency or urgent situation, the flight director is in charge. Cristina, you are flight director."

I gulp in air and jerk upright.

"You'll be in the left seat watching both the nav panel and the warning panel. It's gonna look overwhelming at first, but don't—"

Ryder shakes his head. "What?"

David peers at him.

"You must be…I mean, why her?" Ryder glances around the table. "She has to be the least qualified here."

David says, "Cristina—"

"Don't misunderstand!" Ryder interjects. "I like her, I really do. She's bright and she has a knowledge of historic rockets. But face it, she's not an engineer. So, I don't comprehend this. Can we talk it out?"

The silence goes on for several seconds. Mikki chuckles softly.

"Are you finished?" asks David.

"Me? Yeah."

"Cristina is flight director. I chose her. Is that understood?"

"I'm just curious why you chose her, that's all." Ryder turns to me. "Aren't you curious? Because I sure as hell would be. Curious and totally, totally confused."

Mikki sighs. "You made your point."

But he's not done. "We're pledging our lives. We need to vote on this."

"I'm fine with that," I tell him.

David exhales. "The instant you're in flight you can do whatever you want. Until then, you'll do as instructed."

Mikki leans across the table toward me. "What are your qualifications, by the way? You admitted you never went to university. I hold an engineering degree." She turns to David. "Why should I listen to her?"

The room sways sideways. Heavy waves? Ryder and Alison grab the edge of the table to keep from sliding off their chairs.

I level my eyes at Mikki. Sometimes nothing's going to work except for a bit of no-bullshit resolve. "Once we're up there, we'll work this out any way you want to work it out. Today, we're going to listen and learn."

"All I'm saying—"

"Shut it and listen."

"Can't I—"

"Shut it!" I bark at her. "Or I will pound your face."

TWELVE

The ship's rocking motion goes from bad to ridiculous. By noon we can't sit without swinging left and right. I'm dizzy and queasy, like a bad stomach flu. David braces his body against the wall and never stops teaching us.

A big roll sends Shuko's juice bottle sliding across the table. His face is pale. He murmurs, "Can we take a break, get some fresh air? It might help those not feeling well."

Paige clutches a trash container under her chin. "Taking this with me."

The view outside is magnificent, the ocean a menacing shade of dark metallic gray. Huge round waves roll alongside the ship, and the wind whips up tufts of foamy water. The fresh breeze, plus the change of view, calms my tummy-flutters.

David shields his eyes from the pelting raindrops. "Low pressure system ahead of us. Increasing swells and high winds over the next thirty-six hours."

When we return to the classroom, a heavyset orderly has set up a food cart. His chubby cheeks show the remnants of acme and I doubt he's much older than we are. "Call me Zach. If you can get something down, there's chicken soup, scrambled eggs, crackers, hot tea."

Only Ryder and Mikki approach the cart. Their paths zigzag as they stagger across the pitching floor. Dr. Ordin sticks her head through the doorway. "Try to eat. This is the last regular food you'll get. I'm switching everyone to a low-fiber, high-protein diet to acclimatize you to printed meals."

We eat and David resumes talking. Every aspect of the flight plan will be regulated by the Guidance, Navigation, and Control system, GNC for short. The technology evolved from the guidance systems used on the Chēngzhǎng and Apollo flights.

"My first post-doc position at JPL was with the spacecraft systems group. We managed the Opportunity and Curiosity rovers and the InSight lander. Those spacecraft navigated to Mars with essentially the same GNC system you have aboard *Liberty,* except yours is modified for a faster and heavier landing profile."

He warns us: The systems are reliable, but expect the unexpected.

"Emergency actions! This is the most critical part of today's material. Before you go to sleep tonight you'll know what to do for all ten alarms. We're gonna drill until you're dreaming about emergency actions."

An image of the Caution and Warning Panel appears.

"First alarm, low cabin pressure. Nominal air pressure is thirty-five kilopascals, a little more than a third of an atmosphere. Normal cyclic range is thirty-four to thirty-six, but if it drops below thirty-three point five or it drops at a rate greater than one kilopascal per minute, you'll get the low pressure alarm. If the rate exceeds two kp per minute, it will trigger the decompression alarm."

Everyone learns how to use an Emergency Oxygen Breather, or EOB. They're soft green cups that fit over the nose and mouth. There's a little tube worth fifteen minutes of pure oxygen. We practice the proper technique to get an EOB on our faces fast.

He warns us, "Under no circumstances are you to rely on your EOB if the cabin pressure even approaches ten kilopascals. It won't help you. At seven kp your blood boils."

Blood boiling. That can't feel good.

David adds, "This is why it's critical to distinguish the low pressure alarm from the decompression alarm. Your immediate action for a decompression alarm is to enter the hygiene compartment, which doubles as a pressure-tight shelter."

Ryder asks, "Why not the airlock?"

"The airlock will hold only two people at a time. The hygiene compartment has access to your BioSuits, which are designed for vacuum and the Mars surface. You can depressurize the compartment and rectify the problem. Worst case, you can wear your BioSuits for the entire flight, pressurizing the hygiene department every twenty-four hours in order to eat and evacuate waste products."

Mikki asks, "Evacuate our waste, take a shit, with everybody crammed into that tiny space?"

"Yeah," mumbles Paige. "That is truly a worst-case scenario."

David smirks. "Seventeenth century immigrants crossing the Atlantic in wooden ships had it a lot worse."

Next is the solar particle event alarm for a proton storm coming from a solar flare. That means deadly radiation. Everyone must squeeze into the hygiene compartment for the duration, generally several hours. The shielding is food stock and water tanks.

There's a bus undervolt alarm. Everyone practices manually placing batteries on line and isolating faulty buses using a simulated power panel.

The high carbon dioxide warning activates at 0.3 percent, the alarm at 0.5 percent. We learn how to clear the alarm, isolate the cause, and if necessary use the hygiene compartment as a safe haven.

There's a toxic gas alarm.

Low oxygen partial pressure alarm.

Loss of GNC alarm.

Airlock breach alarm.

David walks us through the procedure for each alarm. He fires off questions on actions he previously covered.

"Low oxygen partial pressure. Paige, what's the set point?"

"Eighteen kp."

"What do you do, Cristina?"

"On the warning panel, verify all three channels. On the master control panel, verify all six regulators in auto. Take one alpha and bravo to manual and open two-thirds. Verify they are open."

"Show me."

I bend over the panel simulation and find both control sliders.

"That's three alpha and bravo but that's close enough for now. You're inverted."

I close my eyes. "Sorry."

"Are you done?"

"Check for positive flow. If the partial pressure doesn't rise above twenty, verify all indicated bank pressures."

"How do you know there's bank pressure without even looking at the master panel?"

I shrug. "You didn't tell us that."

"Anyone?"

Ryder answers, "The regulator should start hissing when you override it."

"Good! Plus, you can feel the flow if you put your hand over the outlet."

Procedures, statuses, endless advice. Power supplies, set points, alternate configurations, routine operations. David describes the technical documentation available for research and troubleshooting purposes. There's a tech catalog and knowledge base for searches, but he advises us to use it sparingly and memorize everything backwards and forward.

Nobody had much dinner except for Ritz crackers and sips of juice or tea. The act of resisting the constant rolling motion saps my energy. The rain-splattered window at the end of the corridor has been completely black for hours. David talks about amine charges and HEPA filters but it makes no sense.

"That's enough for today. Now I want you to get a full night's rest, because tomorrow will be another long, tough day."

Shuko mumbles, "Weather?"

"This is what the meteorologists call a pineapple express. Big, nasty system traveling eastward. Happens this time of year. The storm is fast-moving and things should calm down tomorrow afternoon."

I follow Alison into our cabin. Someone has cleaned up. The bathroom is returned to its pristine state with fresh soap and towels.

There's a soft knock on the door. Alison calls out, "Leave us alone."

It's Ryder. He thrusts an index finger in my face. "Bus one undervolt! What do you do?"

I shut the door.

Sweet, sweet darkness. The sheets and covers feel wonderfully delicious. My stomach calms as soon as I'm horizontal. The constant creaking of the ship's structure becomes lyrical. The swaying cradles me to sleep.

✳

I open my eyes. How long was I out? An hour? Something's happening. Footsteps and voices, in a hurry, from above, below, all over.

I drift back to sleep.

Light! I blink back the painful glare. Dr. Ordin stands at the door. "Get up. Briefing in five minutes."

I throw off the covers. "What? Why?"

"You'll be briefed in the common area."

Alison sits up and stares at me. I tell her, "Probably another stupid test or something."

She swings her legs off the bed, but instead of standing she leans forward and holds her face in her hands. "I just can't anymore."

I pull on my coveralls. "Play the game and maybe they'll let us go back to bed."

She falls over sideways with her feet on the floor but head on the mattress and eyes shut. Dr. Ordin comes back, struts to the bed and tosses a cup of water into Alison's face.

"Awake now?"

I tell her, "That was totally unnecessary."

Dr. Ordin throws the cup to the floor. "Get her up."

The others are seated at the kitchen table, faces downcast. Mikki rests her head on Ryder's shoulder. The ship's rocking has subsided to a leisurely but still sickening roll.

David enters from the corridor. Paige asks him, "What time is it?"

"A little after two."

I clear my throat. "What's going on?"

David taps a tiny black box clipped to his shirt near his right shoulder. He points his mouth toward the box. "Status on IMU alignment and OPS-one load."

The black box crackles. "IMU alignment complete, OPS-one load waiting log reset."

"Copy."

Mikki raises her head. "You are not gonna tell me what I think you're gonna tell me."

"Don't know yet," David answers, voice barely audible. The only sound is intermittent hissing from the little box and the creaking of the rocking ship.

Ryder takes a bottle of frap from the refrigerator.

David tells him, "You probably want to lay off the beverages." Ryder replaces the bottle and collapses into his chair.

There's a thin red ribbon around David's neck. A plastic card dangles at stomach level—a pic of his face, much younger, with some printing.

I point to the card. "What's that?"

He strokes it with his fingers. "My JPL access I.D. A minor memento from the past." He sweeps his eyes over the six of us bunched around the table. "I'm going to tell you everything I know. Around midnight we identified two swarms of spotters following our convoy. Military swarms."

The door opens—it's Zach the orderly. He looks at David and receives a head shake as a response. At least four soldiers are near our door, with huge weapons and full military gear.

"Anyhow," continues David, "We anticipated the possibility of getting checked out at some point. There's nothing they would see that would arouse suspicion. These types of ships run themselves, and sometimes they carry maintenance technicians and sometimes they don't." He runs his hands over his face and massages his eyes. "Genesis. That's what we call our project. Almost everyone involved with Genesis is on board a ship. A handful are ashore in order to provide advance warning of discovery. They're supposed to transmit an all clear code every thirty minutes on the UHF band. The code has to be transmitted manually, so when it stops—"

I finish the sentence. "They're gone. Arrested."

"The last code received at twelve twenty-eight was a suicide signal. They ended their own lives before being taken into custody."

So the Autoridad couldn't torture them and find out everything.

Ryder asks, "Are the swarms still out there?"

"Affirmative. We don't know for sure if the spotter swarms and the suicide signal are related. We have to assume they are."

The box crackles. "Systems, OPS-one, GPC, BFS complete."

"Copy." He faces us. "The decision won't come down unless there's no other option."

Mikki lowers the left side of her face to the table. "We aren't trained. We don't know shit."

Ryder says, "Better now than never."

"They screwed this up," Mikki informs us, her words distorted from having her face against the table. "They screwed it all up, and we'll be the ones who get fucked."

Alison says, "We need to stop, think, figure out exactly what we're doing."

I squeeze her wrist.

A burst of static from the box. "Systems, launch control."

"Systems. Go ahead."

"Tanking commenced at zero two thirty-six. Event timer started. Predict tower rotate at zero seven fifty, launch at zero eight twenty."

I stroke Alison's hair. Mikki buries her head in her arms. Ryder sits back and stares at the ceiling.

The communications box spits out more information. "Winds eighteen knots, gusting to twenty-five. Swells five to six meters from the northwest."

"Copy. Systems out."

Mikki raises her face to David. "You told us eight days of training. We got one."

He runs his fingers across the card dangling from his neck. "Forget about that. We're on a contingency cycle now, everything's focused on getting you on your way. Once we begin stage tanking, we're committed. The tanks aren't designed to be filled more than once."

"Look how this thing's rocking," Mikki responds, a note of pleading in her voice. "At least wait for it to stop!"

Paige says, "They have no idea if this has any chance of working."

Shuko asks David, "You didn't plan for a launch in this kind of weather, did you?"

This is bullshit. What did they expect? I slap my palm on the table.

"I'm sick of this place! Sick of swinging back and forth. Sick of being told what to do. I can't take another week." I look at David. "Can you launch us?"

He gazes back and nods his head.

"Then launch us!"

THIRTEEN

Zach gets down to business. He tosses each of us a blue plastic box labeled with our names. Another orderly enters, a petite woman with a hair clipper.

"Yeah, we're gonna cut your hair," Zach announces. "We'll leave you a couple of centimeters. In space, hair is just a nuisance that clogs filters."

The female orderly throws a towel around my shoulders and goes to work.

Zach's voice competes with the whine from the clippers. "Pay attention, because I don't want to repeat myself. As soon as your hair is cut you're gonna shower." He holds up a plastic packet from my box. "This is your soap. Wash your skin and hair and rinse thoroughly."

Ryder asks, "Wouldn't it save time to do a group shower?"

David snorts.

"Disinfectant!" Zach calls out, holding up two brown packets. They're labeled *Hibiclens*. "You will cover your body with this substance, keeping it away from your mouth, eyes and genitals."

Ryder can't keep his mouth shut. "What if we want to try it on our genitals?"

"Go for it!" Zach snaps. He holds up a brush. "Scrub for five minutes. Five minutes! Then rinse."

"Then repeat," adds Shuko.

"You got it, Doc. There will be sterile towels by the time you're done." He holds up a tightly rolled cloth sealed in clear plastic. "Maximum Absorbency Garment. Do I need to draw you a picture? Don't even think about not wearing this. Good chance you'll need it."

The ship rolls and David braces himself. "What, no joke?"

"Hell, no!" Ryder answers. "I fully expect to piss myself at least once before this day is over."

Zach pulls out two final items, a white package and a pair of blue plastic slippers. "Flight suits!" He looks at Ryder. "These go on over your MAG. Last, booties on your feet. When you're done, return straight to this table. Try not to touch anything. We should accomplish all this in one hour."

Dr. Ordin calls from the doorway, "Don't skimp on the Hibiclens. We want to limit the total biological spectrum introduced to Mars. Extraneous mold, fungi, spores, bacteria, mites. Itty-bitty critters can wreak havoc on your crops and ecology."

I take my shower but I can't look in the mirror. So little hair is unnatural. The orange disinfectant leaves a revolting stink everywhere. A headache comes on. Is it from the lack of sleep? The perpetual rocking? The nausea? The stupid haircut? The disinfectant? All five combined?

The absorbency garment is just a big diaper. I pull the top edge above my waist. Comfortable! Would have been useful at SERCENT. The so-called flight suit is a one-piece, long-sleeved coverall with lots of pockets and thick gray socks built into the legs. The seams and cuffs close with Velcro. The soft white material feels like it's supposed to hold up against wear for a long time.

Somebody covered the chairs and floor of the common area with obnoxious-smelling yellow plastic sheeting. Mikki fingers her flight suit and asks, "So we wear plain white forever?"

Dr. Ordin responds, "After you get there, print your own garments any damn color you want. Purple, yellow, turquoise with green stripes."

Zach passes out EOB's encased in clear plastic pouches. "Put these in your right-side leg pockets," he instructs. Next comes a beige envelope. "Air sickness bag. Or space sickness? Two each. Place in your right or left chest pocket."

My rosies are in my right chest pocket. Everything else could go on the left.

Zach has more stuff for us. "Ear plugs and sleep mask. Use the earplugs when you sleep even if you don't think you need 'em. You'll hear alarms. The tone won't be blocked."

We each get a hydration pouch, 380 milliliters of electrolyte fluid.

"Sip it gradually, especially if you vomit. I recommend you keep it in your front left leg pocket. On your chest, it may get under your seat restraint and burst."

David tells us, "It will take a day or two to adjust. Stay seated and minimize head movement. I'd just put on my mask and earplugs and sleep." He checks his wrist. "We can't speed up tanking, but we're bypassing most pre-launch checks to get you on your way the earliest we can."

Paige mutters, "More spotters."

"Correct. And now there's a military cruiser shadowing us ten kilometers off. Every ship has a swarm of spotters buzzing the decks. They're hailing us on the emergency channel."

Mikki lets out her breath. "We're caught."

"We have a few things going in our favor," David says in his best firm and confident tone. "These naval forces haven't had to take military action at sea for twenty years. They don't know what to do. They might suspect us of hauling contraband. They don't know exactly who we got in here. They're waiting for instructions from the higher-ups, and they'll assume there's plenty of time. When we rotate the tower they'll see Big Fucking Rockets but we still have the advantage. The commander won't take action unless his own vessel is threatened. They won't know who made the rockets or why. What if they're part of a classified operation?" He swallows and looks directly at me. "Cristina, you're going to launch very shortly after the tower is vertical. The instant you're vertical, the snap launch option will enable."

"Independent from you?" I ask.

"That is correct. Ideally, we want to launch all six spacecraft simultaneously, as soon as we're happy with your status. This morning isn't ideal. When the time comes, we may not be able to communicate. Executing a snap launch will cancel the pre-launch program, disconnect the rocket from the tower, and fire the booster stage."

"I understand," I tell him.

"Remember, you can snap launch without permission from me."

"Why don't we launch right now?"

"Would if we could. Need to tank eighteen thousand tons of fuel and oxidizer."

Alison touches my arm and I take her hand. On top of the headache comes a growing sense of strangeness. Leaving Earth forever? Today? How could this happen so fast? Yesterday was one week since normal, since Isabel and Nathan, Marco, my Apollo book. Is all this real? Everything around me shrinks and drifts away.

A strange male voice snaps me back to reality. From out in the corridor, mature and gruff, and for a crazy instant I think it's Paco. The door cracks open and Dr. Ordin speaks to someone I can't see. "Did you wash and sterilize it like I showed you? Go in. Two minutes, no touching."

An oldie with intense eyes and short silver hair, every bit of it perfectly combed. He's dressed all in white like us, but it's a uniform, a magnificent, flawless uniform with gold buttons, a gold and white cap, plus a medal of golden wings on his chest. He fidgets with something in his hands, a triangular package of clear plastic over dark blue with white stars.

He stands for a moment, inspecting us. We inspect him back.

"Cristina Flores?"

For some reason I stand. "Yes?"

He stares as if soaking up every feature of my face. "I am Lieutenant Commander Stephen Baines, United States Navy. My father was Captain Richard Baines. He carried this flag aboard the Space Shuttle *Atlantis* on November sixteenth, two-thousand nine."

"The space shuttle? NASA?"

"He was a mission specialist at NASA, yes. This flag was the pall over his casket, and it flew over the U.S. Capitol in his honor. I'm asking you"— his eyes sweep the table—"asking all of you, to carry this flag in the spirit of freedom and independence it represents."

"Freedom!" Ryder echoes. He can't keep quiet when he's tired.

I take the flag from his hands. "Sure. I mean, of course we will."

He nods, and suddenly his body stands straight and rigid. He places the edge of his right hand against the brim of his cap. It's a salute, like in vids. He's perfectly still, so I salute back, awkwardly, my first and probably last military salute. I repeat his words, "Freedom and independence."

Stephen Baines smiles, a half-smile, really, almost bitter—like a condemned man enjoying his last meal. He gives us one last look before leaving the room, closing the door softly behind him.

I place the flag on the table. The whiteness of the stars over the deep blue cloth is dramatic, or maybe fatigue is playing tricks with my emotions. The flag of the America states—first time seeing it. Like religious icons, flags other than Harmony, Alta California, Texas, Alberta, and other official homelands are required to be kept out of view.

Ryder runs his hand across the plastic covering. "Not sure what we're going to do with it. Mars doesn't have enough atmosphere to fly a flag."

Mikki grunts. "You sound pretty sure we're going to get there."

David says, "Our hardware will probably soft land on Mars. The long-term outcome is up to you." He picks up the flag and turns it over in his hands. "Freedom. Independence." He lays the flag on the table and looks at us one by one. "In a little while you'll have all the freedom and independence you ever wanted, more than any of your fellow human beings left on this old Earth. For the first time in your lives, no one will tell you what to do and force you to do it."

Paige murmurs, "Whoopee for us."

"Freedom is your prize," David tells us. "And your most critical challenge."

"Discipline," I say to no one in particular. "He means we need to make our own discipline, and right now we have zero experience in that area."

David continues. "Every minute of your educational indoctrination was intended to form an obedient servant to an omnipresent master. What happens when the eternal threat of instant punishment is suddenly gone?"

Mikki shrugs. "We create another Autoridad."

"I don't think you're going to do that. But you'll have to organize some system of law that preserves freedom and independence. Figuring out how to do that will be just as important as making air and water and power and food."

Shuko opens his eyes from his nap. "Other people through-out history have faced these problems."

"Yes, the lessons of history. Through no fault of your own, you know little about the history of your species, practically nothing about the struggles your own ancestors had to overcome, ordeals not too different from what you'll face over the coming months and years. Hell, that may turn out to be a positive, who knows?"

The flag, the deep blue, the white stars. Paco's words from long ago. United States of America.

Not America states. *United States of America.*

"My father told me a few things about history," I say out loud. I've never told anyone a word of what Paco said to me those times we were on the beach. It was our secret, up to now. "He told me a few things about freedom, too. Freedom is hard, and it needs discipline and honesty or it's not going to work."

"Discipline, honesty. Check," Mikki mumbles.

I'm not going to tell them more because I'm tired and I have to get the details straight in my head first. Paco and I had this talk long ago. I was eight years old and for the first time my Score was crap. These were still the baby Scores that went from two to eight. We didn't get the full-range adult Scores until our teenage years, with high scorers moving into the adult territory sooner.

I was a three and that hurt me deeply. I couldn't sleep at night. I thought I had learned all the tricks to keep it at seven or eight. I sang all the songs praising Harmony and thanking them for our food and everything else. I recited my lessons perfectly, I was sparkling clean, I was polite to everyone.

It wasn't enough. My face betrayed me. My face and my voice. I could make myself say the words I was supposed to say, but my facial expressions, my voice *tone* as they called it, told my instructors my heart truly did not believe. I was a pretender, and high Scores belonged to those who *believed.*

They knew I was a liar before I knew it myself.

When I hurt inside, I could see my hurt reflected back in Paco's eyes. For the first time ever, he didn't know how to help me. This was a problem I never fixed. From Paco, I learned that wasn't necessarily a terrible thing.

"What do you always do for yourself?" he asks, the setting sun casting a red glow on his skin.

"I do my own math."

"Always. You sing two plus two equals five, but you know it's not true."

"My face shows I don't believe it."

"Don't change that, Cristina."

Which means I'm going to stay at three and maybe even hit two. My special privileges gone. Beans and rice for lunch. *And the others now look down on me.* They don't want me as their friend. They don't trust me. They've learned not to pull their own Scores down by coming too close to me.

I hoped Paco would have some idea how to raise my Score, how to trick them at their own game. But they can't be tricked.

"You have the freedom to do your own math, and now you're learning you have the freedom to *believe* your own math. And you do believe it, Cristina. You're thinking on your own, and it shows. That's why they're punishing you. You're an honest person and their system doesn't know what to do with you."

Honesty, Paco taught me, is important for freedom, for making your own decisions. In this world where we are told what to believe and what to say and what to wear and what to think, he taught me about honesty and freedom.

Discipline, according to Paco, comes from knowing what you want and honestly deciding whether or not you're willing to do what's necessary to obtain it, to pay the price in terms of effort.

When Paco was in grade school, he explained, many people got into the habit of neglecting honesty and discipline. This went on for years and grew worse. Without honesty and discipline it became easier for people to trade away their freedoms for what they hoped would be an easier life. I think Paco wanted me to draw the conclusion that the people of the United States of America, and many other places, forgot how to solve their problems. They forgot how to fight for what is right.

Ryder, Jürgen, Mikki, Eric, all of them—do they understand what Paco told me? Do I understand it myself?

My head is against Alison's shoulder. The ship sways back and forth, and we all float toward something like sleep...

The peace doesn't last. A fierce roar from outside! We jolt upright and turn as if we can see though the wall. It grows louder, then recedes. Something just flew past the ship, something huge.

Ryder cries, "What the hell was that?" and bolts for the door.

"Stay here," David snaps. "No one allowed topside."

Another rumble, this one from deep within the ship, a thunderous rush like a waterfall.

"Counter flooding!" David tells us. He checks his wrist for second time in less than a minute. "They're gonna rotate early."

"Is that good?" My words quiver.

The black box on his shoulder lets out a hiss. "Systems, OPS-one. Get them seated."

PART II

Guts are Enough

FOURTEEN

My hand flies to my right chest pocket—the bump of my rosies. Are they supposed to be sterilized like everything else? No matter; they're coming.

Everyone rises except Alison. Ryder and I tenderly lift her to her feet. Our fingers interlace. She trembles and stares at the wall.

The door to the corridor swings open. Dr. Ordin positions herself behind me and within reach of Alison. Is she going to assist with this potential problem?

Paige and Shuko move toward the door. It's time. But Alison's right hand grips the edge of the table as an anchor. Ryder nudges against her but she's not moving. I need words here. Strength? Courage? Consider those who would joyously take our place if they could?

Dr. Ordin's arm flashes past my face. Her hand presses against the side of Alison's neck. There's a tiny orange tube between her fingers. Alison flinches.

No!

I punch the doctor's arm and send the needle flying across the room. I snarl, *"Perra bruja!"*

Alison's eyes blink, her face goes empty. She slumps and Ryder grabs her other arm.

I scream at Dr. Ordin, "Just like the Autoridad!"

She whispers, "Start walking."

Soldiers jam the corridor. Four of them take position ahead of us. They're in full combat gear, with helmets and goggles, machine guns at the ready. Four more soldiers follow as we move forward, two facing backwards and guided by the other two. They scan everywhere around us, as if we are precious jewels to be protected from a hostile enemy.

The walls and floor along the corridor are covered in yellow plastic. I guide Alison with Ryder's help. Her face is peaceful, her blue eyes vacant. When we reach the first narrow staircase, Ryder carries her down with an arm around her waist.

The waterfall rumble grows louder as we descend. David holds his ear against his black box and snaps, "Copy!" He tells us, "Pick up the pace! Don't run, just walk as fast as you can."

Alison understands and keeps up with us. Even so, the staircases slow us down. The rolling ship makes it tough to walk straight and not crash into the walls.

Clusters of technicians watch us. Why are they here? Is it only to catch a glimpse of us? Alright, here we are. None of them says a word; they simply study us with bloodshot eyes. There's a short, dark-haired woman pretty much like me but around ten years older. She stares directly into my eyes as we walk past. There's no expression in her face other than exhaustion.

I shout to David over the roar, "What's going to happen to you and these people?"

"Not your concern! Keep moving!"

We reach the vast cavern enclosing the horizontal rocket and launch tower. The place is alive with the rumble of machinery and the thunder of rushing water. The spacecraft swirls with white smoke—no, not smoke, water vapor condensing because of super-cold liquified natural gas and oxygen. Moving banks of spray heads douse the sides of the rocket stages with green liquid. Directly below, under a metal grate, seawater churns like the inside of a giant washing machine.

Paige screams, "We're sinking!"

David shouts back, "Not sinking, don't worry! Just move!"

More steep stairs, but wide enough to pull Alison up, side-by-side. There's a walkway to the nose section. A pair of technicians await. They're covered head to foot in yellow plastic suits, their faces framed by hoods.

The hatch. This is it. Goodbye, world.

David growls, "Cristina and Shuko first! We'll talk later on the com channel." He takes my chin and gently runs his index finger across my temple. "Go!" A quick glance at everyone else, then he strides away without another word.

Something soft touches my arm. Mikki offers me the flag. The flag! My mouth is so dry I can hardly speak. "Forgot! Thank you!"

The techs guide me to a temporary access ladder positioned straight down through the circular hatch. The hatch itself is narrow, no more than a meter wide. They yank the plastic slippers from my feet. I tuck the flag under my left arm and take a careful step down through the hatch. I reach out and touch the name *Liberty,* then one more step and I'm inside.

The roaring thunder dwindles to nothing. I'm in the airlock, a cramped box filled with pipes and valve handles. It stinks of medical clinic disinfectant, only worse. A panel shows the air pressure in glowing yellow numbers: 100.64 kilopascals.

All over the walls…writing? Rows and rows of signatures, black against pale green. At least a hundred of them, plus LIVE FREE scripted big and bold. Toward the edge someone had drawn a rectangle enclosing a block of small print.

It begins, *The Lord is my shepherd.*

I wince. My stomach churns and my arms burst out in goose bumps.

Paco, dead.

Dead on his hospital cot. A little white paper in his hand. *The Lord is my shepherd.* It's a poem of some kind, a poem or a song about palm trees. Paco must have read this song before he died, which makes it a death song. Why did he do that? Why is Paco's death song here? It's a horrible memory, Paco—small and dead. I took his rosies from his other hand, but not the death song.

But it followed me all by itself.

Three more steps down, and I squeeze through the inner airlock hatch and into the equipment bay. The disinfectant smell is stronger. There's barely enough room to move. Color-coded cables and hoses snake between storage lockers and machinery. There's the power panel, lit up with yellow and green voltage and current readings. There's a constant hum all around me, like I'm inside a running machine.

"Come up forward, Cristina." The voice is soothing and affectionate.

Two faces peer from the other side of a square access hatch, a man and a woman, their heads enclosed in plastic hoods. "Put your leg over this divider," the man tells me, indicating the bottom edge of the hatch. It's the hatch to the control center. "Give me your hand."

I carefully step through the opening with the flag cradled under my arm. He holds me steady against the rolling motion of the ship.

The woman is old enough to be a mamina. She asks, "How are you this fine morning?"

I open my mouth but no words come, not even a feeble okay. My fingers tremble. Muchacha atontado! The missing sleep, the newness of it all.

"You just relax," the man tells me. He tenderly pulls the flag from under my arm. "I'm going to stow this away safe and secure, then we're going to get you situated."

The control center is scarcely large enough to hold six seats. There are two on either side of the access hatch and two further forward. The black seats are bowl-shaped to cradle our bodies from the thighs up, with a separate support for feet and lower legs. They're mounted upright, which means we'll be on our backs when the spacecraft is vertical.

"This is yours, Cristina." The woman guides me into the seat's soft center. Thick black straps go over both my shoulders and connect to a round center piece. Three more straps come together to secure my lower torso.

"This is your rotary buckle," explains the man. "When you want to release your harness, push the front part down and twist to the right." He demonstrates. There's also a strap securing my calves. How rough a ride is this going to be?

He shows me the lever to loosen and tighten the harness. The straps pull and the seat conforms to my body, a pleasant sensation even better than a bed.

The Guidance and Navigation Panel is within reach. Switches, dials, and a shitload of colorful numbers scrolling past. I'm supposed to know what all this means?

21:16:38 PCT 16 Taurus 53

Is that some kind of date and time? It goes to thirty-nine then forty then forty-one as I watch—definitely a clock. But twenty-one hours? After nine at night?

"This can't be right," I mumble.

The technician chuckles. "You're on Mars time, my love."

Shuko sticks his head through the access. "Hello!"

Paige and Mikki follow and take the seats behind me. They're close enough to touch my head. The control center seems to shrink as more people enter. Confined in this little place for forty-two days? No, much longer than that—until we build some sort of housing structure on the surface of Mars. How long will that take?

The mamina positions a black elastic cap around everyone's head to hold a microphone and earpiece. She shows me a round button on the left edge of the nav panel. "This is your com VHF voice channel, and it's pre-set. Push this to talk. You're linked to launch control and the other five spacecraft."

Ryder quietly positions Alison into her seat. How did he get her down that little hatch? I turn toward her as far as I can and force a smile. Her eyes are open but she's not seeing anything at all.

"Whoa, that's tight!" Ryder complains, tugging at his harness.

Mamina tells him, "It's a big rocket."

She says into the com, "Launch control, *Liberty.* Closing out the cabin."

"Copy, *Liberty.*"

The male tech places his hand on my shoulder. He whispers into my ear, "Launch control, *Liberty.* VHF voice check."

I repeat the words, but forget to press the push-to-talk. I try again.

David's words explode in my ear. "Voice check loud and clear, *Liberty.*"

The tech squeezes my hand. "You're doing beautifully, my precious love." He indicates three display screens on the main panel. "You got sight angles at ninety degrees, two-seventy, and straight down. And a window seat. Enjoy the view."

Both techs stare at us for a few seconds then vanish into the equipment bay. There's a faint thud followed by two clicks, then a second thud from far away.

"*Liberty,* confirm both airlock hatches indicate shut." It's David's voice again.

Shuko jerks his head left and right searching for the indicator. He nods, and I repeat into the com, "*Liberty*...I mean, launch control, hatches indicate shut."

"*Liberty*, you should now be in recirc mode. In a few seconds your GNC will start to gradually drop cabin pressure. It should stabilize at seventy-five kp."

"Recirc mode," I repeat. I ask Shuko, "What does that mean?"

He runs his eyes over his panel and shrugs.

Along with the outside vids, the nav panel has a flat rectangle screen displaying continuously changing information. BYPASSED and CANCELED up and down, absolutely everywhere. The warning panel has a similar screen, with too many CAUTION messages to count.

"David, all these warnings…"

"Ignore them. Tanking's completed! Soon on your way."

Something's happening far above us. Out the topmost window, a meter overhead, a thin line of daylight? It's wider—the ceiling a hundred meters above us splits into two huge pieces that separate left and right. Clear sky, pale blue because the sun isn't up yet, with cloud wisps the orange color of dawn.

Shuko peers upward, too. "They dropped the tops of the dummy tanks straight into the ocean."

Crack crack crack crack crack…far-off gunfire? Curls of smoke drift past our windows.

"David…"

"Explosive bolts, should have warned you!"

A female voice on the com yells, "Tower stations stand by! Release! Release! Release!"

BA-BOOM…everything jerks sideways, as if the whole rocket and support structure just jumped free. The control center jolts to the right as the ship rolls. A distant rumble of machinery comes through the seats and vibrates my spine.

Ryder asks, "Are we there yet?"

"*Liberty*, you're going to feel some motion," David tells us.

Mikki shouts, "Yeah, no shit!"

A deeper, brawnier vibration shakes us. The com announces, "Commencing tower rotate at zero seven four two local."

"This is it," Shuko mutters.

"*Liberty*, be aware we got some uninvited guests out there," reports David. "There's that cruiser on us since last night, and now there's a couple more. They're getting nosy. Just ignore them."

Paige blurts, "Gonna be a problem?"

"Thumbs up their asses," David answers. "They don't know what we are. Our transmissions are encrypted. By the time they figure anything out, you'll be far away. We're turning the convoy into the wind. Just expect them to take a closer look as the tower comes up."

I crane my neck to see out the window to my left. It will become a downward view when the spacecraft is vertical. The inside of the ship moves backwards—or it seems that way, because the massive cradle that supports the rocket is pivoting on end in order to stand the spacecraft upright.

A spotter! A big one, with a single red star. It hovers like a wasp just outside the top window and peers in at us.

Mikki mumbles, "Hello, there."

Ryder thrusts out his middle finger.

Out my side window, the top deck of the ship. The relative motion sends it downward and backwards. The ocean! Hundreds of waves roll in the same direction and the wind beats up white foam. The ship runs fast, the water slicing past in a blur. The spacecraft heaves to the right and rumbles like a beast confined in a cage. The structure transmits growls and tremors on every roll.

Mikki murmurs, "Slow down, please."

Ryder asks, "How long until we reach vertical?"

"Fifteen minutes," answers David on the com.

Three silver and black ships close by—the military cruisers. On the right, most of the far window is blocked by Shuko and his seat. The ship David called *Enterprise* is over his shoulder, small and far away, but close enough to tell that their launch tower is about forty-five degrees up. My vid panels show more ships far behind us, plus swarms of military spotters darting everywhere. The one on our window watches with a black insect eye.

The steel lattice supporting the rocket rotates steadily higher. As the tilt grows steeper our seats recline further backwards. The center of gravity of the ship also rises. That means the rocking motion becomes an enormous upside-down pendulum. Worse, every time the spacecraft reaches the extreme left or right side of the swing, the whole rocket stack jolts inside the cradle as if it's about to break free and fall apart.

Big Fucking Rocket.

Ryder yells, "I want to shake the hand of whoever came up with this idea!" He's smiling but his words shiver.

The rocket vents gas and the wind blows it away in delicate streams. Every time the ship rolls the tower sways a little bit farther. What's it going to be like when we're vertical?

"We're going to tip right over," Mikki mumbles.

"We're fine!" I shout back. "Look at *Enterprise*! They're straight up!"

"Keep your cool," David's tells us. "Cristina, you see the snap launch icon? It's at the lower left corner of the nav panel."

"See it!"

"It'll be enabled a few seconds after you reach vertical."

Loud panting from behind, audible even over the creaking and the wind. I loosen my harness and twist around. Mikki's eyes are closed, and her hands clutch the sides of her seat so hard her fingers are pink.

"Mikki! You okay?"

No answer, just rapid huffs and wheezes. Shuko watches her too. "Hyperventilating," he declares. "A precursor to panic attack."

The ship leans a ridiculous amount to the left. Beyond the window, a hundred meters below, a wall of blue and pink wind-beaten waves. I grab the edge of my seat.

Mikki gasps. She sputters "Fuck this shit," between pants. Alison looks like she's about to fall asleep again. Why didn't they sedate us all? Not a good idea; we're supposed to be alert in case something goes wrong.

Ryder reaches out for Mikki's forearm but his own straps prevent him from moving far enough. He tells her, "Mikki, relax, think about good things. We can all use that bottle of wine right now."

She snarls, "Fuck," draws a breath, then, "You!"

Shuko turns to me. "I can sedate her but I need to get the kit."

David orders, "Stay in your seat!"

The tilt must be over half-way to vertical. What if the constant rolling causes one of the fuel or oxygen tanks to burst?

Mikki gasps deep and hard and her eyes screw even more tightly shut. She fumbles with her restraint harness. "Getting out of here…before…whole thing falls over."

Ryder growls, "Mick, no!"

I release my harness, twist backwards, reach behind me and pull her hand away from her release. I cover it with my own hand so she can't get at it. But I can't stay like this. I shout over the racket of the creaking launch tower, "I know what we're going to do! We're going to sing!"

That grabs her attention. She pushes out each word. "You…fucking…crazy?"

Paige cries, "Hey, let's dance!"

"We're going to sing!" I tell them. "And yes, you will sing with me, Mikki. Yes you will. Just follow my lead."

Shuko says, "Singing calms. Defeats the fear response. Sing, Cristina!"

"Got no wine!" Ryder calls out. "So yeah, sing!"

Sing what? The control center jolts to the right. Paige shrieks.

Magistrado Geraldo Diaz.

What did he say? *You have a beautiful voice, Cristina Flores.*

I whisper, "This is for you, hijo de puta."

I reach back as far as possible. "Mikki! Open your eyes."

Rapid head shake.

"I think you can if you try. Look at me. What's your favorite song?"

Another head shake. Beads of sweat fly from her brow.

"Then we'll make one up. But you're gonna have to help me. My singing ain't great."

Think! Find some words, find a rhythm. Better yet, feel.

I face forward. Ignore the endless stream of yellow WARN-ING messages. I shout, "Are we ready?"

Ryder responds, "Sing it, sister!"

The words come on their own.

"On this day I am free! I can't wait what my eyes will see!"

Ryder repeats, adding his own rhythm, "On this day I am free! Can't wait what my eyes will see!"

"I think we have it, Mikki! Let's do this together."

Her eyes open a bit. I sing the words slowly so Ryder can keep up.

On this day I am free!
I can't wait what my eyes will see
I dream about it wherever I may be
It's a day that belongs to me
On this day I am free!

Paige and Shuko join in. The words flow out of my head.

> *On this day I am free!*
> *I flew across the clear blue sky*
> *Never knew I could climb so high*
> *I close my eyes and begin to cry*
> *On this day I am free!*

Mikki moves her lips and mouths the words. No more panting. She's singing, or trying hard.

> *On this day I am free!*
> *Smile and look me in the eye*
> *If this is the day I am to die*
> *I know in my heart the reason why*
> *On this day I am free*
> *No matter what happens to me*
> *On this day I am free!*

Ryder screams out the last line two more times as Paige and Shuko applaud. Mikki grimaces at me but her breath is steady.

I press down on her harness release and lock her eyes to mine. "On this day…"

"*On this day I am free,*" we say together.

Ryder yells, "We're free! Now let's go!"

The rising sun glistens off the wave tops and turns the ocean foam pink. Still more pops and groans with every roll. Will there be an indication when the cradle is vertical? It has to be close.

I squeeze Mikki's hand, turn back into my seat and tighten my harness. "David!" I say into the com. "Do you hear me?"

"Cristina! Tower at eight six degrees. You're almost there!"

He doesn't sound like David. The voice that's always calm now trembles.

Paige cries out, "Look!"

They turn toward the right-side window, which I can't see. Ryder's fist punches the air and he shouts, "Go!"

The vid! A bright yellow flash and a wall of churning smoke. White smoke and orange flame swirl across the glistening ocean.

A female voice on the com reports, "*Enterprise*, you are away at zero seven fifty-six local."

A new vibration hits our rocket and launch tower, a brisk and violent shaking. It's the distant force of the other rocket transmitted through the air. Will it damage us? Then a BOOM strikes, solid and thunderous, like the roar of a Boeing Skylon on climb-out.

The snap launch icon changes from gray to green. Active!

Our turn when? Hit the snap launch now? How much longer before everything breaks apart?

Another BOOM shakes us viciously. *Enterprise* rises majestically atop a massive pillar of yellow fire. A mountain of smoke spreads across the water.

I hit the talk switch. "David! How much longer?"

No response. I touch the bump of my rosies.

A third BOOM vibrates through us, the loudest of all. Paige screams.

Ryder cries, "Shit!"

On the vid: An enormous fireball of orange and black. My gut tightens into a knot.

"No!" Paige cries.

I shout into the com, "David! Hear me?"

The control center trembles. Ryder's words are barely audible. "Blew up!"

Flaming trails arc toward the water. The down-facing vid shows the edge of our ship swept by waves—we're almost sunk. On the back-facing vid, two silver helicopters land and release a squad of spotters and soldiers.

I yell, "What's happening?"

No answer comes.

FIFTEEN

I jab the snap launch icon and scream into the com, "Snap launch! Hear me? Snap launch now!" The navigation panel flashes orange.

SNAP LAUNCH INITIATED – RUNNING TMP
PRE-SEQUENCE

I snatch the rosies from of my pocket and wrap them around my fingers.

Shit is happening. Multiple bangs and knocks from below. Big Fucking Rocket comes alive, rapidly. On the down-facing vid: struts, hoses, cables, and sheets of ice blow off the sides from top down, like a beast casting off the chains of captivity.

CRACK…the entire launch tower falls away, trailing streams of vapor and tumbling shards of ice.

Four hard, quick thumps. Paige screams. The rosies dig into my knuckles.

Ryder yells, "Here! We—" But a giant BOOM cuts him off, a thunderous explosion like guaranteed death. My seat lurches upward, then falls backward, up and down again and again, then shakes side to side, more furious by the second.

The massive rocket below us detonates—just like *Enterprise*. A fireball comes up fast to engulf us and burn us alive.

Let it be over quick.

The roar, the shaking, *STOP!*

Another BOOM from below, then another, plenty more shaking—no chance the rocket can take this much stress and stay in one piece. We're breaking up, that's certain, I just don't want to see it or feel it when the full fury of the explosions tear us apart.

Redness through my eyelids. Sunlight? Is this death?

I open my eyes. The swirling chaos of wind and fire is below us. Nav panel a jumble of yellow numbers and blinking icons. Altitude twenty-seven hundred meters, numbers changing almost too fast to read. Can't be true! Three thousand meters, four thousand meters-something.

My seat jerks back and forth as if shaken by a powerful, invisible hand. A force presses my head backwards. Speed, rising speed. A weird sensation, exhilarating and terrifying. The spotter's gone, torn off by the force of moving air. Flashes of white and pink zip past as we climb through a wispy cloud layer.

Another vicious rumble from below, plus new shakes and trembles. A boiling orange and black fireball fills the downward vid. The violent tremor subsides to jerking and quivering.

Ryder screams something happy.

I yell, "Ten thousand!" but the engine roar swallows my words. The nav panel displays more information than I can process and I can barely read anything because of the shaking. A green message flashes.

TMP SEQUENCER ON OVERRIDE

Shuko's eyes are locked on his panel. He's supposed to monitor cabin pressure and oxygen partial pressure. Does he remember all the specs?

Getting a bit harder to breathe! The acceleration presses down on my entire body. The nav panel shows over two G's and increasing. The ocean is silky smooth. Six fireballs, now far away. Altitude? Passing twenty-five thousand meters, ten times higher than a minute ago. The noise level declines to a dull roar but the side-to-side shudder doesn't let up.

The other rockets? One blew up. Should be four more besides us. Ryder points toward the vid screens. The side view shows two white vapor trails topped by yellow flame. He flashes five fingers for five rockets.

A computer-generated female voice from the GNC panel announces, *"Booster shutdown in three, two, one."*

BOOM!

Numerous sharp bumps, like a fast-moving bus rushing over potholes. I'm thrown forward hard enough to spray specks of spit across the nav panel. The harness bites into my shoulders.

Ryder cries out, "Yeah!"

The GNC declares pleasantly, *"J2X ignition in three, two, one."*

A grumble from below, then I'm shoved backward against my seat. A muscular hum, and acceleration returns. This stage feels different from the booster—a deep, angry drone compared to a savage rumble. The jerking is replaced by relentless vibration. Passing eighty-five kilometers, acceleration three G. I raise my arm a few centimeters. Heavy, as if holding an invisible weight.

Out the window—the whole rocky gray Baja peninsula stretches to the horizon. The edge of the Earth curves and glows against the deep violet sky. Sunlight dances around the control center, but the two windows on the far side are almost black. The engine drone plus the acceleration are a hypnotic combination. Out the window: all of Mexico down to Panama.

A male voice bursts from the com. "This is *Constitution*. If you can hear me, call out the name of your spacecraft." That has to be Eric!

I press the talk switch. "This is *Liberty*!"

Unfamiliar voices call in from *Endurance* and *Resolute*.

Heaviness...acceleration still rising. Head motion harder, breathing is a real chore. How much worse will this get?

Eric says on the com, *"Independence*, report if you can hear me."

A girl responds, *"Independence* reporting, feeling some pressure, all well."

The engine hum changes tone and the GNC announces, *"J2X shutdown in three, two, one."*

This time no bang, just one quick jolt forward, then a rumble-shudder. Sudden quiet except for the hum of fans.

Falling...no, hanging upside-down. Too strange. I stupidly grab my seat.

Another "Wahoo!" from Ryder. I will someday hit him.

I turn my head toward Shuko and that makes me dizzy. Which way is up? Minimize head movement, look in one direction. The nav panel makes good target. It shows our altitude in kilometers—in the 2040s with the last digit changing too fast to read.

From the GNC, *"Maneuvering in three, two, one."*

Paige mutters, "Not again."

Solid bump forward, then back against the seat. This time the head-swim is worse and there's a falling backwards sensation. Earth departure stage. The noise and shakes are softer, but it presses harder—the acceleration rises just past four G. No one speaks. I decide not to move my head at all and just consider two thoughts: Earth, and departure.

The truth of those two words triggers memories. No matter what happens, this is a kind of death. Our past lives are over. The sweet faces of Isabel and Nathan. As far as they know, I disappeared without a trace. Will they ever know the truth? Will they believe it?

Passing four thousand kilometers, acceleration steady at 4.7 G. Each breath is a huff and a puff.

"Escape!" Ryder shouts, blowing out the word. "Velocity!"

Memories jump in from nowhere. Isabel's tears. Dr. Mike, one hundred percent! Red Block. A cluster of six fireballs against the pink and blue ocean below. Is anyone else thinking about the rocket that exploded?

Here comes six thousand kilometers. Over soon? Tired of breathing against the force.

"J2X shutdown in three, two, one."

A rumble, a jerk forward, a final shudder. The dizziness again, but I'm ready for it and keep my eyes open. A black sleep mask tumbles past my face.

Mikki whispers, "Don't throw stuff."

"Alison," I call out over my shoulder. "How you doing?"

"Fine. Heard your song."

Ryder loudly announces, "If anybody wants to know, those absorbency pants work pretty good."

Paige growls, "You did not!"

The GNC sings out, *"EDS separation in three, two, one."*

Bang bang bang! Mild jolts.

"Flight directors, check your panel for warnings." That's Eric again. "Your cabin pressure should be down to thirty-five kp. Check your O2 partial around twenty-four kp with some variation expected."

Shuko scans the warning panel. His face is pale, or it seems that way in the dim blue light. Why is everything blueish? No sun from the windows, just a soft sapphire glow reflecting from the walls—it's the ocean and the rest of the Earth. The sun must be directly behind, blocked by the Trans-Mars Injection stage.

"Oh, yeah!" Ryder squirms his body away from his seat. He twists into the narrow space between me and Shuko. "I can get used to this!" He grabs the underside of the warning panel and pushes himself under my seat, although the concept of *under* doesn't have much meaning.

"Eric, this is Cristina. Can you hear me?"

"Use your spacecraft name, *Liberty*. Go ahead."

"Pressure is good, exactly thirty-five."

Mikki chuckles. "You didn't use your spacecraft name."

I twist my release knob and cast the harness aside. The straps wriggle in the ventilation breeze as if alive. I rotate myself to face Mikki. "Glad you're feeling better. Want to be our official communication person?"

"Pick someone else."

Ryder calls out from the window, "I can see the Amazon, the Andes, the tip of South America!"

"Have a good look," Shuko tells him. "You'll never see anything like it again."

Something grabs my leg; Ryder pulls me out of my seat and closer to the window. The sight wipes out all other thoughts. The Earth—immense, radiant, impossibly colorful. South America is vivid green and dotted with hundreds of tiny clouds.

Ryder says, "Mick, come see our former home dropping away at twelve kilometers per second."

She's wearing her sleep mask. "The man said stay in your seat and sleep, and that's what I'm gonna do."

Rosies! Still clutching them. I open my fist and let them float free. The burgundy beads dance in slow motion and the silver cross glows in the earthshine.

The control center seems larger now. Paige is on the other side, head pointed down. My head should be pointed up, but too many sights contradict that assumption. I decide that the bulkhead separating the equipment bay will be my personal down, no matter which way I'm pointed.

"Something going on here," Shuko reports, words quivering. "TMI startup sequencer, warning messages too." He presses the com switch. "We have warnings. Invalid precheck values, missing RSC authentication. I don't know what any of that means."

Eric answers, "Disregard the warnings. Let me know if you see any errors."

What makes him an expert? He learned these systems in one day?

Paige asks, "Isn't Jürgen supposed to be in charge?"

Shuko responds, "Except for the scientists left behind, I think he knew the most." He keeps his head perfectly still and directed at the panel. Smart man.

"Jürgen should talk to us. He's the leader, right?" asks Paige.

I press the com button. "What happened to the rocket that exploded? Was it *Enterprise*? Does anyone know?"

Ryder mumbles, "I think they put Kim on *Enterprise*."

My heart sinks. *Happy tears, happy tears.* The pains and efforts of the last forty-eight hours wrap around me like a black shroud. My muscles tighten and the dizziness is back. Kim, gone, with five others. Who else left with her group?

"Jürgen," I call into the com. "Are you there? What do we know about *Enterprise*? Can you talk to us?"

But Eric answers. "The vid from launch confirms *Enterprise* was destroyed. That's all I know."

I whack the back of my hand against my seat. "That's all he knows!" I'm tired. And more than a little tense.

Ryder shakes his head. "Easy, tiger."

✳

"Maneuvering in three, two, one."

Sharp bangs rattle the control center, and the universe spins to the left. I have to hold on to the edge of Mikki's seat in order to stay in place. The sunbeams come back and drift across the pale green storage lockers.

We have a vid of Eric's face. His chin shows even more bristly carrot-colored stubble than it did two days ago. "Broadband links are up," he announces. "All five GNC systems just completed their navigation alignments."

In just a few minutes the Earth shrinks from a curved surface to a sphere hanging in a black void, the visible part forming a huge crescent. The colors are even more intense contrasted against the black of space. The tip of the crescent glows brilliant white.

Clicks and thumps from far away, then the lights flicker.

Shuko reports from his panel, "From what I can tell, the TMI nuclear generator is producing power. We're no longer on the battery, all buses shifted to the TMI stage. Haven't seen an error."

"All spacecraft," calls Eric on the com. "My GNC is predicting TMI thruster start at twenty-two fifty-four, less than three minutes. Probably a good idea to get back in your seat. The acceleration will be low, just five percent of one gee, but if you're not ready you can knock against something with enough force to get injured."

We push and twist ourselves back into our seats. Eric doesn't give a shit about what happened to *Enterprise,* but he seems on top of events, and maybe that's the only thing that matters now.

"Maneuvering in three, two, one."

Silence for one second.

"Thrusters on."

A soft buzz, a gentle push from behind, then a bounce forward. The GNC lets out a sharp chime and tells us, *"Thrusters off."*

Ryder exclaims, "What?"

Shuko looks at me, eyes wide. "Thruster failure!"

"What else?" Ryder asks. He's out of his seat and clutching the bottom of the panel.

"All spacecraft stand by," Eric growls.

"Thruster failure," Shuko repeats. "That's all it says."

I clench my fists. The nausea is back. "Has to be more information."

Shuko points at the panel. "See for yourself."

Mikki yanks off her mask. "What the hell's the matter?"

I close my eyes, turn my head, open them again, the only way to avoid dizziness. Paige and Mikki stare at me, eyes wide. Alison is still and wearing her mask.

"Technical issue, looks like," I tell them. "Eric will handle it. He seems to know the system."

"He seems to know," Mikki repeats. "That makes me feel better."

Ryder reads from the warning panel. "Error zero six two. Sys-op, expand error zero six two."

I bend forward to read the information with Ryder and Shuko.

ERROR 062: THRUSTER STARTUP FAILURE. TMP SEQUENCER ABORT

"Something did start," I point out. "For a couple of seconds, a definite push. I felt it!"

Ryder's hand flicks over one of the displays. The panels are slower than the Stream, old-style flat, but the layered documents make it easy to get information. "The GNC agrees with you, Cristina. Thrusters did start. Ran for two point five seconds, went from zero to point zero one eight gees. Then they shut down."

Eric's voice is annoyed. "Obviously we have an issue with the GNC. The same problem occurred on all five spacecraft, so the good news is we're facing a programmatic failure and not a physical equipment failure."

Paige asks, "What's he talking about? Can he fix it?"

I return to the familiar security of my seat. My mouth fills with fluid. I should imitate Shuko—point my head in one direction no matter what.

Where's Jürgen? Isn't it his job to speak to us? To remark on major events?

"These thrusters are supposed to speed us up, right?" Paige asks. "If they can't fix it, how long will it take to get to Mars?"

Ryder answers, "I know this much. Without the plasma thrusters, an ordinary transfer trajectory to Mars takes seven to ten months."

"Ten months in this thing!" Mikki shouts.

"Don't worry about that, Mick," Ryder mutters. "Mars is a moving target."

Mikki covers her eyes. Paige sucks in her breath.

I tell them, "We'll miss it. So we have to make the thrusters work."

Paige whispers, "Can we get back?"

Ryder shakes his head. He traces his finger over a curved green arc on the nav display. "This is our trajectory right now." He zooms out until the curve becomes egg-shaped. "We're climbing away from the Earth, but technically we're in an elliptical orbit around the sun. Unless we change our velocity with the thrusters, we'll fly twenty-four million kilometers beyond the orbit of Mars, then curve back again."

My stomach won't let up. I take a closer look at the nav panel to see where Ryder reads this information. The trajectory is labeled with a solar orbital period of 406 days and the tip of the elliptical shape is 174 million kilometers from the sun. Pretty firm.

Eric comes back on vid. "We're going to do a manual override. Once the thrusters are running, the GNC will take us back to the programmed trajectory."

I ask, "You're going to give us instructions?"

"I'm going to perform the workaround on *Constitution* and then upload the edited module to the other four nav programs."

We wait. Mikki mumbles to herself, "Correct me if I'm misunderstanding. We're not in space for an hour and already we're dead."

"Mikki," I call out without moving my head. "Keep those thoughts to yourself."

"And if I don't? Are you going to sing to me?"

Eric's voice cracks from the com. "The workaround did not result in the thrusters maintaining operating voltage. We experienced the same automatic shutdown."

Mikki whispers, "We're fucked."

SIXTEEN

Jürgen is the flight director aboard the spacecraft named *Independence*.

"*Independence*, this is *Liberty*."

Seconds later a female voice replies, "Tess."

"Tess, is Jürgen planning to talk to us?"

"Talk? Talk to who? You?"

"Me and all the rest of us."

"Jürgen's indisposed."

"He's working on the problem?"

"That's right."

"Words of encouragement would be appreciated right now."

"I'll pass that along."

The clock on the nav panel reaches 00:00:00 PCT and the date changes to 17 Taurus. Taurus? Is that supposed to be the month?

"Tess, we need to figure out how much time we have to get the thrusters working. Is there anyone on *Independence* who knows how to do that?"

Eric cuts in. "I have Indra working it out. And I have other ideas. We're going to perform a GNC reboot. I need a volunteer spacecraft."

Ryder spins around and thrusts his face into Eric's vid. "Reboot? That's all you came up with?"

"The thruster program module is probably corrupted," Eric growls. "There's no other explanation why it shuts down the thrusters when they do in fact run."

Ryder asks, "Can you reload from a master?"

"What do you think I've been trying to do? Each spacecraft has two identical Core Control Units. One acts as primary and the other as backup. When I delete the thruster module on the primary, it just reloads from the backup. When I overwrite it, it still re-sets from the backup."

Mikki calls from her seat, "Overwrite it on both, genius."

"When I try that, the system goes into protected mode and I can't edit anything. They should have given us more flexibility. Anyhow, if we hard-boot both CCU's with the breaker for the primary left open, the backup will automatically take over, and the GNC should fire the thrusters."

I tell him, "Try it."

Eric's eyes turn away. "That's not prudent, not on *Constitution*. If we can't power up, we lose communication. I'm the one person who can continue to troubleshoot the remaining systems."

"We'll do it here on *Liberty*," I announce. That makes Shuko move his head. "But I want you to answer a question. Why are you the one person?"

Eric opens his mouth but doesn't respond.

I press. "What's so special about you? How did you become such an expert so fast?"

"I was going to inform everyone shortly," Eric says. "I've been with Genesis from the initial phase five months ago. I worked with Chao and the rest to integrate systems from NASA, JPL, and Chēngzhǎng."

Ryder snorts. "You were a plant? You didn't volunteer?"

"I volunteered! I volunteered months ago, before any of you, before any of this hardware existed. My job was to ask questions and show you selects this skeptical and perceptive guy deciding to volunteer. We had to do it. It was better than forcing people, or sending up empty seats, or sending oldies. We didn't know if enough selects would volunteer."

Liars are everywhere. Nevertheless, this is reassuring. He knows the systems. "We'll try it. Tell us what to do." I turn to the others. "You didn't expect this to be easy, did you?"

✳

Like most things, it's trickier than it sounds.

Eric has to override a key safety program in order to force our system to run his code. He's doing it as an experiment, yet no one protests.

Ryder tells me, "Cristina, you are flight director. Not contesting that. But if we do this, an engineer should be in charge for the duration of the procedure."

"Agreed."

There's something different about him. His voice carries a strain. Much better to consider Ryder fearless, but that's not possible for any human being. Dread and a touch of anxiety have emerged, just a little, and it feels worse than if it were anyone else.

Paige offers to assist in the equipment bay, but there's no room; the only way to group around the System Power Panel is for her to be half-way through the access opening.

Eric tells us, "As soon as your GNC powers up, it should align, take a fix, and fire your thrusters. The rest of us will do the same. Each local GNC coordinates the spacecraft in formation flight about a kilometer apart."

Ryder manipulates the panel. His fingers quiver. "Opening master breaker."

The panel chimes and flashes red.

NOT RECOMMENDED

Harsh thumps sound out from all around us. The panels, the lights, and the fans die. We wait for our eyes to adjust to the dim illumination provided by a thin sunbeam reflecting off the master panel screens.

"Does it matter how long we wait?" Paige asks.

"I should have asked him."

I open the breaker for the number one CCU, then close the master. It clicks into place. But no lights, no fans. Ryder blinks as if confused.

Paige says, "That should have restored power to the busses."

A sharp hiss explodes from behind the equipment.

Ryder jerks his head. He blurts, "I know what that is!" He spins around and his head smacks against something hard. He winces in pain, then lets out two quick breaths.

"Get out of my way," he snarls at me. This is not Ryder. He grabs the two red airlock levers and rotates both ninety degrees.

I ask him, "Why turn those—"

"Shut the fuck up," he snaps. "Don't you hear? Don't you know what that is?"

Ryder twists the latches on the outer airlock hatch. His body shakes. He twists his head left and right, spraying droplets in all directions. Some of them hit my lips and nose; blood.

Shuko calls from the control center, "What's going on?"

Ryder yanks the airlock hatch open. The cold metal knocks me against an equipment rack. The tiny space is too small to move. Ryder squirms through the hatch and into the airlock.

"Ryder! Get out of there and focus on the procedure!"

Shuko pulls Paige from the access opening. He looks at me, then the open airlock hatch.

"Ignore the hiss," I call into the dark airlock. "We need to get power restored."

"What the fuck do you know?" Ryder yells. I scarcely recognize his voice. "You know nothing. Shut your fucking mouth. Can you hear that? That's our oxygen leaking away!" He rotates another lever.

The hiss is maddening—is it growing louder?

I lock eyes with Shuko. The hiss is an unknown entity, maybe some sort of relief valve in the TMI. Whatever Ryder is trying to do will may make matters worse.

Shuko barks, "Ryder! Stop what you are doing!"

Ryder shoots from the airlock like a charging bull. He grips Shuko's throat. "Don't tell me what to do! You want to suffocate?"

I wrap both arms around Ryder and use my right leg as leverage to break his grip on Shuko. He thrashes and smashes my hip against something hard. He screams, "Get off me!" The top of my head hits a valve handle.

Shuko's fumbling with a package. He bends over and strikes Ryder in the thigh with his fist. Ryder quits struggling.

Shuko whispers, "Sedated."

Power. We need to get it back.

I catch my breath. "I closed the master and it didn't do anything." One of my fingers hurts like hell but it's probably not broken. No matter. There's no power. No lights, no air, no way to communicate with Eric. And the hiss is still going strong.

Is it our oxygen?

Be calm and think.

Shuko pulls Ryder into the control center. Paige is curled up next to a window staring outward at the receding Earth.

Try again? I open and re-shut the master breaker. Nothing. Does Eric know if it's even possible to do this with the primary CCU breaker left open?

I close the primary CCU breaker and then the master. Several loud clicks and the lights come on and the fans hum to life. The panels glow with beautiful yellow numbers. The hiss dwindles away. The moving air chills my damp skin.

The GNC announces, *"Maneuvering in three, two, one."*

Mikki yells, "Shut that damn thing off!"

I brace against the access hatch as the spacecraft rotates several degrees. Eric's voice comes over the com. *"Liberty,* what's your status? Why the delay? Is your TMP sequencer started?"

I answer, "Shutting the master breaker with the number one CCU breaker open didn't work." His idea may not be wrong; it can't be tried.

"So you left your prime CCU up?"

"No choice. Power wouldn't come back otherwise."

The GNC calls out, "Thrusters on."

A brief push from behind, followed by a warning chime. "Thrusters off."

ERROR 062: THRUSTER STARTUP FAILURE. TMP SEQUENCER ABORT

SEVENTEEN

Despite the burning fatigue, sleep is impossible. *Enterprise* exploding, the launch, the failure, then the problem with Ryder. I'm too wound up. So I search the knowledge base and learn about thrusters.

It's complicated stuff. The TMI stage has a set of sixteen magnetoplasma rockets that generate intense electromagnetic fields to ionize argon propellant into plasma, a super-hot electrically charged particle beam over ten-thousand degrees Kelvin. Nothing burns, so it's far more efficient than chemically-powered rockets. The thrust is low, 4717 Newtons per thruster, about 480 kilos, so we needed high-thrust methane engines to boost us out into space. Now that we're here, we need a lot more velocity to reach Mars on the programmed trajectory, the only possible trajectory given the relative positions of both planets.

Each thruster has an independent, computer-controlled starting system linked to the GNC. With five spacecraft, that's eighty thrusters. How could they all be broken at once?

It's after three already. No word from Eric, no word from Jürgen.

My nausea intensifies despite staying in my seat for almost three hours. And I need to pee. The round hatch to the hygiene compartment is less than two meters away, but moving that far might make me puke. One nice thing so far: not puking.

Eventually I'll need to acquaint myself with the female urine receptacle device David described. But not now. I release my bladder. The absorbency thing does work; hardly any sensation of wetness. But what am I supposed to do with it?

At some point in the future—hours? days?—there won't be enough thruster propellant to reach Mars even if the problem is solved. Did they determine how much time we have? Would it be better not to know?

The others stay in their seats too. The three narrow doors to the sleeper compartments go untouched. Maybe we all feel better within sight of other people. The nav display shows Earth distance 157,320-something kilometers, the last digit increasing too fast to read. Over one third of the distance to the moon. The Earth is a thin crescent.

I go on the com. "Eric? *Constitution*? Can you hear me?"

A voice with an Asian inflection responds, "This is Indra on the *Constitution*."

"Indra, we'd like to know the progress on the thruster problem."

A long pause. "Working on it."

Some kind of frenzied breathing in the background. Then Eric, words taut. "I need to consult with Ryder Lawson."

"Ryder's recovering from an injury."

His breath huffs twice. "Why wasn't I informed?"

"Eric, go on private vid with me."

"Who else is an engineer? You got at least three. What's her name, Michaela? And the other girl?"

Mikki is asleep, sedated with a pill from Shuko.

"I'm a chemical engineer," Paige calls from her seat. "I know absolutely nothing about these systems."

"Eric, can you come on private vid?"

"With you? Too busy right now."

His face is beaded with sweat, his eyes bloodshot as if he's been crying. I make my words gentle. "Let's talk, just the two of us."

Eric sniffs. "In your sleeper. Channel two."

The door to the sleeper compartment I'm supposed to share with Alison is a couple of meters from my feet. Just turning my head causes fluid to collect under my tongue. I touch the sickness bags in my pocket, close my eyes, and push off toward the door. I open it by feel and enter head first. Soft red lighting shows two bunks with wide body restraints, plus a com display.

Eric stares back at me. "Go ahead, talk."

"You said you had other ideas. Ideas, as in more than one. What are they?"

"I can't explain anything to you. You're not an engineer."

"Try anyhow."

He blows out a long breath. "The TMP sequencer runs thirty-five checks after it reads the signal to start the thrusters. Every check passes. The thrusters start! We know this because we detect thrust. But the sequencer generates an error code and initiates thruster shutdown."

"TMP sequencer, what's that?"

"The master program that flies us to Mars, that's all."

"Is there any way to fool it into believing the checks passed?"

"What did I just tell you?" he snarls. "The checks pass, but the sequencer ignores the thrust. Which is bogus, because we can feel the thrust, so it's getting the signal, so it's above the threshold."

"Can we somehow bypass it, lower the threshold, fool the sequencer into believing the thrusters are running?"

"What do you think we've been trying to do?" He looks off-screen. "You're not an engineer. You can't begin to understand the procedural-level details unless you've built these systems from the ground up. I still don't understand all of it."

"You're the expert, the best chance we have."

"I'm the surviving expert. Shani was aboard *Enterprise*."

"These thrusters and the sequencer were tested?"

"Of course they were tested, right after the printers finished the main assemblies. Was less than a week ago."

"And the thrusters started and remained started?"

"Take a guess." He rubs his hand across his face.

"What's our next move?"

He blinks his eyes. "Are you listening? There is no next move. Everything works. What am I supposed to do? There's nothing to solve, nothing to fix, everything works!" He punches the side of his sleeper, making the vid jump. "What am I supposed to troubleshoot? Everything is working as designed! The son of a bitch shuts down for not working, while fully fucking working!"

He doesn't have any other ideas, not really.

"There's always a next move."

Eric shakes his head and sniffs. "Do you realize these ships and every piece of equipment except the reactors were printed just last week? A lot of it hand-assembled, so we didn't have time for system testing and damn little unit testing. System tests supposed to be this week, never got the chance. I can't do this. Never should have come out here."

He needs rest. But is there time?

"Eric, you said Indra was calculating how long—"

"She put our GNC in simulation mode and incrementally advanced the clock. When we simulate more than thirty hours in the future, it throws a landing unavailable error. Twenty-eight hours left, max."

I push my feet against the side of the sleeper. Less nausea in this tiny box. Would be tragic to vomit in this clean place.

Eric's frustration is contagious. What am I going to do after this conversation? Go back to reading technical descriptions? He's right, I don't understand it. If he can't figure out the answer, what chance do I have alone?

None whatsoever.

So we're dead.

Shut it out.

Eric needs rest, but even more than that, he needs peace. Peace so he can think. Relentless focus on this one problem takes him away from any chance or peace. Or perspective.

"Why are you here, Eric?"

He sniffs. Closes his eyes.

"You were in this from the start, five months ago, right? You told me you'd be here with me, trying. And here we are, trying. So you can tell me this little bit. What drove you here?"

"Same as you."

"Tell me in your words."

His face vanishes from the screen. I pushed him too far. No, he's back, maybe just wiped his eyes so I couldn't see. Tears don't flow without gravity.

"Haven't seen my mother and father since I was twelve, Cristina. Senior physicists with TKP, and when their project failed they disappeared. I think they wanted it to fail. It was something bad. I don't know. My counselors always told me I had a clean slate. Maybe I did. Anyhow, made a few mistake of my own. Put into what they call a glass box." He chuckles and shakes his head. "Do you know what that means? I sat at a desk and did nothing for ten hours a day."

"And you couldn't refuse?"

"Not unless I wanted to disappear too. Mandated to some hole. I want a challenge, a life not wasted."

"You got one."

He's thinking.

"Question. Eighty thrusters all fail the same way. Is that right?"

"That's essentially what we're looking at."

"What are the odds they all just happened to break?"

"It's not a unit failure, that's clear," Eric says. "Unit failures we can handle. The working thrusters would just run for a longer duration."

"The common thread is the GNC that sends the signal to start."

"No, the GNC tells the embedded control system on each thruster to initiate the sequencer program. And they *were* tested as a system."

"What we need to do is consider the difference between the test and the result we see now. There has to be a difference."

"There is no difference."

"How does the sequencer decide if the thrusters are running?"

"The most direct way possible. The actual measured thrust. And there is thrust!"

"You accounted for the effect of weightlessness? And vacuum?"

Another snort. "Do I look that stupid?"

"What's the difference, Eric? What's the difference between then and now? You're right, I'm no engineer. But you are. You didn't want the glass box. But accepting that nothing can be done is like putting yourself back in that glass box, isn't it? You didn't want them to do that to you, so why do it to yourself?"

✳

The sun shifts to the left side and a yellow beam shimmers across a storage locker. The spacecraft isn't holding a specific orientation with respect to the universe. We're leisurely turning end over end, fifteen or twenty minutes per rotation.

Back to waiting. The absorbency thing burns, smells too. Shuko is the only other person awake. He studies his panel as if striving to find something else wrong. Like me, trying to fix things everything by himself. His face is empty; he's angry, afraid, and exhausted, all at the same time.

I doze.

Five quick pops jerk my seat to the right. I whip off my mask. The sunbeam is gone and the control center is darker than I've ever seen it.

That GNC voice again. *"Maneuvering in three, two, one."*

Eric running a test?

"Thrusters on."

A faraway buzz. The gentle push, but this time it doesn't stop. The seat exerts gentle pressure against my back.

Shuko blurts, "Is this good?"

"It's good!" I answer. The nav panel shows a steady 0.05 G force. "Very good!"

I squeeze the bump from my rosies, then my electrolyte drink in my thigh pocket. Suddenly my arms are weak and my fingers tremble. Time to drink. Sleep, too. And something to eat, anything at all. Then pee. So much to do. I let out a short, point-less laugh and touch the rosies again.

Mikki's awake. "They fixed it? What took so long?"

Eric sounds like a different man. "All spacecraft, listen up. Your local sequencer will be running your thrusters for approxi-mately ten hours. There's some weight returned due to the accel-eration. Be careful when you move around because it will take practice."

That's it? Did the problem just go away on its own?

Indra announces, "Eric found the solution, but he's too modest to brag."

"For the curious," Eric continues, "I'll explain the snag with the thrusters. Your nav panel displays the local time at our land-ing site. The seconds, minutes, and hours look like Earth time, but they're not Earth time. One solar day on Earth lasts exactly twenty-four hours, because an hour is defined as exactly one twenty-fourth of a solar day."

Paige mutters, "The thrusters failed because they couldn't tell the time?"

"One solar day on Mars lasts twenty-four Earth hours plus thirty-nine minutes and several seconds. A day on Mars is about three percent longer than an Earth day. We can't use Earth hours on Mars or we'll slip behind and after a couple of weeks the sun would be setting at five in the morning. Therefore, those seconds you see on your panel are Mars seconds, each imperceptibly longer than an Earth second."

Shuko asks, "That almost killed us?"

"I wouldn't put it like that," replies Eric. "It just presented an unexpected challenge. The TMI thrusters are from a fifteen-year-old Chinese design. They work exceptionally well. Trouble is, their control system uses Earth seconds. Our GNC uses Mars seconds. When the thrusters fired, the acceleration fell behind the required curve by just a hair, generating a false misfire inference."

Shuko lets out a long sigh.

"I edited the TMI kernel to run on Mars-length seconds and mirrored the changes to the other four spacecraft. Your trans-Mars stage is on Mars time and synced with your GNC."

Shouts, hoots, and applause come over the speaker. "Terrific job, Eric," I tell him, partly to remind him of my existence. Do I get any credit?

Apparently, no.

With the thrusters running, the control center acquires a definite up and down direction. The seats are horizontal and the access hatch to the hygiene compartment is on the floor. My body weighs only a couple of kilos so it's simple to drop straight down.

The principle is self-explanatory, at least for the liquid event. There's a soft rubber receptacle for each person, the female devices shaped like a curved oblong cup. It has to be pushed into the end of a flexible hose. A gentle suction makes the activity reasonably clean. I use the hose to vacuum the inner layer of my absorbency pants. Disgusting, but dry enough for now.

Paige finds food. One of the lockers holds an assortment of pre-packaged meals. Regular hot meals will be printed, but the equipment has to be unpacked and set up.

Ryder is still unconscious. Mikki strokes the square bandage on his head. Those two knew each other before the hospital, they had to. Alison is awake but groggy. I give her a fruit bar and guide her to her bunk. The com is alive with people exchanging names, places of origin, academic backgrounds. We set up a mini-table, maybe a meter square, by clipping it into place between the nav and warning panels.

I'm learning the names of the other spacecraft and who's where. *Independence. Constitution. Resolute. Endurance.* Jessica Eagan on *Resolute* announces it's possible to see Mars if we look almost directly upwards against the direction of thrust.

Paige and I are more interested in the crescent Earth. It's in the downward direction but not directly under the TMI, so I can still see it from the window near my seat—a sliver of majesty floating in a black void. I can cover the whole world with two fingers. She squeezes my shoulder, pulls me to the opposite side of the control center, and points upward toward a pinkish star—Mars.

I have to state the obvious. "That's a really small target."

Shuko beckons us to the nav panel. Our velocity is fourteen kilometers per second and increasing. And there's something new:

ESTIMATED ARRIVAL PROTONILUS MENSAE PM1
09:22:00 PCT 3 GEMINI 54

Exact and to the minute!

The lure of rest overcomes all else. The sleeper is quieter than the control center, just the soft purr of air flowing from a ventilation duct blended with Alison's snores. There's a mesh hamper for the absorbency pants. I transfer the rosies to a clean flight suit and edge into the other bunk. My tiny body weight is just enough to hold me against the cushion. A gentle current of air sweeps my face.

Lights out.

I need to sleep, but my mouth fills with thin fluid.

Try to sleep.

But the fireballs come back, more and more fireballs. Thunder. The world is shaking to pieces.

Orange and black churning together. Hideous.

Death.

Wipe it out. Relax. All is well. The vibration from the thrusters is a guarantee. The system works.

David. Dr. Ordin. Zach. The people standing in the corridor looking at us as we rushed to the rocket. What happened to them? So much going on since then. Forget it, nothing I can do. Hide it for now.

The Lord is my shepherd.

Why did someone write those words inside the airlock? It hurts to think of it. I'll wash or scrape it away as soon as possible.

Paco, the hospital, a piece of paper in his fingers.

The Lord is my shepherd.

Paco, dead.

Everyone, dead.

Bile gushes up my throat. I flick the light and fumble for the sickness bag. I left it in the old flight suit! I pop out of the bunk, grab the bag and retch into it. Nothing but gruel, and it burns my throat. I gag again and a bit more comes out.

How many explosions and fireballs today?

Should be just one, when *Enterprise* blew up.

I get back into the bunk and shiver. The fireballs come back the instant I close my eyes. Booster firing. A tremendous detonation directly below, seconds after launch...

Of course. Tons of methane and oxygen remained in the ship.

The whole ship exploded.

David never worried about Harmony capturing them.

I see it all again; six fireballs below us, one for each ship.

More puking. It hurts, and this time nothing comes up but bitter spit.

I slam my palm against the side of the bunk. Can't hold it back any longer.

"Dead!"

I bash my fist into the side panel. "They're dead. They're all dead!"

Paco.

Zach the orderly.

Dr. Ordin.

David.

Kim.

Dr. Mike. Thumbs up. Now he's dead.

I scream one last effort to keep the tears inside, but I lose the battle. I sputter and sob and I can't help yelling, "Dead, dead, dead, dead!" My fist punches the bunk with each word.

Nathan, Isabel, Dottie.

Sorrows old and new explode from me, unrestrained.

Someone's here, and close to me—two people. Shuko, with something in his hand. Impossible to see through the tears.

Mikki takes my shoulders. "I've got you! You're okay. Grab on to me."

I wrap my arms around her and cry. There's only pure release, and the soft vibration of the thrusters. I tell Mikki, "They're all dead. Every one of them. And they knew they would die."

Everything's out of me. I barely feel the pinch from Shuko's needle.

EIGHTEEN

An artificial voice sings, *"Thruster shutdown in three, two, one."*

My forehead smacks against the cool bunk wall. It punches me back into full awareness without hurting much. I float in the middle of the sleeper, feet dangling in midair. The vibration is gone; the thrusters have stopped. Ten hours already?

The hum from the life support appliances in the equipment bay leaks into the control center. Somebody nested the seats together so there's more room. Paige sits at the fold-out table, her butt held down with a lap belt. She floats food in the air and chomps it into her mouth like a goldfish.

Alison tosses me a protein bar. "Feeling better?"

I nod despite a minor headache. The hatch to the hygiene compartment is closed and the OCCUPIED light glows orange. I might need another diaper.

The Earth and moon are two slender crescents, arcs of delicate color too perfect to exist. We've flown 764,300-something kilometers, the last two digits changing too fast to read. The hundred-kilometer digit increases to four and goes up again every three seconds. Our velocity is just over thirty kilometers per second, three times faster than Apollo. What do you think of that, Buzz Aldrin?

A sleeper door slides open and Shuko blinks against the light. He tucks his legs against his chest and uses his arms to launch himself directly to the table.

"Smooth move!" remarks Paige. "Been practicing?"

The three of them eat with their heads pointed in three different directions. An eggy scent comes through my nose clog—yes, they have the printer going. The menu shows hash browns, toast, scrambled eggs, roti canai, and more, all of it counterfeit-style food created from powders, pastes, and oils. Fake, but widely considered tasty.

Alison tells me while chewing, "Try the oatmeal with cinnamon."

I ask Shuko, "How's Ryder?"

His eyes dart to the hygiene compartment. Ryder's in there. I lower my voice. "What do you think happened? I mean, when we opened the breakers."

Shuko sips from a juice pouch. "Simple anxiety attack. Understandable, don't you think?"

"If you say so. How can we stop it from happening again?"

Paige giggles. "Sing a song!"

We girls laugh, and I'm not even in a laughing mood. Alison says, "I thought it was a perfect song." We hug, an inept, unsymmetrical space hug.

Shuko clears his throat, then whispers, "I don't know how to prevent another panic attack unless I shoot him up with benzo on a daily basis."

"What if we have another emergency? He's bigger and stronger than any of us. He needs to be calm until we land."

"Sedated but awake for the next six weeks? I can't recommend it. There could be issues of drug tolerance, dependence, withdrawal. Probably some degree of cognitive impairment such as degraded memory and concentration. I don't think one anxiety episode justifies that treatment."

"I didn't intend it as a punishment."

"I didn't intend to imply you did."

"Scratch the idea. We'll find another way."

"Tie him up," Alison suggests. We laugh again, tres niñas sharing a giggling fit.

The hygiene hatch swings open. Ryder. No bandage on his head. Our eyes meet. He mumbles, "Don't go in there."

I try to think of something to say but Shuko tugs at my sleeve. "While you were asleep I researched the reason one of our oxygen generators keeps shutting down."

Paige jerks her head. "What?"

I don't care about Ryder anymore. On the warning panel—
red text!

> *ERROR 415: OXYGEN GENERATOR UNIT TWO*
> *HIGH ELECTROLYTE TEMPERATURE SHUTDOWN*
> *UNIT ONE IN BACKUP MODE 11:37:41 PCT 17*
> *Taurus 53*

Shuko grabs my sleeve again, which I hate. "Eric says the
same problem is happening on all five spacecraft. Possibly just
a sensor issue. Every trans-Mars stage has three independent
oxygen generators. When the primary unit shuts down, a standby comes on automatically."

"Does the standby get the alarm too?"

"After about an hour. Then the primary takes over again.
There's a third unit as a spare."

My stomach's rumbling and my bladder's ready to burst, so
this oxygen thing has to wait. I tuck legs and try to fly to the
hygiene compartment hatch à la Shuko, but I miss and Ryder
grabs my ankle to redirect me.

Using the space shitter isn't as complicated as I feared.
Waste gets sucked into a tank, and two jets of warm water clean
you-know-where. What makes everything difficult is the fact my
body refuses to stay in place. I'm constantly drifting, rotating, or
both, so any sort of activity requires anchoring with one hand or
using both feet hooked around a solid object. The hygiene compartment does have two foot straps, but I don't notice them until
I'm done.

Dealing with Ryder will be even tougher. I won't ignore
what happened. I won't blame him, either. I'll occupy him. And
I'm going to get it over with now.

The three other girls fuss over Ryder, feed him samples of
what they consider luscious food, and Alison even massages the
back of his neck. I twist into position with my face centimeters
from his. "Come talk with me."

"This exact minute?"

I nod my head toward my sleeper. He delivers a dramatic
sigh, but he follows. I slide the door shut.

Ryder swallows his food. "First of all, I apologize for going
ape-shit yesterday."

We're up against each other, wedged between the bunks and the lockers. But where else can we get privacy? The equipment bay is too noisy for conversation.

"Let's put that behind us. It was a crazy day. What do you know about the oxygen generator shutdowns?"

"I'm aware of the problem." He's close. No question, peanut butter and coffee with his breakfast.

"At the hospital you said you were an applied engineer. I want you to find out everything you can about the shutdowns. Talk to Eric—"

"Shuko's already done that."

"Talk to him again, one engineer to another. This is your priority today."

He bows at the waist just like the Harmony jefes do to each other. A dig at me?

"On top of that, I'm putting you in charge of training. We have forty-one days. Every minute is precious. We have to be ready for any emergency that can happen."

"Well, there's David's eight-day syllabus. It's in the knowledge base."

"That's a start. We need more."

"His work is fairly comprehensive. I don't think we need to add anything."

"Are you an engineer or not?"

"Bachelor in Applied Synthesis Technology, Jiao Tong, fourth in my class."

"Then you should agree we need to adapt David's plan for the fact we're in flight, and we don't have the benefit of his experience. Can you put together some kind of training plan for everybody?"

"It would take time. There's something like seven hundred training vids."

"You'll have help. We need to get everyone organized."

He averts his eyes. "Maybe we should ask what the others have to say."

My throat closes. Keep it rational, don't make it personal. "This isn't up for a vote. Our lives depend on a thousand pieces of equipment working when we need them to, and we already know they screwed up at least twice. And they didn't have time for testing."

"What do you expect from me, exactly?"

"First, we need to understand why the oxygen generators shut down. Then we need to prioritize topics and procedures we should learn first. For example, the syllabus covers BioSuits. We can start there."

"Why worry about BioSuits now?"

"Not worry, preparation."

"They're useless until we land."

"We don't know that. There's always the unexpected."

"I think David and the rest of the senior engineers anticipated what we need to know better than we can. So relax."

Let him save face. "Don't you agree we need to at least catch up before we relax? I want everyone's suit fitted and vacuum tested over the next three days. And starting tonight we'll adjust our sleep schedules to correspond with nighttime at the landing site."

"Cristina, I didn't want to say this, but you put me in this spot. You're an academy kid."

I get a rush of nausea, plus a weird sensation of being upside-down. "I'm not a kid," I stutter. I sound stupid but I can't stop. "I completed eighty-eight units—"

"All of it academy. You have no professional-level education. You can be flight director, Cristina, that's okay by me. Keep in mind that Mikki, Paige, and myself, we're certified engineers."

I search for words. "But no experience with anything real…"

Ryder shakes his head slowly. "Sure. No experience. Unlike you. I'll plan a new syllabus because you're probably right about keeping us busy. We don't want people to have enough idle time to think about what they got themselves into."

NINETEEN

Ryder breaks his promise, but that's not the worst crisis, not even close.

Something has gone wrong with Paige. She was fine that first morning; she laughed with us, made jokes, flirted with Ryder, had fun floating food into her mouth. Maybe the oxygen generator errors got to her. Plus, as Ryder said, she didn't keep busy so instead thought too much about what she had gotten herself into.

Paige was at the window when we couldn't reset the breaker, just gazing out at the beautiful Earth growing smaller and smaller.

Now she does nothing but sleep and cry, occasionally whimpering, "What have I done? Oh, no. Oh, no. What have I done?"

Nobody can comfort her. We feel less and less like trying.

We're all drowsy. My nose is congested. Without gravity we nod off all the time, even after getting several hours' sleep. Genuine rest is difficult; imagine trying to sleep with sparks flashing inside your eyelids. Just cosmic rays, Shuko assures us. High-energy atomic nuclei from the supernova of massive stars. They stimulate our optic nerves and generate the illusion of streaking white embers. Maybe that first night I was too tired to notice.

Night? We're back in the Ninth Circle; nothing distinguishes day from night. Without sunrise and sunset, the GNC clock is meaningless.

People are awake, so it might be our biological morning. No one else in the control center except Mikki. I ask, "Is Ryder up?"

"In more ways than one." She jerks her thumb toward Ryder's sleeper. Muffled giggles come from behind the door. Alison's giggles.

All I can say is, "Yeah," followed by a useless, "Sure, okay." He's exactly the type. The control center is suddenly more cramped. How long do we all have to live together in this tiny place? Barely four days and it feels like four weeks. Six weeks will feel like, what?

Ryder hasn't even tried to talk to Eric about the oxygen generators. At least he studies the problem once in a while, or maybe he's just a good faker. I'm going to have to do it myself.

Shuko and I take turns monitoring the oxygen tanks. They're always at upper ninety-percent charged, so maybe Eric was right. Triple redundancy, extreme low probability of systemic failure. After weeks of this I'll at least know how to talk like an engineer.

Every spacecraft can see a vid of the control deck of any other spacecraft, or every spacecraft, any time we want. For a while I hallucinated we could do vid training sessions for all thirty of us at once. But no, that's not going to happen.

People don't have the Stream to tell them what to do. So they do whatever they want. What they *don't* want to do is train and learn.

What do they want to do? Everything else.

Sleep, especially, and of course plenty of echar un polvo, as Dottie called it. The boys have quite a selection, and people pair up and even squeeze three into cramped sleepers with two small bunks.

Not on *Liberty*, not yet.

We can watch or read millions of vids and books, and that's what everyone pretty much does when they're not sleeping or screwing. Most of the material was hidden away by Harmony years ago, and now we can see any of it any time we want. The vids go back over a century, so I can find out how people lived when Paco and Victor were small. Alison and I watch a few minutes here and there of extremely old vids from the 1950s and 1990s. It's incredible how people lived their lives, bold and confident, without agonizing over Scores or the Stream.

We'll get there.

I still can't believe it. No one watching, no one listening.

No one with any power over us *cares* what we say and do.

If we want to know something or see something, we just find a flatscreen and get what we need. We're back in ancient times in that regard, but that's how *Liberty* and the other spacecraft are set up. It worked fine for all those people in the old vids.

No spotters, no autosystems. I could read anything, see anything, and no one would know it.

It's chaos. It's strange.

If we had infinite time there'd be no reason for concern, but we don't have infinite time. Or food. We have seven hundred days' worth of calories, not counting emergency rations, which we shouldn't be eating—but we're eating them anyhow. We get three menus a day, and the printer makes whatever we pick, but no seconds. I found out it lets me, and only me, reduce the portions and even cancel meals. The instructions say that future selections will vary depending on past selections. The number of food choices will probably become fewer as the printer uses up stock.

I try to set an example by studying the tech manuals and procedures and asking the engineers questions, but no one cares. They don't know the answers anyhow.

Ryder says he's working on our training syllabus, but I seriously doubt it. Shuko? He's an inexperienced physician. I could do a better job of it myself. But the real issue isn't lack of a formal program, it's lack of motivation.

Where's that motivation supposed to come from? From me? I tell people to complete specific training modules, and they don't bother. What am I supposed to do? Come up with some Autoridad-style punishments? Print my own little swarm of spotters and hit people?

There's a simple text feed where anyone can post a message and add comments. This is an efficient way to find out what's on everyone's mind. Shuko's medical colleague Blair Rizzo is dispensing her version of shab. People insult and threaten each other, usually when they're on different spacecraft. Lots of book and vid recommendations. Music, too.

Darien on *Constitution* mentions there's a tremendous amount of technical knowledge we need to ingest over the coming weeks, but he adds there's plenty of time to do that. He's a physicist from San Diego with a concise manner of expressing himself, so I guess he knows best.

People complain they can only see a few stars from the windows. I've been watching the Earth and moon shrink every day. Both are just slivers against the black, too small to make out any features. Why bother to look anymore?

A couple of fights have broken out on *Constitution* and *Endurance*. Reddish-blue facial bruises, one broken nose.

Abby on *Endurance* wants to know if it's possible to somehow turn around and get back to the Earth. The answer is no.

Jürgen hasn't posted a word. But people ask about him. Tess on *Independence* throws out vague hints that Jürgen's planning the details on how to build a city on Mars.

During the brief minutes I knew him, Jürgen struck me as fully mature and level-headed. Why hasn't he spoken to us yet, especially when we need some unity and reassurance?

Jürgen should communicate with us. As soon as possible.

Maybe every day.

Ideally every day.

I pull into my sleeper and flick the vid over to the control center on *Independence*. They're eating what looks like dinner, while we finished breakfast a couple of hours ago. Everyone's out of sync.

Jürgen's face is puffier than I remember, his eyes squinty, and the shorter hair makes him look older. "I can take a very short break from my work to speak with you," he tells me while chewing. He enters his own sleeper so we can have some quiet.

"How are things, Cristina?"

He knows my name; the screen doesn't show that. I know maybe half of everyone's names.

"We're adjusting. Like everybody, I guess. There's something—"

"You were on my grandfather's ship. Or rather, he put himself on your ship."

Drawing a blank.

"Dr. David Chao."

I guess he can see the shock on my face because he smirks, and looks much younger.

"Dr. Chao selected you, Cristina Flores. My grandfather's judgment is widely considered unassailable. Don't let him down."

"Well, no, I won't," I sputter. A mindless thing to say. "You look like him."

Still smirking, patiently waiting for me to say something intelligent.

"He was a brave and dedicated man. A wonderful teacher. I wish I had known him longer. Don't *you* let him down."

Smirk gone. A couple of solemn nods. "What's on your mind, Cristina?"

"I think people have a lot of confidence in you. You're the one who convinced a lot of them to be here."

"I had some help."

For a second that draws a blank, too. *I was the one who helped him the most.* So much has happened since that short time in the hospital basement, the room full of scared teenagers and plastic chairs and a row of stern-faced oldies.

"Keep convincing us, Jürgen. That's what I'm asking you to do. Don't stop. I'll help you this time, too."

His eyes tighten; now he's the one who doesn't know what to say.

"We need convincing to do the right thing, on a daily basis," I continue. "So much work, and every minute is precious. Right now we're a jumbled mess and getting worse. Everybody's going their own direction. Nothing's getting done."

"It's a major adjustment."

"Won't some discipline and focus make the adjustment go smoother? You're our best chance to get on track. Talk to us, motivate us, set out a formal program. Tell us what we need to know."

His gaze shifts all over. "I'm not sure exactly what you want from me, Cristina."

I want him to motivate us. First, I have to motivate *him.*

"You're a geologist? You're studying our landing area, right? Planning exactly what we're going to do?"

"Yes, resource access and development. That's all quite far in the future."

"Doesn't matter. It's an incentive. Fold us in. *Involve us.* Nothing will keep everybody going better than dreaming about what they're going to do on Mars. It's really all we have."

Lights go on inside his head.

It's working, so I press on. "It's the most powerful enticement I can imagine to keep everybody learning and guarantee we know enough by the time we land. And you're at the center of it—you're our geologist!"

The top of Jürgen's head fills the screen. He's thinking. Let him think.

"My grandfather was a team leader at JPL and Chēngzhăng. He could get people to work together in such a way the experience of individual specialists complemented what other specialists brought to the table. And he only worked with the best."

"He brought together *teams?*"

"Teams, yes."

The lights in his brain are flashing furiously. Both of us, really.

"Teams, Jürgen! That's it! Group us into teams. You know, like in fútbol. Challenge us. Are we good enough to be on your teams, teams exploring Mars? Who has learned enough, demonstrated the necessary knowledge, to join one of the teams making discoveries on Mars?"

"Teams," he repeats back, the word barely audible.

"Learn skills, be the best, the most knowledgeable, be part of a team. Everyone else stays inside and cleans the space shitter."

He nods. It's an idea. What's he going to do with it?

TWENTY

Eric thrives in this crazy environment. Or maybe he just likes to talk.

"I got housekeeping instructions to put out," he grumbles on a vid screen. "Don't eat the packaged food! It's supposed to be for emergencies. Your printer does three meals a day and that's enough, given that we need fewer calories when we're not under gravity. Our food will last if we don't waste it. We'll be the first to grow food on another planet. Things can go wrong."

Things are already going wrong. Endless oxygen generator high temperature shutdowns. It worked okay for a while, now it's all going bust. Eric doesn't care; he yaks on about the TW9 component printers. "They work best under lunar gravity or higher, so we'll use them in flight only if we need to make replacement parts. We have enough garments in our lockers. Once we build up stock resources on Mars, we'll print new clothes."

We gather for breakfast, Paige included. Four vid screens show the respective control decks from the other spacecraft, with the heads of about a dozen people all pointing in different directions. The sight doesn't bother my stomach anymore.

I try to listen to Eric as I wait for my food to print. Too much variety on the menu! Toast with butter and jam, oatmeal, tea with lemon and sugar, six minutes. Should be almost ready.

Paige stops playing with floating water balls long enough to deliver her opinion to Eric. "These coveralls aren't even a week

old and look how filthy they are. Do you know how stinky we're
going to be six weeks from now?"

Eric thrusts a round orange object in front of the vid. "See
this? We can be less stinky by observing basic personal hygiene.
Everyone can wipe themselves over, twice a week. Pay special
attention to pits and privates."

Paige and Alison groan and make faces. Mikki uses a pair of
tongs to withdraw a beige container from the printer and she gin-
gerly directs it toward me. Steam escapes from three tiny holes.
The toast is in strips and it looks like real toast. The taste...bet-
ter than real. Deliciously buttery—even the browning is flawless. I spread strawberry jam and sample the oatmeal. I can get
used to this.

"One more thing," Eric says. "Some of the life support gear
needs daily and weekly maintenance. Your shipboard instructor
probably didn't assign who would do what. Therefore, each
flight director is responsible for delegating maintenance."

I swallow oatmeal. "Eric, what about these oxygen generator shutdowns? Are you looking into the cause—"

"Right, Cristina. Jürgen is aware and we're watching the
units closely."

"Is he going to—"

"Jürgen will take care of everything."

He's bringing my headache back. I wave my arms near
the screen so Eric can't ignore me. "Hey! I'm talking about our
oxygen!"

The others glance in my direction. Yes, I'm okay. But my
words go unnoticed. Tess comes on vid, upside down. "Jürgen
Morita will now address us," she proclaims. "Hold your questions until he's finished."

Jürgen's crisp voice snatches everyone's attention. He's in
speaking mode. That sly smile is back; he's about to share
a secret.

"Is there anyone among us who harbored doubt in their
hearts as we began this journey from a windswept sea? Just for
a moment, did you think we might not make it?"

"Never!" whispers Mikki. Alison giggles. Their faces come
alive, even Paige.

"We've chosen to participate in an historic adventure. The
events of our lives over the next weeks and months will be

chronicled among the most celebrated achievements of human history."

Historic adventure? Celebrated achievements? So the lavish language at the hospital wasn't just to persuade volunteers. The power remains potent—everybody gets hyper-energized once Jürgen starts talking.

Me, not so much. But I'm listening, too.

"Eric Rahn, our chief systems engineer and flight director aboard *Constitution*, reported to me this morning all five spacecraft are functioning as expected. We're on course for landing at Protonilus Mensae. Along with our scientists, engineers, and medical doctors, we're fortunate to have in our company two experienced project supervisors: Senuri Kumar, flight director aboard *Endurance*, and Vijay Mehta, flight director aboard *Resolute*."

Cheers erupt from the com. Why am I clapping for two people I've never met? When Jürgen expects something, people go along—for any reason or no reason at all. Call it the Jürgen Effect.

"I've tasked Senuri and Vijay to organize teams for our initial projects during the first ninety days after landing. We have an aggressive schedule to plant and harvest crops early on so we can take maximum advantage of the three hundred and fifty-day spring and summer seasons. We'll also construct shielded living quarters and move in before summer is over."

More shouts and claps. That part makes sense! But still nothing about the oxygen generators.

Jürgen cuts through the noise. "I have a key announcement to make. Shortly after we arrive at Protonilus, I will select three individuals to join me exploring our landing area out to a radius of fifty kilometers. I call this a Discovery Team, and our first goal will be to identify nearby mineral deposits. We can get water and other vital materials from the regolith, but we need to identify sources of copper, iron, zinc, chromium, tungsten, and nickel to provide printer feedstock for construction components. Candidates for Discovery Teams will be selected based on completion of training knowledge and demonstration of competence in equipment operation and standard procedures. This is your direct path to adventure."

Alright, so he's trying it. Will it work?

Half the Main Control Panel displays a spectacular panorama of steep hills in gray and reddish-brown tones. My skin tingles; it's a view from a probe in orbit, but our first detailed glimpse of the peculiar place that will be our home.

"Protonilus! Don't be worried by the unfriendly look. We chose fretted terrain over the smooth regions because all these glacier-carved cliffs, mesas, and valleys expose a wide variety of geologic resources." A green pointer waves across the image. "See these rocks along the bluffs? That's called a lobate debris apron. We know there's water ice just under the surface near these aprons—millions of tons, available year-round, vital to the long-term progress of our civilization."

Ryder claps his hand once and rubs the back of Mikki's neck. Yeah, they knew each other.

The pic switches to a different view of craggy knolls and peaks. Jürgen zooms in on a pale streak in a beige gully. "This is a silica-rich patch less than four kilometers from our landing site, possibly the result of hot spring water or steam coming into contact with volcanic rock. We may be looking at an environment favorable to microbial life, life that may have evolved to thrive beneath the surface. Based on Earth analogs, hydrothermal systems like these favor preserving organic biosignatures, evidence of past or even current life forms."

The vista disappears. All eyes snap back to Jürgen. "We're flying thirty kilometers per second toward an entire world that has never before been explored by humans. While you're getting past the discomfort of our initial adjustment period, remember this—something incredible is waiting to be discovered."

Ryder throws both arms into the air. "Wahoo!"

"One more announcement," Jürgen says. "Many challenges lay ahead, especially given that our training time was cut short. I'm appointing one of our flight directors to supervise our technical preparation and act as a Sergeant-at-Arms to ensure steady development of our systems knowledge."

I know where this is going. He's appointing Eric to oversee training. But what gives Jürgen the right to appoint anyone at all?

"Our Sergeant-at-Arms will be Cristina Flores."

What? Face burn as it hits me. Ryder reaches out and slaps his palm against my right shoulder. Alison blurts, "Lucky you!"

Jürgen stares at me, the sly smile returned. There's a quiet, and he's still staring. Then I get it: they're waiting for my response.

"I appreciate your confidence in me. We're going to train, yes, we're going to learn a lot, because we want to get out there and explore and build. But what about the oxygen generator shutdowns? Shouldn't that be our priority?"

Heads twist. Mikki blows out a big long breath, spreading the sweet scent of blueberry empanada across the control center.

✳

Sergeant-at-Arms. What does that mean?

A lot of the old warfare vids have soldiers called the *sergeant*. The sergeant is a tough, no-nonsense hombre. What's Jürgen trying to tell me? And who's working on the oxygen generator problem? We need to talk, but he's suddenly impossible to reach. Which is ridiculous, because where could he go?

Tess serves as his shield. "Jürgen cannot conference with you today."

"You said to hold questions until after he's finished," I remind her. "And he's finished."

She flicks her eyes toward her forehead. "It should be obvious Jürgen's not taking questions."

"I'm the Sergeant-at-Arms responsible for our training. He can't spare ten minutes for me?"

"Jürgen is an historic figure."

"What?"

"You heard me."

"Tell him to get his historic ass into his sleeper so I can talk to him."

Tess pouts, really her default expression, then disconnects. Not going to happen. Not today.

From behind me Paige whispers, "Jürgen is a visionary. We're lucky he's with us."

At least she's thinking positive now. Ryder somersaults twice. "Did he say he's gonna pick three people for this discovery thing?"

Mikki snorts. "I suppose you think he'll pick you."

He's still somersaulting. How can he do that right after eating? "Of course he's gonna pick me. I'm just wondering who the other two will be. I'll put in a good word for you, Mick."

"Me," Paige says softly. "Please pick me."

Alison shoves the last of her toast into her mouth and talks while she chews. "I wonder if Jürgen was the one who first thought of going to Mars."

"I didn't ask him, but it's possible. He's David's grandson."

They stare back at me with *are you joking?* faces.

"I can see the resemblance now," Alison says.

"He's a geologist, and the closer we get to Mars, the more important he's going to become. Don't forget, whoever gets to go on the Discovery Teams will be picked on the knowledge and skills they acquire between then and now. We all need to get to work because we don't want to be stuck in these plastic boxes forever."

Alison licks jam from her fingers. "I hope he talks to us every day. He makes me feel safe."

I don't feel safe. But there's one thing I can do. Time to act like a sergeant. I grab Ryder by the arm to stop his spinning. "Oxygen generators take priority. Let's determine our options."

We hit the technical documentation library, a monster with a thousand tentacles. The oxygen generator system—OGS for short—is just as complicated. The equipment is based on old Russian designs used on orbital spacecraft since the 1990s. Electricity splits water into hydrogen and oxygen, which is easy to do on Earth but tricky without gravity. The hydrogen is vented overboard, the oxygen compressed and piped into our reserve tanks inside *Liberty*. The troubleshooting section of the manual is twice as long as the normal operating section. But since the OGS units are inside the TMI stage, they can't be repaired.

Ryder rubs his eyes. "They're temperature-sensitive, so they cycle back and forth a lot. That's why we got three independent units."

"So what's the purpose of all the warnings?" I ask him. As if it could hear me, the panel flashes more red. Another high temperature shutdown on unit one, the third today.

And there's red on the nav panel too.

TMP OVERRIDE 06:47:11 PCT 22 Taurus 53

Our predicted landing time is gone. The override happened over three hours ago. If this is a problem, would Eric have informed the flight directors? Or is it another of those Jürgen-will-take-care-of-everything situations?

I twist Ryder's head toward the nav panel. "Isn't TMP the Trans Mars Program?"

He scans the information on the display, which isn't much. Our flight path and ETA are gone, too. He flicks the com to *Constitution*. "Eric, you awake?"

Eric's red-eyed image comes on vid. Ryder asks, "Did you know the whole nav program is on override?"

"Of course I do. I shut the TMP down because it was throwing out inconsistent data and I didn't want to risk that it would fire the thrusters and deviate from our course."

I pull myself closer to the panel so Eric can see me. "So the nav program is defective?"

"I didn't say that. Once again, there are errors yet to be analyzed. Until we understand the errors, I shut the program down as a precaution."

Ryder jostles against me and leans directly into Eric's vid, "You don't trust the nav system?"

Eric peers offscreen, as if watching someone out of view. "Darien knows the system better than me. Our initial TMP burn was perfect. That makes these errors hard to fathom. Until we understand what's going on, we're better off just letting the laws of gravitational trajectories keep us going in the right direction."

That's not good enough. "Let's get all the flight directors together, and Darien too, so we can figure out what to do. And Eric, are you looking into the OGS failures? We've been trying to understand what's happening since breakfast."

"Oxygen production is down only five percent off nominal. I'm going to edit everybody's tumble axis so the units spend more time in the shade, and that'll cool them down."

Mikki thrusts her body between mine and Eric's vid. "What happens if they crap out? We suffocate? They couldn't give us a supply of liquid oxygen?"

Eric shakes his head. "Too heavy once insulation and boil-off are factored. Compromises were made in order to maximize total payload to the surface. There wasn't any way to test the whole configuration in actual freefall."

I think the nav problem takes priority. One more question. "The GNC has an internal clock, right? Would that create these errors? Could this be related to the clock synchronization problem? Earth seconds versus Mars seconds?"

"No, because the GNC and the TMP always use Mars time. That's what caused the bug with the thruster acceleration sensors."

Ryder twists my sleeve. "What you said makes sense."

"Does it earn me an engineering certification?"

He laughs. "No, but I should have thought of it first. I'm impressed."

Peen!

＊

Alison doesn't doze off once all day. I'm supposed to be the sergeant, so I assign her and Shuko the learning modules covering the theory, maintenance, and repair of the carbon dioxide scrubbers and the Sabatier reaction equipment. She finishes all four related exams.

"You got perfect scores," I tell her. "That's a lot of material to absorb."

Her pale blue eyes shine. "If Jürgen sees my scores, I may have a shot for the first Discovery Team."

Jürgen, the motivator. How did he develop that talent?

Eric's idea to cool the oxygen generators actually works. No high electrolyte temperature shutdown warnings since noon, and a single unit runs in primary mode.

But I can't get the TMP situation out of my head. We had a perfect flight path. Now it's throwing errors? The documentation covers the nav panel interface with minimal detail on how the overall system works. Optical devices mounted on the TMI stage continuously sight celestial objects in order to derive our current position and velocity. The GNC—Guidance and Navigation Computer—is supposed to feed that data to the TMP so it can follow a narrow flight path that ends on first contact with the Mars atmosphere. The precise position, velocity, and time of atmosphere contact are critical.

The manuals say the GNC can run in simulation mode even with the Trans Mars Program in override. Why not try it? I make the request and the nav panel confirms and displays *FIXING POS-VEL* for a long minute, then *TMP INITIATED*, then, in red,

PM1 UNAVAILABLE

There's the stomach flutter, again.

PM1 is the term for our landing zone at Protonilus Mensae. What does it mean, *unavailable?* Can't be anything good. I pull myself across the control center to my sleeper. The instant I'm closed within the privacy of my bunk, I get Eric to come on vid. His eyes are now completely bloodshot, exactly like launch day.

"I put the GNC in sim mode," I inform him. "PM one unavailable?"

"It's simple," he answers. "That means we can't land on Mars."

TWENTY-ONE

I release two short, sharp breaths. "Eric! How the hell could that be?"

"Because the guidance system is lost!" he yells back. "It has no idea where we are! And maybe never did!"

"Darien agrees with this? Wasn't he checking?"

"Darien's sleeping."

"Get him up!"

"Don't tell me what to do, okay? He's asleep because there's nothing more he can check. He doesn't have the precision data to determine our true position."

"You have no plan at all?"

Eric squints at me. "Something malfunctioned with the GNC internal system clock. The whole ephemeris is useless. You suggested this might be related to the clock sync problem that caused the thrusters to shut down. I take back what I said earlier. You may be correct."

"We know for a fact this is caused by the second-length discrepancy?"

He rubs his eyes and takes a long time to answer. "No, we don't know that, not for a fact."

"Explain what you do know. Explain in English, because my brain is tired."

Another long pause. "The guidance computer has an extremely accurate built-in clock. It generates a time signal, basically a number that represents how many millisecs, thousandths of a second, have elapsed since the system first activated three weeks ago. The Trans Mars Program needs this time signal input to calculate our position and velocity accurately. Our flight path needs to be precise enough so we hit the edge of the Mars atmosphere at just the right angle."

"And what's that other thing? The ephemeris?"

"The ephemeris is like a database that knows the position of the Earth, the sun, and Mars in the future. The guidance computer derives our position and velocity by comparing the time signal with the relative positions of Mars or the Earth against a set of navigation stars."

"It uses the star trackers to get the relative position angle against the stars?"

"Correct. And you know what, Cristina? As of early this morning, the time signal...failed. It's all wrong. It's useless, which means the ephemeris is useless, which means the TMP has no idea where we are and won't ever again know where we are!"

"We know the nature of the beast. That's the first step toward a solution."

Eric just worked himself into a panic, again. His face is red and tiny bits of sweat fly off in different directions with every word. "You don't get it. We have *no time signal*. It won't work at all without that precise time input. We can't navigate."

"We find a way to produce our own time signal and feed that into the GNC."

"Cristina, if that were possible, I'd have done it by now."

"We'll find a way."

"Yeah, well, Jürgen reached a decision."

I pull my face closer to the vid screen. What does Jürgen have to do with any of this?

"Jürgen decided we're going to keep the trajectory we have," he continues. "Which, by the way, was nearly perfect when the TMP knew our position. The day before we land the GNC can optically range the Mars surface and derive our precise position and velocity so the TMP can do course corrections."

This is too much. "Jürgen decided, did he?"

"He did. Now get some sleep, Cristina."

"Jürgen's a geologist. Since when did he become a systems expert? Don't you and Darien know more than he does? We're wasting time! Show me these error messages. Get every engineer on the com right now, anyone who can contribute. To hell with Jürgen."

✳

The thin walls of the sleeper didn't muffle the conversation much. They know. Ryder has his arms around Mikki and Alison. Paige is wedged up against a window, arms folded, staring out into the blackness. Shuko peeks from his usual perch in the equipment bay, pale face framed by the access hatch.

I say to no one in particular, "So yeah, we have a problem."

"If we're going to die, tell us," Alison says, voice cracking and childlike. "I can't stand not knowing."

"Quit worrying, get back to studying," I growl at her, way too harsh. It's natural for her to wonder if studying or anything else matters anymore.

Vids activate across the main panel. Eric, Tess, and two other faces unfamiliar to me, both with Indian features. Have to start learning people's names.

But no Jürgen. Fine.

No one wants to speak first, so I begin. "Our guidance system doesn't have a time input, and without that it's lost. Eric, can you show us the error message?"

We squint to read the letters, Ryder resting his chin on my left shoulder.

60335 ALL DATUM OUT OF RANGE

I ask, "How do we know that's related to the time signal?"

"The ephemeris tells the guidance system where Mars and Earth should be, relative to the background stars, in order to hold our planned course. The GNC is looking at the time signal, and looking at Mars and Earth against the background stars, and nothing makes sense. It's impossible to calculate our position and velocity."

"You told me there is no time signal."

"I told you it's failed, it's wrong."

"But we do have a time signal of some kind?"

"It's wrong."

"Let's see it."

Eric flicks the display to our vids. It's a big number and doesn't look anything like a time. Seven digits, the last one increasing every second, plus three more digits to the right of the decimal place changing too fast to read. The first two digits are zeros. The total number of seconds since restart is fifty-five thousand something. Do the math, that's fifteen hours.

Eric's voice is more sleepy than agitated. "Basically it jumped backwards two billion milliseconds. It thinks it's about twenty-four days ago. That's why the positions of the planets can't help us navigate anymore."

I watch the numbers change. "All of a sudden, it jumped backwards. For no reason?"

"For no reason."

."Alright. So we generate another time signal, this one correct, and replace it."

"Not possible!" Eric responds. "It's got to be precise to the millisec. No way to sync it."

The flight director on *Resolute* comes closer to his vid screen. He has a narrow face with dark, passionate eyes. "Pardon me, sir. I am Vijay Mehta and my knowledge of space navigation is nonexistent. Tell us why we cannot sync it."

"Because we would have to know the exact standard time the ephemeris requires. An error of a few thousandths of a second would kill us."

Vijay has another good question ready. "How did it get synchronized to start with?"

"With the time signal from BeiDou, Harmony's space nav system."

"Can we re-sync the same way?"

Eric sighs. "We're over four million kilometers out. BeiDou doesn't reach this far. And if it did, we have no way of correcting the speed of light delay. No human being has ever been past the moon. We got a self-contained celestial navigation system. Once time synched, it doesn't need BeiDou anymore."

I don't know what else he's saying because I'm doing more math in my head.

"Eric!"

He shuts up. Everyone stares at me.

"You said the whole guidance system first activated three weeks ago—is that what you said?"

"About three weeks, yeah, because we tried to test as much as we could before the rockets were printed."

"And it's been running since then?"

"Perfectly, and then it failed today."

"So when it failed, when it failed..."

I can barely think. I'm trying to do the head math and talk at the same time. It's got to be one or the other. I close my eyes and there are the numbers.

Ryder rubs my shoulder.

"So when it failed, it jumped back to time zero, the instant it first synchronized with BeiDou?"

"It rolled back. To zero, yes. And it's not supposed to do that."

"These systems, they were used to guide spacecraft to and from the lunar villages. That takes, what, a couple of days? So no one ever ran this equipment continuously for three weeks."

"I don't see what difference that makes, Cristina. It should work forever. Self-contained celestial navigation computers have been guiding robot probes to the planets for a hundred years. Those trips lasted months, years!"

He said it should work forever.

No, it won't.

I scream the words, way too loud. Because I'm tired. "It can't run forever, Eric! It runs for two billion millisecs and that's the end!"

Eric blinks. "What are you talking about?"

"Look at the numbers! Do the math! It's been fifteen hours and eight digits are taken up already. It can't go beyond two billion millisecs—it runs out of digits! That's a little more than twenty-four days. After another twenty-four days it'll reset all over."

"Maybe you solved the puzzle," Tess says. "But that does us no good whatsoever. The time signal is still wrong."

"It's behind by the exact maximum value that can be stored in a ten-digit number."

"It's a thirty-two bit signed integer, Cristina. But Tess is right. Even if you've solved the puzzle, we can't kill the signal and replace it with another and then do the same thing in three weeks. It'd be off by a wide margin. Letting the TMP navigate with an incorrect time signal would be far worse than the prudent action, which is to keep the flight path we have now."

Ryder's mouth is centimeters from my ear and his voice makes me jump.

"But if we *could* replace the bad time signal with a correct signal, that would fix the whole mess for sure, right?"

"No, not right. You'd still need a signal optimizer that accepts the time as an unsigned integer, and we don't have one."

This is a start. "Signal optimizer? Speak English!"

Eric's face is replaced by a diagram of the Trans-Mars Injection stage, the fifteen-meter cylinder that supplies propulsion, power, water, and oxygen to each spacecraft all the way to Mars. A green pointer moves toward a round protrusion on the outer skin of the TMI.

"These are high-precision star trackers, a kind of sextant, three of them, a hundred and twenty degrees apart. They take continuous bearings to measure the angular separation between the Earth, Mars, the sun, and stars like Canopus and Vega. That data is fed into this device here." The pointer moves to indicate a box. "That's the brains of the system, the trajectory signal optimizer that derives our position in space to within one hundred meters, fifty times per second. That's the input to the GNC."

I enlarge the diagram. "We can't fix this because we can't reach it?"

"It would be difficult to access it physically," Eric says. "But that wouldn't do us any good. The problem is still the ephemeris. The ephemeris was hard-coded into the optimizer the day it was printed and it cannot be changed. That's a safety feature in case of power loss. And it accepts only a signed, thirty-two bit integer as the time signal."

A ruffle from behind me. Mikki pushes away from Ryder's arm and twists around. She ducks into her sleeper and slides the door shut. She's heard enough.

I ask, "This optimizer, do we have the pattern so we can print a duplicate?"

Eric's irritated face fills the vid. "I just explained to you— the ephemeris epoch uses a standard time format and it wouldn't work any better than what we already have."

"Can we edit the design?" The question was from the flight director of *Endurance*, a woman with a stern and impatient face that matches her voice tone. Her hair is longer than everyone else's and styled in a neat bun. Did she refuse the shipboard haircut?

Eric clinches his eyes shut. "That would be an enormous risk, Senuri. The sensible option is to follow Jürgen's decision and keep the course we have now."

I bang my palm against the screen. "Jürgen can't do math! And he's ignoring the fact we're supposed to have at least two mid-course corrections during the flight. We'll edit the logic to accept the different format and print another star tracker, then link it directly to the GNC. Eric, Vijay, Senuri, find out who can run your printers. We need a software engineer to modify the optimizer straight from the pattern."

Tess comes back, pout more pouted than usual. "Jürgen has to approve this."

I snap at her, "Why is that? Where is he now? Who appointed him supreme leader, by the way?" I turn to Alison. "How soon can you get one of our printers set up? Paige and Shuko can help you."

Eric snarls, "Cristina, do you realize this new tracker needs to be mounted outside? As in, outside the airlock, in vacuum? Pointing it out a window won't work because optical refraction will distort the sight angles."

Ryder asks, "Can we design and print a bot to go out the airlock and mount the tracker?"

"There's no time." I grab Ryder's upper arm. "Every hour could mean more propellent required to get back on course. No more delays! We need to configure a BioSuit right away."

That draws a grin. "I get to go out the airlock?"

Shuko shakes his head. Do I really want to trust Ryder outside the airlock?

"Not necessarily," I sputter. "You get my suit ready. I'm flight director. I'm doing this, just me."

But Jessica Egan on *Resolute* is an expert on the BioSuits and she nixes my plan. She calls me to her vid. Jessica's face has one of those permanent little smile looks, but her tone is firm. "As a rule, two are safer than one. Especially since the airlock is not designed for use in flight."

"Okay, Ryder will act as my safety checker."

Shuko frowns. What if Ryder panics again? But no one else volunteers.

The warning panel goes nuts again. It flashes another red message:

ERROR 419: OXYGEN GENERATOR UNITS ONE
AND TWO
HIGH O2/H2 DIFFERENTIAL PRESSURE

SHUTDOWN
UNIT THREE IN BACKUP MODE 11:11:29
PCT 22 Taurus 53

Which is a completely different error than the usual high electrolyte temperature shutdown.

Ignore it and focus. It's not an immediate threat. Oxygen still flows from the TMI into *Liberty*, and the O2 tanks are close to one-hundred percent full. The nav failure takes priority. If the GNC doesn't work, all the oxygen in the universe will only keep us alive long enough to know for sure we'll never land on Mars.

*

"We got a printer operating," Ryder calls from the equipment bay access hatch. "I loaded the pattern for the star tracker."

Jewel de la Bora on *Constitution* helps me organize. I remember her kindhearted face from the hospital. Today, we don't need nice; we need knowhow. "You're going to use three special cables. The optimizer pattern will be ready as soon as we're done testing a prototype with the new time format."

Alison sticks her head into the control center. "Tracker's printing. Done in eleven minutes."

Our BioSuits, helmets, and life support packs are stored in a hygiene compartment locker marked Active Compression Garments. Each suit is labeled by name because they're made to fit each person's body within a couple of millimeters. Is that why my body was scanned at the hospital?

I unroll the thin, silvery-white coveralls. Hundreds of blue threads crisscross everywhere—the shape actuators that will compress my skin and keep me alive in the ultra-low pressure of the Mars atmosphere.

Or, if need be, the vacuum of space. And it needs be.

Mikki does nothing but stare at the wall. "Cable fittings have to be checked for compatibility," I tell her. "The star tracker takes a sixty-four channel line connected to one of the hard plugs outside."

She opens her mouth to respond but the master panel interrupts with a chime from Tess. "Jürgen Morita will speak to us."

Jürgen wears his little grin—at a time like this. Everyone stops. Alison whispers, "He's going to tell us what to do."

What? Doesn't she already know what to do?

"I want to thank everyone for the work they've done on the guidance system. Eric and Darien briefed me on our options, and I've decided to keep our GNC's offline. Since we don't have the—"

"Hold it," I cut in. "You can't do that."

Mikki blows out her breath. "The expert speaks."

Jürgen presses his lips together. "Since we don't have the means to properly synchronize our time signal with the Earth standard, we'll keep our current course and make final adjustments when we're close enough to Mars for the GNC to laser-range—"

"No!" I can't control myself. "We're supposed to make mid-course corrections. We need a fully-functional guidance system to make those corrections!"

Jürgen does his thing. His silky-smooth calm spreads across the control center like a gentle musical note. "Cristina, I understand your feelings. But we can't allow our emotions to control our actions. You plan to stake our lives on modified components jury-rigged together. The tech manual doesn't allow that. We'll be safer if we trust the trajectory the GNC already calculated."

Where's Eric? If I yell into the com he'll hear me. "Eric! Did you explain to him—"

"Stop right there," Eric responds, voice on the edge of a slight tremble. "It's less of a gamble to keep the trajectory we know was good as of this morning—"

"You told me we can't land on Mars!" I'm too loud again, almost screaming.

"Yeah, I made the mistake of not trusting my better judgement. I'm correcting myself here. We're on a nominal trajectory right now. I made a mistake."

I twist toward Jürgen's vid. "What did you say to him?"

Eric snarls, "Any new optimizer we print has to be perfectly synced to Coordinated Universal Time on Earth, synced to within the GNC standard of one microsecond per year. Plus, you want to alter a proven design to use a non-standard time format that no one has ever used to successfully navigate a spacecraft. My engineering judgment is to stick to the trajectory the GNC gave us."

He's done.

But I'm not done, not even close.

I twist toward Shuko and Paige. "We need the airlock configured so I can open the outer hatch and mount the tracker. Get the procedure ready."

But they don't move. Something in their eyes tells me no.

"Eric makes a lot of sense," Paige whispers.

My blood races. This is worse than awkward. It's dangerous, and so wrong. "We're working around the problems right now," I say to Paige and everyone else. "We can do this if we try."

"I think we should listen to Jürgen," Alison tells us. "He's our leader."

They're convinced it's somehow safer to do nothing.

No words are enough for this mierda. "Really?" is all I can get out. Jürgen watches me on vid. We stare at each other. How weird to see him not talking. But he's being smart. They're on his side. He doesn't need to say a word, just wait for me to be Idiota with my mouth alone. "Here's what I think," I answer Alison, slowing my words so I sound sure, just as Jürgen does. "We left home because we had no control over our lives. We had to obey the Autoridad. But the Autoridad isn't here. We're in charge. All of us. The nav system is broken. It can be fixed, but there's not a lot of time." I turn back to Jürgen. "Let's vote on this. Let's talk this out and we'll all decide."

They say nothing. I get it. They believe him. They trust him. Jürgen is in charge. I'm alone, and I can't do anything about the tracker alone.

✳

I close myself off inside my sleeper. There's nothing else to do. I need about ten churros, a hug from Faye, and twelve hours of sleep.

There's a text, just two strange lines.

> *Alexis de Tocqueville: Nothing is more wonderful than the art of being free, but nothing is harder to learn how to use than freedom.*

Alexis de Tocqueville? Is that someone on one of the other spacecrafts? The text links to a request from Vijay Mehta, flight director aboard *Resolute*. He wants a private conference, no explanation why. I flick a response and Vijay appears in his own sleeper, his thin, chestnut-colored face simultaneously tough and delicate. Hair combed perfectly in place, even after weeks in space.

"Senorita Flores, thank you for meeting with me."

Fancy grammar! "Call me Cristina, okay?"

"Cristina, you made a simple and powerful statement earlier. We're in charge." He stops as if contemplating the best way to express his thoughts. "Our tiny clan is in disarray. No one is sure what to do."

"They know what to do. Jürgen screwed it up."

"Cristina, why do you think Jürgen appointed you training Sergeant-at-Arms?"

"Are you going to tell me?"

"I believe it is essential to our survival to establish a basis of fundamental law, a frame of government. Jürgen has been thinking along those lines, too. He appointed you as a step in that direction. Furthermore, I think there's a reason you haven't jumped into this duty with gusto."

"What gives him the right to tell us what to do? Who put him in charge?"

Vijay smiles, closes his eyes, and nods his head three times. "You are a free woman, Cristina Flores. You've possessed freedom in your heart all your life, I can see it. You learned to abide the rules of Global Harmony as a matter of survival. Now the pressure is released and your mind is running in every direction. Am I right?"

This hombre reminds me a bit of Paco.

"Why do they follow his every word?"

"Cristina, Jürgen is what we Hindu refer to as a bol bachan. A smooth talker. He can be inspirational, highly credible, charismatic. Such a person can accomplish much benefit, and much damage. He can be exasperating. Don't let that keep you from doing your duty."

"Such a brilliant leader, why doesn't he supervise technical training himself?"

"People need a guiding figure, but at the same time they don't want to be bossed around. Jürgen sees himself as a true leader, and as such he must be remote, hard to get to, almost like a god. But the supervisor, the Sergeant-at-Arms, watches everyone and makes sure we do what we don't want to do."

I fold my arms. "This supervisor won't be loved."

"Not loved, maybe even disliked, but perhaps respected. Jürgen may prefer them to be angry at someone rather than dwell on their fears."

"I'm supposed to be the new queen bitch?"

"You don't really want to be loved, do you, Cristina? Not the way Jürgen and most people want to be loved. Jürgen sees you can step on toes. Perhaps you enjoy doing so. This is a natural role for you. You are the Enlightenment, the reason for the first amendment."

What's the first amendment? "Is that why you wanted to talk, to convince me to get off my ass and do my job?"

"One minor reason, yes. More importantly, we need to begin thinking about a framework of self-government, a simple foundation of law."

Didn't David talk about making rules and law?

"Laws? We didn't come out here to make another Autoridad."

"Of course not. I meant a simple and concise basis for our leadership structure and our decision-making process. We need a single elected leader with specific powers, a small governing assembly, and a formal expression of our lawful rights and responsibilities."

"You've given this a lot of thought."

"Cristina, it has occupied my full attention for the past two days."

"How do you know about these things?"

Vijay's eyes soften. "I am a graduate of the National Law University at Jodhpur, and I am a member of the Bar Council of India. Although it may seem contradictory, the basis of liberty is the law. Harmony subjugated the United States before we were born. They eradicated almost all information on the history of the western nations that codified principles of due process and limited government. These ideas were never taught to you. Even where I come from, censored history must be laboriously uncovered...a dangerous undertaking. I made the mistake of discussing some wonderful ideas with a few trusted...friends ..." He looks downward as if embarrassed. "Cristina, I apologize for rambling like a crazy man."

What did he just say? "Our own government. A method to reach our own decisions instead of always looking to Jürgen. We need that now."

Vijay squints and pats his hair.

Our own government. Those words make my heart pound. "Our government. Not a new Autoridad. Our rights. Our responsibilities. Everything you said, plus a single leader elected by all of us."

He waves his hand. "Please do not jump ahead prematurely. This is a matter for we flight directors to consider over the coming weeks. Our survival must take priority."

"Survival! That's exactly why we need this now."

I let the words sink in. Any leader would be better than Jürgen; three critical problems so far, and Jürgen either ignores them or makes a poor decision and persuades everyone to go along. Vijay should lead, or maybe Indra. They won't want me, because I'm disliked and they consider me bossy.

"Cristina, we must learn to walk before we try to run. Sudden freedom requires adjustment."

"The framework has to come first, right? Because the framework has the process of election and other details, decided by everyone together, correct?"

His lips turn upward slightly. "Of course. The election must be fair and open so it will be accepted as legitimate. We have plenty of time to decide all this."

"What if we don't have plenty time?"

Vijay nods. "You're thinking of the navigation situation?"

"Will you help me?"

His eyes narrow; he doesn't like it much, but he understands.

✳

We do it together, Vijay and me. The rest of them shake their heads in bewilderment as I pull them into the control center. We contact the other spacecraft and set the vids so they can see both of us.

"We have a proposal," Vijay informs everyone solemnly.

I center my face on the screen. "Vijay has discussed some ideas with me that I think everyone should hear and consider."

Tess rolls her eyes. "Don't wet the bed."

Am I supposed to take the bait? Instead I get to the heart of it directly. "We propose to create a simple government framework to organize our efforts and our rights."

They don't utter a word, but they're watching. Every one of them.

Vijay says, "Cristina and I believe we should have a written foundation for decision-making, a charter."

"One elected leader with specified powers." I look to Vijay; am I saying this right? "And a governing assembly, and a formal record of our rights and responsibilities."

Jürgen overrides the vid. "I agree with all that. I've scheduled a meeting for that purpose, tentatively set twenty-eight days after landing."

I jab the button. "What gives you the power to make that decision? You're the flight director of your spacecraft, nothing more. These are decisions we should all make. Let's vote on this now, today, all of us together."

Jürgen opens his mouth but an Asian girl on *Independence* cuts him off. "Did you say *rights?*"

"I did!"

"As in, the right to criticize whoever I want?"

I glance at Vijay. He's grinning. "Yes!"

"This is Lane Jong. I think we should do that, the sooner the better. I'll tell you this now. I have the right to say what I want. I have the right to be heard. Are we going to do that?"

Ryder smiles. He even stops eating.

I answer her, "The right to criticize. That'll be our first guaranteed right."

My ears explode under the racket of everyone trying to talk at the same time.

TWENTY-TWO

It's called a deliberative assembly, and once unleashed no one can restrain it, not even Jürgen.

Thirty people can't speak and be heard at once, but they can try. Vijay's firm words cut through the chaos. "Order! We must have order, or we get nowhere!" The clatter diminishes and he continues. "Do I have consent to act as moderator? Yes? Then our first item is simply this. Do we wish to begin now or wait until after dinner?"

A rowdy explosion of "Now!" settles the question.

"Very well. I call us to order, our first deliberative assembly. We have earned this. So let us begin."

One blank doc appears on the net: Provisional Transit Charter. Someone mirrors a copy to the master panel of all five spacecraft. Vijay tells us, "The key is simplicity. It is not our purpose to write a comprehensive set of laws at this moment. Today we focus on the fundamental framework and a leadership structure."

Paige points a food bar at the panel. "We vote on this!"

I answer for Vijay. "That's a given."

Mikki stops chewing long enough to speak. "You better not be planning to run our lives!"

Vijay takes this one. "We all retain our sovereignty. The governing powers we grant will exist by the consent of the governed, which is all of us."

Sovereignty? I'll figure it out later. They're all screaming again. Everyone wants something, and they want to see it listed *right now*.

Our texts stay private from everyone else.

Nobody can stop us from meeting together and talking about anything we want to talk about.

We each decide what's the most important to us.

I touch the bump in my right chest pocket, the rosies. "Nobody can take our possessions away from us."

"No secrets!" barks a male voice. The stubble-coated face fills the vid from *Resolute*. "No lies, no hiding, we all have the right to know!"

"We can't very well protect against lying," Vijay responds. "All legislative docs and the minutes of all policy meetings shall remain public and unlocked."

"This so-called leadership structure, it better leave us alone. No one controls my life anymore!" says Jessica, also on *Resolute*.

Vijay tells her, "Our Charter will limit the powers of the government. We will be free from meddling, free to choose what's best for ourselves."

The idea of free expression comes up again and again. "Get that part in right now!" Paige shouts. "Nobody takes anything off the net, and we can say and write anything we want!"

"Freedom of expression," Vijay assures her, "Is now codified in Article One, Section One."

The Charter lists articles, each article organized into sections. Vijay supplies details for each suggestion, combining some points and responding to changes and disagreements as they occur. His mental stamina never falters. We take short breaks, but Vijay never lets up.

The Charter and the Articles within it apply to everyone. No special cases.

Once ratified, the Charter cannot be changed without holding a special assembly, a convention, and that requires a two-thirds majority vote.

There will be a single leader, a captain, elected or re-elected annually by vote. The captain can be removed by a two-thirds majority. The captain can appoint up to three assistants, each with specified duties, each subject to a two-thirds majority confirmation.

An order from the captain carries the weight of law, except that the captain alone cannot alter or violate the terms of the Charter.

The captain can issue an emergency decision at any time. But matters of planning that affect everyone will be addressed in an open forum, the time for which must be announced twenty-four hours in advance. Anyone can attend. We each get a minimum of ten uninterrupted minutes to voice our opinion.

The captain can call and oversee a disciplinary hearing for anyone accused of serious wrongdoing. No penalties or retributions can be dispensed unless a jury panel of five randomly selected people hear the facts of the case and agreed that a penalty is warranted. Neither the captain nor the assistants are eligible to sit on a jury panel.

How much longer will this take? We still need to vote on who will be captain. And that's probably a hopeless cause. They're going to elect Jürgen and we'll still have the navigation problem.

I drift off during a break and get a poke from Alison. "We're going to ratify."

Vijay's voice is going hoarse. "Flight directors, please confirm your entire complement is present and awake. We shall now consider ratification of our Charter. Does anyone have further points or items to bring to the floor? Does anyone seek a temporary moratorium before ratification, say twenty-four hours? A final chance to mull over the details?"

Ryder yawns. "Let's do it!"

"Before we take a vote on ratification, I would like to read a short preamble. Please note that our little union doesn't yet have a name. I don't think that will pose a problem, because when we arrive on Mars, we'll be the only organized group of beings present. So I hope."

Giggles from all over. Giggling is easier when you're exhausted.

"We citizens," reads Vijay, "in order to form an enduring and effective government, preserve justice, ensure tranquility, promote the general welfare, and to secure the sanctity of self-determination for ourselves and our descendants, do ordain and establish this Provisional Transit Charter of 22 Taurus."

No sound except for the vent fans. Ryder looks at me, then nods.

Scattered applause plus more heads nodding. Vijay instructs us to confirm our agreement by stating our full names. Everyone ratifies in turn, and when his chance comes, Jürgen pronounces his name in a serious tone. Ryder shouts his own name, whoops, and performs three midair summersaults.

"This Provisional Transit Charter is now unanimously ratified on this twenty-second day of Taurus, Mars year fifty-three. Under Article three, I will serve as temporary speaker until we elect our first captain."

Indra sleepily asks, "Right now?"

Someone yells, "Eat first!"

Ryder pulls the meal printer open. "Anything in the rules that says we can't eat and vote at the same time?"

Tess thrusts her face into the vid. "I nominate Jürgen Morita!"

That triggers more applause.

"Nominations will be heard when we re-convene," responds Vijay. "We will now break for thirty minutes. Consider your nominations carefully. This assembly is hereby adjourned until ten."

Ryder rubs my back, but the frown tells me it's not a congratulatory gesture. He nods toward the warning panel.

> OXYGEN GENERATOR 2 HIGH O2/H2 DIFFEREN-
> TIAL PRESSURE SHUTDOWN OXYGEN
> GENERATOR 1 HIGH ELECTROLYTE
> TEMPERATURE SHUTDOWN
> OXYGEN GENERATOR 3 LOW FLOW: 101 L/hour
> 22 percent nominal
> O2 AUTO-BLEED 18:52:01 PCT 22 Taurus 53
> O2 BANK 18.06 bar 90 percent nominal   43 hours
> remaining

I rub my eyeballs with my fingers. "This is almost three hours old."

Eric's already on vid. "Don't start screaming over this, and don't jump to any conclusions."

I bang my fist against the panel. "Three hours! Why no alarms? You turned off the alarms!"

"Yes, because of the meeting, I turned off the alarm annunciators."

"Estúpido!"

Now comes Eric's turn to scream. "Why interrupt the meeting? What's the benefit? It would have been a distraction, a distraction to me, because if there's one person here who can nurse these machines until we land, that's me. Only me. I want respect!"

"We'll make you captain," I tell him as if speaking to la niño.

Ryder places a hand on the back of my neck and pulls himself closer. "We've been breathing oxygen from the reserve bank."

"That's what they're there for," Eric snarls. "Reserves! *Endurance* went almost twenty percent into their reserve this morning. They're back up to ninety-eight percent."

I lower my voice. "I thought you fixed these shutdowns."

"I did! But I need to find the perfect thermal balance and spin all five spacecraft just right to achieve that balance."

Ryder points out, "They're not designed to run inside the TMI. They're supposed to run inside an orbital station, where people can reach them."

"Ironically, it wouldn't help if we could reach them," Eric tells us. "They don't need repairs. They need better heat balance. Too hot, the electrolyte temps zoom out of spec. Too cold, the hydrogen line clogs with slurry."

I notice something else. "Number three is running, but with low flow. Explain."

"If I had to take a guess, it's the seals. O-rings and gaskets. The seals can't take the periodic high temps."

"Eric, listen to me. We need to find a way to keep the discharge line warm so we can manage the electrolyte temps, even if it means going outside the airlock."

"Those units are a meter inside the TMI."

"The hydrogen discharge lines reach the outer skin. Maybe we can run a heating wire into them."

"There are obstructions, and the heating wire would probably just burn a hole in the line."

Ryder folds his arms. "Think it over. That's all anyone can ask."

"Eric, I'm sorry about what I said to you. But I don't think these fuckers are going to last another five weeks. We need to come up with an alternative. Does Jürgen know about this?"

"He does."

"What did he say?"

"Nothing. He trusts me."

✳

Now I'm hungry. Everything on the menu looks delicious. Meatballs in barbecue sauce with noodles always seemed too heavy. Tonight it sounds perfect.

We're barely done stuffing our faces when Vijay is back to business. "All present? We will now hear nominations for the office of captain. As per Article three, all citizens are eligible for nomination. Someone who is not the nominee must second a nomination."

Paige thrusts her arms over her head. "Jürgen! I nominate Jürgen!" She claps her hands three times.

Vijay acknowledges, "We have a nomination for Jürgen Morita."

Tess cries, "I second that nomination!"

Paige giggles. "I beat her."

Jürgen accepts in his crisp and confident tone. Before the cheers end I blurt, "I nominate Vijay." Blank-out on his last name.

One heartbeat.

"Cristina, sincere thanks for your confidence. I must decline the nomination. I feel I have made my maximum contribution for the time being."

I want to respond, but I do another blank out. My mouth is open like a fish. Before I can utter a syllable Ryder roars, "I nominate Cristina Flores for captain!"

A puff of air escapes my lips. Ryder grins wider than anyone in history who hadn't just caught a solid hit of shab.

Vijay says softly, "I second that nomination."

A female voice, possibly Indra. "Me too."

Brain freeze.

Vijay calls, "Cristina?"

Ryder taps the side of my head. I manage to say, "I accept...the nomination."

My mind rejuvenates and my head goes woozy. Ryder and Alison tug at my arms, and that brings some reality back. Reality is five stained white coveralls with legs pointed in different directions. Sunlight sparkles off Alison's golden hair.

A female voice nominates Eric.

"Hell, no! I'm not the captain type. I need to focus on the purely technical aspects."

Vijay requests additional nominations and there are none. Paige asks, "So now we vote?"

"Let's recess to give both candidates a chance to gather their thoughts. In five minutes we hear their opening statements, citizens may pose questions, and then, yes, we vote."

I face Ryder, but he speaks before I do. "You've been acting like a boss, so why are you so amazed you got nominated? Sure didn't think it would be me, huh?" He grabs my shoulders. "You want to be captain?"

"I accepted, didn't I?" Belly flutter. Meatballs in barbecue sauce was a bad choice.

"That's not what I asked."

"I can be a better captain than Jürgen,"

Paige murmurs her annoyance. She's hooked on Jürgen. How many others are too?

"Jürgen knows how to give speeches," I tell her. "And he knows a lot about Mars. But what else can he do?"

"Don't rag on Jürgen," Paige answers. "He's an excellent planner. He has vision and he fires up my energy."

"Energy for what?"

Ryder wipes his index finger across his lips. Shut it. He jerks his head toward the hygiene pit. Once inside he shuts the hatch and faces me. "You got about three minutes to come up with something better."

"Why did you nominate me?"

"Conviction," Ryder tells me. "Jürgen talks pretty. He's ambitious. People like him. I like him. How can we help it? He looks good, sounds good, speaks to our highest emotions."

I snort. "Sounds like you're going to vote for him instead of the one you nominated."

"No, I'm voting for you. So will a lot of people. Inside, we're scared. Make that terrified. Jürgen's good for us and makes us feel better. But you *are* better. You're smart, Cristina, and you have the courage of conviction. Now here's the problem. You see what needs to be done, but people are tools to you—a means for Cristina to accomplish an objective."

"I'll do it all myself, then."

"That's my point! You can't do it all yourself. You need us. I think you can win this thing if you bring us together."

The pit's shrinking. He's a centimeter away, barely touching. I say, "I wasn't planning to tell people, 'vote for me and here's your training assignment.'"

"You have it in you. I can feel it. Now *you* have to feel it. When you got us to sing—"

"Sing! Great idea."

"What I mean is, sing with ideas."

We return to the much better-smelling air of the control center. Alison takes my arm. "I'm going to vote for you, but Jürgen's so mouthwateringly gorgeous I can't stand it."

"I don't know who I'm going to vote for," Mikki announces. "And it probably doesn't matter."

I tell her, "As soon as this is over, we're going to come up with a way to keep the hydrogen discharge lines from clogging."

Vijay is back exactly on time. "We should keep as informal a structure as we can. Both candidates may speak and field questions, then we vote. Is this agreeable?"

Too much happening all at once. Rosies in chest pocket, heart doing some crazy thumping. "Good plan, Vijay!" I respond. "Jürgen, you go first. We all know how much you love to talk."

A gasp from Alison. Ryder frowns. Vijay gives a tense laugh. A mistake? Felt right, anyhow.

"Thank you, Cristina," says Jürgen. "This will be short, as I had the opportunity to introduce myself in the hospital basement. Seems a lifetime ago, but it was only a week." He shakes his head. A new dramatic effect? "Who would have thought, at that time, they would be among the first humans to forge a path to Mars?" He holds up both arms. "I float before you humbled by your confidence in me. You are the exceptional ones here. Two hundred and thirty-five went through that basement. You are the best of the best. Your intellect is in the top one percent, and you know how to learn, and you can endure discomfort and uncertainty." He softens his tone. "There's something more important that ties us together. I think you already know. Call it a spark, a spark of defiance. Your mind has always been free, even if you had to hide it."

I might vote for him myself. Jürgen stops and closes his eyes as if trying to think. But he knows exactly what he's going to say.

"You chose hope over fear. We'll see the growth of a community of free men and women living beyond the reach of

Harmony, and close enough to serve as a beacon of liberty for the rest of humanity. This I believe; this I know. I'm asking you to vote for me today, and honor me with the opportunity to be your captain during this historic undertaking."

Cheers and applause. My stomach spins like never before. Picante graso meatballs.

Vijay calls, "Cristina—"

The words come tumbling out. "A minute ago, somebody said it doesn't matter who's elected captain. I disagree. I think it matters. It matters a lot." Too harsh. Too cold. So what? "We're in a fight for our lives. If I seem strict to you, that's because we have a daunting job ahead. No room for error, and no going back."

Take a breath. For an instant the only sound is the hum from the ventilator fans.

"Why did they launch six spacecraft? Because maybe only one or two will make it. There are thirty of us still alive. I expect all of us to be alive this time next year, and the years after that, so we can fulfill a dream that sounded crazy when we first heard it."

Settle down, muchacha. But the words want to fly. "First it was the thrusters. Then the oxygen generator failures. Look at your GNC. There's no arrival time, is there? We might not be able to breathe, and we're off course. My first act as captain will be to fix those problems. I have ideas—"

"Wait!"

It's Eric, and he's not happy.

Vijay says, "Please retain questions until the candidate is finished."

Eric shakes his head. "I don't have a question. I just—"

"Please, sir," Vijay insists.

I take a deep breath. "So, does it matter? Jürgen is an amazing speaker. I love listening to him. But we need more than a speaker. As captain, I will appoint Eric as my technical—"

What?

My head snaps backwards.

Something, some kind of dark object, drifts past me toward the left. Shouts and laughter from everywhere. I stammer, "What was that?"

Alison cries, "Oh, disgusting!"

I turn back to the vid. Get on track, now. "With Eric as my technical advisor, we'll be in a better position to proactively resolve our problems."

"What is that thing?" Mikki demands.

Alison shouts, "It's crap!"

Paige says, "Oh, no."

"I am not joking," Alison insists. "It's a piece of crap. Look at it! There it is, by the middle sleeper."

What's the use? My cheeks burn red hot. "That's all I have. I'm open to questions."

Mikki growls, "Somebody get it and put it in the suction hose."

Ryder asks, "What am I supposed to use, my fingers?"

"Use a vomit bag. They're in the square blue locker."

I hear my own voice on the com. "…as my technical…What was that?" Someone's looping the vid. The dark blob floats past. My eyes go wide in astonishment, my mouth bursts open. It tumbles out of view.

Roars of laughter. The vid loops again. And again.

Mikki snickers, "Ryder, this is your work."

"Not mine. Mine aren't that dark."

The jokes and giggles die down. Alison rubs my shoulders and offers a pouch of tea. Nobody did this deliberately—it's just bad luck—crappy luck. Bad luck doesn't happen to people like Jürgen.

"Cristina," Vijay calls. "Would you like to continue?"

What else is there? Blank out. Brain a cold rock. "I think I mentioned everything important I wanted to cover."

Dead quiet except for a lone giggle. Eric coughs. "I would like to say something."

Vijay responds, "The floor recognizes Eric Rahn."

"I just want to point out that I'm managing everyone's O2 generators to keep your oxygen bank topped off. Note that your bank is close to one hundred percent right now, except for *Resolute,* which is at ninety-one and rising. I'm a little concerned that Cristina's remarks are going to be taken to indicate these units are broken and there's a life-threatening problem developing. I assure you that is not the case. Cristina's suggestion to stuff a heating element down the vent lines isn't necessary and would probably damage the line and put the unit permanently out of commission. Okay. I just wanted to make sure everyone's got a handle on this."

Such a stupid strategy to rant about the equipment! But what else is there? Jürgen knows what to say. How can anyone beat him?

A girl on the *Resolute* identifies herself as Jade Compano. She asks Jürgen what criteria he would use to select the five members of his team that would search for evidence of life on Mars.

"Enthusiasm is my main criteria," he responds. "Not academic degrees. Simply zeal and ambition for discovery. Someone like you, Jade, with your background in physics, has the same opportunity as a psychologist such as Hannah or a molecular engineer such as Laine."

What happened to technical knowledge as the main criteria?

I can't help myself. "Shouldn't our molecular engineers be managing our printers? Growing food this summer depends on our manufacturing tons of polymer for the greenhouses."

Why did the floating turd have to happen?

My question is ignored. Jürgen takes control. He calls each person by name and he's familiar with everyone's educational background and interests.

Ryder speaks up. "I have a question. But not for Jürgen or Cristina. This is for everybody. Since we left, how many of you have regretted your decision?"

That word *regretted* hangs in the air like a silent fart. All joyful banter vanishes. Ryder's next words ring like two hammer blows. "I have!"

He doesn't say a word for several seconds. Again, just the ventilator hum. "I never would have believed I could feel that way. I'm adapted to most of it now, but it still hits me while trying to fall asleep. What have I gotten myself into? Maybe just made my life a lot more interesting and a whole lot shorter."

He massages his forehead. Alison reaches out and runs her hand down his spine. "There was a point just after launch. I was mentally exhausted, wound-up tight, scared, and afraid of showing it. I flew to pieces." Ryder extends his arm and pulls me into the vid. "This person, just as exhausted, probably just as terrified, kept it together and did the right thing. I'm going to stop thinking about regrets. It's done, we're here. Let's all stop the regrets and do what we can to improve the odds. If Cristina is captain, our odds improve."

It happens so fast, without thinking. I pull Ryder close, I hug him, press into his solid right shoulder. With everyone watching.

Worse than stupid!

That does it. In their minds, Ryder is the friendboy. They all believe that's why he said what he said.

Ryder isn't done. "Cristina has my vote. Jürgen will make a good captain sometime in the future. Before then, there's gonna be one or two truly sucky days. Cristina is who we need for those sucky days. I know this from personal experience."

The vid from *Independence* jiggles and for a moment there's Jürgen's face: eyebrows drawn together, dashing look faded.

Vijay clears his throat. "Does anyone have any additional questions for either candidate?" No one does. "Now we cast our votes. This we will do anonymously. I have created a public folder named 'Captain.' There are two checklists, Cristina and Jürgen. You can open the folder in the privacy of your sleeper and indicate your choice. The folder will only count the number of checks. The number of checks must total twenty-eight."

Someone asks, "What if the vote is fourteen-fourteen?"

"We'll deal with that if it happens. Will ten minutes be enough time for everyone to submit their vote?"

My stomach! Next election, no meatballs.

Ryder points his finger from across the control center. "You're going to win." His arm is around Alison's waist.

I wedge next to the big window and let the sun warm my face. The others duck into their sleepers. Paige will vote for Jürgen. That makes four votes to count on? With Vijay that leaves ten more needed, out of how many? No use thinking about it.

It doesn't take ten minutes. It takes four.

Jürgen is elected captain.

TWENTY-THREE

Our guidance system doesn't work, our oxygen generators are screwed up, no one really cares, and on top of everything, we're all sick.

It's worse than the flu. I want to sleep, but there's too much to be done. As if extreme lethargy isn't enough, everyone's nose oozes syrupy mucus in every color of the rainbow. Ryder dubs it Super Snot.

Shuko blames our weakened immune systems—the stress of adapting to a new environment, plus mild dehydration, irregular sleep, and recycled air. He could give out decongestants, but that won't do any good because there's no gravity to drain our nasal cavities. He recommends increased fluid intake.

The lack of gravity fools the body by reducing the sensation of thirst. The only drinks that still taste good are orange juice and the milky chocolate-coconut frappe, both on the menu only in the morning. So it's water followed by more water.

Jürgen's already on the com as we jam into the control center for dinner. His voice lacks its usual crisp tone. "Blair asked me to reassure everyone these nasty head colds aren't dangerous. We just need to wait it out. On a positive note, Eric has good news about the oxygen generators."

Despite his sniffles, Eric's eyes are cheery and alert. His words gush as if he can't wait to get them out. "Me and Darien stabilized everyone's OGS. It was a matter of finding the right heat balance. Notice that all three of your units are running in parallel."

The master panel does show all of the oxygen generators on line—but at low outputs.

"Running at twenty percent capacity so we keep the electrolyte temps under the shutdown limit, and the H2 discharge stays warm enough to prevent the line from freezing up."

"Brilliant!" Ryder cries. "Can we breathe now?"

Laughter peals from the com. "Breathe, brother, breathe!" Eric shouts. "These units are actually marvels of compact, weight-saving engineering. Taking along six weeks of liquid oxygen would have required heavy tanks and insulation. The planners solved that by electrolyzing ordinary water, which is eighty-nine percent oxygen. This saves tremendous weight, which means the TMI can get us to Mars faster, which means shorter exposure to cosmic radiation, and we can land with more supplies and equipment."

Eric grins during the applause. This is his reward. A challenge met, expertise appreciated. Yes, the main reason he's here.

Speeches over, we're back to our normal routine. They stare at me—Shuko, Ryder, Alison, all of them. "Per Jürgen, I'm still Sergeant-at-Arms. Get ready to review your individual training progress as soon as we're done eating."

Mikki licks her spoon. "No one told you?"

Ryder pats her shoulder. "I'll tell her."

The odor from the printer is obnoxious. "Tell me what?"

Ryder fidgets against the table. "This is probably not as critical as it sounds."

"Get to the point."

"Assistants to the captain need a two-thirds confirmation vote."

"According to our Charter," Alison adds.

"You're not telling me—"

Alison touches my knee. "I voted to confirm you."

Ryder nods. "So did I. You needed nineteen out of twenty-eight. Didn't quite get there."

I clench my arms tighter. "How many?"

"Doesn't matter. In fact—"

"Thirteen," Mikki says.

"So they got another Sergeant, huh? That's fine."

"He picked Walt Cunningham on *Independence*," Ryder tells me. "The title is now Training Coordinator. Senuri is

Jürgen's Discovery Team Coordinator, and Tess is his Administrative Coordinator, whatever that means."

Walt Cunningham is a smug little tipo. I'd guess he enjoys telling people what to do. Oh, and he worships everything about Jürgen.

"And they got two-thirds?" I ask. "I never voted."

Mikki takes a huge bite of what looks like stuffed pita. "They got their nineteen without you."

I slap my palm against the table. "Fine." There are more important things to think about. Three OGS units running, all of them at eighteen percent capacity. The compressed reserve is at ninety-seven percent.

Shuko emerges from the equipment bay hatch. "If you check the logs, the reserve supply has been coming on-line intermittently since four this morning."

"Let me guess. You talked to Eric. He's aware of the situation. And everything's under control." I face the rest of them. "Am I still the flight director on *Liberty*? Or did you vote me out of that, too?"

"You're in charge here, Cristina," Ryder assures me.

"We'll do our exam packs. On top of that, we'll find an alternate source of oxygen. Shuko, how much of the stuff do we breathe?"

"Five kilos a day, the six of us." He glances at Ryder. "Assuming moderate activity."

"So if we electrolyze six liters of water, that's a day's worth right there. We got a couple of portable electrolyzers, but they're designed for the moon so they need at least one-sixth Earth gravity to function." I jab my finger toward the panel. "We can't assume these things are gonna hold together for the rest of the flight."

Ryder taps my arm. "Keep doing what you're doing. Act as if."

"As if what?"

"As if you won."

Mikki says, "She didn't win."

Ryder lowers his voice. "Half of us are on your side. What would you be doing if you got a few more votes over the pretty boy?"

"Installing the new star tracker. That should have priority over the OGS."

"Then do it. Act as if. Trust me on this. People might see things differently at some point. Jürgen has an ego so big I don't know how he squeezed it through that little airlock. Act as if. He doesn't want to appear not in control, so he'll go along."

Shuko asks Alison to assist in switching the carbon dioxide scrubbers and purging the off-line unit. They disappear through the hatch.

Ryder leans toward me and whispers, "After all his smooth talk , his promises, his looks, his way of schmoozing, after all that, you almost beat him. And he knew it. Did you see his face? I think he was wishing for one of those absorbency garments."

I can't stop smiling. But this isn't the time to be funny.

Ryder continues. "We gotta pick our battles. Maintain a low profile, but still get things done. Jürgen is the master of managing perceptions, and we're all used to having our perceptions managed. That's why he got the majority." He locks eyes with me. "Can I ask you about something?" He points to the pocket with the rosies. "I'm just a little curious."

Why is he probing now? I withdraw the bundle of beads and let them float and swirl between our faces. The tiny silver cross glistens in the sunlight. "Rosies. They belonged to my father."

Mikki snickers and pushes off toward her sleeper. "They're called rosaries, dumb ass."

Ryder throws her an annoyed look. She murmurs, "Sorry," as she slides her door shut.

I loop the beads around my fingers. "Whatever they're supposed to be called, to me they're my father's rosies and they were precious to him. He kept them hidden, except he would take them out every night and hold them while on his knees. He never told me much about that."

"He was protecting you," Ryder tells me softly. "Religious icon. Prayer. You know that much, don't you? He would have explained more when you got older, when you were big enough to understand the need to keep it quiet."

"They were wrapped around his fingers when he passed." Speaking it doesn't bring the same pain as thinking it. "I took them, put them in my pocket. I was ten."

Ryder grasps the silver cross between his thumb and index finger. "At a minimum, this right here, all by itself, would have kept you out of university."

I slip them back into my pocket. "Makes no difference, then."

"But you studied hard, took the toughest courses, hoping you could somehow compensate for your low Score."

He has me cold. "I was a lot younger and really stupid."

"The eternal optimist. Thinking knowledge and intelligence would override that Score."

"Bottomed at two-oh-eight, couldn't seem to go any lower."

Ryder winces. "They don't call it a Trust Score for nothing. No one trusted you. Why did you come out here? Just to be able to mouth off? And carry those beads around without worrying about them being taken away?"

"Those aren't good enough reasons?"

"You were the last one they brought to the Ninth Circle, hardly there for a day. They had enough pre-selects. Why do you think they stuck you in at the last minute?"

Jürgen said his grandfather picked me. He didn't say *why*. And he didn't appear happy about it. Is that why I'm not too crazy about Jürgen?

"It wasn't for my education, if that's what you mean. Do you enjoy reminding me?"

"The rest of us haven't figured out how to live without the Stream and the sudden lack of surveillance and harassment. We're not used to deciding for ourselves what we should do. I'm guessing you developed that skill a long time ago."

Paco. I have Paco to thank for that.

"The rest of you better make the adjustment," I tell him. "Because I can't babysit twenty-nine kids all by myself."

"You're doing fine. That's what I want to get across. Keep being you. Forget about the election. Most of all, *act as if.*"

"Even without a genuine university degree?"

He squeezes my shoulder, almost fingers my neck. "You have guts. And guts are enough."

TWENTY-FOUR

I caress our newly printed star tracker, a glossy black sphere of borosilicate glass and alumina ceramic nine centimeters across, including the flat base.

We printed it, we're using it. *We* being Ryder and I, plus anyone else who joins our little rebellion. I told them we require a functioning navigation system in order to make necessary course corrections, and we know how to fix it. The only matter to be worked out: What needs to be done and in what order.

Paige watches me. "You need permission from the captain."

"I'm the flight director on this spacecraft. I'll do what I think is best."

"You're required to obey—"

"I'm not required to do shit. If you think I'm breaking the Articles, ask Jürgen to charge me. I'll get a trial with a jury."

Vijay has taught me useful things.

"Look at the GNC!" I growl at her. "Do you see an estimated time of arrival? It doesn't even know where we are! So no, it's *not* safer to do nothing. We're going to fix this problem."

I get Indra on the com. "You said you could script the GNC and the tracker so that it boots with the correct time."

"The script is ready, Cristina. It adds the correct number of milliseconds to the value we have, and does the same every time it rolls over."

Ryder grabs my upper arm. His forehead is coated with drops of sweat. "I'll switch our GNC mode to local."

He's thinking ahead; Eric won't be able to override it remotely. Shuko checks the airlock control panel, so he's on our side. Alison sets up the printer to make a connection cable.

It doesn't take long before Eric discovers our plan. "If you don't want me to override your GNC I won't touch it. If you're so determined to do this, go ahead. Your life! I just want to find out what kind of course correction it decides to do, assuming it still works after you're done screwing with it."

Not a word about Jürgen.

The most daunting aspect of this task are the BioSuits. We had a week to test them and nobody ever did. We need more help, at least one more rebel.

Jessica Egan on *Resolute* is our most experienced suit expert. I ask her to walk us through the process without telling her why. She doesn't ask, but she can probably figure it out.

Jessica's triangular, elfin face fills a vid screen. "I studied biomechanics at the University of Tokyo. These suits were developed for the Chēngzhăng lunar crews. They're lighter and more flexible than the old-style inflated bubble suits from the Russian and American space programs."

Ryder rubs his suit. "Let's do it. I can't wait to get out there."

Jessica continues. "Compared to the old types, these suits are simple and safe. No nitrogen purge required because you're breathing the same gas mix and pressure as your spacecraft cabin. Over a hundred people used these suits for fifteen years during Chēngzhăng without a single fatality."

Shuko mumbles, "No fatalities they admit."

The suit material is thin and delicate between my fingers. "This feels easy to puncture. Suppose it rips or gets a hole. Won't the air leak out?"

"These suits don't hold in air," Jessica answers. "A tear, even a centimeter wide, is harmless. A bigger hole is painful but not fatal. The actuators maintain a constant mechanical pressure over your body, except for your head, which is kept under pressure by the helmet. The squeeze isn't too comfortable at first, because the actuators have to learn your exact body shape. Speaking of which, strip naked before you put on the liner. No clothing besides the liner, not even underwear."

Ryder wriggles out of his flight suit right in the middle of the control deck. I take my BioSuit into my sleeper. First comes the blue-gray liner, a one-piece elastic coverall that stretches tight against every bit of skin below my neck. The suit manual said the liner protects the inner surface of the BioSuit from abrasion and body sweat.

Next comes the BioSuit itself. The front has a heavy zipper and the inside is lined with a velvety material that glides over the liner. Crunchingly tight! With the zipper shut I barely fit. How much tighter with the actuators squeezing?

Ryder's BioSuit conforms perfectly to his wide shoulders and narrow waist; yes, this equipment was created based on our individual body measurements.

"Let's talk temperature moderation," says Jessica. "The Chēngzhǎng suits used water-tube cooling because the lunar daytime temperature is over two hundred degrees. We don't need water cooling because our problem is protection against cold."

There are dark gray insulated coveralls to wear over the BioSuits, thermals, designed to retain our body heat. They're filled with multiple layers of perforated mylar and other material covered with a durable Dacron weave to protect us from the rough edges of Mars.

I hold the thermals up to the vid so Jessica can see. "Is this thick enough to keep us from freezing out there?"

"You're going to be cold at first," she answers. "Especially since all the layers are porous to moisture. Except for your head, your body sweat will evaporate when the airlock is vented. Trouble is, in a vacuum, you won't have any temperature moderation other than controlling sunlight exposure. On Mars, temperature regulation is accomplished with a fan that circulates air between your BioSuit and the thermal coveralls. No way to do that in the vacuum of space. To be honest, I'm not sure what's going to happen with your temperature. How long do you think it'll take to install the tracker?"

"All I need to do is glue it to the side and plug in the cable. Five minutes tops."

There's a life support backpack to power the actuators and provide breathing air and communications. Jessica shows us how to verify the battery and oxygen charge and let the system do a power-up self-check. A display on the suit sleeve indicates all green. The rest of the equipment—the new star tracker, the connection cable, and two safety tethers—is ready.

"We need some way to cushion the tracker against mechanical shock," Ryder says. He swings toward his sleeper and emerges with an absorbency garment. "Shuko, I'm taking one of yours. At least it hasn't been used."

The helmets are the old Chēngzhǎng style, with a soft head compartment and a hard, curved face canopy of clear sapphire. Jessica instructs us how to establish a seal. The life support pack activates, and a stream of cool, plastic-smelling air swirls around my face. The visor displays yellow numbers that confirm the system is operating and maintaining acceptable oxygen, carbon dioxide, and humidity levels.

Paige decides to help after all. She passes us the insulated coveralls. There are four pockets and one of them is the perfect size for my rosies.

I call, "Jessica, com check."

"Hear you perfectly, Cristina."

I want Mikki by the airlock, but she's still rattled about the whole thing, so it will be Paige. Ryder enters the equipment bay first so he can guide me and pass me the tracker. I cradle it in my gloved hands much like I used to hold newborn Isabel years ago.

Paige twists the handle on the airlock equalization valve. The master panel indicates the same pressure as the cabin, thirty-five kilopascals, but the meter-wide inner hatch will not open. Ryder gives the handle a mighty tug and the soft seal releases with a *pfssst*. The tiny circular window on the outer hatch is coated with silver frost. I can't help glancing at the signatures, the *Live Free* and *the Lord is my shepherd* messages printed neatly on the pale green walls.

Ryder squirms through the airlock hatch. There's barely room for one let alone two. He activates the control panel and nods. The lack of gravity makes it difficult to position every part of my body. Ryder's legs, torso, and arms kept bouncing against me, and the confined space guarantees I can't move out of the way.

Paige connects our safety tethers to a metal loop inside the airlock. She passes me an adhesive applicator and I slide it into the pocket opposite my rosies.

"Closing the hatch." Paige taps my helmet. "Just get it done and get back inside."

I feel a thud and we position the six latches. Ryder touches the front of his helmet to mine. "Cozy, huh?"

I spit out, "Yup!" Dumb answer. Childish, too. If our chests touched he'd feel a heart pounding way too hard, so I don't let that happen. Focus on the airlock panel. A horizontal bar indicates steady pressure. There's also a round mechanical pressure gauge. Is that in case power is lost?

"Ready?" Jessica's voice startles me. "Go ahead and vent down to about thirty kp. The suit will sense the drop and trigger the activators."

Ryder grips a red handle and rotates it before she's done talking. The panel flashes *DECOMPRESSING* in bright yellow letters. I yell, "Suit getting tighter!"

"Breathe normally," Jessica tells us.

There's a clutching sensation all over, strange but not horrible. Inhaling requires a bit more effort than normal. Here comes the cold, just as if someone sprayed my whole body with an icy mist. Skin moisture evaporating, and fast.

"Getting chilly!" I report, teeth chattering.

"Keep venting," Jessica tells us. "Take it down to twenty, then hold. You're going to feel some warmth. The actuators will heat up as they learn to evenly compress to your exact body shape."

A hot, gentle embrace—wonderfully warm against the chill.

Ryder sighs. "Oh, this is good."

"Move your limbs as much as you can," orders Jessica. "Flex your joints, including your fingers. How does it feel? Any resistance to motion?"

"Noticeable stiffness," reports Ryder. "But I can move everything.

"Same, and a little easier to breathe," I tell her.

"Ahhh!" Ryder barks. "Crushing my damn…crotch! Jess, this thing gonna castrate me?"

"No worries! That's a common discomfort. Just move your hips and legs to help the suit adjust. Ready for full vacuum? Not as scary as it sounds."

"Easy for you to say!" I blurt. Estúpido! Everyone's listening.

Ryder turns the handle again. "Venting!"

Ten kp, then five, then less than one. Ryder doesn't move. He stares out from his helmet with a little smile as the pressure drops to just above zero. What was the pressure below which David said blood would boil? No matter; we're way past it.

Eric's husky voice fills my helmet. "Cristina, the venting put a spin on your spacecraft. The GNC didn't react because you overrode it, so I'm firing a couple of your attitude jets to stop the rotation." The airlock jerks sideways and a narrow sunbeam pokes inside.

There's sharp pinching between two of my fingers, as if someone's squeezing with needle-nose pliers.

"Flex if you get more pinches," Jessica says, as if she can read my mind. "It happens, especially with a new suit. Also, the fit won't be as good as it should be because you're doing this under weightless conditions. The suits printed on your body dimensions in your hospital scan. They allow for the lower gravity on Mars by slightly increasing your upper body volume. That effect is more pronounced in space, so it'll be tighter than in should be from the waist up."

Ryder stretches his arms and legs, which means rubbing them against everything in the airlock. A weird quiet settles behind the purr from the backpack and the rhythm of breathing.

The panel flashes *OK TO OPEN HATCH* three times.

Zero pressure.

Ryder flicks off the main light and we're in darkness except for the soft red glow of the airlock control panel. "Let our eyes adjust. Better to see the stars."

Pounding heart, be calm. "Not important. Just want to get it mounted and plugged in."

"You're not nervous, are you?"

"Just pinchy. Sooner we're done, the better."

The thermal coveralls act as insulators. That's their purpose—but here, crammed into the airlock, there's no place for body heat to radiate. My face is sweaty, but the perspiration can't fall away; each bead grows larger then breaks free and speckles my visor or gets sucked up my nose. None of this crap was mentioned in the Apollo book.

"I'm holding your sun angle at ten degrees," Eric reports. "You'll have a nice warm surface temp so the adhesive should set in under a minute."

Ryder announces, "Jessica, we're going to poke our heads out."

"Check your tethers. Make sure everything's secured."

Ryder presses our helmets together. "Ready?"

I nod and he pumps a stubby lever that simultaneously opens eight latches. A ring of light—the edge of the hatch catching the sun. Beyond that is utter blackness without a single star.

Eric's reminds us, "Remember, put it within fifty centimeters of the port. Cable's gotta reach."

I ask him, "You sure it doesn't need to be mounted facing a specific direction?"

"It orients itself using celestial bodies. Just needs to be exposed to space and attached to something solid."

Ryder is closer to the hatch, so he pushes it completely open. I'm not letting him completely out. I'm not letting myself out, either—I can do this with just my upper body outside the hatch. That worries me less than the idea of him going out there and losing his mind.

He asks, "Why don't you leave the tracker with me?"

"You'll just have to pass it out to me, and that's a risk of losing it. Steady my legs."

Can't lose the tracker. Should have tethered it too! We can print another, but that would eat up time. The outside surface of *Liberty* is intensely white even at the low sun angle. The helmet visor adjusts and the light dims to a comfortable level. I see the com port, an oval indentation just an arm's length away.

"Push me out a bit further, just a bit, so I can reach it."

Ryder's hands wrap around both of my calves. I'm not bouncing around, both my hands are free, and that's all I need. I hold the tracker against my chest and withdraw the adhesive applicator. The thermal gloves make it awkward, but the applicator is designed to be easy for fat fingers.

I announce, "Putting on the glue."

Jewell asks, "Is the tracker optical surface completely covered?"

"Wrapped with loving care. Here it comes, one big spoonful." I squeeze the applicator with the tip about twenty centimeters from the port, and a big golden glob spreads out on *Liberty*. Torr-Seal Epoxy, the stuff is called. The pretty color glistens in the sunlight. I press the base of the tracker firmly into the adhesive.

"Hold it until it sets," says Jewel.

"Feels pretty firmly glued on."

"Hold it for one full minute."

I pass the absorbency garment to Ryder. He hands me the cable and I connect the tracker to the port, careful to push both sides completely in until I feel a click.

Paige shouts, "Main panel shows we have a connection!"

Done. I push against the edge of the hatch but Ryder doesn't release his grip on my legs. "Let me get back in."

He ignores me. "Eric, my friend, sorry about putting the GNC in local mode without telling you."

"Yeah."

"Can you do us a favor? Put the sun angle down to, say, negative sixty?"

"What are you talking about?" I demand. "We're finished. Get out of the way so I can get back in." I twist my legs but he isn't letting go.

Ryder asks, "Don't you want to see what it's really like out there?"

I jerk sideways and shadows drift across *Liberty's* white surface. The sun moves, or rather, the spacecraft slowly turns. The light fades quickly and the helmet visor goes clear to reveal the red glow from the airlock.

Ryder shifts his body and blocks the glow. Nothing but black, a total black.

I'm spinning again.

Ryder says, "Let your eyes—"

"Stop!"

The hatch drops from under me and twists. *Rotating, spinning,* the whole spacecraft *spins* out of control. We're both about to be pitched into the blackness!

"What's the—"

"Eric, stop the spin!"

There's nothing to hold, nothing to grab on to, just the black space, and my legs are sliding further out of the hatch. It's the centrifugal force from the spin pulling me outward.

Something grabs my left arm.

"Eric!"

"There is no spin," he responds. "No spin! You're steady in pitch, roll, and yaw."

I'm quivering and I might throw up.

"I've got you," Ryder tells me, his tone gentle. "You're on a tether and I've got a good grip on you. I'm pulling you back in now. Ready?"

Jessica says, "You're experiencing vertigo, Cristina. Control your breath. I'm reducing your O2 so you don't hyperventilate. Let's call it a day."

"Come this far," I pant out. "Let's see some fucking stars."

My eyes were closed. Red glow, the outline of Ryder's helmet. There's the edge of the hatch behind my left knee, the bulk of *Liberty* under my feet. I'm adjusted, oriented, some sense of where I am and where I'm pointed.

"Good girl. Now turn your head to your right."

It takes a moment to see Ryder's arm in the near total darkness. His fingertip hovers near a speck of orange.

"Mars. Seen it before."

"Let your eyes adjust."

The cold soaks through the thermal coveralls and my shivers won't stop. I point my helmet toward *Liberty's* side and the temperature display sinks to minus eighty degrees. In the other direction, a brilliant field of stars. Millions and millions of stars of various intensities and hues. There's a white triangle over my right shoulder—one of the other spacecraft, about a kilometer distant. It looks close enough to touch.

Ryder swings his arm. "The Pleiades. See 'em?"

Yes! And there's the V-shape of Taurus, and Orion with his three-star belt. I can see the wisp of the Milky Way, an impossibly gorgeous wilderness of distant suns, crisp, wild, pristine, beckoning.

I had no idea.

Isabel, Nathan. If those niños could see this! And Faye. And Paco. I grip Ryder's arm before I can stop myself. "One of your better ideas."

The warm air of the equipment bay is like dropping into a hot bath. Everyone stares as if something is different. Alison giggles. "You got a happy new face!"

"I am happy," I tell her. "This will work."

✳

It doesn't work. The GNC won't recognize input from the newly installed hardware. When the signals from the three bad trackers are cut, the panel flashes angry red.

OPTIMIZED SIGNAL NOT FOUND

I ask Paige, "Didn't you say it connected?"

"Connected, but not communicating."

"The default admin account," Eric mutters. "The optimizer isn't going to talk to anything until I reset it."

Mikki folds her arms. "This is bullshit."

Nerves. I offer a pouch of juice which she waves away. "I'll drink when this is over." Like Ryder, her forehead beads with sweat when she's stressed. They understand. If the idea fails, we are navigating blind and that's a fatal situation—regardless what Jürgen tells us.

The GNC panel goes dark, then awakens with flickering icons and scrolling messages, almost all of them yellow or red.

> *PLATFORM ALIGNMENT FAILED*
> *OPTIMIZED SIGNAL NOT FOUND. ERROR 031*
> *R3056b*
> *AUTHORIZATION FAILED*

"I'm getting closer," reports Eric.

Ryder reaches for Mikki's neck. She knocks his hand away. Tiny drops of sweat fly from her head. Alison's breath gushes out strong enough to feel a meter away. She wedges herself between me and Ryder, both hands on our shoulders.

Eric mumbles, "Permissions, damn permissions."

More yellow messages, then green.

> *PERFORMING PLATFORM ALIGNMENT*

I exhale. "Eric, you're a genius."

His vid shows fingers stroking reddish-brown chin stubble. "I acknowledge the accuracy of the preceding observation."

The panel flashes a gorgeous shade of green.

> *ALIGNMENT COMPLETE 02:12:35 PCT 23 Taurus 53*

"That just means it found the nav stars and it knows which way we're pointed, that's all." Eric tells us. "The trans-Mars program isn't running yet."

"Can you help Indra with the time sync?"

"That's why I blocked the TMP. Now that the GNC has a signal describing our orientation in space and the location of the Earth, the sun, and Mars against the celestial sphere, all it needs is a good time signal to calculate our position and velocity."

"Would have been better to do this two days ago," I tell him, despite that it's useless information now. "Indra, go ahead and run your script."

The GNC swims with a hundred scrolling lines of red. Bad, really bad. The walls of the control center move in a little tighter.

Mikki utters something under her breath and launches herself through her sleeper door. I follow her and pull her out by the upper arm. Her eyes are wet with tears that can't run. I whisper, "Stay with me. We're in this together."

Everyone watches the panel. No green. I hold Mikki's shoulders and wrap my legs around a table brace to keep from moving away from the others.

FIXING POS-VEL

Position? Velocity? Who cares? A green message! I wrap my rosies around my fingers. Ryder stares at the burgundy beads.

TMP LOADING...
TMP INITIATED

Mikki mutters, "Is the fucking thing gonna work or not?"

The sweet, gentle voice of the GNC calls out, *"Maneuvering in three, two, one."*

Distant bangs ring out and the control center rotates. A sunbeam creeps across the sleeper doors.

"Setting up for a burn," says Eric. "It wouldn't do that unless it's happy."

Paige mumbles, "Somebody ought to tell Jürgen, right?"

I answer, "Jürgen wanted to run the GNC broken. Let him comment on his own." I press Mikki's head against my shoulder.

PENDING MIDCOURSE TRAJECTORY
CORRECTION 02:35:00 PCT 23 TAURUS 53
ESTIMATED DURATION 00:23:40

"I'm linking everyone's GNC to *Liberty*," Eric announces.

Completely changed his mind. He knew he was full of shit. Why did he go along with Jürgen? What's wrong with Jürgen, anyhow?

The thrusters fire. The control center blurs, the walls move. After days of weightlessness, the one-twentieth G acceleration is strange and heavy. My feet bounce off the new floor and I sway sideways into Ryder's arms.

He touches the rosies, still finger-wrapped. "You can put these away now. Don't want to lose 'em."

Success means time to eat and pee. We wolf food, take turns in the hygiene pit, watch the timer on the GNC count down to zero, and speak little. The master panel calls out, *"Thruster shutdown in three, two, one."*

A slight bump, barely noticeable. Food wrappers and empty drink packs tumble through the air. Just a few seconds of head swim. All eyes turn to the GNC.

> *ETA PROTONILUS MENSAE PM1 09:26:00 PCT 3*
> *GEMINI 54*

Ryder clasps Mikki's hand and puts his other arm around my neck. A touch of body odor, but that's fine.

Alison lets out her breath. "We got our arrival time back."

Mikki mumbles, "Never a doubt."

"Just over one percent propellant remaining," Eric says. "Let's hope that was a near perfect correction. We got six minutes of thruster time left for all future corrections, and this is only day six."

Shuko's been quiet for a while. He positions himself toward Eric's vid. "Thank you for reminding us we may still die before we feel solid ground again."

I say to no one in particular, "We're all tired. Need a good sleep."

Shuko points to the block of red messages on the warning panel:

> *OXYGEN GENERATOR 3 HIGH O2/H2*
> *DIFFERENTIAL PRESSURE SHUTDOWN OXYGEN*
> *GENERATOR 1 HIGH ELECTROLYTE*
> *TEMPERATURE SHUTDOWN*
> *UNIT 2 IN BACKUP MODE*

"I checked the docs," Shuko tells me as soon as everyone clears from the control center. "We have forty-eight hours of compressed oxygen. Then six hours in our suit backpacks."

I study the display. "But unit two is running and producing oxygen?"

"Yeah, but it's supposed to be a triple-redundant system! Now we have no redundancy at all."

I get Eric back on the com. Big surprise, he's irritated. At me.

"I know you have two units down," he grumbles. "So do we, and so does *Resolute*. Everybody's got at least one unit down. I think we'll see intermittent shutdowns for the next five weeks. These units were chosen for their low weight. They do crap out, which is why we all got three. We only need sixty percent of the output of one unit to meet the requirements of six people. Even with two down, your flow is at eighty-four percent."

Shuko says, "It was ninety yesterday."

Eric responds, "Regardless, all five spacecraft are at full oxygen capacity, despite the fact I didn't tweak the roll schedules today. That's why the temps went out of spec."

My brain is exhausted. "We need to watch these things."

"Well, yeah, Cristina, sure. I don't want you to worry, but there's nothing much we can do but try to manage the temps. The Genesis team screwed up the heat balance."

"How much warning before they go out completely? Maybe there's a way to transfer oxygen between spacecraft."

"Won't need to." He yawns long and wide. "Not losing sleep over it. They don't have to last forever, just the duration of the flight."

TWENTY-FIVE

I push off and float, muscles tensed, waiting for the ball to fly.

Shuko barks, "Go!"

Ryder serves—too hard. No real control. After a few random bounces it's easy to block the ball away from the hatch and keep him from scoring until the clock runs out. His strong, compact physique may have been perfect for rugby, but not for spaceball. Spaceball requires agility and accuracy in equal amounts. Brute force is useless.

I block with my left thigh, taking just enough speed off the ball to enable Ryder to smack it again. Two bounces, then he flips backwards to try for another whack. His hand swats air.

The buzzer goes off. Shuko calls from inside the equipment bay, "Switch!"

I wipe my forehead with my sleeve. "I forfeit. Don't want you to smack your elbow like yesterday."

We touch hands. "Another game after dinner?"

I shake my head. "Systems training. For everybody."

"Oh, mom!"

After the first week, *Liberty* became a prison. The sameness of each day—of each hour—squashes all desire to do anything besides eat and sleep. A handful of us make slow progress through the training systems, most of them motivated by the hope of being chosen for a Discovery Team.

Spaceball changed all that. Spaceball is a reason not to sleep. Spaceball is life.

It was Shuko's idea. Regular exercise, plus a bit of healthy competition, to get everyone's juices flowing and promote physiological wellness. Whatever that means, it works. Once we get the table folded away the open space of the control center is roughly the size of my puny old bedroom. Being able to float around makes it seem larger—big enough for serious action, anyhow.

Endurance printed their ball as a little globe of Mars.

We play hundreds of games for two solid weeks. No serious injuries, except when Jewel de la Bora aboard *Constitution* broke her finger in an exceptionally savage game against Indra. Dee Thompson on *Resolute* keeps a ranking posted on the net. Ryder holds second place after Walt Sullivan. No one can finish a thirty-minute game against Ryder. He never quits twisting and tumbling. The pure energy wears us down.

Spaceball isn't his only physical activity. The rhythmic thumping from Ryder's sleeper is pretty obvious. Tonight's Alison's turn. Didn't three games of spaceball tire them out at least a little?

Shuko stares at the main panel and shakes his head as if amazed. I push across the control center and peer over his shoulder.

"Is it the O2 generator flow?"

"The flow's been decreasing but we're still at full capacity." He giggles and taps the panel. The curved lines are cabin partial pressures, not O2 generator flow.

"You see a problem?"

"No, just something interesting." He smirks, not his most appealing facial expression.

The thumps increase tempo.

"When they're in there, our oxygen partial pressure drops by two tenths of a kilopascal. Look. It was at nominal twenty-four point five a few minutes ago. Now it's point three." Another giggle.

How stupid is this? "Who cares? Watch the O2 generators instead, okay?"

He waves the partial pressure history into view. "When he's going with the other two, the oxygen drops by only one tenth. Look, you can see the abrupt dip every time, and in the morning, too."

"I really, really don't give a shit. So shut it."

Why is he showing me this now? Is this amazing biological discovery supposed to somehow stir my desire? Did he imagine the only woman on *Liberty* Ryder has not slept with would be inspired to snuggle-buggle with him?

He presses his left leg against my right, then mumbles something about how chilly it is and how two can keep each other warm. I push away and twist toward my sleeper. No, he might get the wrong idea and follow. I duck into the hygiene pit instead.

Midnight's the best time for a complete and unhurried wash. Yesterday's leftover sponge is still reasonably usable. By the time I pop the hygiene pit hatch and emerge, Shuko's curled up like a newborn infant between the CO_2 scrubber and the power panel. He claims he loves sleeping in there because the white noise calms his nerves like an embryo listening to its mother's blood flow.

The thumps are gone but there's some kind of other strange sound. Yes, singing, growing louder and punctuated by frequent laughs.

> *On this day I am free!*
> *I can't wait what my eyes will see*
> *I dream about it wherever I may be*
> *It's a day that belongs to me*
> *On this day I am free!*

I cross my arms and snort. Wasting time and energy when we should all be focused on becoming experts in operating the equipment on which lives depend. This isn't a game or an academy, where mistakes only hurt your grade.

Ryder slides his door open. He's wearing nothing but a skin-tight white undergarment. He smiles before gracefully flipping into the hygiene pit.

I yell at him before he can disappear, "We have twenty-two days left, and we've done shit for training."

"Whose fault is that, flight director?" He shuts the hatch.

✳

Constitution's three oxygen generators fail at the same time.

Eric tells us, "I tried running unit one at seventy percent with two offline. My theory was the ambient heat from the other units caused the high electrolyte temps. Didn't work, and now units two and three are pretty much frozen solid."

I can't make sense of the long list of yellow and red messages. "You're down to one unit?"

"I didn't say that. I'm confident units two and three will be back on line tomorrow. We all got forty-eight hours of compressed oxygen reserve anyhow. This is no big deal."

"But we're barely halfway to Mars."

"Notice we're still breathing."

"There has to be a fallback, an alternative way to generate oxygen."

He sighs. "Triple redundant units are the fallback. I'm rolling five spacecraft to balance the heat and keep the hydrogen discharge lines from getting clogged with slurry. What else do you want from me?"

"Is there any way to transfer oxygen between spacecraft?"

"With a hose? You're jumping to unfounded conclusions and worrying about what we'll never need to do. In the future, why don't you take this up with Jürgen?"

Jürgen? He's captain because he can make dramatic speeches.

Jürgen is in charge, that much is always understood. Jürgen is the only person not listed on the spaceball ranking. He never plays, and no one bothers to ask why. The answer is obvious: our captain is working on bigger things. Jürgen is above spaceball.

Jürgen makes it easy to listen. His words are an addictive drug. His daily dinner presentations pull everyone in and drive them to think about the future—a greater future than the dull routine of eating, sleeping, defecating into a tube, and looking at the same faces and the same panels every day.

As usual, there's a rush to get everyone's food printed before Jürgen starts speaking. I nudge my steaming box of chicken and rice to the table and fit in between Alison and Paige. The chicken bits are one of the few kinds of printed food that are inferior to the real thing, but they're still tasty.

Eric has taken Jürgen's place on the main panel. He shows his unfocused stare, meaning serious business. Mikki tosses Ryder and Shuko their dinner boxes and their chatting masks Eric's words.

I shout toward the com, "Can you repeat that?"

"He said Hellas Planitia," Ryder answers. "What's a Planitia?"

Eric casts his eyes downward. "It means plain. Smooth landscape, with water ice. The twelve of us reached this decision only after informed debate." He closes his eyes and lets out a long breath. "We believe it will be significantly safer to land on the flat terrain of the northwest edge of the Hellas Planitia than the hilly landscape at Protonilus."

Ryder and Mikki exchange glances.

I swallow chicken. "Hold it. You want to change the landing site?"

"I think we should. Hellas is certain to harbor shallow ice deposits and mineral resources just like Protonilus. Hellas has a lower elevation than Protonilus, so the atmosphere averages seventy percent denser. That means better radiation protection when we're on the surface plus more efficient CO_2 and nitrogen extraction."

I ask him, "Then why did the Genesis engineers choose Protonilus?"

"Seasonal timing. Spring starts in the northern hemisphere in three weeks. Hellas is in the southern hemisphere, which is heading into autumn. They wanted to maximize the hours of sunshine so we can grow more food. But don't think spring and summer at Protonilus mean warmth and butterflies. Summer at Protonilus is like summer in Antarctica. Daytime temps run up to maybe ten degrees, but at night it drops back to minus sixty. We'll still need the reactors to keep from freezing."

Eric's vid is replaced by a south Asian woman. Under other circumstances she'd be pretty—but today her mouth has a grim and irregular twist. "This is Senuri Kumar, flight director on *Endurance*. I want to make clear the reasons we chose this new path. From an engineering perspective, once the landing has been accomplished, Hellas is as survivable as Protonilus. But the landing is the most hazardous phase. Each spacecraft weighs almost one hundred tons. No mass remotely as heavy has ever landed on Mars. The largest so far were the two Russian ExoMars probes, both three tons. That was over forty years ago."

Eric takes over. He tells us he thinks it would be prudent to err in the direction of caution. Flat terrain increases the probability of successful landings. Far fewer hazards. This is why early aerospace organizations like NASA chose flat sites for their first Viking landers. The summer sunshine hours won't do any good if we don't survive the landing. In fact, two separate landing sites gives us a better overall chance. With everyone at the same site, a single unknown hazard could kill us all.

Paige folds her arms. "What does Jürgen say?"

According to the Articles, the captain has the authority to make these big decisions. But Eric doesn't mention Jürgen.

I clear my throat. "This affects all of us. We're supposed to come down five hundred meters apart and back each other up. Now you want three spacecraft at Protonilus, the other two on the other side of the planet?"

Alison asks, "Are you sure flatter is safer for landing? Maybe we should all switch to Hellas."

I remind her, "David expected us to land in hilly terrain, where the resources are. Flatter terrain, less variety of resources."

Eric wipes his hand across his face. "Flatter is safer. The GNC will do a correction burn on or about forty-five Taurus, seven days from now. As a test, I simulated a trajectory to Hellas and it would require very little extra propellant, provided we edit the programmed landing points before the next correction. If we wait, we'll be committed to Protonilus."

Paige, Shuko, and Alison turn to me. As if, what do we do? Mikki and Ryder shove their dinner into their mouths faster than usual.

I ask Eric, "Are we certain we can grow food during the winter months?"

"It would be beneficial to have a higher sun angle and more hours of daylight. The big unknown factor is how long it will take to fabricate and erect greenhouse enclosures. We'll need tons of polycarbonates derived from native resources. The Genesis planners figured sixty to ninety days after landing, but Senuri and I agree that could be wildly optimistic. If there are delays getting the enclosures pressurized, if it takes a couple of hundred days or longer, we'll be more than half-way through our food reserves and heading into the northern hemisphere winter. We may end up entirely dependent on winter crops when our stored food runs out."

Mikki snickers. "That's when we roast your ass on a spit."

"Whatever we do," I tell them, "We do it together. Hellas or Protonilus, all five spacecraft must have the same destination.

Face it, we don't know how many out of five will make a successful landing. We're going to need all the backup we can get.
We have a few days to decide. I propose we consider the question further and make an informed vote. I'm willing to change
our trajectory if that's what the majority decides is the best
option."

"Doesn't anyone remember the Charter?" asks Paige. "This
is up to the captain."

"That's right," snaps Tess on the vid feed from
Independence. Her eyes are still puffy from the last traces of the
super-flu. "Captain Morita will speak now. Hold questions until
he's done."

He's *Captain Morita* now.

El Capitán wears his customary sly smile. In some crazy
way he knows everything will turn out fine. "We're here for a
common purpose," he begins, eyes tranquil and confident at the
same time. "We rejected our comfortable existence in exchange
for the ability to control our own destiny. My colleagues Eric
and Senuri are driven by that same pursuit of liberty."

Jürgen's vid dissolves to a pic of a smiling Senuri posed
with a group standing in a field of deep green vegetation.

"Six months ago, at age nineteen, Senuri was the youngest
person to ever serve as general manager of a farming coopera-
tive in the Republic of India."

Another pic: Eric without his beard, speaking if front of a
group of technicians.

"At age eighteen, Eric was promoted to senior project manager at Nihon Unisys. Neither Senuri nor Eric are likely to make
hurried decisions. It probably is safer to land at Hellas. But if it
were safety you craved, you would have stayed on Earth. Our
purpose is not to be safe. Our purpose is to build a free civilization, and to accomplish that end we need to work together as a
cohesive society. This strategy of mutual help and reinforcement
is as old as humanity itself, and it is a strategy with a record of
success, especially when venturing forth into a new frontier."

I almost clap my hands. It had to happen eventually; El
Capitán is completely correct.

Jürgen displays a diagram of Mars's orbit around the sun—
a slightly-flattened elliptical circle with one side noticeably closer to the sun than the other.

"Landing alive is our first goal. I'm also concerned with our second and third goals, as well as our fourth, fifth, tenth, and hundredth. There are a thousand necessary steps that need to come together before we can have a thriving, stable community."

A green arrow appears on the diagram. "Here's Mars today, a few weeks before the beginning of spring in the northern hemisphere. Notice how Mars is moving into the part of its orbit that brings it further from the sun. As Mars moves further from the sun, it's orbital velocity decreases. Mars reaches aphelion here, during the northern hemisphere summer. This means summer in the northern hemisphere lasts a long time. We'll have about four hundred days of relatively warm daytime temps, with fourteen hours of sunshine per day."

Jürgen's face returns, this time the somber Jürgen. "In the southern hemisphere the opposite effect occurs. Winters are long, summers short. Hellas is heading into four hundred days of little sunshine. A couple of hundred days from now, when we'll be ready to grow food, Hellas will be in the middle of winter with only nine hours of low-angle sunlight per day. Will we be able to keep the plants from freezing during a fourteen-hour night at minus one hundred degrees? If we can't, we starve. At Protonilus, we'll have two harvests stored away before the first winter hits. It will be a shorter winter, less than three hundred days."

No argument comes from Eric, Senuri, or anyone else. A genuine magical wizard, Jürgen could change minds without arguing or threatening. Whatever he decides becomes contagious.

This time it's a wonderful thing.

TWENTY-SIX

The sharpest consequences of tight confinement require a full month to bloom. After a crappy day, there's no place to take a walk, no place to get away. Some days are so horrendous the *rii-iiiip* sound of Velcro on the bottom of Paige's socks is enough to arouse blood-pounding rage.

My dreams are in vivid colors. They start instantly when I fall asleep: eagles flying across a brilliant blue sky, enormous pink-granite mountains, misty redwood forests rich with the aromas of life. Yes, dreams with smells. Sensory deprivation, maybe? The wonders of spaceflight.

We have no real Stream, but all is not lost. David promised a vast store of vids and books, and he wasn't lying. There are millions, far more than one person could watch in a lifetime. Many are from the 1970s, 1980s, all through the 2020s—violent and confusing, but entertaining in a weird way. Are these vids accurate about life in the old America states? Contrary to what we learned at Academy, the people in those times weren't starving or under constant threat of murder. They were mostly happy, and they knew once they were inside their residences nothing could watch them.

Since the equipment bay is his bedroom, Shuko usually does the daily maintenance on the CO_2 scrubbers and HEPA filters. I think I understand why he likes it in there: the ventilation is stronger than in the sleepers and some spots are like an outdoor breeze against your skin.

The super-snot sickness finally fades and spaceball makes a comeback. "Try to get in two games every day," orders Blair Rizzo. "We've all lost muscle and cardio fitness over the past month. This will help prepare us for working under gravity."

On 46 Taurus, Eric announces the GNC will perform a mid-course correction, another trajectory adjustment to compensate for the tiny but cumulative gravitational influences of the planets. "The thrusters will burn for just under three minutes. I don't like this because it will use up more than half our remaining propellant."

This time we avoid the head-spins by lying flat in our sleepers.

The oxygen generators lose one half of one percent of their output every day. The compressed reserve comes on-line intermittently to maintain enough O2 partial pressure.

I ask Eric, "What can we do to get the reserves full again?"

"They're reserves, Cristina. If you extrapolate the decrease, every spacecraft will arrive with a fifty-percent surplus, except *Endurance* might be down to forty. As soon as we land we'll be able to produce O2 directly from the atmosphere with the solid oxide units, before we even go out on the surface."

"That's if your assumptions hold out. We should hedge by cutting out spaceball. Uses up more oxygen, doesn't it?"

Eric frowns. "I'll pass that up to the captain."

"You do what you want. There won't be any more spaceball on *Liberty*."

Schedules drift apart again. Only Shuko is around at every meal—always pleasant, too. Is he still hoping? Clearly not going to happen, so why not communicate his interest to one of the other girls? I mean, it's two-to-one! Why should Ryder have all the fun with the other three?

Finally, a bit of joy. Ten days before landing, Senuri comes on vid. "At nine-twenty Protonilus Coordinated Time, Doctor Hannah Lacy became the first person in world history to see the disk of Mars with her unaided eyes."

Scattered cheers and applause ring from the com. We rush to the big window. Eric says, "I'm going to adjust everyone's attitude so the bulk of your TMI blocks the sun."

Ryder flicks the lights off. Yes—no longer just a point of light, Mars is a teeny pink-orange dot, barely large enough to have a shape. But it's now more than just a speck; it's a place.

Paige whispers, "Still so far away."

Ryder's voice cracks with excitement. "Look close, see if you can spot the moons. There are two, and one orbits in less than eight hours."

Darien tells us, "We're still twelve million kilometers out, too far to see Phobos and Deimos. The disk is only two minutes of arc wide, about one sixteenth the size of a full moon from Earth. Be another few days before we can make out features."

"Bullshit," Ryder snarls. "I can see features right now. I see mountains and I can even see the exact spot I'm going to build a house."

Mikki calls from her sleeper, "You are the biggest liar ever born."

I place my hand atop his head. "Keep lying. Lie until it comes true."

✳

The joy is short-lived. I wake to a muffled voice: Shuko in an uncharacteristic angry tone. Something must be exceptionally wrong.

Shuko's almost snarling. "You're wasting the cartridges. Brief exposure is harmless."

Senuri's on vid. She pulls the EOB from her mouth and coughs. "Easy for you to say! It's burning the hell out of my throat."

I stop my forward motion with Shuko's arm. "What's going on?"

"Air problem on *Endurance*."

"Oxygen?"

"Particulate contamination. Potassium hydroxide."

That's the electrolyte in the oxygen generators. "Get Eric."

Liberty's oxygen partial pressure is what it should be, twenty-four kilopascals. But the output of all three generators is only sixteen percent, compressed reserve eighty-five percent. There's an orange message on the warning panel: potassium hydroxide air particulate 2.6 mg/cubic meter. There's been an upward trend for ten days.

Eric clears his throat. "I expected this. The seals are leaking. There's something like fifty O-rings and polyethylene gaskets in each unit. The high temps and continuous operation create hot spots. This is a known issue. We're not going to suffocate, Cristina. There's some electrolyte precipitating out, but there's an easy fix. Just put a HEPA filter on your O2 bleed. It's threaded to fit."

"So this is happening to everyone?"

"Yeah, because everyone's O2 sets are running hot with low-flow. My projections are holding. Nobody's under seventy percent reserve. We'll land in nine days with forty percent or more reserve."

"Shit, Eric! That's twenty hours' margin, and you're happy?" I face Shuko. "Let's get the filter attached and get everyone up."

We pull the others out of their sleepers, Alison directly from Ryder's arms. They stare at me with identical frowns.

"This is my fault," I tell them. "I promised to come up with an alternative way to produce oxygen. I got nowhere. I need your help."

Mikki mutters, "Imagine that."

Ryder yawns. "Did you have any ideas at all?"

I answer, "No, but we have time, even if the O2 generators in the TMI don't last much longer. Forty kilos of oxygen would protect us against total failure. Eric knows a lot, but he's limited to what's in the manuals. We need to think beyond the manuals."

Alison asks, "Can we print a duplicate OGS and run it right here?"

"Good thinking, but the docs don't carry the full printer spec. In theory we can try designing our own, but a weightless type OGS works with ultrasonics, and they're complicated and difficult to design properly."

"Each of us exhales a kilo of carbon dioxide every day," says Shuko. "The scrubber removes it and vents it into space. Can we redirect that CO2 to a tank and strip out the oxygen?"

I think for a moment. "We have two devices that strip O2 from CO2, the two solid oxide units. They're designed to pull oxygen right out of the Mars atmosphere because it's almost all CO2. But they don't work without gravity."

Ryder grips the table edge. "Why can't we repair the existing OGS units?"

"Eric considers that unrealistic and I agree with him. They're inside the TMI and obstructed by other equipment. If we could reach and retrieve one unit, how would we disassemble it, replace at least fifty seals, and reassemble it so it would work— without a schematic? We need a simple idea that will work."

Paige purses her lips. "I have something, but you're not going to like it. There's a four-ton tank of nitrogen tetroxide on the other side of the equipment bay. Tetroxide is seventy percent oxygen by weight. I'm not sure about the best way to decompose the oxygen out of it, or how to collect the gas without gravity. A centrifuge maybe."

Ryder asks, "Nitrogen tet, that's the oxidizer for the landing thrusters. Would we have enough left to land?"

"It gets worse," says Paige. "Tet is nasty stuff, toxic and reactive. Opening up that tank and dealing with it while weight-less would be a big risk. I don't know how efficient the extraction would be. In theory, we'd only need around sixty liters, less than two percent of the total. But in practice? I just don't know."

I tell them, "It's an idea, and that's what we need, ideas. Let's see what we can come up with by noon today. If we're lucky, the OGS units will crap-out slowly and we'll land with a few hours' reserve."

Except they don't crap-out slowly. They crap-out rapidly, with the total failure of critical seals.

TWENTY-SEVEN

Endurance and *Independence* are the worst cases. Electrolyte leakage causes short circuits and sudden shutdowns. The units on *Liberty* aren't much better off, and by the following afternoon, slightly less than eight full days before landing, OGS unit two goes to zero output.

> *ERROR CODE 004 BC*
> *CONCENTRATOR FAILURE DUE TO A PRESSURE*
> *ERROR*

"Reserves are at seventy-nine percent," Shuko tells us. "About thirty-eight hours, plus six hours in the BioSuit packs."

Eric growls a general announcement. "Do not attempt to manually start a unit that went down with a zero zero four error. Once the concentrator goes, it needs to be physically replaced."

"Then let's print one and physically replace it," Ryder says. "I'll go out there and do it."

Eric shakes his head. "You can't disassemble the unit in-place and re-assemble the parts perfectly. Even if you could it would develop the same problems. We all need new OGS units."

Mikki mumbles, "Thanks for clarifying the obvious, fatty."

Is the control center rotating? I'm imagining it; the sunbeams aren't moving. I grab the solid edge of the master panel so I can think. We discussed a handful of ideas yesterday, none of them workable. A precious day wasted.

Paige tells us, "I investigated methods decomposing oxygen from tetroxide. Doesn't look good. We'd need to print complex equipment, and if something goes wrong the cabin would be lethally contaminated. And I'm not sure if we'd have enough left for landing."

A chemical engineer, and she has nothing. "I didn't like that idea anyhow. There's got to be something else."

Not a word from Jürgen. Is he coordinating? Tess blocks access, as usual. "Maybe he expects you to do something," she tells me in her superior tone. "Like with the star tracker. What are you waiting for?"

Ryder refuses to abandon hope of fixing the existing units. "If they can make it, I can fix it. How do we know we can't do it if we don't try?"

"Get a grip," snarls Mikki. "How could we print parts without the spec? How would you even reach the thing? Use your brain!"

"Use your own! We can print standard size O-rings. I can remove a unit whole and bring it into the cabin."

Mikki snickers. "All the cabling, the tubing, the mounting pins, you're going to just reach inside the TMI, disconnect all that, bring it in here?"

"I can try!"

"The airlock hatches are one hundred and two centimeters wide," Paige tells us. "The OGS units are thirty centimeters wider, even with the solenoids removed. I checked."

It takes less than two hours for unit three to die. Another concentrator failure.

They must know the truth. "The last unit is holding at fifteen percent. Enough to support one person. That stretches the reserve to what, forty-three hours? Then six in our suit packs. We're a hundred and eighty-two hours from landing. Now it's a given. We have to make oxygen."

Mikki's eyes are screwed shut, her arms twisted together in a death grip.

Shuko tells us, "We can reduce the partial pressure. Sleep as much as possible. That would cut consumption somewhat, but nowhere near enough."

Is everyone else down to one or two units? Eric isn't responding. The vid from *Constitution* shows an empty control deck. There's a shadow, and Darien comes into view. Even from a distance his face sparkles with sweat.

"Darien!" I call to him. "Pull Eric out of his sleeper."

"You know what's going on?" He's barely audible.

"Get Eric!"

Darien's face fills the vid. His chin trembles. "We're not going to make it. Not all of us. That's what they're saying now."

"Who's saying that, Darien?"

"Eric, Senuri, Norberto. They're calculating how many people each spacecraft can support. They think three at the most."

A sniff from behind. Mikki, now curled up into a ball. Alison asks, "What does that mean?"

"Don't worry about it," I tell her. "Pure bullshit."

Shuko mumbles, "No, it's logical. Not enough reserve for six."

"We're going to make oxygen. Enough for everyone." I point to Paige. "You said you know how to pull oxygen from tet. Can we do it in two days?"

"It would be hard, Cristina. We screw up, we're dead."

"We can try!" Ryder yells. "I'm not ready for some kind of random-selection suicide."

"Who said random?" Paige shoots back. "We're going to start another generation. The number of females is all that matters. We have cryonic sperm—"

"Paige!" I bark. "Don't mention that again. Not going to happen. Do we have the specs for the equipment? And a procedure?"

Paige wipes her hand across her eyes. "I'll have to write the specs. We're going to need about ten kilos of copper stock, then design a centrifuge to separate the O2 from water and nitric acid."

What did she just say?

I grab Paige's arm. "Centrifuge!"

"To separate the gaseous oxygen."

"A centrifuge! Because your equipment won't work weightless, needs an acceleration force."

"That's right," she answers. "The OGS uses ultrasonic separation. A centrifuge is less compact, less efficient, but it'll serve the purpose."

Ryder slaps his palm against his forehead. "Son of a bitch."

✳

This is no longer a matter of oxygen. This battle is mental. Ryder and Paige aren't finished with the design, but I have to get it out now. If fear grabs hold, no solution can work.

"We can make more oxygen. You won't need the OGS. We're going to replenish our reserves and land with one hundred percent. Do you hear me? All of us. One hundred percent!"

Senuri disagrees. "We conferenced with seven engineers. Do you realize that very shortly there won't be enough reserve for any of us to land alive? The numbers show thirteen can make it—"

"Shut it, Senuri! Has El Capitán told you to pick anyone for suicide? Then listen—"

Eric growls, "Now you listen. You're getting ahead of yourself. You don't understand the situation or the numbers we're dealing with. *Endurance* and *Independence* are both below seventy percent. If they act now, two can land alive, two females. The rest of us, it'll be three females." His voice cracks. "We can't wait. The numbers—"

Screams and shouts drown out his words. I get it. They're fighting over who gets to live. My fingers tremble. What if the idea doesn't work? Some of us must die. Today.

"This is Vijay Mehta, flight director aboard *Resolute*. We are standing by for your instructions, Cristina. Would you please direct our preparations and give us a time estimate to test the solution?"

The uproar subsides. I need to sound as tranquil as Vijay. "Give us one hour for the spec. Everybody! Power-up both your printers. Get the stock out. You'll need a lot of high-density polyethylene and aluminum, steel for clips and nylon for bearings. You'll also need to print two standard motors and a compressor. This is how it works. We're all carrying two portable oxygen generators. They're Chéngzhǎng designs, so they need lunar-level gravity or higher. We're going to spin both of them in a centrifuge. It won't be that big or spin very fast. A meter wide, twenty to thirty revolutions per minute."

Senuri asks, "If it's spinning, how the hell are you going to get the water in and the oxygen out?"

Paige looks up from her screen. "Feed water and oxygen will spin along with the generators. Once the tank is full of compressed oxygen we can stop the spin and replenish the reserve."

Senuri moves closer to the vid. "You have no proof this can work. You're guessing, aren't you? Do you understand if it doesn't work there won't be enough reserve for anyone?"

"So give up, Senuri. Lead the way and be the first aboard *Endurance* to die for the sake of oxygen conservation."

Senuri vanishes.

Eric tells us, "It has to work on every spacecraft and it has to work soon."

I correct him. "One spacecraft can make enough oxygen for all thirty of us, and transfer it through the airlocks in cylinders."

Would the capacity truly be enough? If not, I told a lie. But my lie worked. There's no further talk of impending death.

And not a word from Jürgen. Not one word.

The printers purr and the idea becomes real. Ryder and Paige's spec cleverly uses the oxygen tank as the centrifuge axis. One end anchors to a seat support. Two plastic one-liter tanks for deionized water are mounted above the generator cases. The compressor and motor are close to the axis—actually there are two, for balance.

Shuko pulls the oxygen generators from their storage locker. They're sealed white cases marked with the logo of the manufacturer, Fukai. Alison finds the documentation. The largest outside dimension is sixty-eight centimeters. The subassembly that produces the oxygen, something called a polymer membrane pack, is fifty centimeters long and only twelve wide. The cases are long and narrow so they'll be mounted parallel to the axis.

Ryder says, "We need to figure out what to do with the hydrogen."

I ask him, "What happens to it when the units are running as designed?"

"Vented continuously. But we can't vent hydrogen inside the cabin. Never mind the backpressure, it's explosive and a suffocation hazard."

"Can't we compress it into a separate tank, like the oxygen?"

"Way harder to compress hydrogen," answers Paige. "Even if we print a diaphragm compressor we wouldn't be able to cool it. And it would be huge. We can use hydride pellets to absorb hydrogen and then heat them to vent it off, but there's not enough elemental stock to print the pellets. This is a problem."

Mikki launches herself from her hiding spot just inside the equipment bay. She looks over the spec. Her face is red, and she's sniffling. "Any reason we can't we vent it from a hose off the top of the O2 tank? The connection can be the upper bearing."

Ryder grins. "A hollow bearing! Mick, I think that can work."

She turns away. "Make it work, because I'm not going any closer to Mars without your ugly ass with me to share the misery."

✳

The *Oxirotor*, as Paige dubs it, consists of sixteen subassemblies separately printed and clipped together. This will take several hours, so I upload the spec and get everyone started. If anything needs to be tweaked, we can re-print only the altered parts. People will stay sane if they can assemble something real. They need hope in the form of something they can touch.

We run a pair of six-gauge cables from the power panel to the centrifuge mount. The hydrogen vent line is a five millimeter hose leading to the threaded connection at the end of the Sabatier tank manifold, and from there the vacuum of space.

Things look good until Shuko shows me a red GNC message:

TG0037 PENDING MIDCOURSE PROPELLANT
DEFICIT.

"We'll deal with it later," I tell him. "One disaster at a time is enough."

The subassemblies fit together to form a fat, drum-shaped cylinder just over a meter wide and a meter tall. The water tanks are removable, so they can be filled from the hygiene pit. Fukai oxygen generators have built-in demineralizers so they can take potable water and deionize it before it hits the electrolysis membranes. When the last component is in place, Alison and Mikki wrap an aluminum mesh around the exterior—a barrier to keep us from knocking into spinning parts.

At thirty revolutions per minute, the Oxirotor sings a pleasing *thump thump thump* song. I can't take my eyes off it. Ryder cuts the power and stops the rotation with his hand. He switches the oxygen generators on. "We'll let it spin until the water tanks are empty. That should take about two hours."

Vijay announces the Oxirotor aboard *Resolute* is ready for operation.

"Make sure your vent is open at the manifold," Ryder tells him. "Otherwise the generators will shut down due to hydrogen backpressure. I apologize for the lack of instrumentation."

"My friend," says Vijay. "if this works, and I believe it will, as far as I am concerned none of you will never again need to apologize for any transgression as long as you live."

"Ours is spinning," reports Tess. "No idea if it's doing anything."

Ryder tells us, "The O2 generators feel around half an Earth gravity. They should work."

The *thump thump thump* is hypnotic. Time rushes by in a half-awake daze, but we can't wait a full two hours. Ryder stops the rotation and peers at the tiny pressure gauge. For a few seconds he says nothing and I almost kick him.

"Nine and a half bar!" he yells. "Hear that? Nine and a half bar! How much is that in mass?"

Paige smiles, a new look for her. "We sized the cylinder to be a sixth of the volume of the reserve bank. Twenty bar is full, two days for one person. We got a day's worth, around eight-tenths of a kilo."

"Hear that?" Ryder shouts into the com. "Almost a kilo of oxygen in one hour and seven minutes. It needs to run only six hours a day to keep us breathing!"

Can one Oxirotor put out enough for thirty people to breathe? No, but close. My flight suit is soaked with sweat. And I have to pee.

Paige is in a chatty mood and she finds a way to bring Jürgen into our victory. "Jürgen did the right thing by staying out of the way. He's a geologist, a long-term planner, a poetic idealist. He knew we didn't need inspiration. He had confidence in us. He wisely let the engineers solve the problem our own way and without distraction. He's a perfect leader."

"Yeah, perfect," I answer. Nothing more, not tonight. Too exhausted.

Ryder points a shaky finger at the warning panel.

A new line, in cherry red.

TG0040 MIDCOURSE CORRECTION TERMINATED
DUE TO PROPELLANT DEFICIT

TWENTY-EIGHT

First, sleep. No sense trying to resolve the latest guidance system error with a whacked brain. Ryder claims to be too hyped to sleep, so he babysits the Oxirotor. He plans to run it until the water tanks need refills and then discharge the new oxygen into the reserve bank. Nice to see him hyped about something other than spaceball or Alison's body.

When I wake, the oxygen reserve shows one hundred and three percent, technically overpressurized. Ryder lets out a huge yawn. "Next time there won't be any room to discharge it." We decide to spin it periodically to maintain the correct partial pressure.

How serious is the "midcourse correction terminated" message? The GNC displays our arrival time, a good sign. It can wait until we eat. Hungry! Is this breakfast or lunch? The menu wisely offers selections suitable for both.

Shuko's back in pursuit. He presses his whole leg against mine, softly, sneakily, using his foot as a hook around my calf as he must have seen Alison do with Ryder. I pull away. Can he at least show some originality?

"You were outstanding last night," he whispers. "An ingenious solution. I still can't believe it works so well."

"Didn't design it, didn't build it," I mumble, harshness unjustified.

I avoid eye contact, but he doesn't care. "Without you, I don't even want to think about what could have happened yesterday."

"Thank you, Shuko. Sorry I barked at you." Annoying and clumsy aren't crimes. Even if they should be.

Tess is smiling for once. "Captain Morita will now address us."

Paige waves her spoon. "Please please please be quiet!"

"In six days we'll be home," Jürgen tells us. His sturdy voice fills the control center and spreads a sense of strength. "Our greatest adventures and discoveries will soon begin. Yesterday we surmounted the most daunting challenge we've ever faced. Everyone played a role toward our success, but I want to take a moment to recognize four individuals, four quick-thinking engineers who conceived the...what did you name it, Paige?"

"Oxirotor!" Paige cries. "The Oxirotor!"

"I want to recognize Paige Weber for envisioning the centrifuge solution," Jürgen continues over a rising swell of applause. "And Ryder Lawson and Mikki Tischler for designing the Oxirotor, and Senuri Kumar for coordinating assembly and testing."

Cheers erupt from the com. Ryder glances at me, then Jürgen's vid. Shuko pushes away from the table and flips backwards toward the hygiene pit. Mikki stares at Jürgen, no longer chewing, her face empty of emotion.

Jürgen. Cabrón!

Is he maybe saving it for last? Of course not. No mention at all.

"We'll be facing even greater challenges," Jürgen goes on. "Yesterday we displayed the sort of invincible spirit—"

"Wait!"

All heads snap to Mikki. "Are you fucking kidding me?"

I touch her wrist. "Mick, leave it."

"You!" She thrusts a trembling finger at Jürgen. "Where the hell were you?"

Jürgen closes his mouth and frowns.

She's not done. Not even close. "Eric! Eric, you son of a bitch. Thanks to you, I thought I would die. Or watch my friends die."

A tiny voice replies, "You have no basis to blame me."

Mikki grabs my collar. "This person! We made it because of this person! You had half of us dead. You were sure of it!"

Paige folds her arms. "Jürgen said everyone played a role."

Mikki twists away from the table and assumes her rolled-into-a-ball float position. I wait for Jürgen to respond, but the vid from *Independence* is empty except for someone's leg.

My turn. "Yesterday we had a scare." For a moment the words won't come until I listen to the vent fans. "What did we learn? First, keep calm. I was so terrified I couldn't think. Reminds me of taking math and science entrance exams when I was thirteen. Just tell yourself, work out the problem. Think of nothing but the problem." For some reason I look to Ryder. "Second, we need each other. Each of us can provide a piece of the solution. Everyone is essential in their own way."

What else? The fans drone on.

Eric says, "Want to know what I learned? I should have kept managing the OGS temps like I did the first three weeks. It was working well enough. But people got nervous and threw fits over the shutdowns. Whose fault was that, Cristina? Who was I trying to please by going to the low-flow parallel mode that eventually burned out the seals? I learned to listen to my own engineering judgment and not surrender to the emotional opinions of people who lack that judgment."

Norberto calls out, "The shutdowns were getting closer together! No one forced you to change anything."

I have more. "The first step in solving a problem is to recognize that it exists. We have a new problem to work. Look at your nav. Propellant deficit. A hundred and seventy seconds of thruster propellant remain. Why doesn't the GNC think that's enough to do course corrections? What are we going to do about it?"

Darien responds. I don't know him well. He looks and sounds too young to be here. "Me and Eric looked at the parameters last night. The correction estimates become more accurate as we approach Mars. Yesterday it started thinking we might need more delta-V to adjust our trajectory. We need to hit the atmosphere within a narrow entry corridor. The aerobraking has to be exact. If the angle or the timing is off, we'll either burn up or fail to shed enough velocity and fly past the planet."

Ryder asks, "Didn't we start with a five percent surplus?"

Eric still sounds as if he blames me. "We ate up the margin because the GNC ran the initial ten-hour boost against biased position inputs. The first and second corrections were a lot bigger than planned. Plus, we launched seven days early, which makes our trajectory a bit longer."

"But we fixed the bias," Alison says. "So why didn't the system set us on the correct trajectory?"

"It did set us on the correct trajectory," Darien tells her. "But due to inherent precision limits and gravitational perturbations, it can't set us on a *perfect* trajectory. That's why we need several midcourse corrections. Picture it like a boat influenced by winds and currents. Even if you point the boat in the right direction, in order to arrive precisely at the dock you need to correct with the rudder to counteract all the natural forces affecting your course. Our trajectory is curved by the sun's gravity, but we're also influenced by the weaker gravitational fields of every planet, every moon, every asteroid. The total effect is impossible to calculate in advance so we have to position-check and correct as we go."

Mikki uncoils herself. "Why is this so hard? Automated spacecraft have been landing on Mars since nineteen seventy-six."

I know the answer. "Margin of error. We're moving about six times faster than the old probes and our landing mass is a hundred times heavier. And our trajectory has to be more precise for the aerobraking to work."

Eric reports, "Darien and I came up with a solution. It won't be easy, and the sooner we get started the better. We abandon one spacecraft and transfer the remaining propellant to the other four. The other craft each take one or two extra people. The propellant is argon, an inert gas. Since the pressure is under a thousand kp we can do a simple hose transfer."

I have to point out the obvious. "Land with only four spacecraft? We'll have twenty-five percent less of everything."

"Design safety margin," says Darien. "One spacecraft can actually support up to thirty-six."

Ryder turns to Eric. "Correct me if I'm wrong. It's not really more propellant we need. We need more velocity change."

"Well, yeah, but the thrusters use propellant to change velocity."

Darian's eyes light up. "I get it! Reduce our mass, greater velocity change with the same amount of propellant."

Eric shakes his head. "We'd have to lose tons."

"Not necessarily," Darien tells him. "These deficit messages just showed up yesterday. Twenty-four hours ago, the GNC thought we had enough propellant. The difference between the predicted and plotted velocity vectors can't be very large. It might only be a few meters per second."

I try to keep my tone non-confrontational. "Eric, do you agree the propellant deficit is probably small? Could we wipe out that deficit by losing some mass?"

"I don't know, Cristina. I do know the propellant transfer would work for certain. Darien believes your idea is theoretically possible. But what mass can we give up?"

The answer is water. The designers supplied the TMI with three hundred liters for the OGS to electrolisize. About one hundred and eighty liters remain, plus forty-five liters of electrolyte inside the units themselves.

"I can vent it through the relief valves," says Eric. "Assuming none of it freezes in the lines, that lightens each spacecraft by around two hundred and twenty kilos."

I ask, "How much can we spare from the regular tanks, the potable water?"

That turns heads. Paige twists her mouth. "Our drinking and washing water?"

"It's recycled by eighty percent, so a little goes a long way."

Paige screws up her face. "What do you mean, recycled?"

"Haven't you been learning the systems? There's a reverse osmosis unit that purifies urine and a condenser that pulls moisture from the air. All that goes back into the supply."

She covers her eyes. Ryder strokes her hair. "Where did you think it went after it's sucked down the tube?"

Math time. "We started with four eighty-liter tanks. We're down to a hundred and seventy-five, pretty low because the Oxirotor has been using some of it. We'll need to electrolyze another thirty-five. If we don't wash for the next six days and we find drinkable water after landing, we can dump at least half of what we got."

Shuko tells us, "Lowering the cabin temp will reduce perspiration and body odor."

"Wonderful," Mikki mumbles. "We get there filthy and freezing."

But we get there.

Darien and I work out the specifics. Each spacecraft will keep one hundred liters of water in case finding ice at the landing site proves tougher than anticipated. No clothing or medical supplies will be sacrificed. Food? The hygiene pit is surrounded by stainless steel tanks containing four tons of oils, powders, pastes, and pellets—nutrient stock for the food printer. Anonymous decision: every gram of nourishment will be kept.

Liberty can afford to jettison 295 liters of water. I put the GNC into simulation mode and deduct that mass from the stored value. Numbers flash—the final verdict is green:

PENDING MIDCOURSE TRAJECTORY
CORRECTION
14:20:00 PCT 55 TAURUS 53
ESTIMATED DURATION 00:01:56

"Darien's right," I announce. "A little goes a long way."

Eric runs the necessary commands. Water vents and bursts into vapor outside the windows. The cloud instantly freezes into thousands of swirling ice crystals sparkling in the sunlight. Paige and I press our faces against the cool glass and enjoy the enchanting sight. Is a snow storm something like this? The crystals from the other spacecraft quickly cross the kilometer distance and fill the blackness with countless sparks.

Paige says, "They look more like stars than stars."

The GNC flashes red:

TC0932 PLATFORM ALIGNMENT FAILED.

What the hell did we just do?

Eric announces, "The ice crystals confuse the tracker. It can't find the nav stars."

We wait. The swarming sparklers gradually dissipate. Sometime after midnight Norberto and Darien manually guide *Liberty's* tracker to Deneb, a navigation star separated from Mars by roughly ninety degrees of arc. This lets the GNC use both Deneb and the center of Mars's disk to precisely orient the spacecraft. A minute later the GNC shines green:

ALLIGNMENT COMPLETE 00:39:43 PCT 56
Taurus 53

It rapidly sets up for a course correction. "I'm just gonna point my feet this way and hold on," Ryder says as he rotates his body. The thrusters fire and the wall separating the control center from the equipment bay becomes a floor. The weak acceleration, just five percent Earth gravity, sets everything spinning and swimming—and Mars gravity will be eight times stronger.

Ryder twirls Alison on his left arm. Her body sweeps sideways and momentum sends them both gliding and giggling across the compartment.

A touch on the elbow—qué demonios! Shuko, with a stern frown. He wants to dance? I give two head shakes. "Dizzy enough as it is!"

Bad answer! Does he now believe if not for the dizziness, we would have twirled together?

The GNC calls, "*Thrusters off*," and the floor drops away.

ETA PROTONILUS MENSEA PM1 09:27:00 PCT 3 GEMINI 54

Paige and Alison cheer and Ryder slaps me across the shoulders. Almost a punch, but somehow good—infinitely superior to a flimsy elbow grab.

Eric's voice is drowsy. "We're set for another correction on two Gemini. And with that, I bid everyone good night."

Alison turns to Ryder. "I don't get this Taurus Gemini thing. It means the month, but we have twelve months in the Mars calendar, so why can't it just be December, January, like regular months?"

Ryder releases yet another lion yawn. "The number of days per month are completely different from Earth, and the big orbital eccentricity means the month lengths vary a lot. Today is fifty-six Taurus, the last day of Taurus, the last day of the year."

Shuko says, "If tonight is the new year, there should be a celebration."

I launch myself into the hygiene pit before anyone else can beat me.

TWENTY-NINE

It isn't exactly a celebration, but at least everyone agrees to gather in their respective spacecraft control centers at 23:30 to await the beginning of Year 54.

The expected Jürgen speech doesn't come. Instead, Senuri speaks the two magic words guaranteed to get everyone's attention: Discovery Team.

"The first survey expedition will be on seven Gemini, four days after landing," she says. Her tone is crisp and convincing, the voice of someone accustomed to being in charge—but it lacks charm. "Jürgen and I will select two people to accompany us. This first trip runs less than twenty kilometers so we avoid potentially hazardous terrain—"

"Can I ask something?" I cut in. "Four days after landing? These Discovery Team surveys use the trucks, right? So we need to make methanol fuel plus the oxygen to burn it. Did we factor in the time to get the reactors installed and build up a reserve of water and oxygen?"

Senuri starts to respond but Jürgen pushes his own vid over hers. "Cristina is correct to ask about this. Yes, we've factored in the necessary time. Under no circumstances will methanol production begin until life support reserves are maxed. After landing, the helium tank that pressurizes the tetroxide system will be vented so it can serve as an oxygen container. Sixty-kilogram capacity, twelve days' reserve. Once that's full and we have five hundred liters of water in each spacecraft, it'll take less than a day for the Sabatier to synthesize enough fuel for the first Discovery Team expedition."

All right. He's got it planned out.

Senuri pushes a detailed terrain map, in grayscale except for a bright green oval. "This is our landing ellipse. The immediate area is rugged but likely to contain a variety of valuable resources, especially ice. See these clusters of pits? Probably created when ground ice sublimated to gas. There may also be cavities of undetermined depth just below the surface, so we'll avoid that area until we know more."

She'd learned a lot of geological terms from Jürgen. A soft touch on the shoulder—Shuko, at it again, pretending to need something solid to pull himself closer to the panel. Will he stop if utterly ignored? After all, we got three other girls here.

Senuri continues. "These are the best pics we have, but unfortunately they're also the oldest. They were taken by the Mars Reconnaissance Orbiter in 2009. We don't know how far the glacier edges have moved since then." A wavy blue line appears from the center of the oval and loops back. "This is the route for our first expedition. We'll keep to the smoothest terrain and investigate what we think is a hot spring four kilometers northeast of our landing site. This could turn out to be the most interesting nearby feature, a possible outlet for liquid water during the summer."

Ryder says, "And you're asking me to come along? Thank you! I accept." Mikki tosses an empty drink pouch at his head.

Another casual brush from Shuko's hand, this time across my left hip. Again, copied from Ryder and Alison. I remove the hand. Paige watches from the corner of her eye and giggles a bit.

The excursion talk is interesting, but this can't wait. I poke Shuko's arm and point toward the equipment bay hatch. The machinery hum will mask my words. His eyes dart around, then he follows me through the hatch.

"I want to talk to you about the touching."

He drops his eyes and shifts away. Too tough? Maybe, but this has to be over and done. Keep the words precise so there's no misunderstanding.

"I respect you very much but the touching must stop." I almost say *for now*. Dios mio! "In three days we'll all be with a new set of people. We'll have plenty of time to get to know everyone and form relationships." What else? Mention that with twenty females and ten males, the odds are in his favor?

He nods and makes a fleeting attempt at eye contact. I squeeze his shoulder and guide him back to the control center.

"What were you two doing?" Paige demands. "There's less than a minute!"

Ryder grumbles, "No beer, no vodka, no tequila. Anybody know how to print some shots of Jäger?"

The GNP changes from 23:59:59 PCT 56 Taurus to 00:00:00 PCT 1 Gemini 54.

A new year, and we scream and shout! Do you think being tens of millions of kilometers away from everything and everyone we've ever known will stop us? Ryder plants a wet kiss on everyone's cheek, and I mean everyone. Shuko almost cracks a smile.

Maybe Jürgen's uncomfortable not being the center of attention, so he makes a speech after all, his shortest ever, just a promise to meet with everyone privately after landing. Privately. Is Jürgen un mujeriego like Ryder? He'll keep busy.

I push off toward the hygiene pit, but Shuko's just closing the hatch. Ten seconds later a new text pops up—private. I hold my breath and duck into my sleeper.

Híjole!

Cristina, I think about you every day. Can we share love together? There is no reason not to do this because we are both healthy and I believe reasonably compatible. The worst may happen to us very soon. I don't want to chance it. May I join you? If yes, no answer is needed. I love you.

I slap the sleeper padding. Que desastre!

The stupid shoulder squeeze. But at least I know for sure: He doesn't want to die before romping at least once in his life. Sad…or estúpido? And what about the other three girls?

I text: *You don't really want me*…and stop. Too much like a lover's fight. Tried words once. Success will require action.

Mikki and Paige huddle in the control center whispering. I throw my best pleading look at Mikki and gesture toward the sleeper. She follows me in but I have to wait for her to stop laughing. She utters three badly pronounced words. "Cosechar las cerezas?" Another bout of childlike giggles.

"Funny, very funny. But I don't think it would be right, my being flight director."

That draws extra vigorous laughter. She's in a happy mood. Is there a chance? She wipes her nose with the back of her hand. "Oh, please! Can't you come up with a better excuse?"

"As a special favor."

"For him or for you?"

"I just feel…now is not the time."

She snickers. "Have you noticed there's a lot more of us than them?" One last giggle-fest, then, "I'm breathing your oxygen. That might be worth some kind of favor."

＊

The late night means no one bothers with breakfast. The control center is clean, quiet, and empty. The TMI points sunward so everything's dark and chilly—perfect opportunity to wrap myself in a sleeper blanket and sip hot tea while gazing out the window into empty blackness.

Less than forty-eight hours before landing, yet Mars remains tiny to unaided eyes. It's barely possible to make out a whitish dot near the edge—the polar ice cap—plus one little gray smudge. The orange disk appears oval-shaped because a slice of the night side blends into space.

Shuko's not curled up in the equipment bay. And Alison spent the night in our sleeper—without a single customary snore. Two amazing things, and the day hasn't even started.

The com shows Eric debating his engineering associates, a discussion no one bothered to push to *Liberty*. "We won't be overriding anything," Eric says. "Just like launch, strap in, hold tight, let it work as designed. We hit the atmosphere at twenty kilometers per second. What do you think you could do if something goes wrong?"

Andre agrees. "No one's going to hand-fly these things to the surface."

I don't know much about Andre, another physicist who likes to agree with Eric. He's smug and sure but how much does he really know about the systems?

"The final landing approach will be slow," I butt in. "The last three minutes have a series of events that occur at specific altitudes, speeds, and distances from touchdown. The flight directors should have some idea when and how to take action if the GNC screws up."

"Not like that would ever happen."

Shuko! He's perched a meter behind me, left arm around Mikki. He adds, "We got a long list of faults and breakdowns since launch. Expect another surprise or two before we're on the ground."

Darien says, "I'm not clear on what you're suggesting."

"I'm suggesting we be ready!"

Eric snickers. "You'll be dead before you know it."

"I want you on my side," I tell Eric. "I'm talking about the last three minutes, not the entire capture and entry. Yes, most of it will happen too fast to react. But at eleven thousand meters the GNC is supposed to deploy a parachute."

The hygiene pit hatch opens and Ryder says, "That's called high gate!"

"You've been reviewing the manual. Good! Now what happens when the chute cuts away?"

"Begin powered descent," he answers, quoting the manual. "At thirty-two hundred meters, a hundred and eighty knots."

"Low gate?"

Ryder doesn't hesitate. "Throttle up to reduce ground speed to zero. Altitude one hundred meters, four hundred downrange from touchdown."

Eric grumbles, "Cristina, you're not the only person to ever consider this. It's more likely you'll panic or misjudge. What if someone manually starts the descent engines too high? They'll run out of fuel before they reach the ground." He moves his mouth closer to the vid. "Splat!"

Shuko turns toward Ryder, "Would you switch with me and sit at the master panel during landing? If Cristina agrees, of course. You'll have a better view, and you can be her backup."

I nod and Ryder grins like a niño pequeño opening a birthday present.

"Word of advice," says Eric. "Don't override the engines. Just don't. They spent a lot of effort getting that part right by leveraging decades of experience guiding automatic landers down on other worlds. The system manages the throttles and there's no margin for error. If I had half a brain, I'd edit everyone's kernel right now so you couldn't do it even if you were stupid enough to try."

✳

Brains have gone mushy after six weeks of confinement and monotony. There's no other explanation. We land tomorrow morning, and Walt Sullivan doesn't respond to a request to organize a landing procedure drill for all flight directors and physicians. I ask again and he replies, "Me and Jessica drilled everybody on suits and airlock ops a week ago. Jürgen didn't tell us to do anything else."

He doesn't know what to do, so he does nothing, or defers to El Capitán. Was that the reason he was appointed an official Jürgen assistant?

Act as if.

There's still time to prepare, if we start now. I assign Mikki the responsibility for the reactor installation. Paige will be our resource extraction specialist. Both stare at me as if I'm crazy.

"This is an important job, Mick. Each spacecraft has just one power generator and it's nuclear, so it has to be shielded in a hole fifteen meters from the spacecraft. Paige, as our extraction specialist, you need to be proficient on the Sabatier reaction tank and the electrolysis separator, plus the associated compressors, valves, and control systems. We don't want to be figuring this stuff out at the last minute."

Mikki talks around a mouthful of food. "I'm a nanoprocessor engineer. I wouldn't know a nuclear generator if it bit me on the ass."

"No one's asking you to design it. You're going to take charge of the installation. It needs to be done right because our batteries would run out in a few days."

Alison says, "I don't understand why they didn't give us solar panels."

"Power and weight!" Ryder answers. "We need a lot of power to manufacture plastics and ceramics and bake bricks. We'll need thirty or forty kilowatts day and night. The solar panels to produce that much power would be bigger than a whole fútbol field and weigh a shitload of tons."

Ryder has done his homework. He'll be my backup in case Mikki can't handle it.

I get on the com. "We're twenty-one hours from the ground. Flight directors should know who's going to be seated at the panels during capture, entry, and landing. Whoever's up front should be willing to monitor the landing phase for problems and take appropriate action."

Vijay tells us, "I'll be at the window seat with Naldo. We need some idea how to safe the system in event of failure."

I correct him, "Not only safe the system, but get to the ground."

Eric tells us, "Oh, I guarantee you'll get to the ground. The question is at what velocity."

Fine. I lower my voice. "We're going to increase our chances by reviewing the event sequence together."

Ryder makes himself designated expert. Eric listens—hopefully to correct any errors.

All five spacecraft will arrive at Mars moving faster than anything has ever arrived anywhere. Most of that velocity needs to be lost during the first pass, a five-minute rush through the atmosphere to slow down using nothing but aerodynamic friction.

The capture pass requires total trust in the GNC to keep the spacecraft together in formation while losing enough velocity—but not too much velocity. After we skip off the atmosphere we'll emerge with a sub-orbital trajectory, loop around Mars in an elliptical path and then re-enter the atmosphere for the entry and landing phases.

"If your aerobrake doesn't deploy on its own, do it manually," Ryder cautions. "Look for a GNC icon marked 'deploy aerobrake.' Don't hesitate! It needs time to inflate. There's less than a minute from deployment to atmosphere contact, in case the thing's got a leak."

Ryder displays a graphic of the landing phase. "There are five events that may require override. At eighteen thousand meters your nose fairing ejects and a drogue chute deploys. Main chute at eleven thousand meters."

"Let me get this straight," says Senuri. "I'm going to watch the altitude. If we pass eleven thousand and nothing happens…"

"Override!" I tell her. "Hit the main chute icon."

Ryder continues, "Two preset waypoints, high gate and low gate. High gate is when the main chute goes out. When your speed drops below three hundred knots, the GNC should blow your aerobrake off and extend the four engine nacelles and landing struts. As Eric told us, there's a limited amount of fuel for the powered descent phase, so the engines won't start until we're below thirty-two hundred meters. When the engines are at sixty percent thrust, your main chute releases."

The graphic zooms to the final landing approach. "Powered decent lasts only eighty seconds. We'll be moving fast right up to low gate. At one hundred meters we should hear the engines throttle up to max. The GNC will try to tighten the formation so we land around five hundred meters apart. We hover at thirty meters, then descend straight down."

Eric says, "It is my firm recommendation that no one overrides their GNC during landing."

Challenge his authority? He's only recommending.

Tess does her thing. "Jürgen will speak to us tomorrow about post-landing activity."

Jürgen is captain, his word law. Tess knows it and she's joyful for it. They're lovers, for sure.

"Course correction coming up in a few minutes," Eric announces. "A short one, and that's lucky because we only got forty seconds of thruster propellant remaining."

The correction lasts twenty-five seconds, barely enough time for Ryder and Alison to get in some swing-dancing.

The hours sweep by in a rush. This last day in flight feels different. A last day of life? There are clues everyone is asking themselves that question. Mikki and Shuko vanish inside her sleeper. Alison and Paige study the various inscriptions written on the walls inside the airlock.

Ryder and I watch old vids from decades ago. We hop around a lot, never watching a single story more than ten minutes, because there's just too many and they're all different in unexplainable ways. The catalog identifies vids popular in their own times: *The Wizard of Oz, The Apartment, Breaking Bad, Saving Private Ryan, The Sound of Music, Jaws, It Happened One Night, Mad Men, High Noon*. Maybe Harmony wasn't lying too much about the wars and violence and crime of the past, but no one seemed to mind very much. All those people living their whole lives without Harmony, without the Autoridad, without the Stream. They never knew how good they had it.

Mikki emerges from her sleeper and brings back reality. "What are we going to do with the Oxirotor?"

"Leave it until tomorrow morning," Ryder answers. "I can take it apart and cram the pieces in with the rest of the feedstock."

With two reserve oxygen cylinders filled to capacity, Paige and Shuko watch cabin O2 partial pressure and run the Oxirotor after it drops to twenty kp, about one hour out of every five. I tell them, "We can run it one last time after midnight and then put the automatic bleed back in service."

Eleven hours before capture pass we eat cherry cheesecake cubes while gazing out at Mars. It's the same visual size as the moon seen from Earth. Dark gray splotches cover the orange surface, and the polar ice cap has grown from a spec to a silvery-white oval.

Muffled pops from the attitude jets ring out, and Mars drifts out of view. "Hope everybody got a good look," Darien reports on the com. "We just crossed the seven hundred and fifty thousand kilometer mark. The GNC is setting up to start laser ranging."

The TMI points its back-end toward Mars, blocking the view but enabling the optical rangefinder to bounce laser pulses off the surface of the planet and determine distance and velocity with high precision.

The panel flashes a yellow message.

RANGING INITIATED WAITING RETURN

Nothing happens. What's wrong? Can we land without this thing?

Another flash, this one green.

RANGING OPERATIONAL – DETERMINING POS-VEL

Paige lets her breath out. "Speed of light delay."

We get an altitude, the last four digits dropping too fast to read. Velocity 15,328 meters per second, which becomes 15,327 as I watch. Is that good?

"I'm happy!" roars Eric. "Real happy. Setting all GNC's back to stand-alone. We're done navigating by *Liberty's* tracker."

Why the surprise? Was he expecting it to fail? Are there other systems he's wondering about but not mentioning?

Our orientation changes and sunlight floods the control center. The morning-like glow crushes all desire to sleep. Moira Kellion and Naldo Zamora aboard *Resolute* show us their drawings of living and working quarters. They want to build chambers with vaulted arches buried just beneath the surface. Beautiful designs! Mikki bends closer to the panel. "Sunken baths? Do you really think we're going to have sunken baths?"

Alison closes her eyes. "Going crazy just thinking about it."

I squeeze her hand. "If we can imagine it, we can build it."

Ryder's skeptical. "Where we gonna get all those bricks?"

Moira shows her pale, triangular face. "Mars regolith should make excellent airtight bricks. We expect high amounts of calcium and sulfur, so without any additives the bricks will be almost as strong as concrete. We should also be able to make gypsum and lime."

"I'm no expert," says Alison, "But don't you need an oven to make bricks?"

"You mean a kiln," Naldo answers. His stubbled face is shockingly thin. How many others had lost their appetites during the flight? "We're going to use the waste heat from the reactors. A hundred kilowatts per reactor, so we can get at least a thousand degrees to bake bricks."

Mikki asks, "And it heats bath water too, right?"

Naldo laughs. His eyes shine with a twelve-year old's optimism. "We'll find a way! But before we think of baths, we need to get ourselves under two meters of solid shielding to minimize radiation exposure. Indra and Norberto designed an end-to-end manufacturing system. Bots will dig the regolith, add water, shape the bricks, and deliver them to and from the kilns. We should have around one million bricks before winter begins."

The drawings of underground brick housing are outdone by plants growing under transparent pressurized pyramids. The greenery of life arising from the brown and red sands of Mars. The sight of it, even as a drawing, is the birth of dreams.

Ryder makes chomping sounds. "Carrots, potatoes, asparagus." After what we've been through, we'll laugh at anything.

We're going to make it.

This is a good day. Why end it by sleeping? New faces appear—Dee, Abby, Roxane, Giselle. Did these people spend forty-one days sealed in their sleep compartments? Everyone clusters together shoulder-to-shoulder. I look at the others as if seeing their faces for the first time. Our hair has grown so much—why notice that now? And the spots of stubble all over Ryder's jaw—when did that happen?

Eric announces, "We're entering the Mars gravitational sphere of influence. Don't get too excited. Just means Mars is exerting a stronger gravitational pull on our flight path than the sun. Our velocity relative to Mars will increase."

Sure enough, the GNP velocity goes from 15,236 meters per second to 15,237 and keeps rising. Ryder pulls Alison closer.

"Hold on tight. We're falling toward Mars."

"We'll pick up another five kilometers per second before morning," Eric informs us. "Speaking of morning, wakeup time is five. Doc Giselle here on *Constitution* says try your best to sleep. If you're wondering whether to wear your diapers, yes, wear your diapers."

Ryder pumps his fist in triumph.

I zip into my sack at 22:26 PCT, a little more than six hours before wakeup. There's a text from Vijay just arriving.

Cristina: I wish to express my heartfelt thanks for assisting with the adoption of our Charter, and running for office too! Your words, if we can imagine it we can build it, brought a smile to my lips and energy to my soul. Cristina, my brain spins when I realize that within a few hours we will participate in a great achievement of human history. This is fitting, as we are driven by one of the deepest and noblest aspirations of the human spirit, the pursuit of freedom. Although the rest of humanity will not immediately witness the events of tomorrow, it is my earnest belief that our journey here and our future triumphs will some-day serve as an inspiration to billions yet unborn. Cristina, I know it is difficult to understand the actions and points of view of some of our compatriots. We will all need time to acclimate to this wonderful thing called liberty. There will be adjustment pangs! We are accustomed to being told what to do and what to think, under threat for noncompliance. Many now seek that firm hand of authority and self-assurance. This is understandable, but extreme care must be taken that our better judgment does not suffer in the pursuit of solidarity and status. I look forward to meeting you in person!

Complicated words and ideas. Even so, a kind and thoughtful message. I flick the screen dark and close my eyes.

Tomorrow. It all happens tomorrow.

PART III

All of Us

THIRTY

Ear plugs. Face mask. Perfect comfort, near perfect silence. No sleep.

Bangs and clangs begin after midnight. Eric announces the sounds are nothing to be nervous about, just the TMI transferring fluids.

I check the time over and over and there's no way to stop. Less than seven hours until there's ground under me, *solid ground*. A new home. Is this truly happening? I unzip and pull on an absorbency garment followed by a clean flight suit, the last one remaining. Rosies—no, *rosaries*—in right chest pocket. Sickness bag in left. After six weeks there's enough hair to brush, but why bother?

Everyone's still huddled in the control center. Shuko raises a pouch of some dark beverage. "I diagnose you with Protonilus fever."

I squint at him. "What?"

"Protonilus fever," repeats Alison. "Can't sleep? Join the club."

Liberty's nose still points roughly sunward. Warm yellow beams set everything aglow, especially our shiny white flight suits. We've all been saving our last clean set. Mikki passes around protein bars, the ones we're not supposed to eat; this minor mischief is dwarfed by the magnitude of the day.

There's little talking. Alison pushes my right foot against a Velcro anchor and wraps her arm behind my neck. I'm cradled between her and Ryder and secure from drifting. Sleep finally comes—despite the sunlight and the hum from the equipment bay.

∗

The siesta ends when Shuko presses a clear plastic bag of fluid into my hand. Ryder has one, too. He holds it away from his body as if it were dangerous. "We're supposed to drink this? The whole thing?"

"The whole thing," confirms Shuko. "I want an empty container from every one of you."

Mikki tastes it and makes a face. "Let me guess. Old piss?"

"Saline solution," Shuko says between gulps from his own bag. "One liter of salted water. It's a preventive measure against syncope. Passing out."

Alison and I try a sip at the same time. Disgusting. And there's a lot of it.

Shuko sees our pain. "Long-term weightlessness prevents proper regulation of body fluid levels. We're all slightly dehydrated. Not dangerous under normal circumstances. But problems will occur once we're back under gravity. Our blood volume is low, and unless we build up our fluid reserves, we may faint when we try to stand upright."

Ryder takes three or four huge gulps. "Don't wanna faint. I'm walking on Mars today."

Alison takes a gulp. "I'm not going to be able to eat breakfast after this."

"That's ideal," Shuko tells her. "We want our stomachs empty. Will make it easier to deal with high deceleration forces."

Eric's sour, stressed-out grumble makes me jump. He sounds like he didn't sleep at all. "One last course correction in two minutes. Very brief, just to nudge us about three meters per second. The GNC ranged Mars all night and we have a good trajectory. Also, if you're wondering if you should wear your BioSuit during landing, the answer is no. An impact hard enough to breach your cabin will kill you anyhow. Plus, the joint that seals your helmet to the suit is not intended for use under high G-forces. A hard landing or even normal deceleration during entry could result in neck injury."

The thrusters fire for eight seconds.

Ryder places an aluminum grating over the equipment bay access hatch. Our treasured Oxirotor is gone, the cables and the other pieces coiled up and stored away.

The lights flicker twice.

Eric informs us, "Your TMI just transferred electrical loads to your batteries. My indications are nominal, but I need someone to visually confirm that your fifteen banks are on line and showing twenty-nine volts."

Ryder and Mikki study the master panel. Mikki calls out, "Both busses show twenty-nine volts and all fifteen banks are green!"

"When you put your seats in place," Eric advises, "make sure each of the three anchor points clicks all the way into the receptacle. Double-check they're firmly attached. Check your harness anchor points, too."

Sharp *bing bing bing bing bing bing* noise from outside the spacecraft.

"That's your TMI unlatching like it's supposed to," Eric reports. Is there a nervous tremor in his voice?

We check the warning panel for red or orange. It all works for a change. "First atmosphere contact at seven thirty-three," I tell them. Can they hear the edge in my own voice? "Let's make sure everything loose is put away."

"Checked three times," Mikki says.

The GNC sings happily, *"TMI separation in three, two, one."*

BANG! The control center jolts. Alison and Mikki clutch each other's arms. Thousands of sparklers swirl outside the windows. A sunbeam drifts across the sleeper doors. Paige blurts, "What's it doing?"

Ryder cries, "We're rotating completely over! Gonna get a view!"

The six of us push off to the big window and press our faces against the glass, jostling and nudging for more room. Nothing but blackness and the sparklers—but as *Liberty* rotates the window rim shines orange. My mouth is dry as tissue, even after all that water.

Mikki yells, "Ryder, dammit, you're fogging the glass!"

Shuko and I wipe our sleeves across the window. Our six faces jam the glass side-by-side.

The edge of the planet emerges and features come into view. It's so beautiful I can't speak. Mars is a globe, rich in vivid shades of red, brown, and gray forming three-dimensional terrain. Craters. Canyons. Mountains!

Paige sucks in her breath. "We're here, it's real."

An entire planet floating against the black, enormous and too tangible to accept. Ryder bangs his fist against the window frame. "I see our landing site!"

Those five piercing words sting my ears, but that's fine, that's perfect. He sees it! Where, exactly? His finger stabs the window. "There! See the big round crater?"

I respond, "Yeah!"

"That's Lyot. Toward the polar cap is north, so look south from Lyot to the bumpy strip. That's Protonilus!"

That band of jagged ridges, our home forever? Sunlight glints off the mountain peaks, the pink and blue glow of dawn. My brain cannot deal with it. We're moving so fast Mars glides under us as we watch. More details emerge by the second—crinkles, crevices, and hazy wisps.

Indra shouts from the com, "I see clouds!"

I yell back, "Mist! I see it!"

Eric remarks, "Lovely spring morning at the landing site."

The Lyot crater reaches the edge of the curved horizon and disappears. The relative motion of the planet seems downward toward the surface. A line of ragged gullies slide into view, followed by total blackness. This is the end of the daylight side of Mars. Behind me, the sun is on the far side of the control center. A radiant beam stings my eyes.

Eric tells us, "I know there's quite a view out there, but it would be an excellent idea to get seated and harnessed."

Paige flies to the opposite window. "Look at the sun! Right at the edge!"

The black is draped by a crisp arc of light, the sun approaching the middle. They touch, meld, and the sun flattens and spreads out along the curve, changing from yellow to pink to deep orange and finally a thread of lavender. The control center is dark, the only illumination from the soft yellow and green indications on the panels.

"Goodbye, sun," says Ryder. "Magnificent show."

A piercing whirl from the other side of the equipment bay. Eric tells us, "That's your aeroshell deploying. You need to be harnessed at this time. Atmosphere contact less than two minutes."

I push butt into seat. Ryder takes his place a meter to my right. This time Shuko's next to Mikki, their hands clasped together. I adjust my restraint harness and secure the center buckle.

Shuko advises, "Try to inhale and exhale with short, sharp breaths. Might take some effort, but you won't suffocate. Expect some discomfort—"

"Pain!" Ryder shouts while jerking his harness. "Bring it on!"

"Wa-hoo!" Mikki cries, her tone sarcastically flat.

Outside, still just black, no obvious danger. Tell that to my hammering heart. Don't think about slamming into the atmosphere at twenty kilometers per second, fast enough to travel the full length of Alta California in one minute. Yes, rosies out, finger-wrapped. "Rosaries," I annunciate the correct name. That lures a faint smile from Ryder.

My palms are wet and my fingers tremble, but I do it anyway. I stick my right arm out and Ryder takes my hand. Our fingers interlace. His skin is soggy too, heartbeat strong and fast. Two impossible things at once: arriving at Mars, and holding Ryder's hand.

There it is—a faint vibration—a tiny force pushing upward from the seat.

I squeeze hard on rosies and Ryder.

This is happening.

THIRTY-ONE

Peaceful at first, nothing more than gentle pressure and a far-away hum. The panel flashes.

AEROBREAK SEQUENCE INITIATED

Altitude 125 kilometers, dropping fast; *Liberty* must swoop deeper into the atmosphere so we can exploit friction to cut speed. What did David say? *Shed three quarters of your velocity in five minutes.*

The hum intensifies and the vibration becomes rapid sideways jerking. Backward force drives my shoulders and butt hard against the seat. My head is a rock. There's a high-pitched whine. Now wild sideways jerking! This supposed to happen?

Powerful pressure. Not fun, not fun. A massive weight presses on me like an enormous bag of sand. Can't suck in air! I clench both hands tighter and remember—short breaths!

A pink glow breaks through my shut eyelids, pink with bright flashes. The roar soaks into my bones and the intensity kills thinking. I crush fingers as if that can somehow force air into my lungs. Nothing but gray, can't see at all. Reality is a screaming, suffocating, violently shaking mess and it hurts.

Fading. Falling down a tunnel.

Time passed, but how much? The crushing pressure is gone, the earsplitting roar down to a dull hum, and I can breathe. Ryder's fingers on right, GNP altitude in front, 117 kilometers and rising.

Ryder gasps for air, too. From all around, heavy huffs and pants.

The GNP sings out, *"Aeroshell separation in three, two, one."*
BANG!

The harness pulls across my chest then goes slack. Altitude 140 kilometers. No more force. I'm soggy from head to foot. Teeny droplets of sweat swirl around the control center.

I release Ryder's hand and he flexes his fingers. Is my face as red and wet as his? Alison's eyes dart all over.

"Give me a minute," says a voice unmistakably Eric-like. Someone else beyond *Liberty* is alive, someone familiar with the systems. "GNC reports correct formation. Lost enough velocity. Got elliptical orbit. Intersects entry point nine twenty-two."

Faint words from Alison. "Can't do that again."

I release my harness and push off. A wave of dizzy! I stroke Alison's hair. "We can do it one more time."

Paige points a shaky finger. "Here comes the sun."

A wispy red curve cuts across the blackness. It brightens and orange spreads from the center, then the first wonderful beacon of light peaks over the edge of Mars.

"Hit nine and a half gees," Ryder says, tapping the GNP panel. Then he kisses Alison's forehead. "My brave girl. The rest of it will be easier."

"Mikki…"

She's staring straight ahead, oblivious to Shuko and everyone else and still clutching the sides of her seat. "I'll be all right if I can stay here until we're down. Can you get me some water? All that salty piss water made me thirsty."

Speaking of piss, her crotch is one big wet spot. She sees it and mutters obscenities under her breath. "Your fault for making us drink," she says to Shuko. "Plus I forgot the diaper thing. So there's that. Sorry. I'm changing right now. Not arriving on Mars wet."

We drink small sips of water and rest. The GNP shows an egg-shaped path looping around Mars, passing over the sunlit side then back again to the night side before starting the second and final atmospheric entry, sixteen hundred kilometers southwest of Protonilus Mensae.

Independence opens a connection, audio only. "Jürgen Morita will speak to us." It's Tess, her voice stripped of the usual snootiness.

"We set out to define ourselves," Jürgen says, the words stiff with tension. "We already have."

Ryder and I exchange glances. Is that it?

"We already have," Jürgen repeats with a weak tremble. "See you on the ground."

Nothing else comes. Tess tells us, "Everyone is to remain in their spacecraft after landing. Jürgen will speak to us from the surface."

Shuko tightens his harness. "He probably spent two weeks writing his first-person-to-walk-on-Mars speech."

For once I stick up for Jürgen. "He said what he needed to say. He made us believe we're going to make it and think about the future. That's worth something."

"Second sunset!" Paige calls out. The edge of Mars transforms to a red arc. The colors change slower this time, because we're moving around a quarter of our original speed. The curve is burgundy, then chocolate brown, then gone.

BANGS followed by a steady hiss. Second aerobrake inflating. On the surface in nine minutes. Impossible!

"One... more... time!" I call out, each word loud and crisp.

Ryder extends his hand. "We're walking on Mars today. I believe it. Do you?" I force a smile and we interlace fingers. This is fine, but will be much better on solid ground.

Rosies out, firmly clutched.

The hum is back. Mikki mumbles, "Really, really rather not do this fucking shit one more fucking time."

Now we have a tremor, then a shudder. In my stomach, a hot churn of dread and exhilaration. Is someone speaking over the com? No, singing. Someone, somewhere, is singing over the increasing noise. Vijay's voice, it has to be!

"On this day I am free. No matter what happens to me, on this day I am free!"

The voice is swallowed by the rising buzz. Sideways jerking against the harness, up and down too, like racing over a bumpy road. The force is back. The roar of the atmosphere becomes an overpowering screech. Taking in air is like inhaling honey.

Time mushes again. All is brighter, somehow.

Altitude thirty kilometers! Sunlight on my face! On the left is darkness, but not the black of space. Purple gloom, then mountains the color of chocolate and ashes. It drifts away like a dream, then the purple again. We're spinning, the sun skimming past everything from all angles, over and over.

The world tumbles and the edge of the aerobrake flutters outside the window, trembling against the atmosphere whistling past. A hard BANG shakes my seat. Something big flies off and away. Thin black lines form a striped square quivering against the pink sky.

Ryder yells, "Chute!"

The horizon steadies but at a crazy angle. Why is everything tilted? Now the ground is above us, mountains overhead.

More BANGS and shakes. Nose fairing separation?

Ryder reports, "High gate!"

Machinery buzz. The engine housings extend outward, triggering more vibration. Bumps! Hard slamming back and forth, up and down, worse than entry. Panel flashing red.

The GNC calls, *"Misfire. Misfire. Misfire."*

"Shit!" Ryder reaches for the chute release override.

I grab his arm. "Leave it! Sixty percent! Need sixty percent!" That's the minimum thrust for high-gate chute release.

A throaty rumble, then a steady whine. *Liberty* lurches sideways. What's happening with the engines? One of them fires—just one! More rumbling, then a hard jerk to the other side, then even pressure across the back of my seat. THUMP! Chute released!

I cry out, "We're good!"

A tilted horizon, but at least the ground isn't spinning overhead. Something white streaks past the window, downward and tumbling, trailing a twisted line of brown vapor.

A spacecraft. Too big to be anything else. I screw my eyes shut then force them open.

From behind, choking and vomiting.

The spinning spacecraft is far away, a speck at the end of a trail of smoke. Too close to the lumpy hills...ugly flash of yellow. Exploded, impacted the ground.

Dead.

I turn away, grip the rosies tighter, and reach out. Ryder's fingers are there, warm and wet. The explosion! Don't think about it. Altitude forty-four hundred, last two digits dropping fast. Speed a hundred and fifty meters per second. Distance to touchdown fifteen kilometers.

Hills and ridges, massive and close. We fly over an enormous mountain followed by a plain of craters and gullies.

Flashes of light twinkle on the hillsides—sunlight glinting, but off what?

Ryder calls out, "Low gate!" The thrusters shift tone twice, then up and down every few seconds. The ground is incredibly rough and so close. There! Suspended against the pale sky, a shimmer of sunlight off white. Another spacecraft! The conic shape is missing the whole top section.

The horizon levels. Ground coming up! I scream, "This is it!"

Swirls of dust streak upward past the window. The thrusters change pitch and we drop like going down a fast elevator. Past the churning dust there's a dark gray thing moving straight across the surface directly at me. I flinch—but it's *Liberty's* shadow. Flying grit blocks the view. The engines scream, then lots of DINGS from the outside—rocks blowing with the dust.

BAMM! Our seats bounce up and down.

Another BAMM, softer, then a bounce, then one more. The engines fade to silence.

The GNP displays green:

TMP SEQUENCER COMPLETED AT 09:27:51 PCT 3
GEMINI 54 POS 42.187°N 48.062°E

Ryder throws off his harness but doesn't release his grip on my fingers. He stands, slow and shaky, eyes empty.

"Somebody crashed," I tell him.

"I see it in your face."

He pulls me out of my seat. Heavy. Heavy all over. Mars gravity is two-fifths Earth, but feels every bit as strong. Stronger.

Serious head swim. "Take it slow getting up," I advise everyone. "It's weird."

A wave of swirling dust washes over *Liberty*. A spacecraft meets the ground, the sparkling whiteness a stark contrast against the reds, browns, and grays of the terrain.

That's three. One crashed. We're missing a spacecraft. Six people died. Which six? Did we lose Eric? Alison lies flat with eyes open, her chest coated with gritty beige vomit. She'll have to wait.

"Who did we lose?" I ask, as if they somehow know.

Walking is different, easier and trickier at the same time. I shuffle across the control center and grab the edge of Paige's seat to stop. The sleeper doors are vertical like ordinary doors, but narrower. Ryder and I look out from the windows on either side of the sleepers. We have a complete view of the surrounding area.

Two spacecraft out there. *Two*. One of them rests slightly tilted at the bottom of a shallow depression. The upper section, now flat, is visible against a distant hillside. It would be easy for a spacecraft to hide behind one of the hills encircling us.

I tell Mikki and Shuko, "Look for the other ship! There should be three total."

Eric comes over the com. "We're good. We're good. Check your cabin pressure. Check it holding thirty-five, look at your partial pressures. Don't rely on the alarms. We don't know what's working yet."

So *Constitution* made it. Paige jumps and points out the window. "Over there! Right above the mountain!"

There's a faint dome of brown haze against the mustard-colored sky. "I saw a crash," I tell them. "That could be it. Eric! Where's the other spacecraft?"

"*Resolute* impacted at high speed. *Endurance* is out of contact. They were connected on VHF and the data link until twenty seconds before we landed."

"What the hell does that mean?" I demand. "Where's *Endurance*?"

"Cristina, I don't know. We can see only one debris cloud. That's reason for optimism. VHF is line-of-sight, and the five gigahertz data signal is short range. If they landed on the other side of these hills, we wouldn't be able to talk to them except on single-sideband."

Vijay Mehta. Jessica Egan. Four others and I forgot their names. Dead.

A hot wave of nausea shoots up my throat. I cover my mouth.

Vijay!

The heaviness pulls me down. Ryder and Paige take my arms and support my weight because my legs can't do it anymore.

THIRTY-TWO

The dust settles and the outside vista sharpens. The distant hills are so crisp they appear close enough to touch.

I sit alongside Ryder on the edge of Paige's seat—how did I get here?

Mikki glides to the window on light but clumsy feet. "Three out of six."

I snap, "We don't know that yet!"

Alison sits up and frowns at the puke on her chest.

I call out, "Shuko! Check the master panel pressures, power levels, warnings."

"Did that, Cristina. All perfect."

Ryder runs his hand across my back. "Feeling better?"

"Just the gravity. Too much of everything all at once." I sniff and clench my eyes shut to keep the tears inside.

Not now. Far too much to do.

Eric booms from the com, "I'm in contact with *Endurance* via single-sideband radio. They landed hard but there are no injuries. From the coordinates Senuri gave me they're seventeen kilometers northeast of us."

Ryder punches the wall. "Outstanding!"

I turn to Mikki. "Four out of six."

Is that such an impressive victory?

"I don't know why they landed long," Eric continues. "I suspect it had something to do with engine flutter. The engines hammered and didn't start simultaneously. If one side fired alone after the chute released, the asymmetric thrust set up a spin." He lowers his voice. "I think that's what happened to *Resolute*."

"How do we know there are no survivors on *Resolute*?" I ask. "They might be injured, their radio smashed."

"Cristina, they impacted at three hundred knots. It exploded. I watched the vid twice to be sure. I'm sorry."

Alison says, "*Endurance* is out there all alone. They must be terrified."

Mikki adds, "No more terrified than I am right now."

I remind her, "We're in good shape. Save the terror until there's something to be terrified about."

With *Liberty* under gravity the control center feels tiny, more cramped than normal. Four seats take up most of what's now the floor. The two forward seats are at chest level, blocking off a third of the interior.

It requires effort and focus simply to stand. With the sleeper doors open I can walk about four meters in a straight line. I cover the distance in three easy strides but braking forward motion means grabbing something solid. The bottom of our flight suits are more like thick socks than shoes, so sliding is easy.

We stack the seats so we have space to move. Alison says, "Does anyone else need to pee?"

"Go in your pants," Ryder tells her. "Live a little."

"Seriously, is the pit working?"

The hygiene pit, the equipment bay, and the airlock are now below the control center. Ryder removes the grating from the access hatch and helps Alison climb down.

"What about the people on *Endurance*?" asks Shuko. "They're going to stay out there?"

"I don't think they should," I answer. "But this is not up to me. Jürgen's captain."

I stare out at *Independence*, Jürgen's spacecraft, several hundred meters away. Nothing visible happening. Isn't he planning to make a speech from the surface?

Ryder whispers in my ear, "Don't forget. Act as if."

Those three words trigger memories of the flight. He's right—waiting won't work. Too much at stake. I hit the com. "Eric! Can you show me how I can talk to Senuri? What did you call it? Single side?"

"Single-sideband radio. I can activate yours and raise the antenna. Your master panel will show a channel selector. They're on two one eight two, which should be your default. Give me three minutes."

A female voice yells, "We got an emergency! Jürgen's in the airlock, he won't answer, we can't get it open! We need help fast!"

Eric says, "Tess, calm down! Is he unconscious?"

She screams, "He's not moving! We can't get the door open!"

"Pressure difference," Ryder mutters.

"Listen to me, Tess." Eric says. "Is the outer hatch shut? My indication here indicates shut."

"The outer? Shut? I think it is. How can I tell?"

"You need to equalize the pressure. Open the inner vent now."

Sounds of shouting come through the com.

"They're panicked," says Shuko.

I bend toward the panel. "Tess! Let me talk to Walt."

She yells, "They don't want to open the vent!"

Ryder says, "Oh, shit."

Eric says slowly, "Tess, you're going to need to open that vent. I have no readings from his suit, so I can't tell if he's breathing."

"He's got the outer vent open," says a male voice. The words come fast and trembling. "Know what that means? We override the interlock and open the inner vent, we lose our air before we open the hatch."

"Walt," says Eric softly. "Get everyone suited right now."

"Screw you!"

A different female voice. "Eric, we don't know what happened to him. We're not going to let our air bleed away until we know what went wrong with Jürgen."

That's it. I know what to do. "Eric, I'm going out to *Independence*. I'll secure the hatch from the outside."

"Don't rush this, Cristina. Check your suit. I show minus twenty-eight degrees out there."

Ryder grabs my sleeve. "My suit's tested too."

"Wouldn't dream of going without you."

I put Shuko in charge of the airlock. Paige and Mikki pull the suits and thermal garments from lockers. The documentation says light green side facing out when in sunlight, reverse to dark green for night or working mostly in shade. This time we get to wear Mars boots. They're like hiking boots with thick soles. They fit over the BioSuit so they don't need to be pressure-tight. I transfer the rosies and I'm all set.

The airlock is tighter under gravity, barely room for two people to stand on the bottom grating. Shuko shuts the inner hatch. I got the handwriting all around me again, with The Lord is my shepherd message. Don't look at it! Out of nowhere: a hospital bed, a dead Paco. Am I going to remember that every time I set foot inside this airlock?

Block it! Think here and now.

Isn't here and now enough?

Ryder turns my helmet towards his face. "First humans to walk on Mars."

This is unreal. The little window on the outer hatch lets in a circle of golden light. That's real enough—so much like any other morning sun. The visor display comes alive. Five degrees inside the airlock! Ryder's shivering too; are these thermal garments really thick enough for the lower temperature outside?

"This is Shuko, com check."

"Hear you!"

A vibration from underfoot. "I'm running the evacuation pump," says Shuko. "Conserves air, but it'll take fifteen minutes. Eric wants you to open your vent to speed things up."

Ryder twists the handle. The suit actuators tighten instantly. He smiles. "Who's going to be the first to step out on the surface? Big historic event, you know."

"We both do it at the same time."

"Not a chance. It's got to be you. You earned it."

Why does this even matter? "We step out together."

"Okay. But you say the first words."

The panel shows less than ten kp and dropping fast.

"No idea what to say."

"Better think of something!"

I shake my head and ignore my pounding heart. Which is more overwhelming—venturing across the surface of Mars, or coming up with historic words right this minute?

"I can't think of anything good," I stammer.

Pressure down to three kp. Suddenly too warm. Ryder takes my hand. "Relax. Keep it simple."

I squeeze his fingers. I'm good at that now. "You do it. Say whatever you want."

He mouths the word no. "This is your moment."

Pressure less than one kp. I close my eyes. "We're going to have a free planet."

"That's a start. What else?"

"We have arrived...at a free planet."

Ryder whispers, "Keep it simple."

"Humanity has arrived on Mars..."

The airlock panel flashes *OK to open hatch.*

Stomach tossing all over.

I lock eyes with Ryder. "Humanity has arrived on Mars to establish a free planet."

"Perfect! Say it just like that."

Am I going to be able to remember? I repeat it slowly. "Humanity has arrived on Mars to establish a free planet."

Ryder says, "Shuko, we're opening the hatch."

"*Independence* says Jürgen is moving. But he's still in the airlock."

I bend down and pull the hatch lever. The mechanism turns and the seal gives a tiny pop as the last wisp of air escapes. A bit of dust puffs up from the ground. The surface is almost two meters below the bottom edge of the hatch—too far to step or jump.

"See the handle for the ramp?" Ryder asks. "Can you reach it?"

Mars is there, right there, wide open and waiting. Browns, reds, grays—ordinary colors, but impossibly, intensely beautiful. Or maybe I'm just hyper-stimulated.

"Pull the handle to the right, then up," Eric directs. "That should make it drop by its own weight."

A silver frame sticks out from under the hatch. It drops so the bottom step is on solid ground.

Ryder offers his hand. "Ready?"

The hatch isn't nearly wide enough for two. "You step out first."

Humanity has arrived on Mars to establish a free planet.

He grins and puts both feet out on the top step. I offer my arm and he guides me through the hatch out into the sun.

Madre María. *Focus!*

"Together," I remind him with a quiver.

The stony ground is less than a meter below us. Is he ready? I step outward. He pushes me ever so gently. The surface grit crunches under my boots.

All over—I'm standing on the surface.

Ryder's on the second step. Barely visible through his helmet visor, a satisfied little smirk. He did it deliberately. But it's done. Only one thing remains. Say the words!

"Mars," I sputter.

Shock, confusion, brain freeze.

"Free...planet." I screwed it up! "Shit!"

My breath comes out in three quick pants.

Eric asks, "What did she just say?"

THIRTY-THREE

Wisps of brown vapor escape from the engine nozzles. Except for a few streaks and scratches on the nacelles, *Liberty* gleams pure white. The spacecraft is tiny from outside, especially with the nose faring gone. Our new star tracker is gone too. A palm-sized circle of adhesive serves as a reminder it wasn't easy to get here.

The com crackles. Shuko says, "Mars free planet, shit. That's what I think she said."

"Mars free planet, shit." Eric repeats. "How nice."

The sand under the engine nozzles is blown away to reveal a milky-gray surface. I swallow and regain control of my voice. "I think there's dirty ice here, under maybe ten centimeters of sand."

"Noted," says Eric.

Hills in every direction—the grayness at the base of that ridge—a glacier? The sky! Not mustard, something prettier, a perfect butterscotch. Eerie for a sky; glorious, too.

"I can't believe what I see," I whisper to no one in particular. "An untouched world for us, a gift we'll have to earn over the rest of our lives. Thank you for this."

Who did I just thank? No matter, it needed to be said.

But I'm wasting time. Where's *Independence*? The glistening white cone is far off on my right. Only the top half shows, the bottom obscured by a rise in the terrain. The helmet display confirms it's *Independence,* distance 334 meters.

Ryder is still on the ramp gloating over his victory. I snap, "You gonna stand there all day?" He steps out and the flimsy ramp springs upward as his weight is removed.

Shuko reports, "Jürgen's out of the airlock. Blair is examining him. They don't know if it was a suit problem or what."

"We're going over there anyway," I tell him.

The ground is powdery sand strewn with rocks, some round and some jagged. A few have strange shapes—one rock looks like a squirrel. Clean, somehow artificial, and new—a weird illusion! Ryder springs ahead of me, his strides long and slow. We're doing a strange Mars-shuffle, almost running without trying.

"Walking is easy!" I announce to the world. "It's like a wind is pushing from behind. Just have to watch out for the rocks."

Eric asks, "How do you feel? I'm watching your suit data, but it doesn't tell me everything. Pay attention to the cold. It can freeze extremities in minutes."

"Good and toasty over here," Ryder reports.

"Yeah, actually too warm," I add. "Makes no sense. Minus twenty-six degrees. These thermal coverings aren't very thick, so why aren't we freezing?"

"The atmosphere is less than one percent as dense as Earth air at sea level, so it doesn't conduct away heat very well. It's almost all carbon dioxide, a good insulator. Plus, the sun bakes you with infrared. Look on your arm panel. It should let you increase the flow of cooling air."

Ryder jerks his left arm and stops. It takes me two strides to catch up. The weight of the suit, backpack, and helmet create extra inertia—stopping requires a firm stomp with one foot.

"Problem?"

"Pinching a lot between fingers." He jiggles his hands. "Comes and goes. Under the arms, too. How's yours?"

"Getting me in the left armpit."

I wouldn't have noticed the suit-nipping if he hadn't mentioned it. There's too much to see, too much to think about. New information appears on my helmet display along with the temperature and life support indications: 0.04 mSv/hr.

"Eric, what's this m-s-v about?"

"That's your radiation dose rate in millisieverts per hour."

"Is that normal? Why did it pop up just now?"

"Took a few minutes to determine the rate. And yes, it's typical, given the current solar cycle. We all picked up eighty-six millisieverts during the flight. The rate in space was a bit more than twice what we're getting here. A couple of weeks ago it hit point eighteen because of a small sun flare."

The terrain slopes downward toward *Independence*. It takes barely two minutes to get there. Fewer rocks here, darker with more gray. No ice under the engine nozzles.

We approach the hatch. They should be on com. "Tess, anyone, we're here!"

No response. Ryder yanks the lever to extend the ramp.

"Tess? Can you depressurize your airlock?"

"Cristina, this is Doctor Blair Rizzo. The medical emergency is over at this point. We no longer need your assistance."

"Great! We'd like to come in all the same." I glance at Ryder. "Tired of looking at the same ugly faces."

Long silence. Ryder shrugs. What else to say?

"The airlock might be defective," comes the response, this time from Tess.

"Then we need to test it," Ryder shoots back. "Cristina and I are the most experienced."

No time for la mierda today. I climb up to the hatch, open a round cover and grasp a recessed yellow T-handle. "*Independence*! Venting your airlock!"

Twist to the right…no, wrong way. To the left…the handle turns and a slug of air blows against my arm. Shivering cold! The hatch is on the shaded side of the spacecraft. Deep chill, in less than a minute.

Eric says, "The airlock should be talking to your helmet."

The visor display indicates airlock pressure dropping. Eleven kp already.

"Do you know what you're doing?" growls Blair Rizzo.

"If your inner vent was open, the interlock would prevent the outside handle from turning. So yes, I know what I'm doing." That earns me a shoulder pat from Ryder.

The cramped little box is exactly like *Liberty's,* right down to the handwritten signatures and cryptic messages on the walls. But no sign of *the Lord is my shepherd*.

"*Independence*, the outer hatch is shut and latched, ready to pressurize."

No answer. Ryder flicks the control panel. The actuators release and it feels good. That was what, fifteen minutes?

We enter their equipment bay and pull off our helmets. What a smell! Urine, crap, body odor, definitely some vomit. New faces; they don't want us here. Not now. Blair Rizzo accuses us of spreading ultra-fine particulate dust into their nice, clean spacecraft, especially perchlorates—which she fears are toxic. Yes, our legs and boots are covered in orange dust, but aren't they over-reacting?

"Why take the unnecessary risk?" Walt Sullivan growls.

Is he just being stupid? I should tell him it's an unnecessary risk to be on Mars. But no, I'm going to be polite. Amazingly, Ryder lets me do all the talking.

Their control center is a mess of food stains and litter. Two girls—probably Laine and Kelis—lie back, eyes closed as if they could shut out the world.

"Where's Jürgen?"

Walt blocks the third sleeper. Blair folds her arms. "Jürgen briefly lost consciousness due to temporary low blood pressure, an orthostatic hypotensive event, not life threatening, unlikely to recur, probably caused by a combination of stress and mild dehydration. He's resting and taking fluid intravenously."

Ryder asks, "Did he drink the salty water?"

"Are you a doctor?" Walt snorts. "Then it's none of your concern."

I tell him, "If he's awake, I need to speak to him."

Blair says, "I don't see a pressing need to disturb him."

"If you want a pressing need, think about the six people on *Endurance* isolated from all assistance. Jürgen is captain. Does he have instructions? We need to talk this out."

Tess emerges from the sleeper. Her eyes dart between me and Ryder as if we're ghosts. "Jürgen is resting. He'll address us later today. There's no reason for you to be here."

Ryder moves toward the sleeper. The quickness of it signals he won't be stopped. Walt spreads his legs and thrusts his right arm to block the door.

Ryder seizes Walt's flight suit by the collar. The two of them lock eyes.

I cry out, "Ryder!"

Ryder shoves the arm aside. "Go!" Walt shouts. "See if I give two shits!"

Jürgen lies in the bottom sleeper, under a blanket, bare arms exposed, eyes open. His face is smooth but gaunt. At first he doesn't acknowledge us. How can this be the bold and inspirational speaker from the hospital?

I bend down. "We need to figure something out with *Endurance*. There's seven hours of daylight left. Jürgen, can you understand me? Have you given this any consideration?"

His mouth twitches, his eyes search. "How am I supposed to know what to do?"

What's the matter with him? We're here, alive and functional. Wasn't that his driving passion? We have problems to be solved, and he retreats into some kind of mental shell?

"You're our elected leader," I remind him. "But it's obvious you don't have an opinion one way or the other. That's okay. You rest. I'll deal with it."

✳

Eric links me to *Endurance* through the single-sideband radio, voice only.

"Cristina! Where are you?" Unmistakably Senuri.

"On *Independence*, me and Ryder both. Is everybody all right, Senuri? I understand you hit the ground hard."

"Lucky to live through it. We spun. The motors went crazy. But everything's running."

"Has anyone been outside?"

"Not yet. No reason, right? Tomorrow maybe."

"Senuri, you're eating dinner on *Liberty* tonight. My treat."

Tess snickers and whispers something to Walt.

"You are joking? Do you know we're seventeen kilometers away, on the other side of mountains? Maybe this is something to discuss tomorrow?"

"You can walk it, Senuri. You can scoot along the ground like a breeze. Ryder and I will meet you halfway. I'm looking at the topo map. We got two hills separating us, both eight hundred meters high, but maybe we can go between them."

"We don't like it out here with nothing but rocks, but is it safe to do what you suggest? Do you intend for us to use the truck? The truck will hold only two, correct?"

Does she understand the trucks need methanol fuel—and we haven't synthesized any methanol yet? "I don't know about you,

Senuri, but after six weeks sealed inside a box, I would love a nice walk and change of scenery. It's magnificent out there. What you see from the window doesn't do it justice."

"We should consider this carefully and not rush into a course of action. How would we find our way?"

Good question. "Your helmet display shows the direction you're facing. Like a compass—"

"Not a magnetic compass," Eric cuts in. "Mars doesn't have a magnetic field. Your suit has a gyrocompass, and the heading is derived from solar azimuth. Accelerometers compute your location and can guide you to a waypoint. Developed for the moon, reprogrammed for Mars. Pretty reliable stuff. When your suits are powered up, I can upload the heading and waypoint."

"Senuri, consider the risk of staying isolated without assistance or backup if something goes wrong. There's a reason we're supposed to land in sight of each other. Redundancy!"

No response. Are they talking it out?

Tess asks, "Does this mean we have to cram two more people in here?"

"Senuri," calls Eric. "If you look southwest, to the right of the sun, you should see one round hill taller than the others. Really round, like a fútbol under a blanket. The topo shows the rest of us are about the same distance on the other side of that hill."

A pause. "I see it. We need to climb it?"

"You can go around it," I assure her. "Just a little climbing. Eric, can you tell us how fast Ryder and I walked over to *Independence*?"

"Three hundred and thirty meters in one hundred seventeen seconds, counting the time you stopped. Just under three meters per second."

"That's ten kilometers an hour. Senuri, your suits are good for six hours. You'll be walking maybe an hour before you meet us at the half-way point."

Long silence. Are they stressed over making a dumb mistake with no way out? "Senuri, you're scheduled for the first Discovery Team, correct? Think of this little walk as a warmup for your expedition with Jürgen."

That does the trick. "We decided in favor. But we're going to bring extra oxygen canisters."

Eric announces, "Indra and Darien over here on *Constitution* are cycling out the airlock. They want to go along."

Walt mutters, "Mars free planet, shit."

A new kind of mockery? That's fine. I smile at him.

✳

Indra jogs laps around *Constitution*. "Walking here is fun! Eric, Fran, sure you don't want to come?"

"Next time," Eric replies. "Don't do anything *too* fun; get some experience first. Check the surface in front of you as you walk. The suits don't care about broken bones. They just squeeze harder."

Ryder snickers. "You must like scaring people."

I'm thinking ahead. "Eric, the meeting point on the ridge is almost ten kilometers out. Does the com reach that far?"

"That's within VHF and data range, provided you're in line-of-sight of our antenna, which is fourteen meters above ground. When you go over the crest you'll probably lose the signal."

Eric pushes a heading of 040 and it pops up on my visor as a green triangle pointing in the direction to walk. "You're gonna go straight for the first five kilometers," he instructs us. "Then your indicator will turn fifteen degrees and take you to the meeting spot."

Darien points ahead. "See that round hill? From now on we call it Mount Fútbol."

"Eric, tell Shuko and Paige I want them to get experience on the surface and get samples of ice so we can analyze it."

From two kilometers out, the three spacecraft are like upside-down tea cups jutting out of the rugged landscape. The terrain rises gently and the resistance from the suit actuators draws extra energy. Breathing feels slightly harder. Is that shortening the six-hour oxygen supply?

Minus nineteen degrees—and still too warm! My temp control is set to max cool. "Making good progress. Let's rest for five minutes. I want to try something, an experiment."

The thermal garment sleeves are held in place over our gloves by an elastic insert. I tug it up to expose the silver-gray BioSuit around my left arm. "Refreshing! Wish I could do that to my whole body."

Ryder pulls both his sleeves up. Eric must be watching on the helmet cam because he warns, "Refrain from exposing your BioSuit. You can be frostbitten, and there's no ozone barrier here. The solar ultraviolet will annihilate the material, including the actuators."

Ryder jerks the thermals back down. "Experiment over."

A delicate layer of mist twists between the hills, a river of vapor from a whimsical dream. The mountain range on the far horizon appears like a tabletop miniature only a few meters away. The sky is different from two hours ago, the butterscotch transformed to pinkish yellow with some indigo around the sun. Wispy blue clouds too—yes, blue clouds. So weird, a niños fantasy vid come alive.

Another three kilometers and the terrain breaks up into gullies with steep edges several meters deep. "Walk along the top," I advise everyone. Legs giving out, too. Pretty dumb to extrapolate a long hike from a two-minute trek—after being shut in with only spaceball for exercise. I call another rest stop.

Darien scans the horizon. "Look at this place! We could be the only humans in the universe. Way out here, alone, hasn't even been three hours since we got here."

Is he complaining, or is he happy about it?

The spacecraft are white specks on a broad basin. Less than five kilometers, forty minutes! Not a great pace. I didn't eat anything before leaving, another dumb mistake.

Oxygen remaining: Four hours thirty-six minutes, maybe twenty minutes lower than it should be. The six hours must be a base figure, assuming moderate activity. So what's the true duration? Is it extrapolating or going by pressure alone?

Indra squats down. "I'm a little nauseous. Not too bad, just thought you should know."

We all have our share of misery. "I'm lightheaded myself, especially when I turn my head. Everyone sip water. Can you keep going, Indra? Would you rather wait here with Darien?"

"I'm going with you."

Less than five hours before sunset. I can trust that figure, but what else do I know for certain? The suit is supposed to calculate heading, location, and direction of travel based on the sun's position. Is it correct? Does it contain the same kind of errors that biased the GNP? If they can screw that up, what about the suit systems?

Would have been smart to test everything.

"Eric. Com check."

"Hear you, Cristina. Still have your vid and data feed."

Ask him about the oxygen figure and the navigation system? If we go behind a ridge and lose the signal, is it possible to return by backtracking? The terrain is similar in all directions. Would asking ignite anxieties in everyone else?

Control fear and doubt, and they will do the same.

"Senuri's group started thirty-five minutes ago," Eric adds. "I can't talk to them because the VHF links are line-of-sight."

I pull out the rosies and touch them against a gray rock as Ryder watches. "If my father could see this."

Ryder holds out his hand. "He'd understand why we came here, don't you think?" The soft contact of entwined fingers, even though gloves, delivers a pulse of energy from nowhere. Whatever happens can be fixed—and would be fixed.

"Something's moving!"

Darien's arm is stretched out, his finger pointing toward the flat terrain behind us. "See it? What the hell is that?"

Yes, a curvy tan string coming up from the ground, kilometers away, and *moving,* definitely moving to the left, dragging a cloud of dust at the bottom. It's a really thin tornado.

"Dust devil," says Eric. "I see it on Cristina's cam. It's afternoon, so you might see more of them as the air warms up."

Indra asks, "What if it comes closer?"

"Not a danger," Eric responds. "I studied up. The atmosphere here is super thin. If it ran over you you'd hardly feel the breeze. It'll be gone in a few minutes."

"Pretty to look at, though," I tell them. Unnerving, really, but I don't want them to worry or panic whenever this planet presents more freaky sights.

The gullies end as we go higher and there are fewer rocks. Our pace slows to nine minutes per kilometer, a steady walk instead of a stride. As we approach the meeting point two voices fade in and out on the com. Suddenly Senuri's words burst through clearly—*minerals,* and *cool water.* They're talking about sipping water from their helmet tubes.

I announce, "They're within VHF range. Senuri! Andre!"

Indra spots them, still a kilometer off. Are we over the ridge crest already? Behind us, the three spacecraft are no longer visible; only rocky horizon, looking up slope. We walked over the top without realizing it.

"Eric, this is Cristina. We see them."

No response.

"Cristina, we see you," calls an unknown male voice. Who were the others on *Endurance*? Senuri is one of the few without a scientific, engineering, or medical background. Norberto is a physicist, Hannah a physician, a specialist in psychology. Andre? Drawing a blank.

"I don't know all their names," I whisper.

"We'll forgive you for that," Senuri answers. She approaches ahead of the others. We reach out and clasp hands. The visor hides her face but her words are blissful. "Peace be with you, Cristina Flores."

*

Shouldn't have shown anybody my skin welts. They're caused when blood pools in areas the actuators didn't compress with enough force. Alison and Paige gasp at the raised red blotches inside my elbows. I don't mention the other welts in my groin area.

"Not as bad as it looks. Doesn't hurt that much."

"They'll heal by themselves in a few days," Shuko assures me. "Let me know if they cause you any pain."

After the four of us cycled through the airlock two at a time, the whole equipment bay got coated in fine orange-brown dust puffing off our thermals. It's horrible; it stings our eyes and noses and it takes a long time to clear out of the air. Electrostatic cling—the longer we stay out, the more dust is going to stick to the thermals. We need to install some kind of water washdown system in the airlock to control the nasty stuff.

Eric figured out why we felt overheated toward the end of the hike. There's a filter that's supposed to keep Mars dust out of the fan that circulates cooling air under the thermal garments. The filter has an adjustable permeability and it was conservatively set to max fine, which made it clog quickly. Next time we'll use a medium setting, and that should increase the flow of CO_2 around our bodies.

Endurance splits up two for each of the other spacecraft, with Senuri and Andre aboard *Liberty*. One hygiene pit for eight people, and short two sleeper bunks.

Alison hands me apple juice in a blue plastic cup. Before it's half-drained I get distracted and stupidly release my fingers—a habit developed after six weeks of everything floating around.

Surprise! The cup falls, a bit slower than on Earth. Gravity demands a bit of care, remember?

Paige shows Senuri our slush sample—five or six liters of dirty ground ice retrieved this afternoon. About half of it has melted into a horrible brownish-gray liquid. "I'm going to analyze for suspended and dissolved solids to find out what it will take to purify it for drinking and electrolyzing."

Ryder sticks his finger into the container and thrusts it into his mouth. Alison screams. Ryder reports, "Salty and bitter, with a pleasing oakwood finish and hints of pear and apricot."

Our com picks up a lot of back-and-forth chatter; encouraged by the fact no one has died yet, people are suiting up and venturing out on the surface two-by-two.

"A word of caution," Eric announces. "Top off your oxygen supply before venting all your air. You'll feel mighty stupid later tonight if you suffocate because you forgot to line up and run your scrubbers." There's a pause. "Everybody *did* line up and start their scrubbers, right?"

Our two solid oxide CO2 scrubbers are whirling away, producing oxygen from carbon dioxide, most of it coming from the Mars atmosphere. These were developed for the moon, and they require gravity, just like the portable electrolyzers we used for the Oxyrotor. There's a pressure exchanger that compresses both the outside atmosphere and the oxygen produced by the scrubbers before the O2 goes to our banks. They're close to 100-percent already, even though venting the airlock discards some of our air that needs to be replaced from the banks.

"Sunset is at eighteen ten," I report on the com so everyone on the surface can hear me. "That's a little more than an hour from now. Don't stray too far, and remember that once the sun gets really low and disappears, you'll lose a lot of heat. Thermals should be light-side out."

Alison and Paige can't pull themselves away from the big window. The sky and landscape change color by the minute. At least fifteen people hop and skip across the terrain. Vids from helmet cams fill up our main panel. Jokes, laughs, and happy faces.

"We're going out there," Paige announces. Alison frowns, but she rises to join her friend. Everybody's got to try it sometime, and sooner is probably better. The only potential problem is the low sun and rapidly approaching night. The airlocks can only transfer two at a time. No one has ever been on the surface without the warming effect of the sun. It got cold pretty fast when I stepped into the shadow of *Independence*. What if the Genesis engineers guessed wrong about these rather thin thermal garments?

It's possible to vent the spacecraft pressure quickly from the outside and open both airlock doors at the same time.

Ryder touches my shoulder. "I'm going out there to see the sun set. I think everybody else pretty much has the same idea."

If we all cycle out now, we can catch the twilight. Shuko and Mikki help each other suit up. "My plan was to stay right here until someone builds some decent housing," Mikki grumbles. "Then I realized if all of you croak at once, I'll be the last and only poor, sorry bitch on the planet, and I don't think I can deal with that."

"She's telling us she likes us," Ryder adds.

Eric instructs on the use of the evacuation pump to get the airlock below two kp before venting the last of the pressure outside. This conserves air at the expense of battery power. Is this standard procedure, or has he decided air is more precious than battery reserve?

Installing the power generators should be tomorrow's priority.

There's a lot of people out, maybe all twenty-four of us. They gather mostly around *Liberty*. A few try jumping and find they can leap a meter high. Someone performs an outstanding broad jump of at least six meters. I set my visor to display names. Eric! An athletic type? I ask him, "Didn't you warn us against having too much fun?"

This is our first time face-to-face since the hospital. He wraps his arms around me for a quick hug. "We're allowed one fun thing every day."

I scan the other display names in the vicinity. A yellow icon indicates a private com link from Blair. She tells me, "If you're looking for Jürgen, he's staying inside tonight. Tess is with him."

A health reason? Leave it be. The world is too beautiful. The sun touches the top of a distant hill. It's about two-thirds normal size. The atmospheric dust cuts the glare and makes the disk a spectacular pale blue.

"Look! The whole sky on this side is pink," exclaims Norberto, pointing opposite the sunset. He arcs his arm to the west. "On this side, blue! Backwards from Earth."

Someone asks, "Where is Earth, anyhow?"

Eric responds, "It won't rise until early in the morning."

The last bit of sun vanishes behind the hill and the western horizon deepens to a stunning violet hue. The browns and grays of the surface terrain go black and the ground itself turns velvety blood-red. No one speaks. Two or three helmet lights come on but are quickly switched off. The first stars appear.

Ryder faces me and forms silent words with his mouth and draws a loop with his finger. *Make a circle.* I get it. Another outstanding Ryder idea. And he wants me to be the one to suggest it.

I say softly, "Let's gather around. Make a circle so we're facing each other. We should give thanks. And we should pay respect to those who aren't with us."

Give thanks. Be grateful. Feels right. Again, who are we thanking?

They do as requested. Eric puts his arms around Indra and Jewel. I put my left arm around Ryder, my right around Alison. We're a closed ring of twenty-two.

More stars emerge against the deep purple sky. It's quiet except for the soft, alternating hum tones and occasional clicks from my backpack life support systems.

Ryder nudges. They're waiting. Waiting for me. Got to say something, *anything.*

"Is this real?"

Dumb question? No. Affirmatives and head nods. They're thinking the same thing.

"How could this be real?" I ask again. My backpack responds with another hum and a click. "So many incredible sights in one day. Our third sunset since we woke up."

Some turn upward. A motion in the sky? From the east, a dark curtain crawls across the heavens revealing thousands of stars.

Someone whispers, "The shadow of Mars."

Is the thin and dusty atmosphere somehow doing this? No matter. It's a cosmic drapery tenderly exposing the glory of the universe. I can't touch Paco's rosies without letting go of Ryder or Alison, but they're with me.

"We're here. We're safe, we're healthy, we're free. Think about those who began the journey but aren't with us now, and our friends and family we'll always keep close to our hearts. Let's be silent for a moment and remember them, and those who gave their lives so we can be here today."

"Give thanks," a male voice murmurs. Norberto?

"Thank you," says another, the last word cracking as if he's choking back tears.

The shadow-curtain completes its transit and leaves the sky covered with stars. The western horizon glows sapphire blue, the eastern burgundy. Except for the dim red helmet displays, everything at ground level is completely black. I blink to dry my eyes.

"We're here for a purpose," I tell them. "Something good brought us to this place, this beautiful haven. Can you feel it inside you right now?"

THIRTY-FOUR

A full night on the control center floor. Woke up how many times? The last must have been around five-thirty in the dim light of dawn. Mikki, Shuko, Andre, and of course Ryder clustered around a window to see the Earth. Did they say the temperature was minus one hundred? And people were outside?

Any little movement shoots stabbing pain through my legs and lower back. Standing upright intensifies the soreness of my numerous pinch-point welts. Walking hurts worse, and reveals a fresh discomfort: stinging across the bottoms of both feet.

Ryder reclines and yawns. "A little sore, are we?"

"Just stiff. Need to move around." Almost eight, two hours past sunrise. "Were people outside last night or did I dream it?"

"Crazy Indra and her friend Jewel. They still have all their fingers. I think."

The thin folding table in the middle of the control center isn't big enough for eight. Shuko eats his bowl of nattō while standing.

"Stay away from me," Mikki warns him as she digs into a bowl of oatmeal. "That stuff reeks like dirty old gym socks."

The nattō does stink, but everything else stinks too—the eight semi-washed bodies, our clothes, and most of all the hygiene pit. Matters will improve, one step at a time.

Tess appears on the main panel. "If anyone's sleeping, get them up now. Captain Morita will speak to us in ten minutes."

Ryder raises his cup. "Good morning to you too, sunshine!"

Jürgen somehow regained his distinctive glint and subtle smile. Conversation stops. Alison says, "He's back. Jürgen's back." Paige flutters her hand so we know to be quiet.

"We are participating in history. No, we are history. We're here not only to survive, but to create and discover. My first impulse is to talk about our future, but I'm not going to do that. There's too much going on in the present."

I nod in agreement. Is he going to stick to the practical, the here and now?

"We must direct full attention to replenishing our stockpiles of oxygen, water, and power. After that's done, the second phase begins—surveying geophysical resources in our vicinity. Our schedule calls for the first Discovery Team expedition to depart in less than forty-eight hours. I'm going to announce the team members in a moment."

Paige leaps to her feet. Thanks to the low gravity, her body rises a few centimeters off the floor and then plops back down.

Jürgen continues. "During our flight we were at the mercy of equipment built by others. Starting today our success rests entirely in our own hands. I've decided to appoint Mikki Tischler and Andre Broom to take charge of the reactor generators for *Liberty* and *Independence*, respectively."

Mikki spits out bits of food. Her eyes shine with delight. Jürgen agrees with me that she's the best choice for this job, and now she suddenly loves it? Shuko hugs her and Ryder plants a robust slap between her shoulders. Senuri says, "Congratulations, Mikki. A perfect opportunity to shine."

He appoints Mikki to an important job? After she called his bullshit last week?

All heads turn back to Jürgen. "Eric will be in charge of *Constitution's* reactor installation. Power from these reactors will allow us to produce water, oxygen, methanol fuel, and run our life support systems without draining the batteries. We'll be able to start making fuel for our expeditions." He pauses and licks his lips. "Discovery Team One will consist of myself, Senuri Kumar, Ryder Lawson, and Fran Newman."

Ryder jiggles his head. "Did he just say me?"

"He did say you!" Mikki cries. They wrap arms and bounce across the control center, narrowly missing the edge of the main panel. We all cheer, except for Paige. She snaps her spoon in half and lays both pieces side-by-side.

When the ruckus subsides, Jürgen announces, "Discovery Team One will hold a briefing aboard *Independence* at ten this morning."

So those four people aren't assisting with the reactor installation?

I get no chance to ask. Jürgen pushes a few pics of sunlit mountains and gorges. "These images were taken from ten to twenty kilometers altitude while *Independence* was on landing approach. We've been comparing them to the decades-old probe images we've been using to plan our expeditions. We've discovered significant differences that shed insight on the nature of the local debris aprons."

The last pic shows a thin brownish trail in the top right corner.

Resolute.

Has to be! Did Jürgen crop off the spacecraft image so it wouldn't mar his precious planning maps?

He never said a word about *Resolute*. For all his supposed eloquence, he can't offer a few sentences out of respect? Will he do that at the end of this talk? No. He's finishing. I grind my fist into my thigh.

"Each of us came here for our own reasons, but we share a common dream, the freedom to make our own decisions and control our lives. Paradoxically, our freedom requires everyone's collaboration. We're in a new world that may harbor unknown threats. With team spirit, we will not only survive but thrive."

The com explodes with the usual applause. Another hug-fest. But I won't let go of the image of the brown streak.

Resolute. Vijay.

Not one single word.

I scream at the vid, "I have a question!"

Ryder frowns, something he doesn't do often.

Jürgen acknowledges me. "Keep it brief. We have a lot to do."

"You said three days ago we won't make any fuel for the trucks until we have sixty kilos of oxygen and five hundred liters of water in each spacecraft—"

"And we will," Eric interrupts.

"It's a multi-step process," I continue. "It'll take time. We need to dig up ice, melt it, filter it, purify it. Some of it is electrolyzed into oxygen and hydrogen. React the hydrogen with carbon dioxide in the Sabatier tank to get methane, then react the methane with more oxygen to get methanol fuel. The trucks need more oxygen to burn that fuel. You're going to leave us some oxygen to breathe, right?"

The bad joke falls flat. Senuri coughs and folds her arms.

Jürgen stares at me. "Of course we will, Cristina. Was that your question?"

"My question is how do we know we can complete this entire process in less than two days, including the life-support stockpile—"

"Cristina!" Eric, again.

"That's my question." Finished.

"We're way ahead of you," Jürgen tells me. "*Constitution* already purified and split thirty liters of water this morning."

"With battery power? Procedure requires we use the reactors."

Eric responds, "You know very well, Cristina, sometimes the procedure needs a hack. Otherwise we wouldn't be here."

Jürgen leans his face into the vid. "This is for everyone to keep in mind. We're making history. Every word we say is part of the permanent historic record. Don't forget that our children, grandchildren, and generations to come will study our actions and emulate our example. Before you open your mouth, consider how you want to be remembered by posterity."

Fine. But he's not talking to *everyone*. He's talking to me.

THIRTY-FIVE

Ryder and Andre walk out to *Independence* for the expedition briefing and reactor install. First time in weeks Ryder won't be around. Will he come back to help with *Liberty's* reactor?

Mikki leaps into her assignment with enthusiasm. "We'll be the first on line," she declares. "It'll be a bitch to unload the thing. Masses six hundred kilos. Let's get that done now."

Did she ever read the procedure? No matter—Senuri has. "Before we think about moving the reactor we need to assemble the truck. The crane and drill both run on compressed CO_2, so we need to fill the accumulator before we can run the motors."

Paige hasn't said a word since the Discovery Team announcement. She sits chewing a protein bar. We all crave food that's not from the printer, but those bars are supposed to be saved. I ask her, "Are you ready to set up the electrolyzer, the Sabatier, the compressor, hook it all up and hydro-test—"

"I know what I'm doing," Paige says, swallowing the last of the bar. "Leave me alone. Sick of people crawling all over me."

"They're going to rotate these discovery trips so everyone gets a chance. There's enough Mars out there to keep us exploring for the rest of our lives."

She crumples the wrapper. "I sent him my analysis on all the stupid geologic formations. I thought maybe…"

"We'll go on our own expedition, you and me. Steal a truck if we have to."

She smiles and tosses me a protein bar. What the hell? Ryder eats them all the time.

Senuri is the experienced supervisor but she's careful not to step on Mikki's new authority. "With two working inside and four outside, we can rotate for rest and toilet breaks," she suggests. "Mikki, who are you assigning to operate the drill?"

"You and Cristina can do that. Shuko and I rig the crane."

Senuri and I cycle out. Before getting into the airlock we check the power panel for the battery state of charge: 841 kilowatt-hours, ninety-one percent capacity. Almost a tenth discharged over the thirty hours since we separated from the TMI.

"Big power loads coming today," Senuri remarks.

The suit pinches are milder. Jessica had said the actuators sense swollen tissue and modify the pressure profile over time. Pinching or not, the slight discomfort is worth it to escape the cramped and stinky control center.

Liberty's lower two meters consists mostly of cargo compartments. Bulky equipment can be unloaded directly to the surface. I carry the drill tower fifteen meters as measured by the compressed gas hose. "Mikki, is this spot okay?"

"As good as any other. Jürgen doesn't think the ice is deep here, but there's no way to know until we drill a pilot hole."

It takes an hour to set up the tower because it needs six anchor spikes driven into the surface at an angle. By that time there's working gas pressure in the hose. I switch on the drill motor and a faint purr comes through the thin atmosphere. The pilot drill is small, five centimeters across, only intended to explore and make sure we have the right spot for the full-sized hole.

Our first setback comes just after noon. The problem isn't the drill itself but what it's drilling into. Ice, too much of it. Our landing zone was considered unlikely to be over a glacier. Therefore, there shouldn't be more than ten to fifty centimeters of ice or permafrost under the surface. The pilot hole finds ice pockets down to three meters.

Jürgen comes out to investigate. He walks a circle around *Liberty* while studying the ground.

"We're not on a glacier. Probably just hit a local deposit. Can't bury the reactor in ice. Let's try the other side."

Less than six hours before sunset.

Mikki faces Jürgen. "If there's ice over there too, should we start the fallback option? Surface install with regolith shielding?"

"Let's try at least two more locations first. An underground installation means better radiation shielding. We can extend the cable ten meters further out."

He trudges back toward *Independence* and his Discovery Team briefing thing. Is Ryder following what's going on with the reactor installation?

I'm hot, face-dripping hot. Minus nine degrees, but between the thermals and the sun and the lack of thick air to conduct away body heat, the sub-freezing temperature doesn't matter as much as it would on Earth. The fan that's supposed to circulate Mars air under the thermals isn't working right, filter probably needs cleaning.

Moving the tower, anchoring it, and drilling another pilot hole will take how long?

"Mikki, I'm going inside to clean my cooling filter."

"Yeah, but start the second hole first."

"There won't be a second hole if we pass out from heat stroke," Senuri tells her. "Alison and Paige can come out and move the tower later. You and Shuko can cool off in the shade."

The sweat on Mikki's nose glistens in the sun. "Not even two hours, and you're crying to go back in?"

Senuri walks toward *Liberty*. "This is not a comfort issue. My heart rate is one fifty-five."

My visor shows *HR 153*. "Mikki, you're in charge of the reactor, but I'm flight director aboard *Liberty*."

"*Flight* director. As in, for the flight. Did you notice we landed, genius?"

Mikki pulls up tower anchors while Senuri and I cycle back in. The equipment bay is so packed with hoses and tanks the inner hatch is blocked from opening all the way. Paige says, "We're ready to start the hydro test. Once we get this sweetheart going it'll warm this place up."

The irony! She's inside and chilly, we're outside and sweating. "We need to re-drill. Before you cycle out, make sure your cooling air filter is clean, or you'll stew in your own juices."

I need to sit. Twenty minutes to rest, drink, dry off, and visit the pit. Senuri agrees that Paige and Alison will continue the equipment tests and rotate outside in a couple of hours.

After we cycle back out, Mikki and Shuko resume attaching the wire mesh tires to the truck. I drag the compressed gas hose to the other side of *Liberty*.

Constitution reports rock, sand and ice down to four meters. I start the second hole. It doesn't take long for the first material to ooze from around the spinning shaft—dark gray mush, like mud, steaming wisps of vapor.

Mikki examines the new hole. "Fuck. Ice. Fuck me."

Four hours before sunset. I should have scarfed down a food bar before cycling out.

Darien and Indra report the same, but the ice stops at two meters. I ask Jürgen, "What's the max allowed?"

"Half a meter is the recommendation."

So maybe we landed in freaky ice zone. "If we need to, how long would it take to switch to the above-ground method?"

"I want to try more holes before we consider that."

The sun is low in the west by the time the tower is ready for the third hole. Hunger pangs gone, replaced by cold jitters. At least the crap coming up the hole is different this time, crumblier, not steaming.

Mikki bends over the hole with a measuring stick. "We bury it here."

The nuclear reactor is a silver cylinder maybe fifty centimeters wide and a meter tall. Fins around the edge make it look larger—excess heat radiators, according to the manual. The reactor can generate forty kilowatts of electricity non-stop for thirty years.

Senuri and Mikki rig two cables and winch the small but massive device from the cargo compartment. The nameplate reads: GE-Hitachi 4FTD Fluoride Thorium Generator 40kwe 115v 60 Hz AC APR2048, followed by Japanese letters. A yellow and purple label warns: *RADIATION HAZARD.*

Mikki fastens the bottom to the base while Shuko connects a three-meter tube to the top, the refueling port. Senuri and I mount the winch on the truck and lower the reactor assembly to the bottom of the hole. Paige rigs the power, control, and monitoring cable so it can be connected before everything except the top of the refueling port is covered with rock and sand.

Mikki declines a chance to go inside. Doesn't she need to piss? Alison hot-swaps the compressed oxygen canister in her backpack.

Are we done? Not a chance. I help Paige set up bladders to hold the methanol as it comes out of the catalyst tank. Two rectangular areas four meters long have to be raked clear of rocks and pebbles. We do this on the south side of *Liberty* so sunlight can warm the meth and make it less likely to freeze overnight if the temperature dips below minus ninety-seven degrees.

We lay out the bladders inside the raked areas. They're black and made of heavy flexible polymer stamped 1000 L in the center. Just as we finish, a biting chill soaks through my BioSuit.

Mars: too hot or too cold.

Ten minutes after sunset, Mikki and Shuko are still huddled over the conical dirt pile around the refueling port. Everyone gathers by the control center window to watch them finish. They insist on completing the work themselves. "Put your thermals on over those flight suits," Senuri tells them. "Temp is minus thirty and falling rapidly."

I can barely decipher Mikki's response. "Don't you think we know it's fucking cold?"

She's fixated. "Mikki, the BioSuits have no insulation. Watch your fingers! Without the sun, your whole body's shedding heat via infrared. The manual says at night hands without thermal mitts can be frostbitten in minutes."

"Fuck your manual. We get this done."

Shuko has nothing to say?

A dark figure approaches from the direction of *Independence*. Ryder! He sees them and pulls them both from the dirt pile. No words on the com—did they switch to the private channel? Someone shoves someone else. No need to guess who's doing the shoving.

Mikki and Shuko tumble from the airlock shaking violently. Senuri and I back Mikki against the Sabatier tank, pull her flight suit below her waist and detach the BioSuit collar and front seam. I clasp her cold fingers in my palms. "Can you feel this? Can you move them?"

She splutters, "Done...with reactor."

Shuko drops to the floor. Is the imbécil actually smiling?

Dinner is quiet. The cold creeps inside bones and most of us order some kind of hot soup. Ryder spoons the last of his and tells us what we've already guessed. "Andre stayed aboard *Independence* to finish the reactor startup."

"Their first hole was dry, wasn't it?" Mikki asks. "He got a couple hours jump on me."

Ryder raises an eyebrow. "Mick, who said it was a race?"

THIRTY-SIX

A longer, calmer, darker, better night. The sleeper is plush compared to a blanket on the floor, even if the cushion is just a few centimeters thick.

Already after nine! Paige says, "I don't want to rush you, but we need water, as much as we can get, as fast as we can get it."

"Mind if I eat first?"

"I'm not stopping you. Just saying, once we get the Sabatier going we can all take a real shower. Nothing fancy. A couple of liters each. Wet down, tiny bit of soap, rinse."

Alison says, "I forgot what it's like to be clean!"

Ryder, Senuri, and Shuko are outside working. In brown coveralls? No, their thermals are covered with reddish-brown dust. They dig up chunks of ice and toss them somewhere out of sight.

I ask, "We electrolyzing water yet?"

"Started two hours ago," Paige answers. "It has to be melted in the hopper, filtered, put through the reverse osmosis purifier, then deionized. Slow going. We topped off our own reserve and I'm filling the truck's oxygen tank as fast as the compressor allows."

"Topped off what reserve, water or oxygen?"

"Both."

"Wait. You put sixty kilos in the big tank already?"

She folds her arms. "I topped off the reserve tank, the ten kilo reserve. What tank are you talking about?"

"The big spherical helium tank. We don't need the landing fuel pressurized, so we vent it and fill it with oxygen."

"That's not what Tess said."

Should have seen this coming. "Don't you remember this discussion? We reach full life-support reserves before we make fuel for the trucks."

"They told me to make a specific amount of methanol by six tonight. Twenty liters minimum. I might be able to do it if I can get this shit going by ten."

Jürgen broke his word. Or delegated that job to Tess. Do the Articles require the captain to be honest? We forgot that part. So promises don't matter if the captain says they don't.

"Put the first sixty kilos of oxygen in the big reserve tank. I'll vent it and line it up."

Paige shakes her head. "I'm not going to let everybody think I'm an idiot because we're the only ones who couldn't contribute our share of fuel."

Mikki hunches over the power panel with a mug of tea. Battery state of charge stands at 762 kw-hours, eighty-three percent capacity. Lower than yesterday morning. That makes no sense. I ask her, "There's a delay in the reactor start up?"

She jerks her head from the panel. Her eyes are pink. "Not really. What makes you say that?"

"The batteries are down compared to—"

"Yeah. Drew two hundred amps to start the thing. There's a plug of thorium salt that had to be melted from minus thirty degrees, and a CO2 loop and a thermionic generator to be brought to operating temperature. All that takes power."

"I understand. But we're producing power now. Shouldn't the batteries be charging?"

"That almost got me too, but Eric cleared it up. Between melting ice, the electrolyzers, deionizers, three compressors for CO2, hydrogen and oxygen, plus hotel loads, there's a massive drain on the bus and that shows up as a low state of charge."

"So we're charging the batteries?"

"Yes. But with a big current deficit."

Must have happened late. Was *Liberty* first on line? Her eyes say no. "I did the startup without any help from Eric," she adds. "He's not as essential as people assume."

She hasn't been to bed at all.

"Was there a problem starting up?"

"Not really. The internal sequencer brings everything to operating temperature, then I had to manually run a script. That's to make sure the thing never starts itself. There were some issues with timeouts. After I learned to read the TRAC, I realized it was already running."

"Read the what?"

She yawns. "Transient Reactor Analysis Code."

Complicated. But it's running.

A late breakfast, then Alison and I cycle out to assist gathering ice. Ryder greets us with, "Welcome to the ice mines of Mars!"

The ice just under the surface varies in thickness and clarity. Some of it's milky white, but the rest is full of pebbles and sand grit. Unfortunately, the cleanest ice tended to be only one or two centimeters thick.

Shuko uses a shovel blade to uncover patches while Ryder smashes with a pick. I copy Senuri, tossing ice chunks into a square metal hopper just inside the cargo compartment. A gravity-fed mechanism crushes the pieces before they drop into a heating chamber.

Ryder leans on his shovel. "By this time next year we'll have three or four Jacuzzis going."

"I'll believe it when I see it," responds Shuko.

I point to my helmet, meaning my brain. "You have to see it here first. That's the first and hardest step."

✳

Going full-blast, the Sabatier chamber heats *Liberty* nice and toasty, just as Paige promised. But there's a price: the din from the associated pumps, regulators, and fans combines into a constant rumble-whine. Noise for warmth, a fair trade-off.

"Sweet, sweet methane," Paige announces. "Next is the tricky part, single-stage oxidation to methanol. The Sab condenser recovers most of the water we electrolyzed. It's pure, so I'm sending it straight to the potable tanks. No more drinking purified piss."

Ryder yells from the control deck, "I've grown to prefer the subtle flavor of purified piss."

The frequent cycling in and out of the airlock spreads fine brown dust everywhere. It stinks like burnt toast. We try to keep all dirty boots, thermals, and coveralls in the equipment bay, but in practice there's no place to hang everything.

"Nasty stuff!" says Alison. "Impossible to brush out. Hair's turning orange."

Mikki sniffs mockingly. "Poor baby."

"At least there's only a trace of perchlorates," Senuri informs us. "Irritating but not dangerous. Like a lot of things, we'll have to get used to the feel of it."

The first batch of methanol doesn't go to the bladders. Alison prints two ten-liter containers with handles. Jürgen wants the stuff ready to go before nightfall, so Paige babysits the slow stream as it fills the first container. She measures the depth every few minutes and pleads with Ryder and Alison to stay outside and keep the hopper filled with ice chunks

Always calm Senuri screams and points out the window—a moving truck! It's kicking up dust, rolling along at the speed of a fast bicycle. The sight of it makes my skin tingle. Plus, we get to see a new person face-to-face, a rare event.

The driver turns out to be Darien. I climb down into the equipment bay as he steps through the inner hatch. But he's not interested in me or anyone else. The instant his helmet is off his eyes turn to the power panel. State of charge: 727 kw-hours, seventy-nine percent capacity.

Small talk can wait. I tell him, "Our loads seem to be exceeding the reactor power output."

He examines the data and strokes his faint golden mustache. "Eric says this is fine, exactly what he expected."

I want to stick to this subject. "I don't understand why total charge is still going down. At this rate we'll be discharged in a few days."

"Eric's modifying the software."

"Software? But this is a power—"

"It has to do with measuring the state of charge."

"So when he fixes it we'll see an accurate charge?"

Darien lowers his eyes. "I don't know. We got five battery packs, one on line and four charging. Eric says once his fix is complete we'll have a better indication of total power."

Jürgen gets his compressed oxygen and methanol truck fuel. Not enough to go far, but enough to go somewhere. The first Discovery Team expedition needs just two trucks, and they'll stay close in case a breakdown make it necessary to walk back.

"Tomorrow's expedition will cover a thirty-six kilometer circuit," Jürgen reveals during his dinner speech. "Six planned stops, each one with a different scientific purpose. We'll also start to map out the distribution of nearby mineral resources."

Eric offers his own contribution. He designed an alarm system to watch for solar flares "A big flare can deliver enough radiation to kill an exposed person," he informs us. "The good news is, as long as we know about it, we'll have one or two hours' to get inside our hygiene compartments so we're shielded from protons. Trouble is, Discovery Teams will be out of VHF range all day. So my idea is to shoot a small rocket about a kilometer up so it can broadcast a radio alarm."

We applaud Eric's little black rocket, and he smiles in satisfaction.

"The first humans to explore another planet!" Jürgen reminds us, as if we forgot. "Imagine what any scientist in history would've given to be in our place."

Ryder does come back from *Independence*, and promptly vanishes into his sleeper—alone, for once. Wake-up time is five, expedition to depart at dawn.

Battery charge down another ten kilowatt-hours since this afternoon. Eric says don't believe the indication, but what if it's accurate? Except for fans, the Sabatier tank consumes no power once the exothermic reaction kicks off. Shouldn't that lower the rate of battery discharge? And why is the indicated charge wrong, anyhow?

If I don't talk to Eric now, I won't get any real sleep.

He's awake, but with the same squinty-eyed weariness exhibited during the thruster failure and the oxygen generator breakdowns. I show him the charge trend over the past twelve hours and ask about the accuracy.

"Depends what you mean by accurate. Those values are derived from coulomb counting and voltage comparison. They're calculated, not measured. With the reactor up, the inverter is powering your main DC bus loads, not the batteries."

"Eric, I'm no electrical engineer."

"That's right, you're not."

"But I understand basic physics. I know energy input and output have to balance. You're telling me the reactor is draining the battery?"

He sighs. "I said nothing of the kind. Pay attention. There's no accurate way to directly measure the charge of lithium-ion polymer cells. This is a technology I'm familiar with, and I can tell you it behaves predictably if somewhat strangely. You can't gauge state of charge as you would pressure or temperature."

"So we're measuring it indirectly. It might be wrong. How do we measure it right?"

"It's complicated. Been working on this all day. Look, don't lose any sleep. There's an error in the derived state of charge, and I'll create a workaround. Put it out of your head."

"You're confident the batteries are fully charged?"

"Didn't say that. Get some rest, Cristina."

THIRTY-SEVEN

People get up to laugh and chat while it's still utterly black outside. I stay bundled in a cocoon of blankets, a pillow wrapped around my ears to shut out the gibberish. Sleep comes, but dreams of rocks and ice chunks spoil the early morning hours.

Golden sunbeams flood the control center. Paige sits alone, eating a bowl of fake oatmeal and watching a vid loop of Jürgen's pre-expedition speech. My sleepy brain absorbs two facts: the first Discovery Team has left, and battery state of charge is 685 kw-hours, seventy-four percent.

Paige says, "You missed the departure."

"Oh, no. I am so devastated."

There's gotta be a way to determine if the batteries are actually being charged—and whether the reactor is truly generating power. It must be possible to do this independently, without interference or contradictory information. I gulp a breakfast of eggs and sausage while reviewing the electrical system manual. Shuko and Andre are outside digging up ice. Mikki emerges from her sleeper and joins Paige in organizing the day's activities. If a test is possible, now is the time.

We have five Sony battery packs, each a meter square and thirty centimeters thick. A System Management Bus keeps one pack online, one pack charging, one in standby, and two in maintenance mode. In flight, the AC loads were powered by an inverter connected to the battery. The TMI reactor charged the battery. But the inverter shouldn't be powering anything now, because the buried reactor is supplying AC.

I wrap my fingers around the four thick cables from the reactor. They carry every load on *Liberty,* currently forty-six amps according to the power panel. Equipment to melt ice, electrolyze water, compress hydrogen, oxygen, and methane, condense methanol, plus purify our air.

Yet, the cables don't feel warm. Aren't they supposed to be?

Suppose I disconnect the inverter from the battery? Nothing should lose power—if the reactor is actually supplying the AC busses. There are two breakers, both in a common control box under the power panel. I slide the safety latch and press both breakers downward.

Liberty goes dead. No lights, no ventilator fans, no panel displays. An alarm buzzes—must be powered directly off the batteries.

Mikki's face hangs from the access hatch. "What are you doing?"

I close the breakers and our equipment comes back to life. "Mikki, the reactor isn't powering the AC loads."

"You did that on purpose?" Paige shouts, nostrils flaring. "Don't you realize the Sab is outputting methane into a compressor?"

"The Sab is exothermic. It doesn't draw power."

Paige jumps down into the equipment bay and scans the Sab readouts. "The reaction is self-sustaining. But the compressor pulls methane out. You could've over-pressurized the main chamber, popped the reliefs, screwed up the whole thing!"

"I had to—"

She shoves me aside. "Don't touch what you don't understand!"

Eric connects on the com. "*Liberty,* your AC busses were down for nine seconds. Anyone playing with the system?"

"One guess!" Mikki snarls.

"Cris-teeen-naaaah," Eric calls softly, as if to a child. "What did you do?"

"I determined the reactor isn't powering anything. The question is—"

"I don't have time to teach you basic electrical engineering today. All you need to know are these three words. Leave it alone."

He's going to answer me whether he likes it or not. "If the reactor is supplying AC power, how could we lose the busses just by disconnecting the inverter? We shouldn't need the inverter!"

"You're confused. Let us worry about what we need."

"You want something to do?" asks Paige. "I know the perfect exercise. Break some ice! I want to make a hundred liters of methanol by the time Jürgen's back."

✳

The state of charge drops to 659 kw-hours, seventy-one percent. When I return to the equipment bay sometime after noon it's ninety-eight percent. Like magic!

Just as strange, there's no triumphant announcement from Eric. He fixed it. Why not explain how, as he always does?

"For my own understanding," I ask him, "Where did I go wrong this morning?"

Eric blinks at me. No trace of pride, just exhaustion. "Don't be hard on yourself. I might have done the same, before I became an engineer. The SMB didn't know there are five stand-alone battery packs on one bus. They were tested one at a time, which is standard procedure. I had to rewrite the SMB kernel to correct it."

"But only one pack is on line at any given time."

He stares at me. "How did you get that idea?"

"The manual."

"Well, yes, there's one battery pack discharging at a given moment. But if the SMB looks only at that one pack, the state of charge is invalid."

"I'm still confused. I thought it's designed for one pack."

"It is, Cristina. But we have five packs."

"So your fix makes it look at all the packs?"

"I think you've finally got it."

There are missing pieces. But more questions will trigger Eric's defensiveness.

An hour before sunset the Discovery Team trucks round the top of a distant hill and come within VHF line-of-sight range. Ryder contacts us first. His voice shakes with excitement. "Snow volcanoes, three of 'em! Would you believe it? Fucking snow volcanoes. I'm serious!"

That's all anyone wants to see—vids of the snow volcanoes. Slush, mud and steam geysers, actually. They erupt in irregular puffs from the bottom of a ravine. The steam condenses into ice crystals, real snow, that swirl like a bona-fide mini-blizzard. Pretty bizarre.

"We didn't expect snow volcanoes," says Jürgen "I believe this is a phenomenon of the spring thaw. Icy mud flows down until it reaches a geothermal heat source, then it erupts to the surface. We traveled thirty-eight kilometers total, nine stops, sixty kilos of mineral samples. An incredible day of historic firsts!"

"Fuel usage six percent under projection!" Ryder gushes from over Jürgen's shoulder.

"Tomorrow we're loading three times more fuel so we can cover a one hundred kilometer route." says Jürgen. "Our objective is a range of cliffs to the north. Orbital pics show evidence of sporadic flowing water."

Paige yells, "A hundred and twelve liters of methanol in *Liberty's* bladder!"

An endless stream of pics follows. Jürgen describes taking atmospheric samples for traces of natural methane. The max reading was two parts per billion, but there shouldn't be any methane at all. Ultraviolet radiation from the sun breaks it down within a few decades. From where is it being replenished? Biological activity near the surface?

"We're going to find out," Jürgen promises, the glint back in his eye. "We're breaking new scientific territory, a privilege that cannot be squandered."

I order a light dinner of soup and dumplings. With the first spoonful comes the purr of the airlock compressor. Ryder and Senuri. Isn't the discovery gang planning to hang out at *Independence* and bask in the remembrance of their deeds? Why walk over here just as night is falling?

Ryder climbs up to the control center with his helmet on. He pulls it off to reveal his sweaty red face, nose dribbling like a three-year-old. He grins at me. "Don't forget to say thank you."

"For what?"

Senuri pushes *Liberty's* vid out to *Independence*. She winks in my direction. "Get ready for a surprise."

I hope that doesn't mean what I think it means.

"Discovery Team Two!" cries Jürgen. He pauses so everyone can stop whatever they were doing and wait for him. Paige sits, fingers over her mouth.

"Our second Discovery Team will depart at dawn to explore the northern reaches of our yet unnamed valley. Joining me will be Tess, Cristina, and Darien."

Alison screams in my ear and hugs me from behind. Paige bangs her fist down on the tabletop with enough force to fling drops of chicken soup onto my face.

"Ryder did this, you know," Senuri tells me, eyes beaming.

I say it softly so only Ryder can hear. "I'd rather not." He responds, but the noise surrounding us muffles it. I tell him a bit louder, "I need to show you something."

Later, alone in the equipment bay, I hold his fingers against the reactor power cables. "We've been drawing forty to fifty amps all day. Shouldn't these cables be warm?"

"We charged the battery banks over the past two days," Ryder says. He points to the state of charge indication. Ninety-nine percent. "We're topped off, so the generator isn't putting out full current."

"Eric says the AC loads come straight from the reactor, not the inverter."

He squints. "What's your point?"

"We have a power deficit, and the battery charge isn't accurate."

"All right. I don't agree with your reasoning, but I can talk to Eric about this tomorrow while you're in the field."

"I'm going to see Jürgen," I tell him. "Right now. I want you to come with me, but I'm going even if you don't."

✳

The western horizon glows vivid blue over jagged black peaks. It should be beautiful, a promise of adventure on a pristine world. Tonight, it's a stark reminder of our isolation. There are no rescuers here, no teachers willing to forgive our mistakes.

Ryder and I walk to *Independence* hand-in-hand. The visor's night mode shows every rock in sharp grayscale, so the Mars quick-shuffle style of walking is safe in the dark. He hasn't given me an argument yet, but he doesn't know what I'm going to say. And to be honest, neither do I.

We remove our helmets while still in the airlock. "He's extending an olive branch. Don't underestimate him. Sure, he has a high opinion of himself, but maybe that's justified."

I rub my face. He's lecturing, and nothing I can do will stop him.

"Jürgen's a brilliant planner, and he's got a nose for the right direction. You might participate in one of the greatest discoveries in history. With Jürgen, it could happen."

Ryder grips the inner hatch handle but instead of twisting it open he holds it shut. We have a few more seconds of privacy before entering *Independence*.

"Tess told me a couple of things about Jürgen and I want you to be aware. He's a determined and ambitious man. He didn't want the curriculum the university told him to study. When he stopped attending classes he was arrested and put in a cement hole for two years."

Did he just say *a cement hole?*

"That's right, two years solitary confinement. His grandfather intervened, probably saved his life. Jürgen's destiny is to explore—"

"Fine! And there will be a time for that. But this fixation can't be allowed to interfere—"

"Not a fixation. And it's not interfering with anything, except maybe in your head."

"That's what we're here for. Let's talk it out."

Two years. How big a hole? Why didn't they just kill him? And what did he think about during all that time?

Jürgen's in the control center, alone, examining a scientific chart or something. Did he order everyone else into their sleepers?

"Cristina, good to see you. You look well rested."

There's something about him so likable, and the effect is more powerful in his presence. Is this whole talk a mistake? Let Ryder and Eric handle the engineering?

I bow my head slightly, a stupid habit drilled in from a young age. "Thanks for picking me."

"You were the logical choice. Everyone respects your problem-solving abilities."

"There's a problem I'm working on now."

His mouth twists. "Tell me about it."

"I don't think the reactors are charging our batteries. I think we're running out of power. We shouldn't produce any more truck fuel until we find out for certain if the electrical system is working correctly."

He stares for a second, then turns to the main panel. "Our banks are at ninety-seven percent."

"This morning they were seventy. Eric altered the software, and suddenly all our batteries are maxed. I have reason to believe they're not actually being charged."

Jürgen looks to Ryder. "What's your opinion?"

"I can work with Eric and conduct some tests. What Cristina's saying is physically possible, I guess. Remember all the other problems we've had. Not much of a stretch to suspect there's something wrong with the charging."

That's as good as I'm going to get. "I want to participate in your expedition, especially if we're surveying for minerals. But we need to figure out this power thing first."

Jürgen pushes a vid to Eric on *Constitution*. "I agree. That's exactly what we're going to do."

Eric's eyes go wide when he sees I'm with Jürgen. "Yes, I had to alter the code. It was necessary to correct defects in the battery charging management software."

"You hacked it," I point out.

"Cristina, what haven't we had to hack to stay alive?"

"You insisted you could work around the oxygen generator failures. You promised and guaranteed right up to the point they all shut down."

Eric shows a mean little smirk. "Is this some kind of revenge for losing the election? Making the rest of us look bad?"

"Shut it, Eric," Ryder says. "That's not what I want and you know it."

Jürgen opens his mouth to speak but I cut him off. "I isolated the battery this morning and we lost all AC. How could that happen if the reactor is generating power?"

Eric snarls, "Because you disconnected the whole AC bus!"

Jürgen says, "Eric has the experience here."

"Nobody has enough experience. You know that."

Unnecessarily antagonistic!

Another mouth twist. This time it lasts longer. "Cristina, there's a reason I'm organizing these Discovery Team expeditions as early as we can make fuel. The reason is momentum."

"Momentum?"

"Momentum is necessary for morale and attitude, the mental elements that will make us or break us. We didn't come here just to survive. We came here to do remarkable things. Historic things."

"You want to be the first person to discover life on another planet."

Huge mouth twist.

Estúpida chica!

He juts his chin upward. A rare event, Jürgen's at a loss for words.

"I'm going to figure this out myself," I tell him. "Replace me on tomorrow's expedition."

✳

Paige cries when I tell her the news. "Tomorrow? As in tomorrow? Me, tomorrow?"

"As in seven hours from now. You better get some sleep."

"Should have let me go to bed and woke me at five and told me then!"

I pull two electrical system manuals to the main panel. Would opening those breakers truly isolate the entire AC bus, or just the inverter?

Ryder says, "I think we should talk." He slides my sleeper door open.

"I have work to do. And didn't we just now talk, me and you and everyone else? We said our piece. We all know where we stand."

He pushes my manuals off the screen. "I haven't said *my* piece, Cristina. I saved it for just me and you. Do me this courtesy, please."

The door is closed for two seconds and he blurts, "Two oh eight. That's the lowest Score I ever heard."

He's got to be kidding. "What the fuck does that matter now?"

"I think it matters very much, Cristina. You were…at whatever academy, you were…toxic. Friendless. You threw yourself into your studies hoping it would somehow make you special, make you liked."

"I had a close friend, one good friend. That's all I needed." Harmony wants us to have many scattered friends. He's holding it against me I didn't do what Harmony wants?

"I'm going to take a wild guess and speculate it was your one good friend's mission to help you raise your Score, which would make their own Score zoom up into the stratosphere."

Son of a bitch. "You know everything, don't you?"

"We don't have Trust Scores any more. What we do have is plain, ordinary trust."

Paco taught me more about honesty and trust than Ryder or any of them could ever know. "What about honesty? I'm being honest here. I'm not going to lie to you or myself and agree that thing is putting out power."

"I don't think you're being honest with yourself, Cristina. And that's the most important kind of honesty."

"You have no idea what's in my head."

"If we're going to get along out here without an Autoridad to lord over us and watch us and tell us what to do, we have to trust each other. And respect each other."

My face heats up. "Is this the obvious bullshit you wanted to tell me? Are you done?"

"You're fighting the wrong battle. The environment here is the enemy, not us. You made some good calls during the flight, but ask yourself this one question. Could you have solved any of those problems by yourself?"

"I never claimed I could."

"Even so, it's not a rhetorical question. If you had been by yourself, you'd be dead. Eric saved us, Indra saved us, Paige saved us, a dozen other engineers saved us, people with knowledge and creative initiative, which is why they were selected to begin with."

"So why was I selected? To dig out ice and clean the shitter?"

"You have cojones. But they were made for a different world. We all have to adapt and give up our old ways. Think in terms of working on a team. You need us, and you can trust us. And that's perfect because we all need each other." He takes my shoulders in his hands. "Your father, Cristina. Did you trust him?"

"Of course!"

The instant the words come out I know it's a lie. Ryder sees it too.

I love Paco. He will always be the anchor of my life. He taught me so much, and would have taught me much more had the cancer not taken him. He made me, and without Paco I wouldn't be here and I'd never have a chance to be free.

I'm eight, and Alex is gone.

Alex is gone, and Paco did nothing.

Ryder waits; how much time passed?

"Paco did nothing," I tell him, and crunch my eyes shut so he can't see the tears.

Ryder waits some more.

"He did nothing."

"What could he do?"

"You have no idea what I'm talking about." I turn away because there's no chance of hiding anything now. "Alex! My brother. So small. They pulled him out, and Paco did nothing. He did nothing to stop them, didn't even try."

Ryder says gently, "There was nothing he could have done. They would have killed him."

Yes. But I didn't understand when I was eight. I only understood they took Alex and Paco did nothing.

Paco never taught me to fight for what I want. He taught me many things, but not that.

I face Ryder. My face is wet, but so what? "Why just Alex? Why didn't they take me, too?"

Ryder holds me for a while.

"There's a reason," he whispers. "You're here with us now. That's the reason."

"If they had taken me," I sob, "I never would have known Paco, not really. I'm not going to *let* any of you…"

I can't finish. Ryder's arms grip tighter. We're alone, bodies entwined, but he won't sleep with me like he does the others, because that's not what we have between us. That's me, all on me, and that's the way I want it for now.

"Trust us, Cristina. Every last person here has been through their own personal hell. We don't know each other's full story, and maybe that's a good thing. Mikki and I worked together." He sees the surprise in my eyes. "You probably suspected we knew each other. Well, we did. They had us on a physiological control project, mind control really, and we both should have refused… because, what that would have meant to so many people…"

Ryder, for once, is out of words. We look anywhere but at each other.

"It was wrong, this project, but we both knew, refusal could be a death sentence, or at a minimum a wasted life. Our friends, my younger brother, what about them?"

"We're all cowards, is that what you're saying?"

"No. What I mean is this. We learned from a young age to deal with painful truths by avoiding them, or by pretending better truths exist. This made us tough in some ways, but it also makes it hard for us to look at ourselves honestly."

I sit up. "That's what I've been telling you. Truth is hard. The hardest truth is about ourselves. Harmony wants selfless people. The focus is on the group, always the group, always a quest to please the leader, to appear perfect in the eyes of the leader and everyone else. Don't you see? This is what we have to overcome."

No, he doesn't see.

"What I want you to know, Cristina, is that you can still salvage your situation. Jürgen's forming a leadership circle. We'll be the ones in charge as our population grows."

How is this different from how we were taught to behave at the Academy? Trust others to tell you what to do, and keep your own opinions to yourself. Don't speak thoughts others don't want to hear. That would be arrogant.

I pull away from him. "You're in this great leadership circle, I suppose."

"Yes I am. With Eric, Tess, Senuri, and Andre."

"Tess? *Tess?*"

"Don't underestimate her. But that's not my point. Do you realize you had a shot at becoming part of the core leadership?"

"While you're all patting each other on the back, I'm trying to understand how the power generator works."

"That's why I like you. You speak your mind. You were a problem for the Autoridad. That's why you're here. But if you can't adapt, if you can't be part of our team, you're going to be an outcast. Is that what you want?"

✳

Right now I just want sleep. But there's one last hurt.

Tess pushes me a text.

*Jürgen opposed your selection for Mars. You got the
chance only because his
grandfather and Michael Gusman convinced some
others on the Genesis team.*

I stare at the words, unable to think. My stomach rumbles and a cold wave sweeps my face.

Why did Jürgen oppose my selection?

Who else knows this? Who has she told?

Tess is one of the people I'm supposed to *trust?*

I re-read some of Vijay's old texts. *Cristina, I know it is
difficult to understand the actions and points of view of some
of our compatriots. We will all need time to acclimate to this
wonderful thing called liberty.*

Better, for a moment.

But who has she told?

THIRTY-EIGHT

Jürgen's first expedition changed everything. People smile more. A symbolic hurdle has been cleared. We're making this planet our home. The low-level dread that clung to their souls since they left Earth is replaced with excitement.

Mikki and Ryder take charge of *Liberty's* methanol production. The day's quota is two hundred liters. The Sab tank and the catalyst bed make oxygen and pure water as byproducts of the reactions, which means a daily shower from now on—two minutes max.

The entire hygiene pit serves as a shower stall. I make the water as hot as it will go and stand under the wonderfully wet flow. My hair is filthy—but at least it's still short. I soap up fast because there's an automatic shutoff timer.

We have a shower timer, but no way to determine battery charge.

Maybe there is a way. The issue is whether the AC bus is energized by the reactor generator or the battery inverter. If all five battery banks were isolated, a voltmeter applied across the reactor cables would tell the true story. A voltmeter is integral to the system anyhow. But how to isolate those cables?

Eric and Ryder are best qualified to guide, but they already decided it's wasted effort. I'll have to do it alone.

Or maybe not. Darien pushed a message late last night, subject line batteries. Six strange pics of the equipment bay on *Constitution,* strange because they used an infrared sensor Darien had printed. Pics of heat instead of light. The reactor cables were cool, and only the on-line pack was warmer than the others. The charging pack was no hotter than the standby packs. So how could it be charging?

Did he show these to Eric?

He did, but Eric explained everything.

Figure this out alone, but alone with Darien. Except Darien is out on the second Discovery Team. Darien helped solve the propellent deficit problem with a cool rationality. He didn't let himself get sucked into the delusion of the crowd. He analyzed and calculated a solution.

Focus. Is there something wrong with the reactor? Mikki says no.

The manual is complex with lots of terms that need referencing. Natural convection. Secondary loop. Stability margins. Inlet subcooling. Startup rate. Reactivity feedback. Movable reflector. I know neutron flux—that's basic physics.

The reactors are intended to be operated hands-off, as the manual puts it. Self-contained, self-maintained, few moving parts, started by running scripts. This is proven technology, used successfully at the Chēngzhǎng lunar outposts for years. But there's nothing to test, nothing to see.

Eric says the cables are cool because the batteries are fully charged. Heat image shows only one warm cell, the one discharging.

Apparently this is a day of rest for everyone not on the Discovery Team. Once they know the methanol production chain has an ample supply of water, Ryder and Senuri watch vids of their snow volcanoes and exploration sites. Alison and Mikki analyze the mineral samples collected yesterday. Norberto and Irene test a spotter they designed for the third Discovery Team. The idea is to scout ahead of the trucks for obstacles or anything interesting. The thing has to be extremely light to fly in the thin atmosphere. By late afternoon the thing is flying around *Liberty* and peering into windows.

Just what Mars needs—spotters.

They spend the rest of the day watching old Mars-themed vids: *Mission to Mars, Red Planet, Last Days on Mars, The Martian, Angry Red Planet.* I can't help sneaking a few peaks. The people who made these vids portrayed Mars in dull red tones, nothing like the diverse textures and vibrant yellows, browns, and grays on the actual Mars. And the spacecraft interiors are always so huge. In *The Martian* they had a separate gym room in their enormous rotating spacecraft, the gym alone at least ten times the size of our whole control deck. Why did people think spacecraft would have such vast interiors?

Allison wants to know the frequency of dust storms. The Mars vids show lots of storms killing people and wreaking all sorts of havoc. Senuri informs us that due to the incredibly thin atmosphere, dust storms and high winds are not dangerous at all, but large amounts of dust in the atmosphere can attenuate sunlight down to a fraction of normal.

The second Discovery Team returns just before sunset. They boast about reaching fifty kilometers. What if both trucks had broken down? The mountains block VHF radio communication. They had plenty of oxygen, Paige asserts, and they could have walked back by midnight.

"We spent two hours at the edge of an exposed glacier," Jürgen says before taking a bite of dinner. They hadn't eaten all day, subsisting on a watery nutrient fluid sipped inside the helmets. "We found hundreds of spots where ground ice converted to gas and left a void. This is a hazard, so I'm asking everyone to study these pics so you can recognize these formations and avoid them. The surface crust can cave in under your feet. Happened to me three times! Fortunately, the voids weren't deeper than my knees."

Mikki is named for the third Discovery Team.

"You made two hundred and six liters," Paige complements her. Paige's eyes are red and beat. "That's twice my output. You deserve to get out there." She glances at me, opens her mouth, but decides to say nothing at all. People want to please the Captain. That's what matters the most.

✳

Doing this alone isn't working. Darien also suspects something amiss with the batteries, but he doesn't make any public announcements.

"Darien, did you show those heat images to anyone else?"

He casts his eyes down. "I don't want them to know I'm questioning their word."

"All right. Fine. You have a degree in physics? How is it possible for the AC bus to be down with the reactor connected?"

"Physics, not engineering."

"You must have some kind of theory. Look. I promise this conversation is private."

He pushes a complete schematic of the electrical system. "Do you know the meaning of the term C-rate?"

"It has something to do with discharge rate."

"It means the rate a battery will discharge relative to maximum capacity. One C means the present current will discharge the entire battery in one hour."

He indicates a row of figures next to each battery symbol.

161C   163C   160C   159C   161C

"They're almost all the same," he says. "And they're too high, at least for the online bank and the charging bank. They can't be all fully charged all the time, not if the SMB is doing its job. They're supposed to cycle."

It hits me. "Did Eric tell you about re-writing the battery software?"

Darien glares back, his cheeks moving with each breath. He doesn't know?

"Eric rewrote some of the code," I inform him. "He said it was necessary because the system wasn't calculating charge correctly. The indicated charge jumped from the low seventies to ninety-eight percent."

He nods. "This is what we would see if he made the SMB treat five cells as one and use the total voltage to derive state of charge. The true state of charge would be a lot lower than indicated."

"Darien, is it possible the reactors aren't charging anything? Have we been pulling all this power directly from the batteries and nothing else?"

"I don't see how that could be. All that energy has to dissipate somewhere."

"Suppose the reactors aren't operating?"

His eyes dart left and right. "All three of them? All this time? I can ask Eric to verify the status, but he's been doing that on a daily basis."

"Eric's been wrong before. Go out there, disconnect the reactor power cables, apply a voltmeter. That will tell us for sure."

"No, it won't. The generator shuts down instantly on no load."

"Thanks for saving me from making a total ass of myself," I tell him with a forced smile. He smiles back, but the rest of his face is joyless.

"I'm going to take this directly to Jürgen," he says.

"Good. They don't take it seriously coming from me."

"There's an old maxim that goes, it's not a problem unless you have a solution. I think I can make a case for temporarily stopping fuel production and conserving our oxygen and battery power until we figure this out."

"One hundred percent," I assure him in my best Dr. Mike style.

THIRTY-NINE

A perfect peaceful night's rest. On track to solve the power anomalies, finally.

I bypass the pit and go straight to the power panel. But the panel's blank, except for two orange words.

ADMIN LOCKED

They're working on it. Why else would it say that?

Eric pushes a text to everyone. He has taken control of all electrical and life-support systems in order to increase reliability. Nothing to be concerned about. Methanol production is to proceed as usual.

Ryder and Paige begin a new project—printing parts for a surface mining rover. Once assembled it would cover hundreds of square meters of ground and accumulate a massive pile of rock-free sand for making construction bricks.

"We'll be baking bricks in a few days," says Paige. She assigns Alison and me to assemble and test each part that comes out of the printer. The rover will be powered by a small methanol-oxygen motor.

Just before lunch I push a text to Darien. No response comes back.

He must be immersed in a deep technical troubleshooting process with Eric. Ryder says he's been asked to hike out to *Independence*, no reason given. I start to mention Darien—but no, I cannot. I promised the conversation would be private.

Once again the Discovery Team returns as the sun touches the western mountains. Mikki and Ryder stay on *Independence*. Jürgen reports that multiple sources of phosphates, copper, and nickel have been identified within fifteen kilometers. He expects polymer production to begin within twenty days.

And they discovered flowing water. From the base of a small glacier, meter-wide brooks of water roll over rocks and down gullies, the low gravity creating an illusion of thickness and slow-motion.

"Mikki Tischler made this discovery," Jürgen says. "The water's briny and it lasted almost an hour before it evaporated."

There's a vid of Mikki and Andre at the edge of a shallow pond splashing each other. Mikki floats an empty sample container, the lid fashioned as a sail. Jürgen remarks, "Witness Mars's first sea-going vessel."

All they want to do is watch spotter vids of today's newly-discovered landscape. I text Darien again. A full day since our talk, and nothing has changed—except *ADMIN LOCKED*.

How private is private? Should I assume Eric has already been informed about my supposedly private conversation with Darien? I text Eric. No response.

No dinner, and no sleep either. Focus my mind on something? But there's nothing else, just a cold emptiness, an aloneness, like when Faye wasn't around, or just after Paco passed.

What's the use thinking about such things here? Different planet, different life.

Eric does push a vid, but not about batteries. It's dust he's worried about. Dust is tracked inside every time people cycle through the airlock. It blows inside, too. He shows pics of the edges of the outer hatch on *Independence* encircled by a ten-centimeter wide smudge of red-brown. Ultra-fine dust is picked up by the wind and somehow migrates past the hatch seal.

"Short of smearing the hatch gasket with petroleum jelly, which we don't have, nothing can be done about it," he informs us. "Blair says the stuff is harmless, just don't snort it. But watch out for the abrasiveness. It'll eventually affect high-precision equipment because it can find its way anywhere. One of our challenges will be to invent a means of accessing our future living quarters without admitting any dust."

That's it? He's scared of dust?

I examine the ring of red around *Liberty's* hatches. The dust has a burnt stink most noticeable inside the airlock. Memories come, the sickening stench of Lysol in Paco's hospital room.

There's a little card in his dead fingers.

The Lord is my shepherd. Don't look at it. It's there. So what?

The Lord is my shepherd means Paco is gone.

The rosies don't help. The rosies are Paco alive and healthy. Strict, but patient and understanding. His knowledge, his intelligence, his optimism.

A little white plastic card. The Lord is my shepherd.

Why did Paco cling to that little white card while he was dying? What's so good about it?

Paco's dead. I'm alone.

The Lord is my shepherd. It's a death song. No wonder the nightmares.

The dust is abrasive? That could be a useful property. I get a damp wash towel from the pit and drag it across the dust around the hatch. Rub circles around The Lord is my shepherd, the whole multi-line message. Written neatly in black pen, maybe covered over with a clear paint to make it last against accidental destruction. What about deliberate destruction?

Red swirls across the writing. Yes, it's coming off. In a minute every trace is gone. Only a blank pale green rectangle remains.

Victory.

Then why the tears?

FORTY

They secretly spoke with Ryder about the battery—what other possible reason could there be to make him walk out there? But he doesn't say a word. Still in his thermals, he slides to the equipment bay floor and pulls me close. He wipes around my eyes.

"Here's something I think you'll like," he whispers. "A lot of us are getting together early tomorrow morning to see Earth. You haven't seen it, have you?"

"Not since we left."

"It's an incredible sight, trust me. Everyone's going to be there, kind of like an Earth party. I think you should join us. Say a few words. Wouldn't be the same without you."

The rest of the night passes in a flash. People are awake and cycling through the airlocks soon after five. Heavy thermals, Eric reminds everyone. A frosty minus sixty-nine degrees out there.

I do this because Ryder asked me. Despite the chill, I feel better outside. The eastern horizon glows an exquisite indigo blue, with lavender higher up. The hills are absolute black. Orion sets in the west.

There it is! A brilliant bluish-white star just above some mountaintops. No, two stars—the Earth's moon is a much dimmer star next to its companion.

Jürgen is out and about. Why not? Discovery Team Four will soon depart. He reminds us, "We are the first to see our home planet from the surface of another world."

Ryder plants himself between me and Alison and drapes his arms across our shoulders. The sky brightens and individual rocks become visible. But the surface isn't the same deep red as it was after sunset. A thin sheet of hazy white coats the ground and rocks.

"Carbon dioxide frost," Eric says from the vicinity of *Constitution.* "Dry ice. It'll be gone ten minutes after the sun comes up."

Darien's probably over by *Constitution,* too. Should I confront him? What would that accomplish? Focus on something else. The Earth and moon are beautiful against the pale yellow of dawn.

Liberty is surrounded by a dark border a meter wide—the heat radiating from the spacecraft prevented carbon dioxide from precipitating as frost. My eyes trace the AC power cable to where the reactor is buried. The gray metal fill port sticks up half a meter above the mound.

It's coated with frost.

I push Ryder's arm away and walk toward the reactor. Yes, frost. Frost all over the mound and the fill port itself. Thick frost, the texture appearing almost fuzzy.

"Ryder," I call out, voice quivering. "I want you to look at this."

Alison and Mikki come with him. This is Mikki's reactor. She buried it with Shuko. Almost froze her fingers doing it.

I ask them, "A hundred kilowatts of heat. How could there be frost?"

Mikki answers, "It's deep, over two meters under."

"But it's hot," I snap at her. "The top is supposed to be nine hundred degrees!"

"It doesn't always operate at full power," Ryder says.

"It's still hot. The fill tube is metal, and it connects directly to the top of the reactor. It conducts heat. How could there be frost?"

The light is brighter, the seeing better. The darker, frost-free zone around *Liberty* is undeniable. The methane bladder and the mining rover have no frost. Only a tiny amount of heat was necessary to keep those surfaces clear.

Now I'm certain.

I point to the ground. "It's not running!"

Ryder says, "Cristina—"

"Listen to me! Don't you have eyes? The reactor is cold, not doing anything, not charging the batteries."

I need to get back inside. Ryder intercepts me.

"Calm down, okay? It's under a ton of cold dirt and that's a heat sink. It's supposed to be a heat sink. That's the idea."

I pull open the hatch. "We need to find out if the other two are cold!"

I try to close the hatch but Ryder wedges himself into the airlock. "Quit screaming! It's not helping anything, Cristina."

"This is wrong! People are lying, hiding information."

"Not a single engineer agrees with you."

"There's a voice inside your head speaking the truth. Listen to it!"

He hesitates, but answers back, "I'm out of my depth with this reactor shit and the way they have the battery rigged. But Eric knows everything's running as designed."

The instant the airlock is fully pressurized I push open the hatch and yank off my helmet. Shuko's in the equipment bay, waiting. He blinks with sleepiness. "Cristina, be calm. Let's sit down and talk things out. Please."

"Listen to me," I plead with him. "There's no frost around the reactor. It's cold. I think the other two are the same. Do you know what that means? We're not getting power!" I point to the window. "Look for yourself!"

Shuko doesn't look.

Ryder says, "Cristina, I'm going to get you a hot cup of tea, and we're going to talk, okay?"

People cycle back inside and plan breakfast meetings to discuss the day's activities. Who will be the first to fire bricks? Produce ethanol and plastics? Mikki, Paige, Alison, they all chat happy banter. Ryder claims he wants to talk, but he does no such thing. He simply sits and practically forces me to drink tea.

Eric pushes a vid to all spacecraft. "I have information to put out," he says, speaking slower than normal. "I don't do this gladly or with any sense of vindication. I'm doing it because there's a critical lesson to be learned. Jürgen directed me to investigate the reason *Resolute* crashed, and why *Endurance* missed the landing zone. I had a hunch it had something to do with the engines burping or misfiring, and I was correct."

I ask, "Why talk about this now?"

Eric's face is replaced with a diagram of the landing configuration at high gate, thrusters and parachutes deployed. "We don't know why the engines didn't fire immediately. These things happen when liquid-fueled equipment is kept at near cryogenic temperatures. We can't eliminate every failure. What matters is how we ourselves react to the unexpected. There's the answer to your question, Cristina. I want to get this out of the way right now, for all of our benefit."

The image zooms out so that the full parachute is visible. "When we reached the high gate position, all four thrusters were supposed to fire continuously and then the chute automatically breaks away. The sequencer knows to wait for stable thrust before releasing the chute. The aerodynamic pull of the chute provides directional stability to the spacecraft."

The pic shows the chute flying free.

"Suppose the chute is released but the engines misfire, especially if one or two of those engines provide more thrust than the others."

The image spins out of control.

"This is what occurred on *Resolute*. We don't have the data or the vid, but I'm certain that Naldo or whoever was seated at the GNP released the chute manually as soon as they reached high gate. They overrode the system, something I have specifically and repeatedly recommended against. We lost *Resolute* because the thrusters could not recover from the fast spin that began when the chute was manually released."

A deep cold washes over my body.

Shuko asks, "Why didn't *Endurance* also crash?"

"I'm guessing pure luck, as the data shows they recovered after sixteen relatively slow spins. By that time, they were too low and too far northeast to land in the programmed zone."

Senuri covers her eyes. "I released the chute." She glares at me. "You told me to override the landing sequence if something doesn't work."

"The thrusters on *Independence* and *Constitution* fired as designed," Eric continues. "*Liberty's* thrusters shot all over the place, putting all kinds of off-axial forces on the spacecraft, yet they did not spin. Why? They didn't release their chute. It stabilized them until their engines recovered. But why did they hang onto their chute?"

A new vid, all jittery—inside *Liberty* during the landing decent! The image bounces and sunlight flies all over the control center. The memory sets my pulse racing.

The sound of thrusters banging. A lot of vibration, hard to see.

The GNP announces, *"Misfire. Misfire. Misfire."*

Ryder screams, "Shit!" The vid slows to show his arm extending to the main panel. He wants to release the chute.

I grab his arm and shout, "Leave it! Sixty percent! Need sixty percent!"

The control center jerks and throws us sideways against our harnesses. Then the engines roar and the shaking subsides.

A *thump*. The chute breaking free?

I yell, "We're good!"

The vid ends. Eric's worn-out, scruffy-bearded face comes back.

"I do this without joy. I do this because it's necessary. Cristina didn't listen to her own advice. If she had, she'd likely be dead, along with everyone else on *Liberty*. Moral of the story? Follow the procedures. The biggest danger facing us is failing to properly operate the tools we have been provided. The results can be fatal. Don't make these kinds of decisions on your own. Talk to me, or Darien, Ryder, Paige, or Norberto."

I don't want to look at anyone. This is a punch to my gut. No, a physical attack can't come close.

If not for me, everyone on *Resolute* would be alive. Vijay Mehta would be alive. He could experience the freedom he dreamed about. Now he would never do that, and one person is responsible.

My skin tingles. Ryder places his hand over mine, but I jerk back as if to avoid contaminating him.

"I deserve to be punished!" I scream as loud as I can. "So punish me! No matter what you do, I'll live with this forever. But that doesn't change the fact. We're not getting any power! Get your sand rover to dig a hole through the mound. See if it's hot. I'm going to do that right now."

I rise but Andre blocks my path. He's light. Am I mad enough to shove him aside? But Ryder's powerful grip seizes my upper body and pulls me away from the access hatch. "Sorry, Cristina. I can't let you do that."

"I can prove it if you let me!"

Shuko fumbles with something in his hands. Ryder grasps my head and holds tightly. He forces my face toward his.

"Relax. Please relax."

Shuko mumbles, "Mental exhaustion."

I scream, "Screw you!"

A sharp, hurtful pinch on my neck.

Ryder's face blurs. The control deck shimmers into curves. Vision fading. Words from far away. Then silence.

Then black.

FORTY-ONE

A whisper. "She's waking up."

Dark shapes, just blurs. Not enough light. Only a faint red glow.

Piercing headache, right in front. Breathing, panting, from someone else. Faces, and close.

"Cristina?"

Gentle hands, but cold.

"Cristina. Can you hear me?" That has to be Alison.

"Drink this, Cristina."

A cup of apple juice, slightly warm. Sweet and wonderful.

I jump forward in the sleeper. Ryder? Shuko? What are they doing?

Alison gently positions me against the cushion. Everyone's eyes are tense, almost wild, and their chins quiver. From the cold, or from fear?

"Drink it all, Cristina," says Senuri. "Need to wake up."

Time and thought become real. Alison steps backward. Her breath rolls out in puffs of vapor.

"Why is it so cold? I have to piss."

"Sure. One step at a time. How do you feel?"

"Like shit."

It's night, and it's been a long time. Since the struggle. What was that about?

The reactor. The batteries.

I toss the empty cup to the floor. "What the fuck is going on? Tell me right now. Better be the truth!"

The sleeper door slides open. Ryder.

I murmur, "Estúpido bastardo."

Ryder squeezes into the tiny compartment with his eyes cast down. He wears thermal coveralls, they all do. Don't they know thermals are supposed to be kept in the equipment bay? Maybe it doesn't matter anymore.

Ryder takes my right hand. Alison shifts to make room for him to lean forward. "I'm going to take you into the control center, okay? Ready?"

Alison and Senuri back out of the sleeper. The room sways. A trace of the drug, or something else?

The cold! It has to be zero degrees. And why so dark? I pull on thermals while Ryder's grip keeps me upright. They're cold, damp, and gritty. The control center is dimly lit by yellow emergency lights. The usual hums from the vent fans and the equipment bay are almost gone. Unnaturally, weirdly quiet.

People! They're packed into the cramped space, bunched around the table and seated against the walls. Everyone from *Liberty*, plus Senuri, Andre, Darien, Jürgen, and Eric. Eleven total. They stare at me. Terrified children, clutching each other, wriggling fingers, weakly rocking back and forth. Jürgen is different. He's thinking, thinking hard.

"I have to pee," I tell them before carefully descending into the hygiene pit. It's a freezer that reeks of stale urine. I poke my head into the equipment bay. Only one CO_2 scrubber running, plus one of the six vent fans.

The power panel flashes a lot of red.

UNDERVOLT DISCONNECT

Batteries exhausted.

Then it was true all along. The reactors never put out any power. Current time 11 Gemini 01:39 PCT. Out for almost twenty hours. No wonder the weakness and hunger.

Mikki gives me her seat. Ryder is directly across the table. He whispers, "I'm sorry, Cristina."

I run my hands over my numb face. "Are the backpacks charged?"

Eric and Ryder answer at the same time. "Yes."

"A few aren't fully charged," adds Darien. "But they all have at least five hours' oh-two and power, not counting the thirty-minute reserve."

I look at the tabletop. There's a perfectly round stain from some beverage. "Is there any possibility of getting power from the reactors?"

Eric's words are low and soft. "No possibility. Cold start up requires a minimum of eighty amp-hours at twenty-five volts. We don't have the charge remaining, even if we wired the cells in series to get the voltage up."

"What about using the trucks as generators?"

"The fourth Discovery Team used all three trucks, and practically all the methanol we had left."

The silence hangs. In the dim light Eric is just a beard, a mouth, and a pair of eyes.

"I have one more question. Do we know why this happened?"

Paige grumbles, "What difference does it make?"

Eric leans forward. "The reactors are an early series. The startup scripts failed, but they didn't generate a specific error message. The reactors can't be tested because once the core goes critical, they're radioactive from fission decay even if they're shut down. There's a movable reflector ring, and it wasn't in the expected position. I've edited the sequencer that writes the script, and I honestly believed the reactor was at criticality based on the neutron flux."

Andre nods. "I saw the same. No errors."

"I knew my scripts were timing out," Mikki says.

I glare at Eric. "How can you say you didn't know those reactors weren't generating current? How could you lie about it, given that eventually the batteries would go out?"

Eric lets out a slow breath. "I didn't lie."

"Then you didn't understand what you were doing."

"None of us had a deep understanding. When the charge dropped below seventy percent, the SMB automatically started isolating banks as a protection against a short circuit or other accidental drain. I edited the kernel to keep that from happening, and I got what I thought were accurate readings. I believed the other two reactors were producing power."

I look around our tiny, cramped space. "You assumed even if your reactor wasn't charging, the other two were. You assumed it, you believed it."

Mikki covers her face. "I didn't want to be the only one who couldn't do their job. My stupidity killed us."

"Shut it," I snap. "Darien! You're the physics kid. Do you understand what happened with the reactors?"

Darien raises his head. "The key is the startup rate. I believe we didn't get the expected result because the fission fuel is a couple of decades old, and the higher gravity here compared to the moon might be a factor too. But if we had enough electricity, we could script the reflector ring to the bottom range and move it up a couple of millimeters at a time to keep the startup rate below the trip threshold. If we could do that, the reactor will achieve criticality and produce rated power."

"Eric, can you try all that with the *Endurance* reactor?"

He nods.

Jürgen says, "I have a plan."

"We have a plan," Eric repeats. "We worked out the numbers."

I stand on shaky legs. "Good. Suit up, depressurize, get the others out. We leave now."

No one moves.

Ryder says, "There's something else you need to know."

"Talk while we get into our suits. No use cycling out. We'll depressurize the whole cabin and open both hatches."

Still, no one moves. Jürgen says directly to me, "I worked out the numbers with Eric and Ryder. Our plan is to maximize the number of people we save, given the resource constraints we're facing."

"What the hell are you talking about?"

Ryder stands and takes my arm. "Cristina, it has to be eleven of us. Eric and Darien took a realistic look at the situation, did some estimates, ran some numbers. Eleven of us, including you."

I pull my arm away.

Ryder goes on. "Eleven of us can start the reactor at *Endurance* and produce power and enough oxygen and life support, like CO_2 scrubbing. Twenty-four is too much support load. With all twenty-four, the load would decrease the likelihood of success. We'll come back as soon as possible for—"

"No!"

Dry throat. Maybe the knockout drug. The words come out hoarse but intense. "All of us. We're going to *Endurance*, every one of us."

Eric says, "The numbers—"

"*All of us!*"

Nothing but the huffs of us breathing bad air.

"Eric worked it out," says Paige, words trembling. "We can't all go."

"Did you fucking hear what I just said?" I move toward Paige. "You'd leave everybody else here and walk away?"

Paige's voice cracks. "I don't want to die."

"You're not going to die. There's been enough death. We're going to do this together, all of us."

Jürgen clears his throat. "I am the elected captain. I have made this decision."

Ryder whispers, "Twelve people already died. What difference will another thirteen make if it saves—"

I swing my right arm with all my strength. My palm smacks Ryder directly across his face. The crack from the blow rings through the control center. He stares back, stunned. They're all stunned. Good.

"You talk about trust and respect! *Trust and respect!* Now you turn your back on your friends, people who trust you!"

Ryder blinks as if he's about to cry. I turn and look into each face. Most cast their eyes downward.

Jürgen isn't done. "I've made the decision."

"Oh, go fuck yourself," I throw back, as forceful as my throat allows. "What a joke! Day eight, and this how we start our new civilization? Sentence half to death? Then what's the *point?* What's the point of being here?"

Eric mutters, "It's just too much load, Cristina."

"They're not loads, they're *people!* I'm a load too, so why didn't you just put me out of my misery while I was sleeping?"

Jürgen still isn't done. "We can't put twenty-four people into *Endurance.*"

"Shut it and listen. Here's what I want. Consider yourselves already dead. Now you don't have anything to be afraid of. You're going to do exactly what I say. Understand that? Exactly what I say. I'm depressurizing this cabin in two minutes. We're getting the others, *all of them.*"

The soft buzz from the CO_2 scrubber and the fan stops. The power panel emits three angry beeps. Now the silence is total.

"Eric! Have you considered navigation between here and *Endurance*?"

Will he answer at all?

"We walk heading zero four zero. You walked half the route, Cristina, Senuri the other half. We move steadily, four hours' total time, arrive shortly after dawn."

"That's it, then. Heavy thermals, with mittens and boot covers. Suit up. Now!"

They do it without another word. Even Jürgen. And they do move as if they're already dead. Ryder whispers, "I'm a coward. Maybe I deserve to die."

"Shut it and focus on what we have to do," I tell him. "We'll need the best from every last one of us."

When all helmets are sealed I climb down into the equipment bay and open the airlock inner hatch. The control panel is blank. Eric comes down the ladder. "Inner has to be closed to override. It's a double protection."

I shut the hatch and Eric rotates two red handles between the airlock and the power panel. I re-open the inner hatch, and Eric twists an L-shaped handle recessed into the ceiling. Seconds later the BioSuit actuators tighten. *Liberty's* cabin quickly depressurizes through two wide valves under the floor.

Rosies. Shit.

"Everyone file out and test your night systems," I tell them. I climb back to my sleeper and retrieved the rosies from a crumpled flight suit. I also pull out the triangle-folded flag. Dark blue, white stars. That's coming, too.

The equipment bay is already empty. The outer hatch is wide open to the hard blackness of the night.

FORTY-TWO

"Helmet lights to red," I call out. The remaining white beams switch color, but the ground swallows most of the illumination.

Alison asks, "Isn't it too dark with red?"

"Our eyes will dark adapt in a few minutes. We'll be able to use a lower setting on the image intensifier. Helps spot small rocks. Trust me."

All of you, trust me.

Paige points to the flag under my arm. "Why are you bringing that?"

"It's lucky."

"Why do you say that?"

I stuff the flag into the largest pouch on my thermals. "It got this far, didn't it?"

Constitution first. Their com is working, so I instruct them to suit up and depressurize their cabin. No argument whatsoever. They move with heaviness and inattention—what's the correct word? Apathy. So much decline in twenty hours.

Minus eighty-three degrees. Even with full thermals, the cold soaks through. Need to make this quick before people get other ideas.

Jürgen connects with me on a private com channel. "Do what you want."

"If you have anything to say to me, do it later and in private."

He snickers. That's not like Jürgen at all. "What if there is no later? We're probably going to die, Cristina. Think about preparing yourself. I'm prepared. I'm ready to die."

"You've come this far just to die? Just stay out of my way."

Back to channel one. Hungry. Should have forced down a food bar.

I announce, "Everyone gather near *Liberty*. Stretch your legs! Get the blood flowing! We leave in two minutes."

A semi-circle forms, each person facing me. Clusters of twos and threes, arms interlaced, only a few standing alone. Walt asks, "Would it be better to wait for first light?"

"No more power to run the inside CO_2 scrubbers, and our suit packs are good for five hours. We leave now."

I pull off the mitten on my right hand and withdraw the rosies. I hold them high for all to see. "These belonged to my father. I kept them with me for seven years. They're part of me, my reminder of my father's goodness and his belief. His belief. Belief in something greater than himself. Belief that life has a purpose besides just survival."

I step toward the hatch and wrap the rosies around the release handle. The beads and the little cross swing gently. "I'll leave them here for now and come back for them in a few days. I know they'll be safe, and we'll be safe. We're here for a purpose. Do you believe that?"

A chorus of *yes* fills my ears.

"We'll move steadily, fast enough to keep warm, not so fast we're tripping over rocks. Watch the ground in front of you."

I swallow. Throat and mouth are still parched from whatever drug. Concentrate on keeping the shiver down. "Eric and Ryder, I want you both up front. Everyone else, a single line behind them. Walk directly behind the person in front of you. We'll rest if we need to, but better to keep moving."

"Let's go!" Indra cries. "The bottoms of my feet are freezing!"

I feel the need to tilt my head back. The visor image of the stars is strange, like a child's drawing. Orion is directly overhead. "We're going to make a new start. Again."

That draws a few soft laughs.

"This time we have an advantage. We're better. We're better than we were yesterday, and the day before. We already took some hard lessons. Expect some more. We live and we learn. So let's get moving and get warm."

A quick count as the line forms; all present. The end of the line is the best observation position. Some hold hands or walk with arms around someone's shoulders, but no one needs physical support.

I pull Eric into a private channel. "You were pretty sketchy about the reactor problem. Do you have a firm procedure, or are we in troubleshooting mode?"

"I know what to do. We were looking at the wrong start logs, for one thing. So yeah, I understand what needs to happen. With the reflector too low, it times out before the internal battery fades. With the reflector too high, it trips on high startup rate. Matter of finding the right position."

"I want you to keep Darien and myself informed on every stage. In fact, he'll assist you directly. I want you to give me the news in plain English and without delay. Do I have your promise?"

"Yeah, Cristina. Sure."

Walking doesn't do much to ward off the cold. The mass of Mount Fútbol blacks out a curved chunk of stars. The pace quickens—a universal subconscious craving to reach shelter and safety, probably. But there would be no true safety until the *Endurance* reactor generates power, and before that it needs to be installed. That will require power, and time. Were the batteries in good shape? Would they be affected by the cold?

Shut it. It's not a problem until it's a problem.

No conversation, not even on the general channel. Some people walk with their helmets pressed together, maybe speaking privately through sound conduction. Jürgen and Tess march arm-in-arm near the end of the line. Does she have any idea he was about to leave her for dead?

Phobos due to rise a few minutes before four, but there's no glow on the eastern horizon, ahead and to the right. I switch off the imager to see in natural light. No Phobos. Are we walking in the correct direction? I turn—there's a milky radiance behind us. Phobos is rising above the hills to the southwest. I forgot! The little potato-shaped moon orbits Mars close and faster than the planet rotates, so it moves backwards in the sky.

We hit an incline several kilometers before the terrain crests. This was the meeting point on day one.

"All downhill from here," I announce. "It'll start getting light in less than an hour. By that time we might be able to see *Endurance*."

We walk with purpose. The eastern sky glows and I switch off the imager to enjoy the natural spectacle of the Earth and the moon against the deep blue. Orange light sparkles off the moun-taintops.

The line stops, people cluster. They point ahead. Trouble?

Norberto says, "Three klicks at the most."

Far away, yet so crisp, a tiny white bump stands among the brown ridges. *Endurance*.

We'll need to fit twenty-four in a volume too small for six. A fishbowl with way too many fish.

No one cares. It is salvation. It is life.

FORTY-THREE

Endurance is slightly lopsided and appears minuscule even though it's the same size as *Liberty*. It rests on a gentle slope, the bottom marred with black streaks from atmospheric entry.

Everyone gathers by the hatch. I wave Eric over to me. "You and Darien cycle in first, recommend whether we enter two at a time or depressurize."

"Cycling everybody in would take two hours, twice that if we don't use the compressor."

"Forget it. Vent it so we can all go in and get warm."

Eric and Darien cram into the airlock. Someone touches my shoulder. Ryder. We switch channels.

"What?"

"I didn't know what I was thinking. That's what."

"You weren't thinking. Now drop it. Do you have your head on straight today? Focus on the present. Can the cargo hatches be opened from the outside?"

"Ah, no, the latches have to be released from the main panel."

I switch back to channel one. "Norberto! You and Ryder stay out, assemble the truck and the winch, plug it all in, pull the reactor. Jürgen!"

The name grabs attention. Heads jerk, people stiffen. He comes to me. "You're going to assist with the truck and reactor. Shuko! Alison!"

"Here, Cristina!" Alison answers instantly. She actually sounds cheerful.

"You're in charge of setting up the drill. Start going as soon as we build up gas pressure, which won't take long. Mikki and I will assist in half an hour."

Brown dust blows out from underneath *Endurance*. They're depressurizing already.

Ryder presses his helmet against mine. "Seize this day."

Both airlock hatches are open and people hurry inside. Tess turns her head toward the hatch and back again. Jürgen motions her to go in. She rubs his upper arm before leaving.

Once inside, I find there's no way to exit the airlock. The inner hatch is totally blocked by bodies, four in the equipment bay alone, crammed into two square meters of floor space. People shift and I squeeze through. Eric and Darien are at the power panel.

I yell, "Make room! Everybody exhale!"

The suit actuators release. When the pressure hits thirty-five kp helmets and gloves come off and everyone rubs freezing noses and fingers. Powerful burnt dust smell! Eyes dart all over as if danger lurks. There's hardly any room to move. We're packed together shoulder-to-shoulder. Need to wedge more bodies into the sleepers.

They must not sense any doubt from me, not even a tiny bit. Panic would be instantly contagious. "Five still outside, so everybody's thinking, are we really going to fit more in here? Can it be done? Yes, it can be done. We can't afford the luxury of doubt. We'll do it vertically. Small people lie on top of big people." That draws nervous chuckles. "Take your thermals off as soon as you're warm so they don't get damp with sweat. One pisser for all of us. We should put our helmets in the equipment bay so no one's tempted to use them."

Weak joke, more thin laughs.

The vent fans blow warm air and the compressor starts to build up working pressure for the drill and winch. Food bars are passed out.

Eric peers up from the equipment bay. "Pressure for the drill in ten minutes." But the words crack, and his eyes are empty.

I'm afraid to look. Battery charge 489 kw-hours, fifty-five percent.

"It was warm in here before we vented," Eric whispers. "They left the life support running. But we're good. We're good. Eighty kilowatts for a startup, spread over forty minutes."

And how much for life support until the reactor starts? What about all the power to simply install the reactor? What's the use of asking? There are no other options.

Eric says we're good. What else is he going to say?

Shut it. No fear. No doubt. Not even a tiny bit.

Purpose is the antidote for panic.

"I'm not going to bullshit you," I tell their anxious faces. Golden sunbeams spill through the windows. It feels bright and exciting. Enthusiasm! Harness it. "We have a lot of work to do. No one has the day off. We need to watch our power. Turn the printer off. We'll get hot food as soon as the reactor's running."

The flag. No use carrying it any longer. I set it against the top of the main panel, white stars facing everyone. "Reminds me of the sky."

A short girl with freckled cheeks stares at me. Abby. She whispers, "Do we have a chance?"

I shake my head as if confused. "What makes you think we don't?"

Keep everyone thinking, contributing, helping in some way. "Senuri! We need to devise a plan to remove the battery cells from the three other spacecraft, move them here, recharge them, and put them back. Can you work with Paige and Andre and give us a plan by the end of the day?"

"Absolutely, Cristina."

Paige says, "Might be better to produce methanol and oxygen here, move it in tanks, use it to generate current with the truck motors."

"Determine which method can be done soonest with the fewest trips. Blair, Tess, Jewel. We need a six-month plan to get ready for winter. A year from now we'll be up to our eyebrows in fresh fruits and vegetables, but what do we grow first? Did anyone ever estimate how much plastic we need for each greenhouse?"

"Depends on design and construction materials," says Jewel.

"Figure out how much growing space we can create this summer. There must be some estimates in the manuals. Refine them based on what we learned on the expeditions. We dream of the day we can move out of these things, but the truth is we'll have to build greenhouses before the residence structures, so get used to smelling each other."

Kelis says, "I'll be sleeping in the greenhouse."

"I might join you," I tell her. They're exhausted, filthy, the men's chins covered with stubble, lots of nervous grins. There must be no doubt in their heads. "The walk over here, wasn't it beautiful?" They gaze back at me and some nod. "Think of the faces of your own children. They'll grow up free in this pristine place. We're here, alive, and that means anything's possible. We control what happens to us. We made it this far, together on this sunny morning, all of us, and we're free. That's something to think about. Does anybody wish they kept the life they had before?"

No one does.

✳

First hole, ice pockets down to four meters. No surprise there.

By noon we have seven slender holes drilled around *Endurance*. Too much ice. The reactor is attached to the winch and ready to lower, but there's no suitable location. The power cable and compressed gas hose are both twenty meters. This limits the area in which the reactor can be buried.

"What about an above-ground installation?" I ask Mikki.

"You're talking fifteen cubic meters of material. The regolith here is hard and frozen, so we'll need to break it up by using the jackhammer attachment on the drill. That uses up a huge amount of compressed gas, and therefore a lot of power."

Charge 433 kw-hours, forty-seven percent, the big drop caused by continuous gas compression to run equipment, plus life support for twenty-four people: oxygen generation, CO_2 scrubbing, air heating and dehumidifying.

I tell Eric to shut off the heaters. Will be okay for a while, but after sunset comes the supercold. And it looks increasingly unlikely the reactor will be running by sunset.

The depleted BioSuit backpacks need recharging before noon. They're swapped with those that still have about four hours remaining. By mid-afternoon there are only four partially-charged packs left.

Mikki, Eric, and Darien debate solutions. Above ground would take more time and use up a lot of power—but yield certain results. Or, print a ten-meter extension for the power and air cables, allowing holes to be tried as far as thirty-five meters out.

The extension method will be faster and use up about half the power of the above-ground method. But the results are uncertain. What if drilling further out doesn't produce an ice-free hole?

The sun drops behind the western hills.

If the extension doesn't work, will there be enough power remaining to try the above-ground method?

Eric calculates. Yes, but barely.

He recommends the extension method first. The ground thirty meters south is different, not as flat, with more rocks. Before we start the printer, Ryder finds a pick-like tool in the cargo hold and pounds out a half-meter hole in the new area.

No ice.

He swings non-stop down to a full meter. No ice. But it's over thirty meters from the receptacle.

The printer completes the gas and cable extensions in under an hour, but the power reserve sinks to 357 kw-hours, thirty-nine percent. And we don't yet have a hole big enough for the reactor.

I devour a food bar as the sky darkens. It takes longer than usual to chew and swallow. No one talks. They know this is taking too long. The windows go completely black and soon acquire a thin coating of frost.

"We've have to prioritize on comfort," I remark casually. "Scrubbing CO2 and replenishing oxygen are necessities, warmth merely optional."

The joke falls flat. They're back in thermals. I lower the lights to a minimum red glow to encourage sleep. Every centimeter of floor space is occupied and it's easy to step on people.

Just after ten Ryder and Mikki emerge from the airlock shivering and covered with dust. The reactor is installed and connected.

284 kw-hours, thirty-one percent. That's over four times the power needed to start the reactor.

I tell Eric's bleary eyes, "Whatever it takes, my friend, do it."

He sets to work. I lie back on the equipment bay floor with Ryder and Alison. Sleep comes. The nightmares start immediately. Starry nights and display panels with bad news. A web of cables and hoses to be untangled, the price of failure imminent death.

I wake with a jump. Dull throb under the forehead. Eric's imposing frame directly above me, fingers flicking across the power panel, eyes narrow in concentration.

"Time?"

"After midnight. Go back to sleep. Let me work."

More sleep, then Eric shakes my arm.

"It's running?"

The look on his face tells me it's not.

FORTY-FOUR

There are decisions to be made.

Eric stammers, "Still a chance."

"What went wrong? You promised to tell me everything."

"I put the reflector at the bottom of the range and moved it up incrementally. The script works. But I think I should have started higher. The problem is the startup rate. If it's too high, the reactor shuts down. That's a safety feature, impossible to disable. But if the rate is too low, the startup takes too long and the program times out. That's also a safety feature to prevent the internal power supply from depleting."

"The thing's got its own power?"

"Yes, but only to run the local CPU. We have to supply a lot of kilowatts to get the process going, liquify the sodium and bring it up to design operating temperature. Right now the flux levels are increasing slowly. If I put it too high, the whole thing shuts down. That happened three times, and we can't afford a fourth."

"Why?"

"Current draw—"

"Shit, Eric. Shit. You told me eighty kilowatts for forty minutes—"

"I didn't lie to you, Cristina. That's the nominal requirement when the auto-sequencer does a routine startup. That's not what we're doing. I drew a lot of power."

"Get to the point."

Ryder stirs and sits up.

"I turned off everything except the emergency lights. We got twenty-four volts and low oxygen and CO2 is dangerously high. I can probably start the reactor with the power we have. But we're down to a hundred kilowatt-hours. With the rate I've been raising the reflector, it's going to take six to eight hours to increase the flux enough to sustain fission and produce power."

Every bit of energy drains from my body. "Can we breathe that long?

"I figured it. We still have a reserve of compressed oxygen. We can bleed oxygen in to replace what we use, and purge air out to reduce the CO2 buildup. We'll have to bleed nitrogen too, to keep the O2 partial pressure reasonable, but we have enough."

"Do it, then. Get the reactor—"

"Cristina, I figured it and refigured it. Can't do it for twenty-four, not for eight hours, not even for six. We'll all suffocate in under four hours. If I try to speed up, it'll trip on high startup rate and it'll take more power than we have to try again."

"You're telling me we can't keep everyone alive until we have power."

"You wanted the truth!" he growls. "Those are facts. And we tried to tell you this, Cristina. We tried to tell you this. You didn't want to listen."

Ryder leans back and covers his face. Alison is awake too. She lies motionless, eyes fluttering, tongue licking her lips over and over.

There's a stirring above. Three people at access hatch. Hannah, Tess, and Jürgen.

They heard it all.

I pull myself through the hatch and look around. The dim yellow glow reveals cold, wild-eyed faces, mouths releasing puffs of vapor with every breath. Jürgen stands and motions with his hands. He's stronger than anyone.

"Half of us can survive—"

"Sit down!" My voice fills the compartment and stops him mid-sentence.

"We want to hear him," Giselle says. "We want the truth."

"The truth?" I repeat. "Here's the truth. We're going to live, all of us."

Walt sits up. "You have to tell us exactly what's happening."

"I agree. So here it is. There's been a delay. We're making progress." I turn to Eric. "You want to confirm that?"

"Progress, yes. Power in six hours. Or not."

"We don't have enough oxygen for all of us, now that we shut everything down," snarls Hannah. "We heard you. You expect us to go back to sleep and give you a chance to kill us with a needle? I'm not closing my eyes again!"

I face Jürgen. "You have a right to speak. But you don't have a right to create panic. So I'll tell you again. Sit down." I scan the entire control center. "You're going to do exactly what I say. We're going to conserve energy and air until this is over. Once we have power you can sleep, scream, cry, eat, shit, I don't care. For now, you're going to listen and get a fucking grip. I'm scared shitless the same as you. You think your fear right now is any worse than the fear felt by all those people on the ships? Knowing they would be burned alive the instant we launched?"

"You're using too much oxygen right now, sweetie," says Blair. "With six hours to get power and more oxygen, we have the right to decide among ourselves what to do. Some of us may need to leave so that others can live. I'll take that over all of us suffocating together."

Senuri's head is barely visible from the top of her thermals. "Cristina, we may pass out from lack of oxygen sooner than we anticipate. We must face facts and make a decision while we can."

"I've made the decision, Senuri," I tell her evenly. "All twenty-four of us will live."

Giselle growls, "And if you're wrong, all twenty-four of us will be dead."

Eric's head pokes up from the access hatch.

I tell him, "Move the reflector higher, start producing heat and power."

He stares back, expression vacant.

"Eric," I call softly. "Write a script to raise the neutron flux so we can generate power. Do it now. We don't have a lot of time. But we have *enough* time, I promise you that."

They settle down, even Jürgen. We defeated panic, but as the air grows thicker it will return. And it's already an effort to breathe. I climb down into the equipment bay. "Ryder, do you know how to do the O2 bleed? Get more oxygen in here. Get it up to a minimal level, above twenty."

"I can write a new script and raise the reflector higher," Eric says, voice low, "But it will use up the last of our power. I can isolate some banks and rig in series, keep the voltage from going too low."

"I'll help you."

We re-wire the batteries with jumper cables from the emergency repair kit. Over the next hour Ryder periodically bleeds the cabin pressure outside to drop the carbon dioxide concentration while bleeding in oxygen and nitrogen from two storage tanks.

"We got zero oxygen," he reports. "When I open the valve there's no hiss at all."

I lose track of time. We can't breathe without gasping. Eric says, "Point of adding heat in less than an hour. Or not. Unlike you, I promise nothing. The cross-connected cells are keeping us above twenty-one volts for now. This is it. If I positioned it too low, the flux won't be high enough to sustain a positive startup rate, go critical, generate power. If it's too high, the system will trip and the core cools down. Then we are done."

My brain is fogged with rotten air. I lift myself up the ladder. People pant in short puffs, their eyes staring ahead. Everyone touches someone else. I sit for a while listening to the breathing. Jürgen and Tess are in each other's arms, her eyes nearly closed, his staring back at me. Not hostile, just empty. He trusts me too, in his own stupid way.

Below me, Eric is no longer at the power panel.

The panel flashes red.

UNDERVOLT DISCONNECT

The battery voltage is below the critical level. It's now impossible to run any equipment except for the panel itself, not even with the banks wired in series. No more oxygen, and no more power.

Eric blinks and mumbles two words.

"I'm sorry."

FORTY-FIVE

"What do we do now?" asks Shuko, tone more annoyed than terrified. "Wait to pass out?"

I can't keep the trembling out of my voice any longer. "Eric. Run another script. Move the thing higher. We've got to try."

He shakes his head slowly. "The system...can't do it with voltage below twenty-one. Just trips. Even cross-connected, don't have the voltage to try again."

"We got eighty-seven kilowatt hours. You said it takes eighty."

"At the proper voltage. If we series more...it just trips out. I'm sorry."

Jürgen rises to his feet.

"Our only choice is how we die," he proclaims, voice clear and crisp.

He pulls Tess to her feet. She faces Jürgen and says, "I love you," in three gasps.

Walt and Abby pull themselves up, then Norberto, then Paige and Indra. We're all so tightly squeezed, there's no room to even turn around a look them in the face. Shoulders jostle me, then someone's suit pack slams me in the hip and knocks me into Abby.

Indra says, "Goodbye, my friends. I love all of you."

"You're not going to die." My voice shakes and I can't stop it. "No one's going to die."

But their eyes go to Jürgen. "We can stay here, go to sleep. A hundred years from now, someone will find us huddled together, fearful little animals in a cave, beasts who died where they happened to be. Or, we can choose to face death with courage and daring."

I need to kick him, kick his cojones, anything to shut him up. But my leg can only lift a tiny bit. No energy left, all empty, all gone. But maybe enough to choke him. I stumble, clutch at his thermals. I try to shake him, hurt him, but he's solid as a tree.

Anger provides new strength. I say to his face, "Found your voice now?" I turn to the others. "No one is going to die. Eric, solve this. Solve this now!"

Eric hangs his head, defeated. He even quivers.

Walt covers his face to muffle his sobs. That gets Eric crying too, wiping and snorting his nose like a niño pequeño. "I tried," he stutters through tears. "Tried so hard. I just can't. I'm sorry, Cristina. I just can't."

I check their faces. Wild eyes, clutched hands, furious panting.

Ryder? A blank. Neither scared nor brave. Empty. Useless.

"Suit packs still have a few minutes of air," says Jürgen. He's confident, even while gasping. "We don't have to die crammed into this place, not if we don't want to. I don't want to. I'm going to suit up and spend my last minutes under the stars. Who will join me?"

"I will," says Tess.

The rest of them shift positions, grab hands, pull each other from the floor. One last time.

"Help me do this," Mikki says to Alison. "Don't want to die alone."

"You won't be alone," Alison answers.

"Let me out," someone whimpers from behind me. "Let me out, let me out, let me out..."

My legs bend. It's over? Like when Paco died? Like cancer? A problem that can never be solved?

The Lord is my shepherd.

The death song.

It's here.

Why now?

The death song, the card in Paco's fingers.

Why did he clutch the death song? What use was it to him?

Paco—smart, rational, competent.

They put on BioSuit packs and helmets. An elbow shoves me. Everyone's standing.

The Lord is my shepherd.

I take Ryder's hand. "I need your help."

"I'm sorry I won't get to fully know you," he says. "But we still have a little bit of time to share. Let's do this together."

I stare at him. It's so hard to think.

"Cristina, wasn't it almost suicide when we volunteered? Just took longer than we expected. We shared some times. Seen some sights. Lived free, for a while. Think of those things. We'll be under the stars, together."

"I need your help."

He doesn't understand. The low oxygen makes us a bit stupid.

I close my eyes.

The Lord is my shepherd.

When there is calm, there is hope.

I swallow and manage to shout, "Wait!"

They stop what they're doing, all of them. Don't cry. Think of Paco! "I can't do this. I can't do this alone. I need your help. Please help me."

They stare at me.

Ryder whispers, "How can we help you, Cristina?"

"I'm asking all of you to do one thing for me. Please. Do this one thing for me, this one last thing to help me. Because I can't do this alone." I find Eric. His lips tremble. He's in a panic, unable to think. Same with Darien and Andre. "I need you to calm your mind. I need everyone calm, calm and thinking. That would help me very much. But I can't do this without... you. All of you."

Jürgen's moving, helmet on. The depressurization valve! Blow the air out, he'll do it. He wants to have this his way. I pull myself between Jürgen and the access hatch and brace against the frame. But it's no good. I'm too weak. He shoves me out of the way like a piece of trash.

Ryder's arm lashes out against Jürgen's face. A solid thump, then two flailing bodies twist wildly. Both men grip each other's throats and throw punches with their free fist. They fight on top of everyone else. Ryder pulls away and wraps an arm around Jürgen's head, locking him in place, rendering him powerless.

"Did you hear her?" he pants, one breath per word. "She asked for help!"

No one moves. Our breathing fills the small space with short, rapid huffs. They watch as I run my fingers over the main panel. I search for it, find it, and push the text to every panel on *Endurance*, the whole block of words, the whole of Paco's song. We can all see it.

"This gave my father peace. Now we read it. Together."

FORTY-SIX

Mouths open. Eric shakes his head. Kelis squints and points a shaky finger. "What's this?"

I suck in a lungful of thick air. "The Lord is my shepherd."

Most just stare. A few repeat tentatively, "The Lord is my shepherd."

I speak the first line again, driving each word out firmly. Ryder places his hand on my shoulder. He gets it. We lead the others through each line.

> *The Lord is my shepherd; I shall not want.*
> *He maketh me to lie down in green pastures;*
> *He leadeth me besides still waters. He restoreth*
> *my soul;*

Blair gasps, "Why we...doing this?"

I continue reading out loud. More voices join.

> *He leadeth me in the paths of righteousness for His*
> *name's sake. Yea, though I walk through the valley of*
> *the shadow of death, I will fear no evil; for Thou art*
> *with me; Thy rod and Thy staff they comfort me.*
> *Thou preparest a table before me in the presence of*
> *mine enemies; Thou anointest my head with oil; my*
> *cup runneth over. Surely goodness and mercy shall*
> *follow me all the days of my life, and I will dwell in the*
> *house of the Lord forever.*

I start again. Immediately, no hesitation.

"The Lord is my shepherd…I shall not want."

How many speak with me? Eric says each word, and he is the most crucial. Only a few remain silent. Blair, Jürgen, Tess.

We reach the end and I begin again.

"The Lord is my shepherd…I shall not want."

Blair screws her eyes shut and cries.

Don't stop. Repeat. Repeat. Repeat.

Never stop.

Fourth reading, all of us speak as one. Yes, Jürgen too. Mikki sniffles between lines.

Six readings.

"The Lord is my shepherd…I shall not want…"

There's no air, but we somehow find breath for seven readings.

We're one tight ball of hands and arms and faces, all of us, clutching each other, no one outside our mass of individuals, no one alone. It's good.

Tranquility. A new calm. Our minds ease, our minds rest.

Eight readings.

Time loses meaning. It's no longer necessary to breathe. It becomes an unconscious act, the pain forgotten. Eric speaks with his eyes shut, each word puffed out separately.

Ninth reading.

Nothing matters now. The words are our only reality.

Eric's eyes, closed. He's thinking.

"The Lord is my shepherd…I shall not want…"

Eric screams, "Stop! Stop! Just stop!" He wipes his hand across his face. *"The power panel is a voltage drop."*

No one moves. Just quicks pants and huffs.

Norberto asks, "What?"

"Everything here, a voltage drop. Switch everything off." Eric huffs in three breaths. "To get the voltage higher. Lights, panels, sensors, fans. Everything. Including the power panel. There's a whole sub bus…under that."

Ryder mumbles, "Shut down the whole panel?"

Darien says, "No! Can't run the script without the panel."

Eric's words are calm and clear. "Script eighty-five millimeter position. Schedule the script to run in one minute, disconnect, shut down the panel and the sub bus. Reactor still on internal local power, absolutely nothing else draws. Take the whole power panel out of the equation."

"No!" says Darien, shaking his head. "No way to get information. No way to know if it works or not."

Norberto adds, "We'll be blind. Know nothing about the status."

"So what?" I growl through my burning throat. "Eric! Listen to me! Schedule a new script to set the reflector at the higher position. Then shut everything down, just like you said. Everything! *Do it!*"

FORTY-SEVEN

Endurance dies. Only the people within live and breathe.

Eric gives the signal and Darien throws the breakers. The cabin, every panel, every readout goes dark. The only illumination is from handheld lights, set to red to preserve night vision. Ryder releases Jürgen, and props two of the lights upward so they shine against the ceiling and bathe the compartment in a dim red glow.

"In forty minutes it will work, or not," says Eric. He's at his end. "No, wait. Even after the point of adding heat, need time for the thermionic generator to put a sustaining charge on the banks. Thirty minutes more."

Ryder is next to Eric. "How do we know when enough time passed?"

"I can count seconds," says Indra, her voice barely audible. "I did that…when I was a little girl. See how accurate I could be. I'll hold up my finger when I get to sixty."

"I'll count seventy minutes," Laine says. She can scarcely pronounce the words.

It's so dark. Fast huffs and pants from all around. Paige and Norberto bleed all the remaining compressed oxygen from the suit packs. It isn't much. Now CO_2 is the problem. Massive headache, hard to think at all.

Time passes without knowing. Indra and Laine no longer counting off minutes—but no one notices. Or cares. Minds fade fast, fast and unseen.

"Twenty minutes, I think." I force myself to announce. "Indra, still counting?"

She turns her head slowly. "Messed up."

All their gasping grows louder.

"Jewel!" I call across the darkness.

A faraway voice answers, "What is it?"

"How many children...do you want to have?"

She doesn't respond. "How many—"

"Heard you!" She growls, the words hard. "What kind...of stupid question?"

"How many?"

"Screw you."

"Okay, Jewel. Just...think about it."

"Three," calls out another female voice. Senuri.

"No kids," gasps Mikki. "Hate diapers."

"Stupid," snorts another voice. Irene? "Don't you feel it? We're dying."

I struggle to think of words. "Irene. I bet you...bet you..."

Ryder slides to my side and wraps his arm around me. "Be still," he mouths. "Conserve air."

Is it happening? Truly, truly dying? Too gone to know it?

That's what it's like to die. You don't know it.

"Indra!" I rasp. "Counting?"

No answer.

"Been an hour," says a gruff voice. Andre?

Ryder's breath is warm and good. He shifts his weight, leans his head closer. "Need to get...breaker. Now. Before."

I nod. I don't know why.

He rises to his feet but almost falls over. "Eric. Almost time."

"No!"

"An hour?"

"Wait. Do it before, will trip...system. Wait!"

Ryder leans against the wall. What's he worried about? Oh, the reactor. A cake, baking. Is it ready? I know—the frost will tell us.

Frost, or no frost.

Is it possible to stand?

Which window? Opposite the hatch. I grab at blackness. Ryder pulls me, and I stand on floppy legs, two straws really. Now the window. All iced over. I wipe it with my arm.

Ryder holds a light against the glass. Rocks. Frosted over. There's the cable. There's the mound.

And a big dark circle around the mound.

I pant out three simple words. "Big, dark, circle."

Ryder peers out. He must see it too. He wipes the glass more and squeaks, "Son! Son of a...bitch."

Legs feeble, I'm going down.

Heads rotate, just a bit.

Eric mumbles, "What?"

I'm on top of somebody. "Eric. No frost."

"No frost!" Ryder repeats. "Hear that? It's...*hot!*"

Big dark circle, with no frost.

"Shit," says Eric.

I tell him, "Ready."

"No. Not yet."

We'll all just sleep if we wait. Ryder crawls toward the access hatch. The breaker. Shut the master breaker, turn everything back on.

When? Now? Time passes. Ryder sits at the edge of the hatch. "Hold me," he says.

I take his arms. He puts his legs inside the hatch.

And drops.

Something rude slaps me in the face. My face against the cold floor.

More time slips. Can't even see except straight ahead. Like a hole. Is this death?

Lights.

It hurts! Bright yellow, bluish too. Panels. Buzzers wail, three or four of them. Painful sounds! A wind comes. Soft, warm, wonderful. Sleep takes it all away.

FORTY-EIGHT

Alison leans forward, smiling.

"Your favorite stuff," she says, placing a cup on the table in front of me. "Nice and hot this time."

"Relax." That's from Ryder. He strokes my hair tenderly. "We're safe."

Sunlight, delicious air, joyful faces. The light is funny. Someone unfolded the America states flag and hung it over the large window. The low morning sun shines through the red and white stripes. The stripes are beautiful and somehow, in some crazy way, happy. Captain Stephen Baines, United States Navy, do you see this?

"Reactor running?"

They burst into laughter. "I guess so," says Mikki.

I gulp tea. Yes, nice and hot. Everyone's here, everyone so close together. "We rest for one hour," I tell them. "Then we get to work."

Another explosion of laughter.

Their eyes will not leave me. They grin and giggle even as they stuff their faces with mush. That's fine. A sunbeam peeks from behind the flag and plays on Ryder's and Alison's faces.

"When you're feeling better," Senuri says to me, "You can take a hot shower. Then sleep. Or whatever you want. This is a holiday, whether you like it or not."

A third round of laughs and hoots.

"Reactor performing perfectly," Eric says. "I'm not touching that bastard ever again."

I drain the tea. "Need to figure out when we can get back to *Liberty* and pull the batteries."

Ryder says to me, "Plenty of time for that. Since this is a holiday, we need to do something special. We should name this place."

"The whole valley?" asks Indra.

"The whole planet. We earned that right." Ryder places his palm behind my neck and caresses my skin with his fingers. "For thousands of years, humans looked up at this planet and saw a little speck in the sky. They invented names for it. But they never came here, did they? Why should they get to name it? From this day forward, this place, this place of ours, this big ball of red grit, will be known as Mars Free Planet."

Cheers and applause from all around. I close my eyes and smile.

Shuko says, "Mars Free Planet, shit."

"Mars Free Planet," Ryder corrects him. "This is official." He gazes at me. "What is the name of this place?"

All their voices merge as one. "Mars Free Planet!"

I take his fingers and press them against my cheek.

He runs his other hand though my hair again. "Get used to it. Let's say it again, nice and loud, just to make sure we remember. What is the name of this place we call home?"

"Mars! Free! Planet!"

Breakfast goes on forever. Maybe it will take all day. Alison and Darien slide piles of used food trays back into the printer. Irene asks, "Where's Jürgen?"

Tess looks away.

"Sulking in the airlock," says Kelis.

Someone snickers.

Senuri says, "Cristina, you might not like this, but I propose we hold a common meeting at this time, an assembly. I believe we should discuss and vote under Article One on the question of whether to remove the captain and elect a new one." She glances around. "We're all here."

"You're right, I don't like it," I tell her. "We should wait until we're rested and had some time to think. We can set a date for an assembly."

Vijay would have been helpful figuring this out.

Senuri says, "We should focus on logistics, is what you're saying."

"Exactly. Not sure what that word means, but it sounds good."

They laugh. None of my jokes can go wrong.

An alarm clangs, a blaring *BING BING BING* from the warning panel.

There's a hiss from the equipment bay.

The panel shrieks, *"Low cabin pressure! Low cabin pressure!"*

Ryder shouts, "Hatch vent!" He jumps down into the equipment bay and twists the vent handle. The hiss stops. I drop down the hatch. At that instant a massive *BOOM* shakes the floor. Sudden sunlight streams through the little airlock window. I put my eye to the glass. The outer hatch is wide open! No Jürgen. Wait!

Jürgen, on the surface, with no helmet. He lies still, legs splayed across the ramp, the rest of him on the surface of Mars.

Ryder says, "He blew right out!"

How much time?

"Help me!" I leap at the two red L-handles between the airlock and the hygiene compartment. I rotate them together.

Ryder yells, "What the hell?"

He pounces on me and grabs my arms. I'm not letting go of the handles. I kick him with all my strength and it catches him by surprise.

Air jets from my nose and mouth. Someone shouts, "Oh, shit!"

Another alarm, a deep drone. The main panel cries, *"Decompression! Decompression!"*

All noise fades, like diving under a wave at the beach. I hurt all over, and there's a gray mist.

Pull him back. Possible? Yes. Now, open the inner hatch. But it won't move.

Latches! Pull hard!

Wetness, everywhere. Why?

I swing the inner hatch open, push it into Ryder.

Sunlight. Too bright! The rocky brown surface, all bare. I'm in the airlock. My lips and tongue are thick. He's face down, ass up. Grab his legs. Cold! Heavy!

I pull hard and fast and fall backwards through the hatch. A smack on the temple. All is gray.

A ROAR...Ears popping, and I hurt, so I'm alive.

Cussing and crying—from other people. Eric shouts, "Get the nitrogen line!" They're venting gas into the cabin. A clear thought bursts into my head: Do we even have enough oxygen to replace the air we just lost?

The outer hatch is closed, but I didn't do it. Ryder clutches the handle. Eyes shut, mouth twisted in pain, knee firmly on my chest.

I scream, "*Shuko!* Down here!"

Head hurts all over. Ryder's off me so I pull Jürgen's upper body from the airlock. He's cold, stiff, and his blood smears my flight suit. Is he even breathing?

"Shuko!" I yell again. "Blair!"

Fade out, then back again.

What's happening now? Shuko's sitting on Jürgen, going up and down on his chest with both hands. Blaire squeezes something that sticks into his mouth, a device from the medical kit, a resuscitator.

I sit up so I can cradle Jürgen in my arms. He moves, sucks in air, then dribbles a thick gob of saliva across his cheek. Blaire pulls the resuscitator off his face and he gasps, coughs, and squirms against my arms. His nose is the source of most of the blood.

"Jürgen! Can you hear me?"

His eyes open and he nods.

Paige mutters from above, "That was stupid."

"Stupid!" someone agrees. Norberto?

Stupid? Who was stupid, Jürgen? Or me?

Full life returns to my brain. That triggers a scream directed at all of them. "What's wrong with you?" I stroke Jürgen's bloody head and hold him close. His heartbeat throbs against my chest.

We look at each other for a while, but it's not fear in his eyes. It's more like amazement.

Shuko listens to Jürgen's heart and examines his head, eyes and mouth. Ryder turns to me. "Almost killed us."

Darien pushes his face through the hatch directly above. "You crazy?"

I take Jürgen's icy fingers into my hand and squeeze tight. They all watch, sniffing and coughing, staring, just waiting for me.

"*All of us!* I said all of us, and I meant it!"

No response except huffing. That's fine. There are a few things more they need to know.

"We can survive this environment. But lies will kill us. We made mistakes. We'll make more. So right now, we start fresh. We have to. Look outside! Look! *There's no one else here!*"

Ryder shakes his head and there's a weak smile. I gaze upward into the packed control center.

"Life is precious. We won't last long without respect for every life. Protect each other, or everything we've been through was for nothing."

Will it be enough?

Is this the *purpose* Paco spoke of?

The answer must be yes, because hands and arms reach out to me...

...touch me...

...pull me to my feet, and clutch me, so we are together...

All of us.

ACKNOWLEDGEMENTS

I am tremendously thankful for the insights and contributions that a variety of people have made to this novel. First, my thanks to Cori McCarthy, Amy Rose Capetta, Tom Fagan, Diane Elliot, and Dolores Lowe, who provided critical feedback during the earliest phase of my writing and encouraged me keep trying and maybe shape something out of that raw first draft.

Also, I'm grateful for everyone who provided their expertise during every phase of development. Naomi Long helped me better understand the themes expressed in the story, and Tom Ligon supplied his engineering know-how to improve the authenticity of the technical struggles besieging the characters. Laura Montgomery and Jeffery D. Kooistra generously gifted me their time and thoughts when I most needed my spirits re-ignited. Special thanks to Robert Bidinotto for his "tough love" criticism that enabled me to see the light.

Finally, I would like to thank the following people for their ongoing confidence and encouragement: David Hannon, Mark Kirsnis, Dan Bohlke, Peggy DiGiacomo, Mark Bottorff, Gene & Joyce Gonzales, Doug Roberts, Dena Ellison, Karin Divens, Dave Terman, Nolen James, Saurabh Saneja, Michelle Medhat, Tamara Wilhite, and my brother Paul Damato.

ABOUT THE AUTHOR

Glenn Damato studied physics and astronomy at the University of Iowa. He served in the US Navy as a nuclear propulsion plant operator aboard an attack submarine. He has worked as a short order cook, a taxi driver, a car salesman, a loan officer, a debt collector, a private investigator, a technical support engineer, and a software instructor. A lifelong space and aviation enthusiast, he holds a pilot's license and while at sea level he enjoys sailing. He is the author of the bestselling memoir *Breaking Seas. The Far Shore* is his first novel.

Made in the USA
Las Vegas, NV
31 July 2021